DISTANCE

BETWEEN

ECHOES

Brayden Bechtold

ISBN-13: 978-0995907409

Oathkeeper:

I am exhausted. I can only see the light when I close my eyes, yet I need them open to proceed forward.

This is the most important thing that I have ever done with my life—aside marry my best friend and have my sons. I have to keep both my feet planted while keeping my head in the clouds. Gravity isn't my friend. Reality isn't my world. Fantasy is my realization.

This both depresses and inspires me. Takes me back to a time I can never relive. A happiness that is but memory. A forward motion that is beyond the notion of present time and space.

As my dream expands, my reality crumbles. As it crumbles and my family builds, I realize that fantasy is but preferred reality. The one that I live everyday.

I am only tired because I keep dreaming with my eyes open. Days filled with my wife's smile, and my boys' laughter.

To Laura, Kaito and Takato.

ACKNOWLEDGMENTS

Thanks to Drew, who made this most amazing cover. My god! Thanks Daniel Pod for helping me edit and always challenging me to write better.

Thanks Justin for encouraging me to see this through; plus all those nights editing over nachos was amazing!

And a totally different Dan who said this story was the stupidest idea he'd ever heard (paraphrasing here). To him I say, fuck off.

Chapter One: Ordinary Girl

March 4th

Blue eyes stared upwards to a white plastered ceiling; freshly sanded and painted from last year's heavy rain. Vala's mind's eye saw past the water damage, the ceiling, the roof of the house, into the sky and focused on the large Saskatchewan clouds that she knew were there.

Heavy eyelids fought to stay open, falling shut again every time they stretched to their widest. A numb mind fought sleep as Vala tried to remember her dream.

Silence broke. A commanding mother, well past irritation, called from the kitchen. "Vala! It's seven-forty-five!"

Eyes shot wide as numbness was replaced with urgency. "Shit." Vala sprung out of bed with the grace of a one-legged unicyclist.

Pink bedspread swirled into a knot around her ankle during Vala's ascent. The sheets caught on the other side of the bed, tightened. Vala fell forward, reached out, and turned the collapse into a harmless stumble, thanks to her trusty desk.

"Thanks, Trusty." Vala spoke openly to the old oak desk, littered with magazines and nail polish. Vala turned to face her bed as if it were her arch nemesis, how dare it assault her so; but a smirk crossed her face as it was in fact her favourite friend. With three swift kicks, Vala freed herself of the blanket.

In the washroom, Vala stood on the scale. Brushed her teeth. Weighed again. Popped a calcium tablet. Raced back to the bedroom to choose between a white tank top and black jacket or that new blue spaghetti strap with the white transparent sleeve top. Undeclared, Vala weighed herself again.

Decisions about pants were easier, so jeans were slipped into. Mid equipped, Vala stumbled on her left leg, fell onto the desk again, this time to her back. "Thanks, Trusty."

Back on the scale, Vala played with her belly. It was beginning to get a bit flabby again. Back to the room, she used the mirror to judge her outfit, realized the spaghetti strap was quite tight around her stomach, showing off the extra two pounds gained from crisp February days.

Vala headed down stairs, her loose tank top and open black jacket covering most of her skin, snagging the black cap she'd had left on the banister. She slid the cap on and tucked as much of her unwashed, hip-long, blonde hair into it as she could.

Ahead was the kitchen, the most dangerous route out of the house. To the right stood two objects that terrified Vala. One was a mental terror; the fridge that held foods of sugar, starch, grain and whatever gluten was. The other, an emotional enigma that moved and spoke not in English but in lectures and stern glares.

Four paces through the kitchen and three from the door, her eyes locked so tightly on the objective that she didn't pause as sound found its way to her ears. Pretending like all teenagers do, that sound took time to process and translate into words.

"Your lunch, Vala." Her mother held up a brown paper bag from the kitchen counter.

Not missing a beat of the heart, Vala curled her lips into a convincing smile. She turned on her last pace, white knuckled the doorknob hidden behind her lower spine. "Chelsea's buyin', Mom. Love you." Vala was out the door and two paces down the steps, without confirmation of acceptance.

Four powerful strides crossed the room. Vala's mother's trembling hand reached for the door knob. The sound of approaching footsteps brought pause, and she lowered her hand. Vala's mother looked down in defeat, as she put the paper bag in the trash can. Her husband walked in, as the lid finished rocking back and forth.

With smiles they shared a lie, because it was easier to.

Vala smiled as she rushed into the warm rays. March was bringing its warmth to the crisp days of Regina. Her nostrils welcomed the smell of thawing dog poop as the snow slushed to expose the grass below. As every Saskatchewan resident knew, this was the first sign of spring.

Vala tugged up her pants from exposing her thong. It had been a year and yet they still didn't fit right. Vala tried to keep pace as she looked over her shoulder. The window was still sealed by curtains. No one was coming after her.

Standing by the front gate was Chelsea. A pale girl with blonde, shoulder-length hair, wearing a white dress and too much jewellery. Earrings looped on lobes while rocks sparkled through cartilage and gold fell flat on the upper ear. She wore two necklaces; one a short, silver dolphin and the other a long, golden chain that mostly fell behind her shirt where it ended in a Star of David. Three multi coloured, plastic bracelets adorned her left wrist and one jade around the right.

The two friends didn't bother exchanging words. Lies could have been traded, but instead Chelsea lifted up a piece of toast to go against her scowl.

Vala spun around gloomily, her arms extended while she looked up at the heavens attempting to be comical. "Ugh, you too?"

"You're fifteen, not a supermodel." Chelsea handed over the bread to her friend. A stern look made sure Vala was aware of the accompanying milk awaiting in Chelsea's other hand.

"Whatever. I'm happy with my body." Vala put the toast in her mouth, aggressively pocketing her hands into the jacket and crossed them to hide her torso. As far as Vala was concerned, zippers were last week's fashion statement.

As they walked, Vala ate without hands. Slowly pulled the toast into her mouth as she chewed, with her head tilted low to fight the wind's attempt at removing her cap. Chelsea followed at Vala's pace, a walk that was much too slow for how close the bell was to ringing.

"Good. You should be." Chelsea smiled, hoping the pause was unnoticed, and leaned forward to look at her friend from an odd angle. "You're beautiful."

Vala rolled her eyes. Tilted up the bread hoping it somehow was big enough to cover her blush. "I know. I know."

"Vala." Chelsea stopped. "How many times did you weigh yourself this morning?"

Vala sighed. Stopped a few steps later and let the bread fall to an open hand. She turned to her friend and very sincerely spoke with blank expression. "Chelsea. I. Am. Eating."

Chelsea looked up with lowered eyebrows. "Promise?"

Vala tilted her head as she engulfed the rest of the toast. With a full mouth accompanied by a smile, "Pinky swear." Pieces of whole wheat sprayed through the air.

Their fingers locked. Shook. *No lies, not this time.* Vala gave her friend a quick embrace. "Let's get to school, huh?"

They passed a few shops, each new window a chance at giggles from cute outfits the other should buy or laughter from the ridiculous pricing of out of season wear.

Conversation ensued and soon Chelsea was informing Vala about the new fortune teller that was all the rage with the girls at school. None of it interested Vala, though it may have a year ago. She attempted to fake interest, but a part of her knew that Chelsea knew that she knew that she was faking all of it; but even so, the act was appreciated.

4

"Jessica was talking about taking a group of girls to get our fortunes read. I could ask if you want to tag along?" Chelsea nervously cupped her thumb with her other hand's digits, while her teeth gripped her lower lip.

Vala suppressed the urge to ball her fist at the mention of Jessica. "Sure." Her eyes wide and a smile cross her face, she relaxed her hands. "Let's find out if I end up with a black guy." Chelsea still hung out with everyone else, Vala would do her part to pretend it was all okay.

Soon the school would be in sight. With only one last road to venture down, the two passed an alley as a soft meow caught the tip of their ears. They paused.

"What was that?" Chelsea peeped her head over to the alley.

"A..." Vala sarcastically grinned, "... cat?"

Curiously, Vala made her way into the alley. It was early morning but sun touched most places so there wasn't much need for hesitation or fear. Chelsea stood her ground outside the alley. With the bell being so near, she didn't want to encourage the distraction.

Only a moment passed before Chelsea was unable to handle the building pressure. She had to say something. "Vala. It's almost nine!"

"Hang on." Vala waved over her shoulder as she continued her journey, looking around trash cans and parting dying bushes. "When have I ever been on time anyways?"

"Never." Chelsea frowned. "But between you and my wristwatch I manage a 60/40 relationship that I'm aiming to make a 10/90 by the end of the year."

"Yeah. Yeah." Vala rolled her eyes. "Math. I get it."

Tucked behind one more trashcan sat a damp cardboard box. It was turned on its side so one flap fell to the floor of the alley while the other hung low making a small doorway while providing a nice dark hiding place.

Vala knelt down to the box, pulling back the flap to reveal a set of green eyes. A smile crossed Vala's face as her eyes met the gaze of a dusty brown cat with little shine to its coat. A scar crossed the right side of its jaw. Its build thinner than you'd want as it nervously fought between fight and flight.

"Chelsea. Come here." Vala hissed over her shoulder. Paused for effect before grinning. "It *is* a cat."

Chelsea shifted her weight as she looked down the road at the inviting school that felt only an arm's reach away. So close, yet—

"Dammit." Chelsea stepped into the alley. Quickly she scurried across patches of ice and cement to Vala's side.

"It's starving." Vala carefully cradled it into her arms. "Give me that milk you brought me."

There was a pause between the girls. Chelsea stiffened her back as she worked up the courage to meet Vala's wide eyed expression with her own tight and watery one.

"Vala." Chelsea broke the eye contact as she played her fingers along her thumb. Her voice was turning distant as thought processed behind her tightening eyes.

"I'm not finding a way out of eating, Chelsea." Vala frowned with narrow eyes and a pulsing temple. "I'm just feeding a stray."

Silence took over Chelsea as she looked away.

Vala sighed. Her eyes closed softly, as her voice matched in compassion for Chelsea's position. "Seriously?"

"My mom says I'm supposed to stand my ground with you, Vala." Chelsea stopped fiddling and made eye contact. Her eyes were solid, the tears never fell. "I can't be an enabler."

"Jesus Christ, Chelsea." Vala shook her head, taking a step back so she could tilt backwards easily on the ice, balancing the cat in one arm while she dug into her pocket with the other. She fished out a toonie. "Buy me another at lunch, okay?"

Chelsea slowly took the coin, and with a world's weight of hesitation she put it in her dress pocket.

Chelsea removed the lunches she had packed for herself and Vala, making her best effort to squish both sandwiches into a single container to use the now-empty second container as a makeshift bowl.

"What do you think happened to it?" Chelsea squatted down, using her hands to keep her dress from touching the pavement. While she filled the bowl, she tried to get a closer look at the cat's scar. "Do you think its homeless?"

"Dunno." Vala eyed the poor creature, it brought a feeling of familiarity. "Must be a badass to survive the winter without a home, though."

The bell went off.

"Crap." Both girls took into a sprint.

The cat watched the two run off. It licked its lips clean then went back to lapping more milk.

Wade W. Wilson Collegiate was less than a decade old, its main building was bright red brick turned brown after years of prairie dust. A white arch enclosed the duel glass entrance doors, which had survived the colour change from being the janitors priority. The school extended outwards to an undersized parking lot with plastic portable extension units.

Past a set of bike racks and through the doors, the girls blurred onward to class. As they turned on the tile flooring, they drifted, their sneakers squeaking as they went, leaving slight brown tracks from the slush outside.

The hallways oversaturated with a cocktail of lemon and vinegar which tried to mask the natural urine scent that had infused itself into every tile and wall.

The girls came to an opening door, swinging wide as the Janitor came out backwards. Chelsea slid past the door with an arched spine, pressing her back against the lockers in the narrow hallway.

The gap was now too narrow, and Vala too slow. She attempted to skid to a stop, only to collide with the janitor, sharing an awkward glance as Vala ricocheted against the lockers. Without losing pace, Vala looked over her shoulder with a scowl. The shaggy blond haired janitor just stared at her lower back as she ran.

Creep. Vala face twisted at the way he stared at her. *Ugh.*

Chelsea and Vala were the last two students to enter room 204 that morning. Vala had managed to catch up to Chelsea as she slowed to a snail's pace several metres from the door. Chelsea hoped the lack of speed into class would seem more natural and draw less attention. Vala however simply rolled her eyes and matched Chelsea's pace.

To the girls' shared relief, Ms. Harrison happened to be running late as well. Both girls glanced upwards at the clock to see they were ten minutes late. Something was off about Ms. Harrison's behaviour. Chelsea started a one sided conversation, gossiping possibilities to Vala as the two made their way to their desks.

The door slid open. Ms. Harrison emerged on their heels. Chelsea found the aid of gravity and almost slammed herself into the plastic chair. Vala was caught mid motion, still removing her chair from under her desk.

A growly Ms. Harrison swayed towards her desk, the classroom door left open. She was hunched, a hand to her temple, her face firmly planted into her palm.

"Vala. You're late." Ms. Harrison peered through parting fingers. "That's the third time this week. I'll have to write you up."

Vala's mouth hung open. Her arms moved in sync as they swayed towards Chelsea, "Come on," Vala's own desk, "are you," to the door, "kidding me," then finally the clock where they collapsed to her side. Chelsea giggled behind the camouflage of a closed fist. Vala sighed, sat softly at her desk while she buried her head into crossed arms in defeat.

Ms. Harrison found the safety of her own desk, using it as a brace to slide into her chair. Slowly she pushed away from her desk. Ms. Harrison looked up to the ceiling as her and her chair spun around in place.

"Wow. Ms. H looks hung over, huh Vala?" Chelsea made sure to lock her eyes on the teacher and lean close to her friend. Chelsea dared not let her words drift too far.

"Yeah." Vala eyed a pendant pinned to Ms. Harrison's breast pocket. A gold swirl escaping a star and bursting upwards into cursive to spell 'Perfect'. "Isn't that a pendant from *Love Thy Self*?" Vala was referencing a Christian talk show that had been around for a year now. Women would write in about their struggles and, if read, would receive a pendant via mail. A sign of glory for the fans, that they had the strength to present the darkness within to the light of the world.

"Oh my gosh, Vala!" Chelsea was hit with sudden realization. "I bet she was Ms. H."

Vala stared long and hard at her friend. "Yes, Chelsea. I believe you have solved the case. Well done. Medals will be rewarded, parades assembled and songs formed of this day. This moment. This glory. Your glory."

"Oh don't be a jerk, Vala." Chelsea shook her head as she opened her notebook, clicked a pen and began to mimic the words that Ms. H had begun placing along the black board. "I mean from last week's episode. A woman wrote in about her abusive boyfriend. How he had hit her and forced her to give up her unborn child. Oh Vala, it was heartbreaking I tell ya."

"Yeah?" Vala broke her attention from Chelsea, to study Ms. Harrison with a bit of clarity. Vala's frown on edge of disappearing. "I guess teachers are people too."

*   *   *

The walk home was at a slow pace that day. Vala dragged her feet along the way with a low head and drooped arms. Thanks to the miracle of multiple choice testing, Vala was able to have her science test graded before leaving class.

Chelsea walked normally, a bit embarrassed at the scene ahead of her. Overseeing others leaving the school pointing and giggling at Vala's misfortune, Chelsea decided to quicken pace to her friend's side.

"Oh, come off it." Chelsea attempted to cheer up her friend, by penetrating the thick atmosphere with a fragile smile. "Vala, it isn't that bad."

"This isn't *that* bad?" Vala held up her 20% test paper. Nostrils flared, eyes wide and mouth open. "Are you comparing it to Hiroshima or something? Cause yeah, then it's not bad."

"Vala." Chelsea shook her head with closed eyes and breath firm as she touched the Star of David under her shirt.

Continuing her walk without realizing what she had said, Vala stared down at her paper.

Chelsea changed to a more upbeat voice. "It was a tough one, you know? I only got a 70%."

"I'm stupid," Vala crumpled the paper. Struggled to get it into her pocket. Jeans too tight. "And fat."

"Don't say that about yourself." Chelsea crossed her eyes with a burst of anger.

"You're right." Vala shifted her mouth to the side, lowered her brow and slit her eyes. "I'm not stupid."

"*Exactly!*" Chelsea skipped into a bit of a hop to get closer to Vala.

"Just fat," Vala spun to match her body and rotating eyes, forcing Chelsea to duck the extended arms.

"You're not fat." Chelsea brought her spinning friend to a stop with a swing of her bag.

"Ow," Vala rubbed her side. "That hurt, Chelsea. The hell's in there?"

"Textbooks." Chelsea studied the bag.

"What are those for?" Vala hunched her back and held a raised eyebrow.

"Hitting you." Chelsea took the time to mimic her friend with rolled eyes and twirled with extended arms. "Apparently."

"Whoa." Vala stopped walking. "Do not." Shot her arms out.

"Not what?" Chelsea smiled as she leaned forward with rosy cheeks.

"Not my thing." Vala pointed a finger and waved it to bounce along her words as if an adult lecturing a child. "I roll my eyes in this relationship, not the other way around, missy."

"Perhaps." Chelsea hopped onto both feet a half a metre away, elevating her voice into a bit of a shriek, "We should go shopping?" Then Chelsea's face fell into that of a sly dog, with shifty eyes as if to watch out for spies. "Maybe check out the new ballroom? Mom says it's a Greek wedding. Oh, Vala, you have to see the designs. It's enormous!"

"Perhaps." Vala tapped her chin with folded arms. "Perhaps shopping outweighs the anger of two gloomy frowns."

"Huh?" Chelsea shot her spine straight as she pulled herself back into lifted eyebrows.

"Parents... cause they're clouds or something. Metaphors aren't my thing." Vala shrugged. Clasped two hands around Chelsea's free hand, as a grin wider than the equator slide mischievously across her face. "We should get sundaes and go try on some slutty clothes in front of that pervy manager."

"Okay," Chelsea giggled. "Just don't get any chocolate on them this time. He won't always give you discounts."

"Oh," Vala took two strides backwards with cuffed hands behind her back, her lips ducked with eyes up to the clouds. "I'm sure my adorable looks can turn your words into lies."

"Whatever." Chelsea shook her head with a smile across her face. *This is my friend.* She grabbed Vala by the hand and began taking into a run. *The one I'll always have.* Looked back over her shoulder to Vala, their smiles matched. *The one I fought for.*

Sundae's Skor-ed. Frowns now smiles. Doubt now laughter. The two girls made their way down the mall towards the second floor escalators where the mall attached to a bridge that extended over the street below and into a neighbouring hotel.

Chelsea's mother had been a manager of the hotel's ballroom for as long as Vala could remember. She was very good at it as well. She always helped couples design the most beautiful rooms to create the perfect wedding.

Maggie, Chelsea's mother, would tell Vala about the days she use to model, and how one day she wore a designer wedding dress. The backdrop for the shot was a relic, uninspired by modern times and simply awful, so Maggie had the shoot completely redone with a new backdrop.

It was a mess. Hours went by for the team to make it to Maggie's liking. However, the picture was a success and a buzz about the backdrop was all the rage for the next few months. Maggie had decided she had more talent for this, and was past wearing the imagination of others anyways; she sought to be a creator. So she lost a few digits from her salary, but with age that would have happened eventually.

For Maggie, though, it was what closing your eyes at night all was about. The dream. "Only with eyes open," Maggie would always say with a smile.

The thought made Vala smile; one day she hoped to be like Maggie. Unlike her own mother, it was hard not to respect a woman who had control of her life. *Able to do whatever the hell she wanted*, Vala always thought.

Vala respected the uniqueness of Maggie and looked up to her in many ways. She found it amazing how someone could be so talented yet grounded. Staying in the backyard that they grew up in. Who wouldn't want to ditch Canada to see the world? Especially rural community Regina. *Bleh*.

"Oh," Vala bit down on her last piece of ice-cream. She cringed as the cold touched a newly discovered cavity, her shoulder instinctively kicked up into her ear. "I can't wait to show your mom my new sandals. I can't wait to ditch socks."

Chelsea laughed. "Vala, it's March. We're lucky enough not to be covered in snow."

"Luck has nothing to do with it," Vala spoke deeply as she spun her spoon in the air as if it were a wand. "I am but a grand wizard of grey. A wizard does not wait for the seasons to change, but commands them to. Arriving for sandals just in time as she wishes to place them upon her mighty feet."

"You failed English, but you've managed to read every Lord of the Rings book." Chelsea shook her head unimpressed. "People our age watch movies, Vala."

"I only read it because I mistook the title for a romance novel." Vala tossed her sundae container into a trash can. In a moment of weakness licked her hands clean. "Don't trust a book by its cover, they say, but they never warn you about titles." Vala brought her hands up into fists. *"Bastards."*

"Wait." Chelsea's pace seized. Titled her head towards Vala with a raised brow, and bluntly put words through oh-ed lips. "How?"

"I thought it was about a lord who gave rings out to maidens. Like the Bachelor, but you know, thou shalt take my rose for thou has the shortest of skirts and the flattest of navels."

"You sound like a perverted Jesus, not a wizard." Chelsea cupped her hands around her giggling lips. Her religious side a bit guilty at the joke, even if she wasn't Christian.

"Critics." Vala shrugged it off.

The two girls came into the sky bridge. *An odd name given it's only like six metres up*, Vala thought. It had white tiles chalked with dirt and grime. The windows were well kept but had finger prints if you looked out the side that faced the midafternoon sun. Nothing special, but what it lead into was beyond words.

So here are those words…

The hotel was five star. The floors a bright sapphire blue with black swirls that were either flowers or leaves, Vala could never really tell. The walls were an egg shell white. Golden baseboards outlined the rooms. The ceiling the same colour of the walls but with golden decor hanging with diamonds, likely fake.

Vala grinned. She loved it here. Everything was spotless and so well kept.

"I so did not need that chocolate." Vala breathed in the clean air. It was well vented, chilled and not dusty like the rest of Regina. Vala found escape in this beautiful atmosphere.

Happily the two girls made their way across the main hall, located on the second floor. A glass balcony overlooked the entrance of the building. A water fountain shot up water in loops and curves. The pattern was hypnotising. Busboys hurried here and there, helping the new attendants. The escalators moved silently and grime free, only the odd patch of someone's recently muddy foot, but that was to be expected in a melting Regina March. Slush was everywhere. Past the balcony there were five massive double doors, each leading into a main ballroom.

The ballroom was one giant room divided up by sliding walls. Depending on the space being rented, the hotel would divide the room into many sections. The entire room was identical to the hall outside, but the diamonds hanging from the ceiling were very much the real thing. Or at least of a higher quality, if the ones outside were also real.

Vala could feel the sparkles of light dance off her face. It was all in her head, but she would curse out Chelsea anytime the best friend brought it up. Chelsea, confused by Vala's transformation in this new area, had learned to ignore it. An acceptance of the lack of manners was enough for Chelsea to get by on. Seeing a mature Vala was quite irregular.

The room at this time was one complete section. Two workers were halfway through putting white sheets and red bows over the chairs. The remaining exposed chairs had golden frames and sapphire cushions, each table already set for tomorrow's event with white sheets and a series of decoratives.

A glass centrepiece housed sparkling gems of all kinds, branches of cherry blossoms with each leaf covering a well-hidden white Christmas light. A single row of beads trimmed the top of the glass while three off-pink stripes ran along the base of the glass.

Each table decorated with about half a dozen unlit candles, three gold plated wire frames that would be later used to house bottles of wine. White plates, red napkins, silver utensils and red ribbons were neatly set to each table.

Vala's jaw dropped. She had never seen the entire room rented out. Everything was overwhelming. The raised head table had three sections. The top for the couple, the middle likely for the wedding party, and Vala assumed the bottom for the parents and family of the couple.

The walls had designs in the process of being hung up. Vala couldn't yet tell what they were, but she couldn't help but crush her eyes and stomp in place with glee. "This is amazing!" Vala shouted across the hall at the directing Maggie.

A smile crossed the woman's face. Though her head was turned from the girls, she knew exactly who had just shrieked with glee. Maggie may not have been the perfect role model that Vala made her out to be, but she certainly loved to pretend to live up to it.

Maggie turned to the girls. She was wearing a long black dress suit, perfectly maintained with silver cuffs and a bow tie. Three silver buttons closed the suit. Her long, straight and well-groomed red hair fell to her waist. It was pinched in the middle with a black, long strand of cloth and a silver buckle. Her blue eyes were much brighter and wider than Vala's. Vala *envied* those eyes, especially the full lashes that went for miles.

"Well hello, girls," Maggie smiled softly. She briefly returned to instructing the workers, then put down her notepad and walked over to the girls.

"Hey, Mom," Chelsea smiled as she removed a yet to be sheeted chair from the table. She dropped her oversized purse onto it. "You seem ahead of schedule. I thought you normally didn't start preparing until six."

"This place looks beautiful!" Vala cut in, her cheeks red and eyes wide, while lips trembled.

"Thank you, Vala." Maggie laughed. It was a gentle laugh as sweet as sugar, perfected from her days of modeling and chumming around in the big leagues. Vala was even more envious of Maggie's non snorting laughter. Vala hated her own pig laugh.

"You see," Maggie turned to her creation to take it all in, before turning back to her daughter. "The bride's mother is a bit of a bag. She wants to be here by six to do a full inspection. Normally I tell them to deal with it. Wait till seven or eight for everything to be *perfect,* however it is rare to rent an entire room out so—well you know." Maggie blushed at her own trailed-off thoughts.

Vala squealed a bit on how cute Maggie's blush was. Both Maggie and Chelsea gave Vala a concerned look as they didn't understand what she was squealing over. Vala sunk into her own blush, brought up her shoulders and dug her chin into her chest. Hoping to vanish from existence.

"She giving you a hard time, Mom?" Chelsea too enjoyed her mother's work. However, unlike Vala, it was more of person with an eye for art enjoying a painter rather than an art student gunning to be the Michelangelo that stood before them.

"Yes." Maggie pulled each girl a chair to sit in before sitting herself. "She calls every hour, on the hour. The conversation is fifteen to thirty minutes long—" Noticing the girls faces Maggie added more "—I wish I was making this up, girls, I sometimes only get a half hour break. It is *insane.* Horrifying."

"Tense." Vala attempted to redeem herself from embarrassed banishment. "Let me unravel that worry with an excellent sale I found. The price tag matches the number on my scale." Handed over her new sandals to Maggie.

Maggie smiled. She enjoyed Vala's sense of humour and when her guard finally would fall to reveal herself. "Yeah right," Maggie looked over the pair. "Try adding about thirty more bucks."

"Rude." Vala went tight eyed and into a frown. Folded her arms to top off the effect. "It is a wonder how Chelsea ended up so polite."

"From her father." Maggie laughed. Turned to Chelsea still holding her wide smile. "Can you run up to my office and grab my Advil? My head is killing me, and you know how I am with stairs, heels, and migraines."

"That's a tonic which always leads to hilarity." Vala grinned ear to ear.

The three laughed. Chelsea rose. "Sure thing, Mom. Vala, I'll be right back."

"Sure thing," Vala saluted.

"Thanks, Hun." Maggie smiled.

Chelsea wasn't gone for long. Vala and Maggie started to talk about school, her family, and, of course, the conversation Vala never talked to anyone about. A conversation that left her low, dark and miserable. However, Maggie herself had once been there, so Vala felt okay with talking about her anorexia.

"Why don't the three of us go shopping?" Maggie suggested, once Chelsea had returned. As a responsible adult, she felt it best to bring up the spirits of Vala by rewarding her good behaviour.

Vala used her balled fists to push herself up into the back of her chair. "Yeah?" Vala was wide eyed, she never went shopping with her own mother, so this was a treat for her. "That'd be great!"

Chelsea swung her purse over her shoulder. "Let's get going. Heard they have a sale on jeans and skirts at Jennifer's."

The walk was detoured as the three stopped for smoothies, a treat from Maggie to the girls. Chelsea for her good marks and Vala for her continued efforts. They did manage to pop into a few other stores along the way. A fifteen minute break extended well into an hour, but you got to do all of that when you were the boss. Maggie even let the annoying bag's call ring over to voice mail.

Vala jumped in the air. "Hey!" Turned to the other two. Vala had just found the perfect skirt, and Jennifer's sale made it quite affordable. "Check this shit out!"

"Yeah, right," Maggie waved her hand without looking back. "Chelsea, don't let Vala buy squat... No way would her father let her wear anything they have on these shelves."

Vala frowned and turned to Chelsea, who was already glaring with folded arms. "*Ah*, come on!" Vala almost fell to her knees in a plea. "I'll only wear it to the beach, I swear."

"Sorry Vala," Chelsea laughed as she put the skirt back on the shelf. "Plus why the heck do you want something so expensive anyways?"

Vala didn't answer. Pushed her index finger into an empty hanger. Watched it sway back and forth as she marinated in her own depression.

Chelsea sighed. "Vala, you don't need to dress slutty to get boys attention."

Vala nodded, slide her mouth into a momentary grin. "Thanks, Chels."

"Yup." Chelsea slide out a pair of jeans. "Plus, these are in your size, tight enough to cut off circulation, and leave little to the imagination."

"Nice." Vala grabbed the pair, wide eyes danced along the fabric. "Dad can't say no if I'm still covered." Vala jumped in the air on her way to the change room.

Maggie shook her head as she studied her daughter up and down.

"What?" Chelsea frowned and wrinkled her nose.

"You are evil," Maggie hugged her daughter. "You are going to make one special boy too happy, and your father bald before he is fifty."

Chelsea pushed away her mother, but not too hard. "Mom. Please." Her green eyes darted along the heads in the store to see if anyone saw the embrace. "People are here." This made Maggie laugh a bit too hard. Heads did turn this time. Chelsea went flush.

∗   ∗   ∗

Now at home, Vala stood in her bathroom, naked aside from her underwear. The scale below, her exposed toes bounced two pounds higher than she had hoped. Her head fell. *Ice cream, for reals?*

"If I weren't Caucasian, you'd make me a racist." Vala grabbed her bunny hug—a hooded sweatshirt with a pouch that ran across the navel area—which hung over the sink. She pulled the extra-large bunny hug over her head, the sweater's waist falling to her thighs. "You white piece of crap." Vala flipped up the hood.

Vala's reflection caught her eye. Looking over her body, she pulled down the bunny hug's neck, then one side up to look herself over.

Red jagged stretch lines down most of her pale skin. Permanent reminders of a year of fluctuating weight, a dangerous dive below a hundred pounds and the fearsome climb upwards. Vala paused at her hips. *Idiot.*

The stairs leading to the main floor were steep and turned tight. Vala hated vacuuming them. It was a juggling act of man, machine and *slippery ass hardwood.*

Inside the kitchen, Vala's mother silently cleaned up after the family's evening dinner. Vala was able to sneak in as her mother's attention was turned to the sink. Vala took two exaggerated strides towards the table, turned on her heel, and sat, folding her arms to hide her face as she crouched to hide her head from the world.

Thanks to the dark evening, Vala's mother noticed a reflection in the window, her little girl hunched over the table. A moment of hesitation came over Vala's mother as she finished her current dish. Last time Vala had come to the table to engage in this matter it had begun a confession that was a four month uphill battle of honesty and dignity versus saving family face.

Vala's mother slowed her pace on the dishes, unconsciously giving the same dish a third trip through the nightly ritual as she felt the guilt pull on her shoulder. The dish placed neatly in the rinse water, she turned to her daughter. Resting her spine against the cold counter, arching her back with two hands on the marble, as if to retain as much distance as humanly possible between herself and her daughter.

A deep breath.

"What's wrong, honey?" A forced high pitched voice, an over the top smile with closed eyes.

"Seriously?" Vala sprung up. Back straight, eyes wide and mouth low with disbelief. A few darts of Vala's eyes scanned the kitchen as if expecting an audience, but it was empty. This was the third face burial in this exact spot since overcoming the battle, and the first time her mother found the rarity of motherly concern.

At first reluctant to bite into the question, Vala pulled her chair closer to the table. She adjusted her bunny hug to cover her exposed bottom. "I gained two pounds from depression." Vala let her eyes fall to the ground. Emotion left her face.

"Vala..." Vala's mother drew out the name. Shifted her weight. Decided to sit. Second guessed and stayed standing. "You're still..." Placed her dish cloth to the side. "...Eating, aren't you?"

"Mom, I'm fifteen." Vala crossed her eyes with breath escaping clamped teeth, vision still turned to the floor. "Not anorexic." This wasn't exactly the way Vala wanted this conversation to go. An intense pressure pulsated from within her skull. Thought locked on the accusation rather the justification.

Vala's mother felt like backpedalling, but the daughter didn't pace to give her time.

"I can comment on my weight and how at times, not always, I do feel fat." Vala's eyes were tight and voice harsh as she borderline spat unraveled thought. Vision raised to her mother's level. "How I want boys my age to try to catch a peak of my bra and not mock my arm fat. Maybe girls would smile or giggle if we wore the same thing to school that day, instead of turning red faced with embarrassment. Maybe someone would even ask for my number for a change instead of saying they'll text Chelsea to text me."

Vala's mother eyes were low, lip bit and hands fidgeted. A pause. The concern transitioned into tightened eyes, clenched teeth, hands balled into white knuckled fists.

Unsure what to make over the quick change in expression, Vala sat up straight and very slowly slid backwards in her chair as if to prepare for flight. Fighting was out of the question. The adrenaline pulsing through her veins needed to go someplace. Right now, a quick sprint felt like a good idea.

Very slowly. Very Carefully. As to not twist words into hate, Vala's mother spoke with thought lingering on each syllable. "You failed a test, huh?" The soft, fake, familiar voice was replaced with something closely resembling Satan.

"Whaaaaa?" Vala looked around comically. A smile crossed her face that wouldn't fool the blind. "No, Mom. Only stupid people fail tests. I'm not stupid, ask Chelsea." A last second chuckle escaped on its own. Sealing the reveal. "Just fat."

An extended hand was all Vala got out of her mother. The hand was open palm upwards to the ceiling while the other dug its middle and index finger into her temple. In the open hand, between clasped fingers, was a folded white piece of paper. Vala's mother had retrieved it from her pocket so quickly that Vala hadn't been able to notice.

A sigh. "Vala..." Vala's mother slowly and softly placed the test on the table. Quivering hands smoothed out the folds. "You're not stupid. You know what you are?" Her soft voice, and shaking hands did not match her angered facial expression.

"Fat?" Vala sighed with rolled eyes. Slid down in the chair with arms folded as if she were a lawyer that just rested her case.

Red had never crossed her face so quickly, not in all her thirty-eight years; Vala's mother slammed her palms down on the table. Vala jumped back into a straightened spine. "Try. Grounded."

"Grounded?" Vala knocked the chair over as she stood, the unintentional impact increasing the rage in her mother's eyes. Guilt clung to Vala but the staring contest with her mother converted guilt into fuel to fire up her rage. "*For what!?*" Vala didn't give a *damn* about the nice chair and pretty tiles, not anymore. *The hell did I fucking do?* "The *hell* did I fucking do!"

"*For not applying yourself!*" Vala's Mother waved a hand. Stepped backwards towards the counter. Voice trembled and she shook her head to match it. Unable to look at her own daughter directly, Vala's Mother chose the reflection of her ungrateful brat. "For wasting my Goddamn time."

A drought in vocabulary was brought on by a dimming mind. Vala's eyes shook as they darted around her mother as if searching for an opening. A weakness. The right answer to exploit the woman. To change the mood and shift blame from Vala to her mother.

In her head, the silence was a minute, but in reality it was longer. Vala twisted her face in confusion. Hung her face to the side with shame to break eye contact. "I..."

"You. What." Vala's mother had her eyes tight. This was no question, but someone waiting for stupidity to flow.

"I'm sorry, Mom." A pause. Vala slowly turned her face back to eye contact. "I just... it's hard."

Vala's mother stood in silence. Crossed arms were not welcoming.

No longer able to see her mother as a woman, but as a towering giant whose shadow eclipsed the fiery sun that had once been Vala's anger. Vala felt her chest collapse on itself as breathing became difficult, filled of panic.

"I can't always do the right thing." Vala chuckled a bit to herself. Face tilted to the side, still not confident enough to fully lock eyes with the woman ahead. "Even when I really try, Mom. It always feels like the right thing is on the horizon and no matter how far I run, or how far I reach... I can't catch it."

It was all in her head, but Vala couldn't fill her lungs from her desperate grasps for air. She felt the room shift out of focus and spin, balance lost as she tried to backpedal.

Vala slouched, reaching for the table for balance, a hand searching for a new chair as she kept looking at her mother. She guided herself down. Face fell to the table, away with shame. "I screw up, a lot. Then I just feel empty. Hollowed. At first I seek out food but then I feel full of guilt. Solid. Like a rock falling into the waves and I can't get out. Can't breathe. Can't swim. I keep sinking."

A cold hand touched Vala's temple, the sharp pierce of its chill snapped her head up a moment as it took several seconds to realize it was her own hand.

"S-sinking." Vala sobbed. Wiped a tear from her eyes. Heart quickened. Breath dried. Teeth chattered. Chest condensed. "Sinking until it's only darkness all around me. Until I can see nothing but the glimmer of light and as I reach for it. I can't reach for it. I just managed to block what remaining light I can see with my fat, ugly, dumb hand."

Vala's mother looked over her shoulder to her daughter. The sight was disgusting. Turning back to the sink, Vala's mother covered her mouth with a free hand. Tears fell from her eyes.

Vala looked up to see her mother in tears. Through painful, blurred vision, Vala slowly moved away from the table. With well-placed steps, as if an actress in a movie, Vala found her mother's side without having to look for objects in the room. A puff of air so fragile it would be an over exaggeration to call it a whisper, "Mom... please don't be mad at me."

"You unbelievable, detached, self-centred child." Vala's mother jerked her head towards Vala, her dark eyes dug into Vala's like daggers. Lips contorted as teeth dragged along each other. "Last year I held a dying daughter covered with my own tears!"

Vala's mother quaked through the anger as she fought off guilt. Pain slowed her tears. "And now you sarcastically and ungratefully weaponize that memory. To guilt me into not punishing you. O-over what, Vala?"

Vala back-stepped. Tears falling in front of her. The twisted face was not that of sadness. It was anger. Years of suppressed emotion bubbled to the service of her mother.

"Mom—" Vala reached out. A smile half believed. Eyes wide for forgiveness.

Vala's mother batted the hand away. Looked away. Couldn't stand the sight of her *own* child. "Over a test? A thing you did poorly on in school? Instead of allowing me to punish you like a parent. To teach you that you need to apply yourself. You rob me of that duty with guilt of something that you did to yourself? Something that I spent months afterwards in depression over. Sought out counselling? Even debated about leaving your father?"

Vala stopped moving. A slow gulp was all she could muster.

There was no reply. Vala's mother just stared off into the nothingness. Vala didn't know what to say or do. *What is she thinking? Is she mad... is she? What have I—How can I?"*

Vala finally reached out. "Mom I—" She couldn't stand it. What was she doing to herself and her family? How did she think her mother was so empty of thought, or heartless enough to ignore her? In reality, if Vala let herself be truthful, she was there the entire time. More than others may have been willing to be.

"Just go, Vala." Emily rubbed her temple. Possibly for the first time, Vala was seeing her mother as a person. A human being that had her own wants, needs and dreams. A person that was pushed passed anything Vala would have ever been willing to endure. "Just. Go."

Vala took a few steps away while still looking at Emily. When there was no returned concern, not even a glance her way, Vala took off.

Out of the kitchen. *Stupid. Stupid. Stupid. Stupid.* Up the stairs. *Stupid. Stupid. Stupid.* Around the first post. *What the hell were you thinking?* Around the railing and onto the second floor. *What were you doing?* Down the hall. *You fucking moron! Vala you are a fucking moron!* Past the washroom. *Idiot—*

Vala stopped mid stride. Shifted her weight backwards onto her heels. Looked over at the scale. A moment between the two as they exchanged the weight of guilt.

Vala entered her room. Slammed the door. Immediately regretted the expression of aggression. Sat on her bed.

Silence. For a long time.

Eyes quaked as they looked down at her open hands. No sound. No sound from anywhere in the room.

Vala grabbed a textbook from her bookshelf. Sat down at her desk.

The desk was cluttered with makeup, wrappers, nail clippings and other things. Slowly and precisely, Vala began to put away her clutter. Only once everything was perfectly where it should be, Vala opened her textbook.

Eyes locked onto the fonts below and Vala lost herself in the words of others. Reality slipped away as knowledge poured into her. Much more clearly than it had in months. Silent, though; Not a sound.

Sound was words. Words were thoughts. Thoughts made mistakes. Vala was past mistakes. Past guilt. *Past the bullshit.* Onto reality.

Droplets fell from Vala's eyes, staining the pages where they fell. Blue eyes looked past the wrinkled paper as if it wasn't even there.

CHAPTER TWO: NOBODY'S PERFECT

March 5th, 00:02 hours

The window slammed shut. Vala jerked upright. Heart raced. Head spun as darkness and spots over took her vision. She swung her hair around with each snap of the neck. As the blood returned to her conscientiousness, Vala steadied her mind and stilled her heart.

She had fallen asleep studying at her desk. A quick memory of the fight with her mother brought on an audible curse.

Vala rolled her eyes, as she realized the bedroom window had slammed itself shut. It was always closing itself and waking her up in such a fashion, Vala cursed its existence; like the rest of the house, it was *shittly put together like some retard had found a hammer one day.*

She dragged her heels across the floor of her room. Her frown cemented and eyes hung low as her mind began to replay events from the evening. The distraction kept her from noticing the cat on her bed, until she had opened the window and sat back at her chair.

A skinny frame, with worn, shineless, brown fur, stared up at Vala. Still half asleep, Vala entered a confused staring contest with the cat. She struggled to keep burning eyes wide while she attempted to figure out where she knew the intruder from. The cat seemed to not care about the contest, and broke the ice by slowly licking the back of its paw, to brush behind its ears.

"Hey. You're—" Vala noticed the scar on its chin. "Did you follow me home?"

"Yes," the cat answered, *in a British accent, of all things*, "I did."

"*Holy fucking frog shit!*" Vala backed up and out of her chair onto the desk; between shifting weight from the two, the chair gave way, rolled and crashed against the bed with great force.

Vala fell to the ground, cracked the back of her skull against the desk and slammed her butt on the floor. Her hands came up defensively to the back of her head, but the pain became unimportant as Vala's mind caught up with itself. *A talking cat!*

With pain now ignored, her sanity felt like it was slipping away. Deciding the event at hand outweighed a possible concussion, Vala lowered her hands into her lap as her eyes cautiously rose to look at the feline.

The cat transitioned from bed to the spinning chair. The momentum depleted just in time to line the two up eye to eye. An eerie shiver shot up Vala's spine.

A series of mental gymnastics were being performed in Vala's brain. Bypassing a lifetime of paradigms to accept a talking cat didn't come easy. A few moments passed until finally all of that became unimportant.

"I'm not sure," Vala's gulp got caught halfway through her dry throat. She coughed, which flushed her cheeks. "If that was creepier than you talking. Either way, I'm pretty sure demon kitten should leave."

The cat rolled his eyes. "A hundred lifetimes searching for the Echo Army, and the first one I find is more suited to be a jester than a knight."

"Yeah?" Vala knew she would be matching wits with a feline, but an insult was an insult, and she was willing to stoop to any level, no matter how low. "Well at least when I clean myself, my hair clogs the drain and not my throat."

A pause.

"Hilarious." The cat hopped back onto the bed. It begun to speak as one would to the dim witted. "My name is Rift. In your native tongue, it'd be easiest to refer to me as a Light.

"My purpose is to seek out the reincarnated souls of knights that were once members of the Echo Army. I am to find these souls and awaken them at the arrival of the Dragon."

Vala was slow to get to her feet, used her hands to find the desk behind her; eye contact with Rift never broke. Both her eyes and breath were stilled as she leaned against the desk for support. Finally, she drew in a deep breath.

"I," Vala patted herself off, "am confused." Ran her arms down each other before folding them.

"Really." Rift rolled his eyes with a sigh. Possibly shrugged. Vala was sure cats couldn't do this, but he did. It was weird. "Perhaps a demonstration is in order."

"Hey," Vala went red faced. Took a step towards Rift with a raised fist. "Listen you little—"

Fur peeled back as muscle and skin were vacuumed into a silver skeleton structure. Rift's bones collapsed into themselves as they flattened into spinning spades that twisted at the joint where the body met the skull. The mouth stretched and pulled back over itself as a green jade sphere took its place.

Vala stood very still as her jaw fell, and eyes quaked. Her voice only a cracked whisper, "**S**hit."

Rift now floated above Vala's bed. A silver device the size of two balled fists. A jade stone with thousands of tiny shards all around it to make a jagged ball. Eight shards left its base and though their tips never left the ball, they moved without chains or joints. An invisible force kept them in place. A strange black dot moved over the jade as if ink swaying in a pool of green. Vala recognized this as his eye. The shards on Rift's body shifted and rotated in a pattern that evoked lungs breathing.

The shards broke off the ball to expose countless amounts of golden chains, each ending at one of the shards, but so intertwined that Vala couldn't tell where any of them led. The chains rotated and looped over themselves. A strange gravitational pull came from the dancing chains. They vanished any time the spades returned to touching the jade orb.

Vala reached for the device.

On contact strings wrapped around Vala's arm violently. It wasn't painful, but forceful. Her body was jerked forward and she was forced to take a step to avoid falling over.

Vision blurred as everything solid, liquid and gas meshed into one shared form. Lines crisscrossed everywhere in a strange mix of coloured strings, gold and pink, yet they retained their original colour all at the same time.

The universe unwove itself into a clump of everything and nothing.

Vala was well aware of the space in her chest cavity. It had a strange hollow sensation that was quickly replaced with a warmth she had never felt before, and yet felt more natural than anything had ever felt in her entire life. The sensation elevated into a boil as her soul unwove her own body to join the universe.

The strings, at one time believing themselves to be a teenage girl, wove themselves through the universe. Her soul focused her mind on a level that Vala had never before dreamed possible. Picking and choosing as it weaved through reality, the soul pulled at the strings.

Once the soul had what it needed, it retracted itself out of the universe and wove it self back into the teenage girl that it had originally been.

With her body came the fabric of reality, the gold and pink strands of the universe wove through her skin. Creating a tight lace of raw energy all over her body.

The universe hardened around her person into a tangible material. It's durability beyond question, yet its flexibility felt more elastic than her very skin.

A high collar sat on top long sleeves, which expanded off the wrist into a loop around her middle finger. A skirt wrapped around her hips and heels buckled tightly around her feet. Angel wings stitched over her shoulder blades. The entire armour an emerald green, save the mocha brown torso.

A hollowed sound shook at Vala's ears as her entire skeleton vibrated. Air was forced out of her lungs as a life time of pressure was removed around her being. She fell against the bed. Straightened her arms to catch herself. Her legs buckled under her weight and she fell to a knee. Hung her forehead against the soft quilt as the room spun.

The spinning continued for a moment as the universe rebuilt itself around her. The strings reshaping themselves back into the oxygen in the air, the desk in her bedroom and the expired pumpkin spice latte that sat on the bookshelf.

Her lips opened slowly to draw in air. The cold rush brought thought back to her mind, which steadied the room. Vala used the bed as a crutch to stand back up.

Vala shifted her weight, then slowly opened her eyes to see Rift floating ahead.

"How do you feel?" Rift's orb glowed with every syllable, his shards twirling about him. "I've been told it is 'quite the rush.'"

A moment wasn't lost before Vala displaced insanity for immaturity. "You little jewelry-producing, talking, best friend kitty-cat!"

She reached out for Rift's enchanting orb, and in doing so she noticed her fingernails had been painted brown. She pulled them in to look them over and saw the fabric around her hand. Curiosity took over and her eyes ran up her arm to her shoulder, down her torso to end at her skirt. Reality sank in that her clothes had been transformed.

"Do you ever maintain concentration long enough to be serious?" Rifts voice was flat, his shards still.

"Only time I'm serious is when Will Smith is shirtless," Vala ran her hands over her stomach to test the feel of the cloth against her hands. She looked up to Rift in time to see him blink. His top and bottom shards passed over the orb, making his eye vanish for only a moment.

A pause came over Vala, as it took her mind a moment to realize what had happened. She cocked her eyebrows in confusion.

A mixture of her defensive humour juggled with an honest curiosity, lacking reason, sanity or a grip on what was happening at this very moment. "Jewelry will buy you two minutes, though."

"I am not jewelry." Rift let his shards of silver shift over top themselves.

"I'll say." Vala ran her fingers around Rift's silver shell, it was warm to the touch. "This is gorgeous," Vala tapped the orb, Rift didn't seem to mind.

"Please refrain from smudging my eye. It is impossible to wipe myself clean in this form." Rift took a moment to transform back to his cat form. Rubbed his eyes a few times then returned back to his Light state. "I happen to be the universe's most powerful weapon," Rift hissed.

"The universe's most powerful weapon didn't come equipped with a windshield wiper?" Vale raised an eyebrow as her mouth curled into a grin. Before Rift had a moment to reply, Vala plucked him out of the air and turned to her mirror while holding him in a position as if he were a necklace. "Cat. We are totally square on the milk thing. Get me some string and I could wear you as a pretty cool necklace."

"Great." Rift slid down and out of her grasp. "I am glad you think so."

Vala shrieked.

"*My hair!*" Vala shoved her face against the mirror. Her breath fogged it up as she clawed her nails through brown strands of hair. She gripped the stands tightly as she twisted her wrists to tighten them. The dye in her hair was gone, and her cosmetic contacts missing. Vala stared at herself as a brunette, brown eyed girl. Someone she hadn't seen in many months. "My eyes too! My... my money! That shit costs a lot." She jerked back and frowned at Rift. "Dude!"

"All material objects on your person will return when you end the transformation," Rift sighed, unimpressed with what Vala deemed important. "Your contacts and dye will return as will your clothes."

"They better or there'll be hell to pay." Vala let her hands fall in defeat.

Vala took a moment to play with her skirt, trying to lower it down to her knees. "Dad won't even let me wear makeup..." Vala's voice was distant. She felt like her own body was a million miles away.

"This is the uniform of the Echo Army." Rift hovered just behind Vala's ear. "With this armour's power, you'll be able to stop the Dragon's Queen, and her River Army."

Vala could feel it inside of herself, that Rift was speaking the truth. A memory unwove just half a heartbeat before the words left Rift. A sense of responsibility overtook Vala, and for a moment she could feel the weight on her shoulders. But her tendency to brush off the important took hold. With the defense of humour and naivety. Vala brought herself back to reality.

"I'm fifteen! I can't wear this shit!" Face bright red, she grabbed a pillow to cover her lower self. "Are you kidding me? How can this be armour? I'm barely covered. What is it going to protect me from?"

"It's simple." Rift returned to his cat form and dug his paw into his temple. "The armour is crafted from a scale of the Dragon. It's virtually indestructible on four of the five planes of existence."

"And it's only covering my torso. Why?" Vala tossed the pillow aside. Fell back against her desk. Gnawed on her lip. "My legs aren't important?"

"You lack a full grasp on the nature of the universe. It'd be impossible to explain it perfectly to you," Rift lowered his paw from his forehead. "Imagine that everything is connected to everything else, does that help?"

"I'm failing most of my classes." Vala leaned over to grab the pillow off the bed, holding it in her lap to pinch the corners with each hand. "No idea what you're talking about." Tugged up the corners one at a time.

"Well." Rift cleared his throat. "To put it simply, all matter is connected to each other as if with strings. Everything is connected to everything else."

"Ok. Strings." Vala nodded. "Concepts." Vala sighed and let go of the pillow. "I don't get it."

Rift continued. "Billions of years ago, near the dawn of the cold war, an army of knights attacked the Dragon. They were able to loosen a single scale, and only one returned with it in hand. We were limited on spreading the armour among all our knights."

"Wait. We're fighting the Russians?" Vala slowly shifted her eyes as she mentally back pedaled.

"No," He continued his explanation, with or without Vala. "The science is beyond your comprehension. The blacksmiths found a way to network the armour so it is strung throughout your entire being. Contrary to your senses, the armour is covering your entire body. You only perceive it to be covering part of you."

Vala shook her head. "So what can this stuff do anyways? Can I take a bullet or something?"

Rift smirked. "The armour is designed to stop an Echo, so I doubt that a high-velocity projectile would be of any consequence to you."

"Okay." Vala twisted her lips and darted her eyes. "Say I follow you, because I am." She held up her hand to tilt it back and forth. "Sixty-forty." Rift took a moment to roll his eyes. "Let's back this up to the army bit. I'm some kind of knight for what army, what country and… what war?"

"Finally, some intelligent questions." Vala met his words with a frown.

"First thing you need to accept is that this universe is not the only universe. It is a fairly young universe. Billions of years are but a blink of an eye on the scale of the greater universe.

"A being of great power created this universe. We refer to it as The Voice." Rift closed his eyes to visualize it himself. "The Voice is a most powerful creature. We are but in a Womb for its child, your soul but an atom, a small fraction of its infant."

"Wait…" Vala felt the warmth in her chest expand outwards and flatten. "I feel funny."

"Every single person you have ever shared a positive connection with is intertwined with the strings closest to you. The transformation has awakened that connection. You draw from that power. The more people you love, the more strings will appear."

Vala looked down at her chest. From her left breast five golden strings fuzzed into vision. Very curiously Vala grabbed them with one hand. "Mom." Vala carefully shifted the string to her right hand. "Dad." The next string. "Chelsea." Vala stopped on the two other strings. She followed one to Rift. "Rift?"

"Yes." Rift smiled. "We are bound, Vala, though I am only yours until we find the Echo, as she reincarnated herself for when the cold war turned hot. I have other Lights that are dormant. When I go to her aid, I shall give you one of the other Lights to use."

Rift came up to Vala's face, his paw on her chest. "Your interaction with me yesterday has awakened what was already there. It's why you found me, before I found you. You aren't powerful enough yet, but there are many more strings connected to you. Ones you have forgotten."

"Forgotten?" Vala looked at the fifth one. "I don't know who this last one belongs to."

"Oh?" Rift sat up straight with a tilted head. "There are five then?"

"Yes." Vala looked over at Rift. Held the remaining string as high as she could take it before it tightened. "You can't see them?"

"No." Rift shook his head. "Unlike you, I have no soul."

"Weird." Vala looked down at the fifth string. It was the brightest of them all. "This one is important, but I don't remember who or why."

"Perhaps it is the Echo. She was the one that created the army in the first place. She is likely connected to all of the knights, as you draw from her power to transform. By spreading her powers out among the knights, she was able to become small enough to use the strands of Distance... something the Dragon would never do. Luckily.

"There is an awesome power inside of you, Vala. Once we are ready and have awakened more knights, we will seek out the Echo. We can not risk awakening her when we don't have the means to protect her."

"I have to protect a god?" Vala went wide eyed. She let her strings go as she stepped back and brought up her open hands. "Whoa. I am not cut out for this. Rift, I can't even parallel park."

"Not just you," Rift chuckled. "That would be something though, wouldn't it? I hate to admit it, but my scanners aren't working perfectly. I can not tell exactly what you are Vala, but judging from your connection to the Echo you are likely an Angel. You may not be a god, but compared to anything you've ever experienced, you may as well be."

"I don't..." Vala sat. "What's expected of me, Rift?"

Rift lowered his head for a moment of pity. "Everything, Vala."

"I…" Vala ran her tongue along her inner cheeks to try to mossen it. "Rift…"

"You are the first that I have found." Rift fell next to Vala. "But you will not be the last. We will find others, and as your numbers grow the responsibility will be divided, but don't mistake the fact that reality itself rests on your shoulders."

"Rift…" Vala felt her heart quicken. Breath became short. The room started to spin. "I think I am having a panic attack."

"Relax." Rift almost purred. "We will spend the next few weeks trying to find what knights we can. Then we will seek out the Echo. End this before the Dragon can finish making his move."

Vala cringed as if she had just been hit in the gut. Stumbled forward a few steps before collapsing over her bed. Golden threads ignited as her armour unwove itself and then trailed through the air as she fell forward.

Vala used her arms to brace her fall. She was back to her normal clothes. Sweat ran down the side of her face as she struggled to catch her breath. Eyes trembled as she fought to keep her vision in focus.

After a moment, she rolled over to her back and slid down the edge of the bed to the ground. She brought her legs inwards as she hung her arms and head over bent knees. Sighed. "I can hardly think straight… what happened?"

"Hmm." Rift fell to her side and circled Vala before stopping in front of her. "Perhaps your mortal body isn't accustomed to transforming. We will have to train you a little bit."

"Sounds good," Vala rolled over to her stomach and pulled herself up and onto the mattress.

Her head fell straight into a pillow, her left leg hung half off the bed while the rest of her sprawled out. Vala fell asleep with the lights left on.

The alarm buzzer caught Vala's attention. Sprung her upright. Red eyes blinked twice in disbelief. Vala groaned as she turned to smash the off button with a fist. Unimpressed with the time that it displayed, Vala contemplated ripping it free from the wall socket.

Rift meowed from behind the alarm, with a smile.

"Saturdays. Fifteen." Vala tightened her eyes and dragged her teeth over themselves. "No. Alarms."

"Well." Rift chuckled. "Be that as it may. We have a lot to accomplish today. We are going to train so you can last more than a few minutes in your armour. Do you know of a place that people won't see us?"

"Ugh!" Vala rose from her bed. Tossed the pillow as hard as she could but Rift dodged it. "I'll get dressed."

"You are incredibly barbaric," Rift frowned as he hid under the bed. "It's very dirty under here. Does your family not possess a vacuum cleaner?"

"Whatever." Vala grabbed a towel that hung on the back of her door. "I'll be back in about an hour."

"Twenty minutes." Rift appeared from under the bed, the bed spread falling just around the back of his skull to give the illusion of a pink mane. "Why would it take that long to bathe?"

"Showering." Vala ran her fingers through her long greasy knotted hair. "Takes a long ass time to look this good."

"We are going to be training, Vala." Rift shook his head. "*Not* picking up boys." Rift looked up but Vala had already vanished.

Vala closed the door to the bathroom. Tossed the towel on the sink. Stripped. Weighed herself.

A pound higher than the day before. Vala sighed as she started to run the hot water.

An hour and a half passed before Vala returned to her room. Rift was waiting for her on the bed. Vala kept the door open.

"Out in the hallway while I change." Vala extended her arm towards the open hall.

"I am a cat, I hardly see why—"

"You can talk, and you have a penis." Vala went crossed eye. "Out!"

Rift left the room. The door slammed, millimetres from catching his tail. He arched his back with a hiss.

Inside her room, alone, Vala sat at her desk for the first few minutes. Legs pulled inwards with hands cuffed to keep them in place. Water still dripping from the towel she wore.

Blue eyes lost at the blank wall ahead of her. Vala felt exhausted by how normal waking up to a talking cat was.

Vala checked her phone. No new texts. Used her laptop to check any status updates. Shared two pictures and liked Chelsea's test result post. Turned the computer off and tossed it on the bed. The towel following to cover the laptop.

It took about ten minutes for Vala to decide on her clothes this time. She grabbed the jeans she had bought yesterday. Shifted through several tops before coming across a green t-shirt. Shrugged. Put it on. Fished her jacket from behind the desk. Opened her window to test the weather. Judging by how red her hand got, she grabbed a toque on her way out.

"Well that didn't take forever." Rift rolled his eyes. "Anything else you need to take care of?"

"No." Vala picked up Rift. Slipped him into her coat. "Mom hates cats. What are you thinking staying out in the middle of the hall?"

Rift was silent.

For once, Vala grinned as she zipped up her jacket.

Downstairs was busy this morning. The living room was buzzing. Vala's father watching TV, the kitchen sizzling with bacon and eggs from her mother. Vala picked the lesser of two evils and left through the living room.

"Hey Dad," Vala waved. He didn't look up from his newspaper.

Hello Vala. Vala slipped on her shoes. *Hey Dad. Jets doing good?* Grabbed her mittens. *No, not this year... hey is that a new jacket?* Grabbed the key off a hook near the entrance. *Yup...* Vala looked back at her father before leaving out the door ... *You should know. Cost you 250, ass.*

The sun was bright and warm to Vala's bare face. It took a moment for her eyes to adjust to daylight. It'd have been a perfect day, like all Saskatchewan days, if there hadn't been a strong wind. However, there was always a strong wind. Always.

Vala opened her jacket and from it fell Rift. He walked in a circle for a moment to grasp where he was.

"Don't say anything, please." Vala began walking with Rift trailing a metre.

The two did not speak as they made their hour long walk. Vala content to enjoy the cold breeze, her heart matching her numbing hands and face.

Vala and Rift found themselves in front of the football stadium. It was a large cement building, about 70 years old, wrapped by green chain link fence.

"Correct me if I am wrong," Rift looked around to see most of the street empty. "Is this not a large gathering area for human beings? Won't we be seen?"

"It's an open field," Vala had her arm extended out to the fence, the tips of her fingers dancing along the green chain link. "They can't use it this time of year because of all the snow inside."

"Wouldn't it be locked?" Rift matched stride with Vala.

"Easy." A wide grin was met with tight eyes. In Vala's hands were a set of pliers. "We got the key right here."

"You—" Rift looked about. "—are not serious?"

"Robot." Vala frowned. "This isn't my first rodeo." Vala span the pliers in her hand. "No one is going to see us."

"Oh my..." Rift hissed. "I cannot believe that the first knight I found is a common thief." He paced as Vala got to work.

"Whatever, man." Vala began pulling back the wire. "I use to do this all the damn time when I was a kid."

"You are still a child."

"Whatever." Vala pulled away the link. "Get in."

Vala slipped through the hole she had created. Once on the other side, she put the fence back near the pole and bent three loops back in place, hoping to keep it from being noticed.

"Follow me," Vala led while spinning her pliers. "I will give you the grand tour. We pretty much win every Grey Cup."

"Is that a trophy?" Rift allowed himself to trail behind Vala. Looked this way and that. "You know our culture uses metals for almost all purposes. I wonder if there is some relation there."

"Yeah it's a trophy." Vala pocketed her pliers. Buried her red hands into her jacket pockets. "I would have no idea."

"I suppose not." Rift sighed. He let his eyes follow Vala's heels.

The two came to a towering hallway. Vala smiled. This was her favourite part. The dusty scent still found its way to her nostrils even in the crisp wind.

"This is it." Vala breathed in deeply. "I use to come here all the time with my dad."

Vala shook her head and waved her hands slightly. "My dad was Saskatchewan born and raised. People think Canadians are hockey fans, but the fact of the matter is the prairies are about the pigskin."

Her grin vanished as her eyes fell to the ground. Shoulders raised as Vala shoved her hands back into the pockets of her jacket. "I use to come to every game, until I was eight. Dad got busy with work. My mom only used football for social status. You can only pretend to give a shit so long, when the person next to you isn't waving a flag and a green finger, but flapping their mouth the entire game."

"I see." Rift closed the gap between the two. "Is loyalty important to you, Vala?"

"Yeah." Vala stopped. Slowly shoulders slacked, back straightened and a smirk found its place. "It never was until Chelsea. My other friends—they didn't stick around when things got hard."

"You two do seem very close," Rift smiled. Now in front of Vala he tried to roll his neck and point his head to the opening in the hallway. "Let me show you something."

"Sure." Vala took into a jog. Her smirk curled a bit more on the edges. "So when do I get to tell Chelsea that my cat can talk?"

"I am not *your* cat," Rift shouted from the lead. "I'm not even really a cat. It is just what us Lights were programmed to do. We are organic computers, we simply take on the form of small animals near the people we wish to keep ties with."

Vala cringed as Rift's fur and muscles retracted into his Light form.

"This is my true form." Rift whizzed back and forth around Vala's head. "Impressive, is it not?"

"It is something." Vala swatted Rift away as if he were a fly. "But I've already seen it."

"I'm surprised you aren't stunned to see my transformation." Rifts voice held a frown.

"Seriously?" Vala laughed through wide white teeth. "A talking cat was scary. Over it. A weird robot is pretty normal."

"Your generation is very jaded. Only a hundred years ago and every time someone saw me transform I would get a marvellous reaction." Rift floated over Vala's left shoulder. "I must admit, I am a bit upset that I did not get to see you fall on your behind a second time."

"No kidding." Vala let herself fall into a walk as they came out of the hall. Her heart raced as her breath was heavy. "Dude. I am out of shape."

"I can tell." Rift shook his head.

"I can't believe you just said that to me." Vala held no expression as her feet froze for a theatrical moment.

The hallway led them into the middle of the field, surrounded by empty seats to hold twenty-eight thousand, the stands divided by red, yellow and orange plastic seats. North and south field goal posts with cement walls half way up, where the stands rose and curved inwards.

"Let us begin." Rift floated himself into the middle of the football field. His jade eye blinked sapphire twice. "The security guards don't seem aware we are here."

"Whoa!" Vala waved a hand at Rift as if trying to bat a misbehaving animal. "You were freaking out earlier about being caught and you could have just scanned the place?"

"Sure." Rift transformed himself back into his cat form. "If it had been dark enough to take on my robotic form."

"Great." Vala shook her head as she rubbed her temple. "They could design a robot that can turn into a talking cat, but not one that doesn't lose all of its cool abilities in the process."

"Do not mock my creators." Rift showed his teeth as he glared. "It takes a lot of CPU to manage a circulatory system. You wouldn't believe how complex it is to behave alive. I must be able to blend in perfectly. We had predicted your technology to be a hundred years ahead of what it is now. We couldn't have predicted that your religions would have muddled the advancement of science so greatly."

"Yeah?" Vala let gravity take her as she slumped into the snow. Tilted her lips as she played with the tip of her sneeze-edging nose. "How is that anyways? You haven't explained everything."

"Then I suppose it is time that I do just that." Rift snuggled into the white powder. "This is incredibly cold."

"Look here," Vala pointed to Rift as if her hand were a gun. "Get used to it. If you wanted someplace warm you should have found someone in Hawaii."

"Right." Rift sighed. "I should probably begin from..." Rift stopped from the look on Vala's face. She had a goofy grin with tight eyes as she fought to contain herself. "What?"

"Were you going to say the beginning?" Vala laughed. "Cause that is where one would begin a story."

"I can not believe you were the first knight I managed to find." Rift rolled his eyes. "Lucked out on that one."

Vala frowned.

"At the beginning of time there was the Voice." Rift began from the beginning. "The Voice created five core elements; Earth, Fire, Metal, Tree and Water. Everything you can see, taste, touch, smell and hear are made up of these core elements.

"A sixth element was created. This one was called Void. It parted every core element from itself. This way, separate objects and people can exist. A seventh element called Distance does the same thing, but for realms or dimensions.

"The point of the universe is to be a womb for the Voice's infant. Everything is an intricate web of reality and flow of energy to one day form a new god. Mankind was created for this purpose. Every time a human is born, they are given a soul, and whenever they die, their soul returns to the womb of the infant. Each soul is like an atom to a god, thus we mostly refer to humans as Atoms of God.

"When everything was created from the extreme power of the Voice, certain pockets of power were formed. These pockets grew consciousness, and became the Echoes. These creatures are almost as powerful as the Voice. They can manipulate matter in the same fashion, but they are unable to create or destroy matter.

"One of these Echoes was the Dragon. He lived in the River. One day, he found out about the Atoms of God living in Eden. His goal was to make his own form of life. He hid among the masses to learn their ways. Stole a few for experiments until he found a way to make his own artificial souls.

"From here he created his Dragonborn—more or less human, but they aren't Atoms of God. This caused an imbalance in the Womb and its energy, poisoning the infant. So the Voice aborted the infant, moved Atoms of God to the Garden, Earth, and left. The Echoes followed.

"Before the Voice left, it destroyed the seventh element, Distance. This was to trap the Dragon in the River. Only trickles of Distance still exist, but not enough for something that large to pass through.

"One Echo stayed. She believed that Atoms of God could be cured. She created an army of knights, or the Echo Army. Using her abilities, she had her army put into the reincarnation cycle of humanity. The one string, the one where you couldn't tell who it belonged to, is likely connected to her power source where all the suits of armour draw from."

"So… I am an Angel or something?" Vala took a deep breath. "Can I fly?"

"As I said last night, I believe you are an Angel." Rift took a step towards Vala. "There are many species that exist. Each with their own purpose to our army. Dragonborns were spies, Angels once caretakers now warriors, and the Kitsune our blacksmiths."

"What is a Kitsune?" Vala jerked her head.

"Think half human, half fox," Rift's tail divided into nine. "Depending on their age they can have up to nine tails."

"Okay." Vala nodded her head. "That was almost fall on my butt worthy. Please return to a single tail."

His tails drew into themselves so only one was left. "Why don't we start practicing. Try transforming."

"How flashy is this going to be?" As Vala stood she brushed the snow off her person and looked around the empty stadium.

"It should be fine." Rift transformed back into his Light so he could scan the arena one more time. "No one is around."

"Cool." Vala pocketed her hands and started to walk, stopping where she felt was the centre of the field. "It's cold. Will I lose my jacket if I transform?"

"Yes." Rift nodded. "However, your armour should bring you to regular body temperature in almost any climate. It may take a minute to adjust but it shouldn't be uncomfortable for long."

"Okay." Vala sighed. She tossed her jacket to the side, closed her eyes and tried to remember the feeling of the chains along her body.

"It will come back—"

"Nope." Vala shook her head. Transformed. Wrapped the jacket around her waist. "I am not letting anyone see me like this. I don't trust you."

"Seriously?" Rift rose slightly then fell back to his original height. "That won't stay on. You'll wreck it or lose it."

"Please." Vala tilted her grin and shook her head. "What are you expecting me to do anyways? This outfit is only good for one thing and I don't see any poles."

"You are..." Rift shook his head. "Just jump."

"Jump?" Vala raised her eyebrow. Looked up into the sky and then back down to Rift. "Why?"

"Jump." Rift floated a metre into the air then fell. "You do know the concept? Jump as high as you can."

"Whatever." Vala shook her head. Stretched a bit then crouched low. "Here we go—"

Vala leapt into the air. In a second she rose thirty metres, eyes and ears on full alert with mixed information. At the peak, gravity gripped her stomach and forced her back down. If anyone had been paying attention from outside, they would have seen her clear the walls of the stadium.

The snow did not move from her impact, as tiny threads of brown and green escaped the bottoms of her heels. Senses overwhelmed, Vala fell to her knees.

Vomited.

"That was pretty good." Rift floated down to be at eye level, he tilted upwards a moment then back to her. "I'd say almost at your peak on the first go. Nicely done."

"What..." Red faced and heart racing, Vala glared. "The hell, Rift! Warn someone next time eh?"

Rift laughed.

"Ugh." Vala spat the disgusting taste out of her mouth. Used the back of her knuckle to clean the edges of her lips as she sat up on her knees. Noticed her jacket swaying in the wind as it landed on a bleacher. "Goddamnit…"

Chapter Three: As I Am

March 5th, 16:23

David was a tall man with dark hair and deep, brown eyes. A brooding aura lay about him, which allowed him to pass through the crowd in an easy mixture of fear and ignorance.

Favouring his right leg, David moved with the aid of a cane. Hand-crafted, deep brown, oak at his side, it intentionally went well with his expensive black suit and dress shoes.

As he traveled through the crowd he held hunched shoulders. He only smiled when it was instigated by another, usually married women on their second or third drink.

With no intent on waiting among the crowd, David passed the line. Stink-eyes found their way to the back of his skull, but quickly became eyes of guilt once they fell to his limp.

A white board displaying the seating arrangements sat on a table just inside the doorway to the hall. David grabbed his name which was held by a pin next to table seven.

The bright light of the room penetrated the paper, revealing a faint 'hidden' text on the other side. He rolled the pin along his fingers while he turned over his name. A poem sat on the back printed in a cursive font that caused the need for squinting to tell an I from a J.

"If magic isn't real..." David rolled his eyes at the first line. Without finishing the poem, he crumbled the paper and tossed it in the small trash can that was tucked under the board. Pushed the pin back in place.

Before taking his place at table seven, David walked around the outer layer of the tables. His brown eyes danced along the crowd with curiosity to see if he knew anyone at the event. Thankfully, he did not.

The bar managed to find its way to David. Perhaps it was merely luck, his Irish blood or the layout of the room; but whatever the case, it had found David and like so many times before, he was very welcoming to its visitation.

He was the first out of a possible eight guests to reach his table. Placed his ice cold rye to the side as he tackled the issue of balancing his cane next to his chair.

Once the cane found the right angle to support itself, David returned his attention to the room. Drew a long taste of his drink while he jumped face to face, taking a second glance to make sure no one he knew was here.

A face brought on memories of a kind face, and a wonderful person. The redhead had filled his high-school fantasies for many years, but back then she had been a blonde.

David rose and walked over to the beautiful woman. She was busy instructing an employee about getting more cream for table three. She had her back to him and almost jumped three centimetres off the ground when he spoke only half a metre behind her.

"I swear you could still be seventeen," David's smile was genuine, but awkward. When her green eyes dropped to his grinning teeth, her eyebrows raised, so he dispatched the smile in a state of embarrassment.

"David?" Her words were slow and tones rose then fell. "David Bywaters?"

"Hello, Maggie," David smiled again. He couldn't help it.

They shook hands. The contact of skin caused his eyebrows to fall, mimicking a sick dog. He felt guilty, but he couldn't risk someone walking away and knowing he had been here.

The look only lasted a heartbeat and went unnoticed by Maggie. The two made small talk before a dropped glass from table five stole her attention. She apologized and returned to work.

With a sigh, his brown eyes dead locked on the rye back at his table. David made his way to his seat, his hands almost shook when he grabbed the glass.

Minutes passed while Maggie worked the floor. She felt her skin crawl a moment as a shiver ran up her spine. She didn't pay it much mind, blaming her goosebumps on the room being too cold. She checked the thermometer, but it read normal.

"Who was that?" Chelsea asked when her mother returned to the kitchen. Chelsea had noticed through the small windows in the doors. She was helping with the understaffed event.

"An old friend," Maggie sighed. "I guess he knows one of the couple."

"You guess?" Chelsea juggled her tossed salad while doing her best to shoot her mother a raised brow. "Couldn't be much of a friend if you didn't bother asking that."

"Hey." Maggie glared. "Don't be a smarty pants."

*   *   *

Vala sat in her underwear and bunny hug at her desk. Both hands clamped around her right ankle, as she attempted to work the tension out of her burning muscles.

"I need an ice pack or something," Vala leaned to look up at the ceiling; while still grasping her ankle.

Her mind drifted to the different drills she had ran. Learning to jump and fall, arcing forward to use her jump to cover a lot of ground quickly and one last ability...

"Well." Vala brought up her hands. Slowly she stepped off the chair and stood, her right ankle flared up on contact with the floor. It wasn't sprained, but severely abused from the strain the armour brought on. Her thoughts drifted to the back of her mind as she focused on finding her soul to call its energy forward.

Her blue eyes became brown, and hair brunette, as she transformed. She stared down at her upward palms as a soft green glow, the size of a penny, started in the centre of each hand. To anyone else, it was light, but Vala could see tiny threads of green swaying. She was manipulating the universe at its most basic form.

She held her breath, as she tried to strain the dot further, over a minute's time and two breaths, she wove the energy to glow all around her hands.

"This green stuff feels so *weird*." Vala moved her eyes along every curve in her hand to search for some kind of crack or wrinkle. Something to remind her she had actually used her hands a few times in her life. The energy had healed everything it touched.

"Could you explain it?" Rift was in cat form, sitting on the bed.

"It's like they're vibrating, but they're still." Vala twisted her lips. "I can't really put it into words aside from that... isn't this crazy?" Vala held up her palms to Rift. "Dude, my hands don't even have those bendy things anymore."

"The energy heals, Vala." Rift sighed, while shaking his head. "I already explained this, you know."

"Sure." Vala nodded. "You certainly did, but I've looked at bendy things all my life. It's kind of a mind fuck." Vala looked down at her palms to see how long it'd take for them to wrinkle. "Guess I haven't come to grip with the fact that all of this is real… I still can't believe I am talking to a cat. Shit, what if I'm insane? Like laying in a hospital bed, talking to a dead rat I found in the ventilation system.

"My mom's looking through a one-way mirror, cradled in the arms of my father. Tears stain cheeks, as she buries her face into his chest. She cries out to God 'my poor baby!' My father places his firm and powerful hand on the back of her skull, as he pulls her in with his other arm, and just stares at his only child with a cold look, that says he is dead on the inside from years of juggling his troubled child and crumbling wife."

"Why," Rift began to question, but decided not to entertain her hypothetic fantasy. "Why don't you practice using your healing powers?"

"On?" Vala looked up. Her eyes went wide in horror as her ears caught a sound she wished she had never heard.

A snap, like a twig, but more chilling. Rift had put his front leg between the bed posts and cranked his weight with all his might in a different direction. His right paw was bent in entirely the wrong direction.

Acid found its way to the back of Vala's throat, as the room became a swaying liquid and the Lord's name escaped her mouth several times. She took a step forward to steady herself as her lips were brought up and her eye twitched.

"Place your hands on my wound," Rift sat with his paw now extended to Vala. His voice didn't shake, nor did he flinch from the pain.

"Doesn't that hurt?" Vala slowly took a step forward, as she reached out and touched his wound.

"It would," Rift removed his now healed arm from her grip. "If I was a real cat, but I am not. I can command my pain receptors to be placed to low or off."

"That is so twisted." Vala shook her head, as she pressed her eyes together. The sound of Rift's broken bone came back to her ears. It kept repeating like a scratched record. Her face was knotted, as she tried to push the sound out for good.

"What are you doing?" Rift lowered his body and looked up to try to get a better look at Vala. "Are you sick?"

"No." Vala placed her hand to her lips, as she took a deep breath then swallowed. "Just don't ever do that again." Her breath was difficult to catch, voice hoarse and face flushed.

"Humans are strange creatures." Rift made his way to the bed's pillow. Taking great pride in his mimicry of a cat, he made himself a bed by clawing up the covering, before planting himself down.

"How original of a concept." Vala fell back into her chair. Sighed as she pressed her hands to her own feet. They cooled instantly as the energy penetrated her skin, to relieve the pain. The sensation felt amazing. "A robot who finds it difficult to understand humans."

Time passed quickly for Vala, as she moved her hands from ankle to ankle. They were cured upon the first touch, but she couldn't get over the cold sensation. It was blissful. She put one hand to each ankle, closed her eyes and leaned back to relax as if she were at a spa.

"You should be careful not to overdo that," Rift yawned from his pillow. "You could potentially mutate the cells."

"Pffft," Vala shrugged with her eyes still closed. "Some people smoke, and some people drink. I restore the cells of my body to pristine condition—"

The world fell forward. Vala felt herself lifted from her seat in a state of slow motion. Her eyes widened as something reached inside her chest and pulled her across the room. She brought her arms up in time to brace herself against the window seal.

"What happened!" Rift leapt to his feet and across the bed to Vala's side. "Are you okay?"

Vala stared down at a golden string that was knotted and vibrating. The string made her stomach twist and her throat dry up. "Chelsea." Vala brought both hands up to cradle the string. "Something isn't right."

$*$ $*$ $*$

Vala landed on the roof of the mall next to the hotel. She had been following the string across town for the last five minutes. Leaping from house to house and across fields until she found herself now facing the sky bridge that connected the mall to the hotel.

Night had mostly masked her movements, but for those that did see and would tell others, no one would believe their story. Even the boy who caught her on his phone and uploaded the video to the internet would be seen as a sham.

"The hotel?" Her breath visible to the world. She drew in air very precisely as she attempted to still her beating heart. She still cradled Chelsea's string.

The golden string was tighter and knotted more than it had been when she was in her room, though Vala wasn't quite sure how she knew this. It was a bad sign.

With a breath that sent air down a bottomless pit of despair, Vala moved forward. Her first three steps were made of lead, but by the seventh she was lighter than air. Swiftly, Vala crossed the sky bridge to enter the hotel.

She ducked her head as she leaned her shoulder into the glass window. The event was anticlimactically cut short as she was pushed backwards.

"Shit." Vala swore as she landed on her butt. She twisted her torso to fall on her right side as she gripped her throbbing left shoulder.

Rage fuelled her tight eyes as she glared from the ground upwards to the splintered glass. Cracks ran all over the window, making it almost impossible to see the details of the hotel interior. Vala felt mocked by a distorted set of shiny lights through the cracks of her defeat.

"That was possibly the least intelligent thing I have ever witnessed a person attempting," Rift floated above in his device form. He bobbed as he studied the window. "Your eyes say Angel, but your might is still very human."

"Screw you!" Vala grinded her teeth. With controlled core strength she pulled herself up to a sitting position without the aid of her arms. "That freakin hurt."

With the use of her healing powers, Vala numbed the pain. In a few short seconds, the numbness was replaced with normality.

Stumbled to her feet. Locked eyes on the glass ahead of her. Slammed her fist to finish the job.

"Whoa." Rift twirled his shards. "I didn't expect that."

"Yeah." Vala placed her heel on the frame and dragged it along the bottom to clear shards away, then lifted herself through the opening. "I'm pretty much a badass." Rolled her eyes.

Inside Vala found onlookers staring in dismay. A few recovering from the startle brought on by the shattering window, while others were baffled by Vala's outfit.

"Yo," Vala gave a wave before heading towards the ballroom.

The golden string slowly dissipated as Vala neared the closed doors. Vala shifted her focus from finding Chelsea to potentially protecting her.

Repeating her mistake, Vala leaned into the door with her shoulder. This time more confident in her might, she had expected it to work.

Vala was thrown backwards. Slid over the carpet about a metre while a glimmer of black crossed the oak doors.

"You are a slow learner." Rift hovered from above.

"Yeah," Vala brought herself up, tried to ignore the snickering onlookers. "This stupid thing has a fricken forcefield. How is that even a thing?"

"Well—"

"I don't care." Concern for Chelsea enhanced her tone. "How do I bring it down?"

"I'm not quite sure," Rift scanned the forcefield. "Its being generated by Water based magic. Your Tree element should be able to penetrate it."

"Sweet." Vala took a deep breath.

Both of her green fists slammed into the barrier. The light grew out of Vala's hands and like roots of a tree, they quickly spread along the entire surface. Criss-crossing over and over until the black was replaced entirely with her green light.

With great force, Vala proudly hurled her shoulder through the doors. This time expectations were met with success.

The room was as Vala remembered from yesterday. Save for the cowardly crowd all gathered to one side of the room, with a dark figure holding up a panicking girl.

The crowd rushed past a frozen Vala. One even connected shoulders with her. She didn't notice that her torso was forced to twist as her eyes quaked at the girl ahead.

Blonde bangs almost covered her gentle green eyes. Though at the moment, they were hard pressed and watering, only opening for quick reminders of the horror ahead. Hands clasped around her attackers wrist, trying to keep the strain off her neck. Her legs dangled loosely below, about thirty centimetres off the ground.

"Vala!" Rift swayed into her view. "Wake up. You need to help her!"

Fists balled followed by a violently shaken head. With closed eyes she pushed her freeze up out of her mind. With newfound clarity, Vala opened her eyes.

She took two steps before leaping up and over the room. Shifted her weight forward as she brought her right arm around and over her shoulder.

The fist indented the face of Chelsea's captor. Vala felt her skin and cloth drag along the almost reptilian skin. A damp thickness stained her knuckles as blood was spilt.

Landing on a knee, breaking the captor's grip, Vala turned to her friend as she fell. Chelsea violently coughed as she frantically fought to fill her lungs with precious oxygen.

"Chelsea!" Vala turned to the dark figure. Threw a fist without a thought then turned back to Chelsea ignoring the body being thrown backwards. "You okay?"

"What?" Chelsea was on her knees while using one arm to brace her weight while the other massaged her throat.

When she looked over to Vala her tight eyes were forced wide. "Vala? What..." Her head shook in confusion. "What happened to your hair?"

"Didn't you know, brunettes are making a comeback?" Vala grinned. Fell to Chelsea's height to place a hand over her friends back. "What's going on?"

"My Mom—" Chelsea's choke replaced by panic. "Watch out!"

"Huh?" Vala looked over her shoulder in time to catch the back of a hand across her face.

The force was great. A strain burnt where Vala's skull connected with her spine. If it hadn't been for her armour, she believed she would have been decapitated.

However, her soaring ragdoll body was the least of her concern, nor her straining neck, or the broken tables and shatter glass that embedded its fragments into her exposed skin. Her concern was a familiar face.

A loving, caring face that belonged to a woman she saw as more parental than her own mother. A love that was poisoned and twisted. A distortion into a mangled mess. Something almost unrecognizable.

Yet it was. Vala's quick glimpse had been enough to know it was Maggie, but something was awfully wrong with her.

Slowly Vala stumbled to a standing position. With great hesitation she brought her eyes up along with the rest of her. Ahead stood the creature that once was known as Maggie.

The creature held the right body frame. Its skin no longer silk smooth, but now bumpy and cracked. Delicate red hair perverted into a dried tangled mess. Eyes blacker than the absence of any light could ever naturally be.

The eyes sent a chill down Vala. When the shiver passed her stomach, Vala bent over slightly as she fought the urge to vomit.

"So you are here." It spoke. Its voice echoed itself while playing backwards off separate vocal cords at the same time it played forward.

The distorted voice continued as the creature began walking towards Vala. "I will be seen as a god when I return with your head on a spike."

"Wha—" Vala shook her head as she took a step backwards.

"Vala, you need to do this." Rift edged her from behind. "You need to subdue her, then you can heal her." He bumped her in the upper back.

With a deep breath Vala retracted her back pedal and replaced it with three forceful strides before striking a powerful stance. Voice steady and deep. "What the hell are you?"

"According to the woman screaming inside of me, I am apparently the closest thing you have to a mother." The creature curled its lips. It made it look more demon than Vala could ever have imagined. "She keeps begging me not to peel your flesh free of your bone."

The claim panicked Chelsea and simultaneously enraged Vala. As Chelsea sat up to reach out to her mother, Vala white knuckled fists as she sprinted forward.

As Chelsea spoke softly through cracking syllables, "Mother?" Vala shouted while pulling back her fist. "Bitch!"

Vala leaned forward as she pushed off the ground. Rocketing forward to close the five metre gap almost instantly.

Cracked bones rang through Vala's ears as her fist embedded itself into the demon's face. Unlike when Rift's bone cracked and left her woozy, this sound fuelled her.

She fell to the ground. Followed up with a hook from her left fist. However it never made contact. Her assault interrupted by the demon's own follow up.

Blood filled the air. Crossed Vala's face as her lungs filled with the backup caused by a crushed nose. The demon had punched her.

"Goddamnit," Vala back pedaled as she curled over herself. Grabbed her throbbing face with glowing hands. She peered through watering eyes just in time to see the demon's hand morph into a claw.

The hand tripled in size as the pinky and ring finger, then the middle and index fused into two claws. Torn skin and shriveled thumb left to dangle.

"Jesus." Vala snorted blood as she heaved backwards in full startle. The motion opened herself up for the demons next strike.

The claw started at her left hip and dragged across her stomach and chest to finish skimming her right shoulder. Blood spilled into the air.

The force lifted her and threw her across the room. She landed on her side. Slid a metre before coming to a forceful stop when the back of her head collided with the metal box at the heated buffet table.

Darkness over took Vala. Without a second thought, Rift sent a power surge through the golden string that connected the two. His jade lost its inky iris as he fell to the floor with chains sprawled out. A golden aura covered Vala's body while she was unconscious.

"Vala!" Chelsea screamed as she got to her feet. The demon turned and slapped Chelsea with the back of its claw. She caught most of it with defensive arms, but the force lifted her and she smashed her back against the wall. Slid down. Blacked out.

The only remaining attendee stood up from his table. His lips emptied the final sip of spiced rum before he reached below the table for his cane.

David placed himself between Vala and the demon. His brow low as his moppy demeanor hide the curiosity behind his dark eyes.

"That's enough." David's voice was collected. There was no sign of expression in it or his face. He didn't cheer for Vala nor did he show empathy. He was indifferent. The experiment had concluded. "Release the woman."

The demon laughed. The twisted voice made David cringe. He collected himself as he brought up his cane. Aimed it at the beast as he demanded his presence to be acknowledged.

"Let her go before I forcefully dispel you," David narrowed his eyes ever so slightly.

"Please," The demon waved its hand to brush David's words aside. "You may have conjured me but you are *our* tool. You hold no authority over me."

"Do it." David allowed anger to slip into his words. "*Now.*"

The demon stopped its laughter. Tightened its eyes as a strange surge of energy rippled from its core. Darkness overtook the room as the energy erupted from the beast. The power to the entire building was cut, the only light source to the room the soft red glows of the exit signs.

The demon's breath became louder and more violent. Though David knew it was still fifteen feet ahead of him, he could feel its breath on his face. The disgusting smell of sulphur brought queasiness to his stomach.

With a steady set of hands, David found a metal ring just below the curve in the cane's handle. He pinched two metal indents and twisted the handle free of the shaft.

Gears inside the hilt revved up and from them ignited silver sparks. An eruption of plasma spewed into the air. A gravitation force extended off the hilt and pulled the plasma back into itself. The photons clashed in quick succession until they beat themselves into a hardened state of matter.

A metre long, silver blade extended off the hilt. The gears continued to rev in ten second intervals. Each rotation destabilized the brand which sent a shiver that serrated the blade. The stabilized weapon was known as a brand, a weapon that drew off the power of the human soul.

David held the blade like a rapier, standing so his body was thinnest towards the assault, hiding his bad leg behind his body. The demon threw two tables as he began to backpedal.

Two quick slashes sent each table crumbling to the side. At first the hardened light pushed the wood to the side, but it wasn't more than a heartbeat before the heat cut through the wood.

The table cloth freed themselves from their respective tables. Though the candles on top fell free and were blown out by the rush of air, the cloth still lit up. The blades heat had started the fire.

Each tablecloth floated to a new destination where their flame would begin to spread.

His eyes tightened as they studied the darkness quickly but carefully. David held the room's main light source, which left him at a disadvantage as the demon perfectly blended in with the darkness.

A flame flickered from a rush of air passing by. Eyes had been elsewhere but the sharp sway in the light reflecting off the remaining crystal on the tables allowed him to make an educated guess as to where the demon may be.

Without waiting to confirm the demon's location, David swung his blade horizontally through the air. He caught nothing in its sluggish, but powerful swing.

He took in a deep breath to still his heart. The move had been sloppy. His blade didn't require force to penetrate flesh. The swifter the move, the better. David would not make the same mistake twice.

Two more tables came, the sound of shattering glass gave their location away. He directed his blade towards the assault. David didn't bother finishing his turn before cutting twice through the air, same as before.

David laid the blade to his side as he studied the room. His blade illuminated his left side top to bottom but it did not fully cross his body horizontally. The blade was useless for him to use as a light to seek out the demon.

Suddenly water fell from the skies. Covered every inch of the room. Soaked the flame out of existence. The room dimmed considerably, returning back to a thick darkness.

The sprinkler system continued to rain down. David adjusted his collar as his suit gained weight from absorbing the liquid. First he released his tie then began undoing his jacket buttons, all the while watching the darkness.

Mist ran up his arm and over his shoulder as each droplet vaporized over the blade's heat. With every movement of the blade, no longer was there just a trail of blinding light, but a thick trail of steam.

David swung his right arm free of his jacket then passed his blade from one hand to the other. Doing his best to ignore the sirens of the fire alarm, David studied the room.

The jacket fell to the ground. His frown thickened as his white shirt became skin tight, the feel of the fabric annoyed him; the annoyance enhanced to a frustration as any movement he made seemed to tighten the fabric.

"You can still walk away from this." David squinted as water ran down his brow and into the curves of his eyes. He pinched his eyes with both thumb and index to relieve them of the liquid. It didn't work and so David tilted his chin low in hopes it would help.

Laughter was the only verbal reply that David received. The distorted voice crept all over him and got under his skin. He stepped towards it.

His limp kept him from closing the distance quickly, but the laughter wasn't moving. It continued as it lured David in for what he assumed the demon assumed would be his final moment.

This bothered David because the beast could potentially be correct.

The beast came first. The laughter suddenly cut out, which caused David to straighten up right in a startled state. As he did so he instinctively swung his blade upwards.

David saw a greyscale set of teeth and glaring eyes just before it collided with his face. His blade had cut Maggie from hip to shoulder so the skull had been lifeless on contact, but the force was still great from its forward momentum.

David first stumbled into a back pedal, then fell as his right leg couldn't keep up to his left. He came down on his back. Air rushed out his body.

He coughed violently, seeking to fill his lungs, but with his face up to the falling water his coughs quickly turned to outright choking.

He rolled to his left. Let his blade free which cut its power. Curved his right arm over his head as he tried to keep the water away from his airpipe. From this position he struggled for a moment before he found his breath.

Lungs strained and throat burned as he fought to swear. "Dammit." His voice hoarse. The air was heavy and every breath felt like it was getting caught in the back of his throat.

Though he was now breathing, he felt just as restricted as when he was drowning. With a woozy mind he fought to fish through the darkness for his jacket, then his hilt.

Slowly he stood. Put his jacket back on but kept it undone. Took a moment to search for the rest of his cane before the sounds of sirens met his ears.

It was difficult to tell as the walls muffled the noise but both fire and police seemed to be outside.

Without time to spare, David limped over to the unconscious Vala. He ignored the sobs of Chelsea blindly searching through the rubble.

He was halfway out the back door with Vala over his shoulder when Chelsea found her mother's body. The scream was deafening.

"Chelsea?" Vala opened her eyes slightly. She caught a vaguely lit Chelsea curled over Maggie's body. Her eyelids fell as she blacked out.

*   *   *

Vala fell from the edge of her window frame. Her mind felt empty of thought. She kept trying to draw upon her memories but everything was fuzzy about the evening. Vala didn't know how Rift or her had made their way into the parkade. She barely remembered calling Chelsea's father to tell him he needed to get down to the hotel, and she had been awake for that part.

"Mister Grayson," Vala's own words echoed in the back of her head. "Something bad happened…" She didn't remember what that something bad had been. How she had gotten Maggie killed. All she knew is she had to leave without facing Chelsea.

With defeated thought, Vala reached into her soul to command the armour to dematerialize. Vala stood in her room back in her clothes of the day. She felt naked and ashamed. Exposed to the world even while in the safety of privacy.

Disheartened steps guided Vala across her room. Eyes danced on the cracks of hardwood beneath her. With only memory alone, and not with the aid of vision, Vala grabbed the chair that still rested next to her bed.

She sat down on her chair and used her heel to shift the seat so her legs were under her desk. At first she slouched but found the arms to the chair weren't adjusted properly. This infuriated her. Two shakes of frustration to force the arms into position burnt her out. Exhausted with the day, Vala let her own arms fall to gravities whim.

Rift stepped into the room from the open window. Looked over his shoulder to the street below a bit more concerned about wondering eyes, however no one seemed interested in anybody else's business.

A few soft hops and Rift was on the bed behind Vala. He paused a moment before clearing his throat. "Vala, I think we should talk about tonight."

"Get out." Vala's teeth grinned as her head fell to the side.

"Vala," Rift took a step forward, about to jump to her shoulder. "I—"

"Get out!" Vala rose as she spun around swinging. Her contorted body caused the chair to flip over and crash into her bookcase, every novel and textbook fell to the ground. Each a grenade of expressive anger. The entire world shook from Rift's perspective and he felt a lifetime's worth of guilt pit in his stomach.

Green eyes shook with a mixture of panic and concern, but blue eyes glared with anger that mudded the mind and caused Vala to fall short of thought. Neither of the two exchanged words, but sat in each other's gazes. Both wishing to reach for the other, but neither understood if they wanted to or should.

The bombardment of books to floor had echoed through the entire house. In the kitchen Emily had been enjoying a book, without bothering to bookmark her page, she stood. "Vala, honey?" Emily called up the stairs and quickly followed her voice with concerned steps.

"Vala..." Rift finally let his dry mouth slide open. So much hesitation behind his shaking voice as he attempted to fathom the words a teenage girl may need.

"Just don't say anything." Vala let her shoulders fall.

Eyes matched her defeated stance. They danced along the patterns of her blanket, her mind hoping distraction would ice the pain, and numb reality. "I'm too sad to be properly mad right now."

"Vala you had to—" Rift tilted his head to attempt to get into her line of sight. "She—"

"I'm sick and tired of people!" Vala balled her hands. Knuckles strained white as nails stabbed into her palms. "People thinking because I'm fifteen that I'm stupid. I know what happened, and why. Is it confusing? Yes. Am I mad? Yes."

A second passed that lasted longer than life itself. "But more than anything Rift, I'm sad."

"Do you hate me?" Rift felt his eyes shake with a new sensation. One he was certainly not programmed with.

Vala looked up for a moment. Mouth oh-ed but then her exhaustion kicked back and she let her expression blank before her face fell to the ground again.

Her voice was low, shivering with hesitation. "A year ago I was in the hospital. For a while I was anorexic. After a week without eating or drinking anything, I finally passed out during class one day, almost died. Chelsea visited me. Everyday. Was the only one who did. My father kept his distance. Ashamed. And my mother was in denial. Said I was just a girl pushing herself too hard. Took her time to come to terms to what had happened. There was only one person willing to admit I was depressed, and it wasn't even me."

Vala whipped tears from her eyes with the back of her hands. "When I came back to school girls teased me, some of them I had considered my best friends. The boys just avoided me. Only Chelsea was there. Even though others isolated her to get to me, she stayed around."

A picture over top her bed had the two smiling during mid falls frost. "I've just hurt the only person who was willing to hurt to make me happy. You have no idea how I feel right now."

The door opened, Emily stood in the door frame scared to step in without permission. Her eyes darted from her daughter to the cat on the bed. Confusion ran through her entire body as her ears attempted to figure out the words of Vala's that she had caught.

Before a thought could muster itself into parental action, Vala had embraced Emily. Arms tightened around her body so hard that Emily found it difficult to breathe. Her vision locked on the wall across the room as sounds of her daughter weeping touched her ears.

"Vala..." Emily slowly looked down at her daughter. Ran a hand across the back of her head. "What..."

"Mom." Vala's voice shrieked. Her face was red, eyes crushed, with every breath her chest expanding to its limits before imploding on itself over and over again. "I'm sorry. Please don't hate me."

"H-hate you?" Emily grabbed her daughter's chin and forced it upwards for eye contact. "Vala, what for?"

"Don't hate me." Tremors ran through her entire frame as she pushed her face down again. "Don't hate me."

"Why would I hate you?" Emily felt her steady body begin to shake.

"Don't hate me." Tears flowed from her as she dug her face deeper into her mother.

Emily tightened her arms around her daughter. Without a word the two spent the night crying together, while Rift watched from the distance.

CHAPTER FOUR: ASSOCIATES IN CRIME

March 9th, 07:00

Vala opened her eyes. Blue vast oceans empty of thought. The white ceiling above Vala was unfamiliar; sure she had seen it every day of her life, but something about the ceiling felt foreign.

With a deep breath Vala sat up. The air felt foreign. Rougher. Colder. Vala could feel the alien gas all the way past her nostrils, down her throat, filling every centimetre of her lungs.

It wasn't that Vala herself was empty minded, but that so many thoughts rushed through her so quickly that it all collided into a tangled mess of blank. Nothing was focused enough to reach out and grab. To hold.

Slowly Vala rose to her feet, careful not to disturb Rift, who was sleeping on the body pillow between Vala and her desk. The cold hardwood floor felt as sharp as knives underneath her feet, but she did not flinch. Vala reached over to her nightstand to turn off her alarm before it went off.

The room felt bigger than usual. It was a chore for Vala to stand and then make her way across the room. She pulled out her chair from the desk. Clothes for the day were previously folded and awaiting her there. Without hesitation or decisiveness, but somewhere between, Vala reached for the cloth.

Black long skirt, long dress shirt that had shoulders that made Vala look twice her age. The suit was heavy, but not as heavy as Vala's heart. With rolled eyes Vala reached for the door knob. Here she hesitated.

What am I doing? Vala's filtered thoughts had pushed the obvious question at hand. *Chelsea won't want me there...*

Today was Maggie's funeral. Pushed a week out to make time for family to arrive. Invitations had been sent out from Chelsea's email address, but Vala had a hard time believing it was her actually sending the invites. The structure had grammar and spelling mistakes, something Chelsea would never have done.

Believing the email to have been sent out from Chelsea's father, Anthony and not Chelsea herself, Vala decided that Chelsea must not have told the police or her own father about what Vala had done. *Who'd even believe her?*

Vala pulled open the door. Made her way down the silent hallways. Every bedroom still closed, the 7 am sky was still pitch black, so Vala made her way around the house from memory alone.

Down the stairs. Through the kitchen. Into the crisp winter air.

The church wasn't far from Vala's house. It was all a haze. She knew she had gone, hid in the back but there wasn't much memory of it. Vala made sure to keep out of Chelsea's eyesight. There wasn't much time to show her respects to Maggie, but Vala did manage to slip by the graveyard after everyone had gone home.

"Sorry." Was the only word to escape trembling lips.

*   *   *

April 5th

Vala opened her brown eyes. Stared up, like so many days gone by, at her unfamiliar ceiling.

Slowly Vala sat up. Shifted around a sleeping Rift, to turn off the alarm before it went off, a second shy of 7 am. Left the bed and stumbled to her feet. Vala grabbed her bathrobe and made her way to the washroom.

The hallway was silent. Like so many mornings before, Vala wondered if her family had lied to her for all of these years. Had they all just woken up a moment before Vala's traditional 7:45? A month ago, this would have been funny. Vala would have grinned.

Once in the washroom, Vala turned on the shower as she stripped. Played with the knob for two minutes before deciding on the proper heat. Turned to her scale during the entire process. Weighed herself. Frowned. Showered. Brushed her teeth.

Noticed herself in the mirror. Ran her hands through her hair as she tipped her chin forward. Sighed as she saw her roots coming in. "Dammit." She cracked open new contacts before leaving the washroom.

Before her family was awake, Vala was already out the door and on her way to school. It wouldn't start for another hour and fifteen minutes, but with a numb mind, Vala didn't care.

As Vala walked, she ate her toast. Both hands dug deep into her bunny hug. Using her mouth to pull in the toast and eat bit by bit.

Rift followed Vala, but no words were exchanged. Not much had been said between the two for the last few weeks. Rift was content with the silence as long as Vala continued her training after school and on weekends. During the mornings he would follow her trip to school from the fence tops.

Ms. Harrison addressed the room, "I know it's been awhile since Chelsea has been in class, but as of today her father has officially pulled her out of this school. For those of you close to her, she wanted you to know you can still reach her through email. It seems the family has decided to move back to Toronto, to live with their extended family."

Vala looked around the room. She was in class. The desk next to her empty. She hadn't even realized she had walked all this way and waited all this time. Was it first period? *Must be.*

"The school is about to wrap up the donations that we've been collecting for the Grayson family condolences probably within the next day or two, so if you are donating please do it by then. We want to give it to the family before they move this Thursday. Vala... is it okay if I have you drop off the money to the Graysons?"

Vala closed her eyes to hold back tears. "Yes." Her voice was low. She felt her entire body quake.

Without paying attention to the front of the room, Vala began to prepare for the class. Clicked her mechanical pencil, opened her notebook, and touched granite to a fresh paper. Waited.

"I would like to take this moment to introduce you to a new classmate," Ms. Harrison demanded attention again.

Vala remained looking at her desk, still not having looked up to the front of the class. Mechanical pencil pressed to the first tab of her paper. The lead dancing on a fine line of sturdy and breaking.

At the front of the class, unknown to an ignorant Vala, stood Mei Ling. Shoulder long black hair with a single dark blue streak. A faded bunny hug and worn jeans, both two sizes too big, fell onto her body. The ends of her bunny hug were cut so that her thumbs could poke out to make a fingerless glove. No tan. Pale for an Asian girl. In her left hand a copy of The Gunslinger and in her other the five textbooks for the next few classes. Ear buds in both ears that vanished into a homemade slit just below the neckline of the bunny hug. Her iPod hidden some place beneath.

"This is Mei Ling," Ms. Harrison announced. "She's a transfer student from Daniel Pod College High School."

A quick cut of gossip tore through the air. No attempt to keep their voices masked. Even though the beats pounded her eardrums, Mei Ling heard every last one. Her eyes tightened a moment as she began mental judgement.

"Brainiac alert," came from *a clever girl that looked like she had once been overweight but the lack of eating three meals a day left her with a body that made for poor life choices and likely was fuelled by father abandonment.*

"Ugh that hair," came from *a girl the size of a whale with nose hair a mile long.*

"Heh. Too dumb for private school, eh?" came from *a boy with teeth that would fill the wallet of seven orthodontists.*

"Her clothes..." came from *a girl who was a billboard for every band under creation.*

"She reads?" Came from *a girl—slut—who was five minutes away from her water breaking all over the tile flooring.*

"Still hit it." came from *a boy who'd I'd never let touch me even if his father was Michael Peter Balzary.*

"Why don't you tell us a little bit about yourself?" Ms. Harrison smiled, pretending to ignore the other students to make less work for herself.

Mei Ling sighed. Flicked off her iPod, and removed an ear bud by looping the cord over ear so it wouldn't fall free. "My name is Mei Ling." Favoured her shrug to her right shoulder.

Pause.

No one filled the pause. Eyes began to shift left then right. Everyone wondering why it was silent. Surely there was more to be said.

"Umm..." Ms. Harrison noticed the eye darting. "Anything else you'd like to share?"

Gossip picked up. The silence had been broken, and by teenage law it meant no one could over hear you.

"I have a question," Mei Ling tightened her eyes onto the group of girls midway down the rows. "Do you grade on a curve?"

"Of course." Ms. Harrison grinned. A bit of pride flowed through her strict ways. There weren't too many teachers still willing to challenge their students. "We may not be a private school, but I am sure you'll see we can still challenge our student body."

"Good." Mei Ling began to walk to the only empty desk in the room. While passing the gossiping girls Mei Ling threw her speech under her breath, over her shoulder and in a way that said 'I am whispering' but loud enough that everyone heard the words. "You're fucked."

The gossiping group exchanged confused faces. A few of them looked worried, the others looked as if they didn't even know what a report card was.

Mei Ling stopped at the empty desk. Raised a brow at the collecting dust, stomach turned as she debated life choices. *This place is disgusting…* Mei Ling turned to Ms. Harrison and pointed at the mess. Ms. Harrison nodded, and with that Mei Ling sat next to Vala.

With a frown, Mei Ling balled her hand into her bunny hug and with one quick swipe, cleaned the desk.

"Okay..." Ms. Harrison nervously shifted her weight. "Well let's begin on reviewing chapter four then. Can anyone remind us what's currently happening?"

The sounds of the day began to drown out as a student was voluntold to read.

Mei Ling placed her notebook on the desk. It was covered with graffiti art: a mixture of bold letters done in white-out, highlighter-yellow slanted text and cursive letters in thick red ink. Various monsters were done in a mixture of the three.

Vala looked over, raised a brow. Mei Ling opened the notebook to the first fresh page, the left page held perfect writing. No letter out of place or misformed. Things of interest were highlighted.

Vala and Mei Ling exchanged awkward looks.

Mei Ling smiled. "Fan of the Chili Peppers?"

Vala nodded, slowly.

Mei Ling gave Vala the hanging ear bud. "We're friends now."

Vala slowly put in the ear bud, held her voice low, "What was with all of that?"

"That?" Mei Ling jerked her head to the group of girls. This caused the ear bud to fall from Vala. Mei Ling snickered as Vala put it back in.

"Yeah." Vala nodded. It took a great deal of willpower to keep her moody expression from curling into a smile.

"What's your name?" Mei Ling leaned closer. A fairly blank expression across her round face. Vala was stuck in an honest state of confusion if Mei Ling was squinting or not; Mei Ling was well aware of this and though she kept her expression blank, she was smiling in the back of her mind at how uncomfortable it was making Vala.

"Vala," Vala leaned a bit closer so only centimetres were between the two.

Mei Ling smiled before sitting up straight.

$$*\qquad*\qquad*$$

Classes went by slower than normal for Vala. Though this wasn't out of boredom, it turned out Vala and Mei Ling had a lot of classes together. Mei Ling's presence seemed to bring Vala out of her void and to pay attention to the day unfolding in front of her.

The two decided to stay after school to study on the roof top. Vala hoped Mei Ling might be able to help her catch back up, her grades were slipping even for her. Conversations of the day suggested to Vala that Mei Ling liked having good grades, and Vala wanted to share this.

"How can you remember all of this?" Vala leaned back on the picnic table. The fresh blue sky was very welcoming. Too bad trig wasn't.

"I haven't had a wrong answer. Ever." Mei Ling went back to trying to teach her new friend the mysteries of math.

"Ever, ever?" Vala leaned forward with a crocked eyebrow.

"And even ever-er." Mei Ling smiled. Looked over to her left to make eye contact with Vala.

Warmth came over Vala's chest, her eyes dropped to see a golden string expand towards Mei Ling. Imaginary threads of black and grey wove around her person, consumed her and transformed her into a knight. When Vala blinked, Mei Ling returned to her normal attire.

Mei Ling picked up on the weird vibe, but mistook it. "Are you high right now?"

"No." Vala waved her hand as if to brush an imaginary cloud of thought out of her eyes. Once everything was back to normal she couldn't help but laugh, "But hey, if you're so smart, why are you here?"

"Fits me." Mei Ling shrugged as she turned back to the book.

"I don't understand." Vala shook her head.

"Nobody does." Mei Ling sighed. "My parents don't. Teachers don't. Maybe I don't."

A pause.

"I just know things," Mei Ling turned up her music, which was still split between the girls. "Those other kids at that school earned it and are smug about it. I never had that. I just knew it. There was no pride. I just want to be me. Not a bunch of numbers at the end of a report card."

"Is that why you dress like a burn out?" Vala grinned at her own joke. "But keep your notes so organized?"

"Okay. So I'm a little smug." Mei Ling laughed. "Why can't I take a little pride in my work?"

"Were you..." Vala scratched the base of her skull while she searched her thoughts to find the right words, but there weren't any polite ones. "Kicked out?"

"I didn't get along," Mei Ling nodded. "Things happened. Now I'm here."

Vala stood up, this tore Mei Ling's earpiece free, a smile cross her face as wide as a barn.

"Get your ass down here," Mei Ling pointed at the bench. Yanked her ear buds back. "You haven't finished a single problem."

"Whatever," Vala rolled her eyes. "Just gonna grab a pop."

With a smile, Mei Ling tossed two coins Vala's way.

"What's your poison?" Vala played with the coins in her hand. Slid them over and under each other.

"No diet. Surprise me otherwise," Mei Ling waved Vala away like royalty would a peasant. Slipped her ear buds in.

"Sure thing," Vala placed the coins on the notebook, "but it's on me."

"Thanks," Mei Ling smiled a little as she pocketed the coins.

*   *   *

Vala walked through the hallway. Smile on her face while she twitched her nose; attempting to use it as a wand to psychically command the mound of pop cans not to topple over one another. Even though she had recently lost Chelsea in her life, she felt blessed to find somebody she could connect to so quickly. It was as if divine intervention had decided to grant her a personal miracle.

Down the hall came a tall, pale-skinned girl. A brown pony tail fell to her shoulder blades. Judging from her build and height, Vala assumed she was a year older than her. The darting brown eyes suggested she was lost.

Vala's own eyes fell upon the girl's right eye. It was covered in a purple swirl mixed with jaundice yellow and a trickle of crimson that escaped from the highest part of the swirl.

Eye contact was made. A pause came to both sets of feet. Vala knew she should dart her eyes away in a panic bewilderment, as was proper, but she couldn't look away from the swelling.

"I'm new here." The girl scratched her chin while diverting her eyes to the ceiling. She had a deep voice, the kind commonly mistaken as a boy over the phone. "Where's the washroom?"

"W-were you in a fight?" Vala was still wide eyed. She'd never seen someone hit before, not without her armour pushing adrenaline through and cloudy doubt.

"Yeah." The girl grinned as she ran a hand along the bruise to rub it like one would while polishing a well earned trophy. "Bitch called me fat."

A hard impact to Vala's chest disconnected her from reality as another warmth swelled up and expanded a golden string towards the girl. Orange and yellow threads consumed the girl as cloth tightened around her into knight armour. It didn't last longer than the blink of an eye before it was gone.

"Yo. Air head," The girl brought Vala back to reality with daggered eyes and hipped knuckles. "Help me out, huh?"

"Sure." Vala turned her body. "Uh..." Balanced the pop cans in her folded right arm while taking a moments chance to point down the hall with a wavering left. "Down the hall. A bit more past the yellow lockers. The signs were removed by some dick, but the left door is ours. The right, his."

"Thanks." The girl smiled. Gave a slight bow and waved her hand like a butler from old England. She began to walk past Vala.

"Sure..." Vala paused on her heels as they passed one another. With a twist of her lips she judged the situation before turning back to the girl. "My name's Vala."

The girl paused her steps. Twisted her body towards Vala almost bothered by the entirety of it. "Asa."

With one hand Vala pulled up the bottom of her bunny hug to roll the cans into. "Could you use an ice pack?" Vala held up a pop can next to a smirk.

"Seri—" Asa smiled as she caught the tossed can. A strong warmth in her chest opposite the intensity of the ice cold tin can. Dumbfounded, Asa read the 'diet' label in her hands. "—ously?" The first part of the word sincere, then quite sarcastic.

"Did you just give me a diet drink?" Asa pushed the cold can against her skin.

Vala turned on heel while in mid laughter. "Thought you could use it." Her tone quite joyful.

As Vala vanished down the hall, Asa was left with a smile on her face, "What a bitch."

*   *   *

The wind had picked up back on the roof. Mei Ling pulled her arms to shiver for a moment, before fighting her pockets to retrieve her iPod. She slid the volume low so that when it was her favourite part, she could raise it dramatically, to make it seem louder than normal. The song began with a guitar riff. Slowly she slid her finger to raise the volume as the bass bled into the song.

Mei Ling swayed her head with the flow of the bass. Hands ran across the wooden picnic table to add sensation to touch, in hopes of matching her hearing. She longed for her own bass at home.

Soon the song picked up. Mei Ling leaned back, hooked her legs to keep from falling. Plucked the invisible bass for every memorized chord. Broke into a violent nod as the beats picked up.

The bright world was torn apart and replaced with a blackened stadium. On top of the stage Mei Ling slid her left hand down the neck of her polar white bass. The weight of parental disappointment, isolation from the student body, and reference to time was taken off her shoulders.

The only thing left was life; it was good.

Suddenly Rift hopped on the table. The thud warranted open eyes. Mei Ling looked up at the brown cat ahead of her, still leaning back at an obtuse angle and continued playing her invisible bass. A crooked smile crossed her face as one eyebrow raised.

"How," Mei Ling swung herself forward as the song died out. Ran a hand from Rift's head down to his tail. While her other hand removed her ear buds. "How did you get up here?"

"I can jump really high," Rift purred.

The two stared at each other in silence. Mei Ling slowly, without any emotional reaction, put her earbuds back in.

Mei Ling's heart heaved itself against the inside of her chest, flared nostrils attempted to have insanity removed via music. The bass riff was not doing its normal job; instead of calming her down, Mei Ling was frozen in eye contact with the feline. Unable to muster up thought to issue action.

Passed Rift, though Mei Ling didn't notice, opened the door to the roof. From it came Vala holding her mountain of pop cans.

"I hope you're a fan of Russian roulette." Vala turned and closed the door with a free foot. "I dropped one down the stairs."

"This cat talks." Mei Ling's voice matched the beat to her song. All her mind could do was cling to familiar settings.

Once at the table Vala looked up from her mound of drinks, feeling much more confident in her balancing act while not walking. Down below, she noticed Rift looking up at her. The two shared in a small staring contest before blinking at each other a moment. "Rift?"

"Hello, Vala." Rift smiled. "I wouldn't mind something fruity."

"Oh good," Mei Ling lowered her head to watch her feet. Her stomach was clenching up. "You're friends."

The door opened with a greasy creak. From it came a cleaned up Asa. "Whose friends?"

Mei Ling looked up to shift eyes from Vala to Asa. "Vala has a talking cat."

Asa laughed, as she cracked open her ice pack and swung a leg over the bench. Her face had been cleaned of blood, but still was swelled. "What?" Drank a long swig.

"Everyone's taking this quite well, Vala," Rift purred a bit.

Asa spat out her drink across the table, covering Mei Ling's book and part of her bunny hug.

"Uh..." Mei Ling wiped part of the pop from her face. "Gross."

Asa violently coughed as some soda went down her windpipe. She gasped for breath as she fell backwards, out from under the bench. Twisted her leg awkwardly as it got caught on the way down. Quickly found both breath and footing and took two paces from the table to distance herself. "*Shiiit!*"

Vala laughed hysterically into the bend of an arm. Crouched to get her stomach as close to the picnic table as possible, before rolling the cans onto it. While still laughing, Vala extended her arm to Rift, who used it to climb to her shoulder.

"Mei Ling, this is Asa. Asa, this is Mei Ling." Vala freed a tear from her eye as both girls exchanged looks that expressed 'like *that's* important'. "Girls. This is my cat, Rift. He says things. Words, mostly."

"Pleased to meet you." Rift had a wide smile cross his face.

"Is this real life?" Asa looked down at her can. "Is *this* laced?"

"Vala." Mei Ling placed her iPod on the table. "Question."

"Yeah?" Vala cracked open a can.

"Why does your cat talk?" Mei Ling twisted her head left then right, as if balancing thought in mind. "It's not that I have an issue. I'm not cat-speaking-phobic, but I'm pretty sure if the Bible doesn't have something against this, than you know, science might."

"Well Mei Ling," Vala let Rift drink from her can. "I see your book smarts, and raise you with my street smarts."

Mei Ling opened her can as her mind was beginning to settle itself. "Alien?"

"Alien." Vala confirmed by tipping her can to Mei Ling, then sat down.

"Mars?" Mei Ling sipped.

"No." Vala laughed.

"So if he isn't from the third rock from the sun," Mei Ling ran her hands across her face to finish pushing her worries out. "We dealing with Deep Space Nine stuff?"

Vala shook her head.

"A different galaxy?" Mei Ling tried leaning towards Rift with a raised eyebrow.

"A different dimension," Vala looked over her shoulder for confirmation. "I think?" Rift nodded.

"Checks out," Mei Ling smiled back at her friend. "Past it." Sipped her can.

"I'm glad everyone is in good jest about this," Rift lapped up a bit more pop from Vala's can.

"Hey space cat," Mei Ling leaned closer for inspection. "Are all aliens British?"

"No," Rift looked up. Used a paw to remove some pop from his chin. "My accent is a rarity. Most sound closer to your Earth Boston accent."

Mei Ling cocked an eyebrow to Vala. With a smile Vala shrugged a little, "He has been trying to adopt my sense of humour. Sadly, his jokes aren't quite there yet."

"I respectfully disagree," Rift turned his face away.

"Whoa." Asa fell to the edge of the bench, faced away from the girls. "This Twilight Zone shit is freaking me out. Vala. Explain. Yourself. Please."

"I'm kind of a superhero," Vala shrugged. "It's a pretty big deal."

A pause from both girls.

"Well that sums it up," Asa slowly turned around in admitted defeat. "Thanks."

Asa pulled out a makeup mirror. "How hard did that chick hit me?" Eyed her reflection.

Rift hopped onto the table.

"My name is Rift." Rift announced. "I am a biological device known as a Light. I am the catalyst used to transform the knights of the Echo Army into armoured warriors. It's my duty to be the Light of the Echo. However, in the meantime, I am Vala's Light. Once I've found the Echo, Vala will be given a new Light."

Rift looked up at Vala. "And as group leader it is Vala's duty to find and assemble her team, so that we can find the Echo, then vanquish the Dragon's Queen once and for all."

"I'm team leader?" Vala went wide eyed with the news. *Deal.*

"Yes." Rift nodded. "You are a knight of Eden after all. Possibly the only native-born."

"Rift." Vala was brought to reality. "I can't lead a team. I can't even jailbreak my iPod."

"Bricks?" Mei Ling asked.

"Every goddamn time," Vala expressed through waving arms.

"Vala," Rift's voice became firm while eyes tightened on Vala. "This is not a time for joking."

"Says the talking cat." Asa fell forward into folded arms, kept a space free to eye Rift. "Am I the only one that is having trouble calculating the computing process of... the hell am I even saying? I'm that mind broke right now."

"Don't tease." Mei Ling ran a hand across Rift. "I think Rift's puuuurfect."

Asa raised her eyes passed her arms to glare at Mei Ling. "I hate you."

"Mei Ling," Mei Ling reminded Asa of her name.

"Right." Asa tightened her eyes even further. "I hate you, *Mei Ling.*"

Mei Ling smiled. "Chili Peppers fan?" Offered an ear bud.

Asa sat up as a strange sensation came over her, she was relaxed about everything going on. "More into Britney."

Mei Ling's smile vanished into a frown fuelled by the flames of hell itself. "We are sworn enemies from this day forth."

Vala ignored the other two. "So why are you here?"

"To help you with these two." Rift motioned over his shoulder at the girls.

"They're knights?" Vala looked up at the two girls. "That explains the hallucinations."

"The what?" Rift veered back.

Mei Ling and Asa perked up from their arguement. "We are what?" They spoke in harmony.

"Yes Vala." Rift twisted his head about. "Just like you, they are tied into the destiny of the Echo. Everything has been calculated for this moment. The return of the Dragon's Queen."

Suddenly a scream echoed through Vala's entire being. Her entire body shook as her eyes turned milky white for a moment. She looked down to her golden strings but didn't see any struggles. "Whoa, this is new."

She turned around to face the city through the chain link fence. Blue eyes returned to dart along the land. She began to tremble from guilt of Chelsea's mother and fear of facing another demon.

Rift leapt to Vala's shoulder. "Vala?" His head tilted in an attempt to see the front of her face from his angle.

For a moment, Vala's mind was distant as her thoughts were mute. Slowly a part of her broke through the barrier, bit by bit, until she felt the warmth inside her chest swell up and was reminded of how powerful she truly was. The warmth overcame both guilt and fear as her mind bolded.

"Past it." Vala tightened her eyes and balled her hands.

As she pushed herself up from the table, golden strings ran across her body. They wove in and out of each other. Once the design was complete the strings dimmed into green and brown cloth that pulsated power throughout her being. By the time she had finished turning away from the group, she had transformed. The weeks of training allowed her to transform without Rifts direct assistance, she now only needed a close proximity to him.

The power felt like small tremors through her entire body. Vala closed her eyes to settle the power building within. "I got this." Her voice was deep and steady as her body stilled.

Asa and Mei Ling both dug their nails into the table top out of fear. The golden lights had startled both of them and seeing them consume Vala, then leave her in armour was overwhelming.

With a smile, Vala turned back to her friends. "See, superhero." Vala leapt through the air before either girl could get a word in edgewise.

The girls rushed to watch Vala soar through the air. They both ran into the chain link, without realizing it was even there.

"Whoa." Asa stepped back with a low jaw, but smiling lips. Her heart was beating with pure adrenaline, cheeks flushed with power and her nails dug along her skull for some kind of relief.

Mei Ling stood still. Looked down at her clenched fists, she could swear she felt the universe pulsating through her body.

Vala fell to a long street. Leaned forward and kicked off, rocketing down the street. With the weeks of training under her belt, she had much more control over her actions while in her armour.

Cars shifted from the sonic boom. At the street's end came a building. Vala leaned backwards so her bent legs slid on pavement to gain traction and slow down. Though bare skin ran against potholed riddled asphalt, Vala's armour prevented any damage. Just before the building Vala uncurled her legs last second to send her upwards and over the building.

Came down in somebody's back yard. Slid on her extended leg to drift under a clothesline then twisted her body and spun during the momentum to get to her feet. Jumped again. Passed a street and landed on a roof top. Slid a metre down with waved hands before regaining focus.

Kicked off.

CHAPTER FIVE: RESOLVE

March 9th, 16:40

Jennifer rushed through the park with her boyfriend Edward. The crowd panicked as a creature followed in tow. Jennifer tripped. Cracked the side of her face against the pavement, splitting her pale skin open. Jennifer rolled to her back, just in time to get face to face with her pursuer.

The beast was as big as a bear. Its snout shot out awkwardly from its round head like a dog's face on a melon. The spine curled like a cat and extended into a long thin tail that twisted and knotted. Completely hairless, the creature had dark grey skin with spikes tearing through flesh at every joint; black blood gooped out of the wounds; the beast was in a constant state of blood loss, but never bled out.

Edward skidded to a stop. Turned to grab Jennifer. The young boy only had a moment to reflect on his mistake. Just as he noticed the creatures yellow iris-less eyes, a mighty claw swiped at and through him.

Edward fell into thirds on the ground. Blood splattered Jennifer. She screamed a deafening cry.

A raised claw came down to Jennifer, but Vala landed down the street. Bent low and kicked off shoulder first into the beast. The two tonne beast was hurled across the street and into the side of a corner store. Glass shattered as people screamed.

Jennifer slowly turned to look up at Vala. A crowd of onlookers stopped to see the mysteriously and awkwardly dressed girl. Vala took an unintentional heroic bend at the knee and reached for Jennifer. "You should get out of here, miss."

Jennifer nodded traumatically as Vala helped her to her feet. Jennifer's entire body was covered in the blood of Edward. Vala guided her around and pushed her back to give Jennifer pace.

As Jennifer ran away, she glanced back at the scene, her eyes locked on the girl that had just saved her life. Too afraid to look down at the man she had loved. Her brain unable to process anything besides left leg, right leg, repeat. Jennifer faced ahead. A strange smile crossed her confused face. A twitch and a laughter overtook her.

The beast snarled as it crawled out of the side of the building. Spit escaped its rotting mouth. The grey liquid slashed the ground, instantly browning the grass in the easement and eroding the cement.

Vala tightened her eyes on the beast. It backed up onto its hind legs to reach a towering three metres. "I can spit too." Vala spat to the side, took her best attempt at a boxer's stance. "Don't make me bust out my light." She cringed as the words had sounded more intimidating in her mind.

The beast fell forward onto all fours. The entire block shook from its weight. A scream came from onlookers as the beast leapt towards Vala. Vala rolled to the side. Recovered to her feet. Stumbled. Attempted to weave her green light—

The beast back handed Vala. Like a stone against the water, Vala skipped along the ground. Rag dolled against a light post and fell.

"Ow..." Vala grabbed her rib cage. They weren't broken, but if you had told her that, she'd have called you out on it.

Time wasn't on her side however, as the beast had already begun to charge Vala. She leapt backwards just in time to miss the beasts bone cutting through the steel of the lamp post. Vala landed, eyes wide. "Okay, definitely staying away from those."

The post fell apart. It was as if it had been nothing but paper to the beast. Before the post touched the ground, the beast was already half way to Vala.

With a vault, Vala dodged snapping jaws and two follow up swipes. Landed partly on top of a car. Her right heel caught the windshield. Slipped. Caused her to fall to the side and face planted cement.

"Goddamnit," Vala shook it off. Turned around and wove a green bolt.

In mid sprint, the beast grabbed a car, spun, and tossed it. "Oh, come on," Vala rolled out of the way. The car crashed and condensed into a mangled mess of metals as it bounced across the ground before crashing into the side of a brick wall.

The beast came down on Vala. She slammed a glowing fist into its throat. The energy spread quickly throughout its cells. By overcharging her healing abilities, Vala mutated the cells within the creature, creating large pockets of tumours throughout its throat and down into its lungs.

A violent coughing fit overwhelmed the beast, chunks of grey liquid were hurled forward with each struggle for breath. Vala scampered from under it. Turned to face the beast, slammed a fist into the snout.

The beast snorted before it lunged.

Its jaw open for the kill. Vala leapt backwards. The beast grasped her lower leg in his mighty claw. Spun around and effortlessly sent her down the street.

*   *   *

Cracks littered the faded wooden bench. It creaked as Chika sat upon it. She brushed back her long, black hair and cupped her skirt under her bottom as she sat. She slipped her backpack off to the side so she could adjust her Catholic school uniform. They didn't make the uniform in a size that fit her petite frame and short stature, so it was always getting twisted awkwardly around her body.

She sat on the bench, as she waited for the bus, reading from her notebook. Memorizing the lessons of the day.

The ground shook. Chika looked up over to her side to see the bus rounding the corner. She smiled. The bus driver was an old man who could barely see, let alone drive, but he managed his way day in and out. Always clipped the sidewalk on that same turn.

Chika stood up and prematurely waved to the bus driver. He waved back to her.

The bus pulled up in front of Chika. As the door slide open, he smiled. "I normally don't pick up pretty girls, but I won't tell my wife, if you don't."

Chika blushed, as she placed her notebook in her knapsack—

An explosion!

The two turned to look past the driver's window, but before they could see anything the bus was struck. Chika screamed, wide eyed, as the bus began to tip towards her, but it fell back onto its wheels.

Two quick breaths were all Chika needed to ground her mind. Ran around the bus to find Vala on the other side, embedded into the bus. Glass from the bus was scattered around the street. Metal twisted inwards and wrapped around the base of impact.

"Oh my," Chika dropped her things, as she ran to Vala.

Vala groaned. Eyes rolled out from the back of her skull and looked upwards to see Chika looking down.

"You're alive!" Chika reached out and helped Vala out. The metal was tight around her, but Vala was able to use her strength to bend the metal a little.

Chika's jaw dropped. From Chika's prospective Vala seemed to move the metal almost effortlessly, but that was far from the truth.

Vala fell to her knees. Rubbed her throbbing forehead as she stood up. Stumbled. Chika caught her. Vala's head spun. Was dizzy. "Thanks."

With a smile, Chika accepted the thanks. "Who are you?" a warmth took over her as a foreign sense of excitement took hold and shoved itself into her world.

"Um," now able to stand on her own, Vala stepped away from her crutch. "The name's—"

A blur. Chika screamed. Vala was back in the bus. This time the beast on top of her. Vala had her arm bent with an elbow to the beast's throat, while her other hand wrestled to keep the snout skyward.

Claws on either side moved rapidly trying to find Vala, but they couldn't bend inward enough to slash her body. Instead they kept cutting the metal on either side of her arms. The beast used its strength to push Vala deeper into the bus. Metal bent upwards and was forced into her back. She screamed. Passengers rushed out and away from the scene.

Chika backed up. Hands extended and waving. Not sure what to do. "I'll..." Chika ran a hand across her face, "get help." She ran.

Tight eyed, Vala struggled. Her face turned red as tears fell. The breath of the beast getting closer and warmer, fogging up Vala's iris. Her arms shook, unable to keep the beast at bay much longer.

"*Help me!*" Vala shrieked. It was too much.

Her arms gave.

The snout turned down. The beast's head shot forward. Jaw closed as it shadowed around Vala's head. Just before the teeth touched her skin, the entire beast was removed from the bus.

Hard pressed eyes slowly opened, Vala starred up in confusion. The flare of the sun kept a figure ahead of her blurred. Slowly, a girl's back came into focus and Vala had to decide if she should be confused about why she wasn't dead or who was standing ahead of her.

The girl turned to Vala. She had about a foot on Vala in height, was toned, blonde hair and green eyed. Her armour was similar in design, but silver and white in colour. However, her left arm had a thicker cyan material that darkened as it traveled down her bicep and ended in a navy-blue glove. On her index finger sat a sapphire crosshair. For a moment, Vala thought it was Chelsea standing before her.

"You okay?" The girl offered Vala a hand. The voice wasn't inviting and her eyes were a mixture of disgust and disappointment, but Vala took up the offer anyways.

The girl pulled Vala out of the tangled mess. Vala fell forward to her knees, but the girl caught her and helped her upright. Vala whispered mostly to herself, "Thanks."

"Sure," the girl looked over the bus, "you almost died."

"Yeah, about that…" Vala looked over the beast. It was laying on its back with a snapped neck. Its tongue hung out to the side, its eyes rolled in the back of its skull and strange folds of stretched skin around its neck; where the girl had grabbed and twisted the creature to the point of breaking its spine. "Did… did you snap this thing's neck?"

"Yes." The girl noticed a gawking Chika. Nodded, then leapt through the air.

The rush of wind pushed against Vala's back. "What…" She turned to see the girl was missing. Ran around the bus looking for where she may have gone. "The hell!"

Vala felt her vision blur a moment as she tried to process everything. How she had almost died, the thriving pain in her back where pieces of metal still stuck, and of course there was another knight out there somewhere. She trembled a moment, as she fought to sustain the armour.

Chika walked up to Vala. Looked her over, then the beast. "No offense," picked up her things, "but you're a horrible superhero."

Still fighting to catch her breath and still her heart, Vala glared at Chika as she ripped a piece of metal out her own back. Looked Chika up and down. "Saved your skinny ass."

"Really?" Chika raised her voice. Took a powerful step forward, "I sort of get the feeling you brought the danger to my vicinity. If I were a superhero, I wouldn't put others in danger just because I'm too green to handle the job."

Vala looked hurt as she lifted part of the cloth that was green. Chika shook her head violently. "It's a metaphor, I don't mean you are actually green."

"But I am, green." Vala stretched the cloth further. "See?"

"*Ugh!*" Chika stomped a foot. "You are a simplistic child!"

Vala shook her head. "I swear to God, if you're a knight too, I'm telling Rift I'm over this." With that, Vala leapt away.

Chika watched Vala cross a great distance with a simple jump. Fall and jump again, now out of sight. She was caught up in the amazement for a moment.

"Wait." Chika turned back to the demolished bus. Dialed her cell phone. "Hey Mom, I need a ride. Funny story…"

∗   ∗   ∗

The park was dark. Well past hours of normal operation. Typically it would have been empty at this hour, but two girls sat on swings.

Waiting.

Mei Ling dug the heel of her sneaker into the ground. Chin low and into her chest as she leaned forward. Her eyes danced along the curved roads she created while swaying.

Asa laid back with her arms extended as far as she possibly could with her legs straight to the sky. She let her pony tail drag through the sand, as she swayed. Chin dug into her chest, as her eyes studied her exposed legs. A stiff frown at a spot of hair.

"You think she's going to show up?" Mei Ling twisted her lips around to make faces. She wasn't really sure what she was supposed to be feeling or what she actually was feeling. Expression both purposeful, expected or natural seemed to be distanced at the moment; Mei Ling didn't bother keeping up an appearance. "This is insane."

"Yep." Asa pulled herself up to a sitting position. Dug her toe into the ground and twisted. Brought up her foot and let herself sway side to side. "Why wouldn't she show? I doubt superheroes get cold feet."

"They don't get nervous." Vala called from the edge of the swing's sand pit. Blue jeans, her black jacket and a white tank top underneath. Both girls looked up at her with yearning eyes.

Vala gave a slight wave. "However they certainly get cold." She walked up to the girls. Their blank faces weren't the most inviting of things.

"Jesus." Vala brought her arms inward to grasp her elbows. "It's freezing tonight."

The girls didn't say anything to each other. Eyes danced along each other. Sometimes they found the sky to dart to the stars. Then the ground. Repeat.

"So." Vala sighed. An arm fell straight while a hand kept it tight to her person by securing it at the elbow. She tilted her head to the side, used her eyes to distance herself from the moment by staring into the darkness. "Sorry for ditching you guys back there. I didn't mean to just take off after ripping apart your world and all. I just—" Dryness stopped the sentence.

Vala attempted to clear her mind, but it strained. Instead all she managed to do was draw out the silence, as her gaze kept to the side. Kept to the darkness. Kept her in the distance.

Why was it so difficult to apologize? Why was it so difficult to get things right? Why was it so difficult to not think of Chelsea?

"Don't be a dick." Asa lend forward, arms fell on top her inward legs. "Duty calls."

Surprised; Vala looked up at the girls. Her back straightened from shock and eyes wide with a 'thank you' in them.

"We saw the news. You had someone to save." Mei Ling smirked with eyes locked with her friend. "Someone got to go home to their family tonight, because of you. Don't ever feel like you need to apologize for that."

"Thanks." Vala crushed her eyes in hopes of smothering the need to cry. Face flushed. Hand clasped to her chest. Words strained through thought of Chelsea in her black dress, speaking in front of a crowd. "You have no idea how much that means to me right now. How fucked up all this stupid shit is."

"Whoa." Asa froze up at the sight of Vala's trembling shoulders.

Mei Ling stood up and embraced Vala, catching her just before her legs buckled under her own weight. Mei Ling slid down to the ground with Vala. She allowed Vala to cry into her chest.

*   *   *

"I'm okay," Vala whipped her eyes clean. No one's mind had kept track of the passing of time. "There is just a lot to explain to you guys. I don't know where to begin."

"You have the whole world on your shoulders." Mei Ling left her hand on Vala's shoulder. Their eyes met and Mei Ling smiled. "We don't understand what's going on, but all of this feels right for some reason. Being here, together. Like we've always known each other, or some shit. So let us know what's going on, so we can lift that weight from you."

"For you." Asa backed up with tight eyes. Pocketed her hands. "Always, Vala."

Blue eyes bounced between the two friends. Something strange sparked between the trio, igniting a friendship that spanned millions of years. Vala smiled and found her footing. Now standing, she sighed, ran her hands down her face, pulled the tears out of existence. "Thanks."

"You want to get a pizza?" Vala looked around at a small glow down the street. "I always get hungry when I do anything."

"Seriously?" Asa went wide eyed. "You want to eat? I can't even keep anything down."

"Yep." Vala nodded with a hand over her stomach. "Jumping two hundred feet in the air gets a girl thinking, stuffed crust."

"I'm in." Mei Ling stood up with a wide smile across her face. Touched her butt to make sure she had brought money. "I can pitch."

"Good." Vala pointed down the street. "Cause I ain't got no money. You're buying."

"Okay." Mei Ling shook her head while laughing. "Sure. You save the world and I'll buy two toppings."

"Three!" Vala corrected without missing a beat.

"No." Mei Ling crossed her arms. A twenty swaying in the breeze between pinched fingers.

"Yes." Vala nodded. Turned and raised a hand in the air. "It has been decided. Use the debit card."

"Seriously?" Asa let her jaw fall. Watched her two friends begin walking away. "Are we seriously doing this here?"

"Nope." Vala let her raised hand fall so it was an arrow towards the restaurant. "There."

"For crying out—" Asa shook her head. Stood up then swung her arms violently in opposite direction, palms up. "Great."

"You owe me a pop, anyways." Vala turned back to Asa while she kept walking backwards. She leaned forward with extended arms behind her back and hands cupped together. "I don't take diet though."

"Pfft." Asa grabbed the ten out of her pocket. Jogged to get caught up. "You are getting diet."

"What?" Vala turned to face the parlour. "I'm not screwing around here, Asa. That stuff tastes like garbage."

"You shouldn't be drinking that stuff anyways." Mei Ling piped in with a hop in her pace. "You are a superhero. Shouldn't you be juicing?"

"What?" Vala turned her head to glare at Mei Ling. *I'm being flanked here!* "I can't even think up a word foul enough that it could begin to express how much I loathe you. If I have to resort to drinking vegetable juice, then this blue and brown rock is going up in flames. Carbs save lives!"

"Seriously should at least drink water," Asa laughed along with worries stripped.

"Water? Fish sex up in that stuff." Vala shivered, while lips twisted and eyes crossed. "I'm not drinking that."

The girls continued to laugh and joke their way down the street, through the glass door, and down to their faded rubber seats.

Vala slid into the booth. Mei Ling followed on the other side. Asa sat next to Mei Ling on the edge. Both of the newbies facing their potential leader. Eyes wide with anticipation.

Seeing the wide-eyed girls, Vala quickly opened the menu. Dug her nose deep as she pretended to not already know her order. *Pepperoni, banana peppers and jalapenos, duh.*

The waitress came by. Orders ordered. They shared a large pizza, thanks to Mei Ling.

A weight clung to Vala's shoulder, burying them down. She attempted to clasp her inner thighs and bend her arms to get them back up, but the weight was too great. Her face was even lowered by the force. Eyes fell to the faded oak table.

Silence. Maybe a minute.

"Vala." Vala looked up with wide eyes, blinked twice, she wasn't sure who had called her name.

"Sorry." Vala nervously grinned. Scratched her neck. "Okay. Things. Stuff. Events."

"I'd prefer if you perhaps elaborate on all three." Mei Ling kept her back straight. Eyes locked. They did not sway.

Asa shifted her weight, but her face was just as serious even if she wasn't as confident about it.

A sigh gathered Vala's thoughts, reeled them in one at a time, and brought them to her tongue. "Okay.

"About three weeks ago I met this cat. Only it wasn't a cat. It was a robot. From like before time and space." Vala tried to smile. Her joke wasn't much of one and fell flat. "I met Rift. He isn't really a cat, he is a tool designed to be a *cat*-alyst for people like us. Lights sort of reconnect the reincarnated knights with their original power. We all had to be reborn so we were ready for the Dragon's Queen.

"Everything started with the Voice and Eden. Humans were created to die and live and die. Every time a human dies their soul goes into what is called the Womb. Think of each soul as an atom and the idea is to build the fetus of a God.

"The Dragon poisoned the fetus, so the Voice trapped the Dragon in the River and left the universe. A creature called the Echo stayed to form an army. Reincarnated various species into the Womb so that when the Dragon could make his move, there would be someone there to protect everyone."

Vala held her head low, kept still a moment, slowly raised to look at her friends. Her voice was slow and quaked. "That's us. What we are. Reborn knights."

"So, what are we, exactly?" Mei Ling looked at Asa. Asa had the expression of a child that had just been taught quantum physics. "Angels or something?"

"No." Vala shook her head. "I guess some of us might be. Some of us aren't. Rift would know. The knights were from all the realms. Eden, the River and the Void. Maybe there are more realms too, Rift would know.

"Rift told me some stuff. There are Angels, which are pretty much what you expect them to be. They were caretakers and protectors of Eden, before man was moved to the Garden. I mean Earth.

"Dragonborns are the creatures the Dragon created. Some of them were converted to our side. Rift says they have lizard eyes, but otherwise look pretty human.

"Kitsune are like fox people… with nine tails. They are super smart. They made the armour that I wear."

Vala placed two lights on the table. A black and grey one in front of Mei Ling, and an orange and yellow in front of Asa.

"Rift gave me these." Vala drew her words slowly, "I spray painted them so I wouldn't get them mixed up. Their yours. Take them."

Both girls took the Lights without much hesitation. They didn't bother to see if anyone was looking, not that it would matter much. To everyone else, they would look like chunks of twisted metal.

"These are like Rift?" Mei Ling ran her hand along her Light.

"Do they have names?" Asa looked up from hers.

"I'm sure they do," Vala pointed to a cat sitting outside on the windowsill.

Mei Ling pulled herself over the fencing of the booth to wave down a waitress. "Let's take that to go, please."

Outside, the girls sat in the furthest corner of the parking lot. It was hardly lit. Pizza opened on the ground between the four of them. Vala sat up on a cement block with Rift on her lap. Asa and Mei Ling sat down below cross legged.

"Sorry about earlier." Rift nipped at a bit of pizza that Vala had handed him.

"No problem, dude." Asa had regained her appetite and was eating away.

"How do we activate these things anyways?" Mei Ling pulled off each spicy pepper in a failed attempt to make the pizza tolerable.

"Yeah. Why are they dead anyways, and you weren't?" Vala double fisted pizza. With each bite she altered which slice she fed to Rift.

"They haven't awoken theirs yet. I am special. Once I have found the Echo, then you may have your own Light, but for now I am your Light." Rift purred. "Hope you'll have me."

"Word." Vala took a bite of the last bit of the pizza, then proceeded to fist bump Rift.

"This thing's neat," Asa poked her Light. Suddenly, a bright light blanketed vision.

The device unraveled and expanded. The metal plates twisted and spun. An orange light blinked to life as ink formed in its orb. "Hello. My name is Nither."

"Nither?" Asa looked slowly at Rift. "Why is yours a cat, and mine is a talking robot?"

Rift chuckled before his skin and muscles peeled away as he transformed into his Light form.

"Oh." Asa nodded slowly as she fought to swallow the pizza that had just come back up. "The talking cat is a robot alien, right."

"So we are like superheroes or something, right?" Mei Ling downed her pizza. Fished for her Light to try to get it activated.

"Knights." Rift corrected.

"Superheroes," Vala corrected the correction. "Join me?"

"Pfffft." Mei Ling tapped her Light to life. "Duh."

A grey eye booted up. "My name is—"

"Flea." Mei Ling butted in.

"Am I being named?" the Light had a very annoyed buzz to his speech.

"Yes." Mei Ling answered. "Flea. You are named."

The Light turned to Rift, who offered no assistance, so he turned back to Mei Ling. "My name is Solar."

"I am never calling you that." Mei Ling folded her arms, as she did so she let go of the Light forcing him to steady himself then float at eye level. "Your name is Flea."

"Why?" Solar shook his head.

"Best bass player ever." Mei Ling looked around for back up, but no one understood what she was talking about. "If you're my side kick, then you better be the best side kick. The name is a reflection of that."

"Flea is a side kick?" Solar asked.

"Well no..." Mei Ling tapped her chin. "Suppose he is the badass of the band. But... It'll give you something to aspire to."

"Great." Solar—no, Flea sighed. "My name is Flea."

"Can you guys turn into anything?" Asa let go of Nither, to watch him float about. *This is pretty cool.*

"Sure," Nither shifted his shards. They expanded and the chains twisted into muscle and fur. He fell to Asa's lap as a rabbit. "Does this form please you?"

"This is kind of cute," Asa ran her hand over Nither.

"Dude," Mei Ling went wide eyed at the sight of Nither. "We need to give him a carrot and get him to ask us what's up!"

The other two girls stared at her with blank expressions. With rolled eyes and a sigh of disappointment, Mei Ling was saddened that her joke wasn't well received.

"How do they know about the animals in our world?" Mei Ling looked up at Rift, realizing her rude gesture she turned to Flea.

Pretending to not notice Mei Ling's mistake, Flea spoke. "We are created of every element in the universe. Everything is connected, and when we are 'asleep', we are in a state of rest and we are downloading information. We don't know everything on your planet but enough."

"Oh sweet." Mei Ling grinned as she leaned towards Flea. "Can you be a pug?"

Flea fell to Mei Ling's lap as a black pug. "Yes."

"Ooooh," Mei Ling shook with excitement. "This is the coolest moment ever!"

"You're such a girl," Vala snorted. Mei Ling glared.

With a thud, Vala landed on the ground. Rift swayed over her shoulders and returned to his cat form to land on her left shoulder. Vala used her foot to flip the empty pizza box closed, then picked it up.

"Who wants to practice saving the word?" Vala grinned, as she shoved the box under her armpit. She realized the bottom was greasy, quickly brought it back around, but the damage was done. "Great…" Vala frowned at the grease marks on her bunny hug.

"Oh hell yes," Mei Ling sprung to her feet, leaned forward as she attempted to catch Flea, but failed. He fell, rolled on the cement. Glared as he gave a sharp bark. "Sorry, champ."

Flea snorted, before he stood up on his hind legs to be picked up.

Slowly, Asa stood. She held Nither between folded arms. "I've always wanted a pet. This is pretty cool."

"Yeah," Mei Ling nodded. "Nice to have a pet that is potty trained out the gate."

"Excuse me," Rift leaned forward, "but I don't think it's very polite to discuss the fecal matter of the most powerful weapons in the universe!"

"Rift. It's us, come on. You really think you're going to win this?" Vala raised an eyebrow as she looked over to Rift. They shared a shrug.

The girls made their way around back. Hidden from view in the alley way behind the strip mall. The smell of old milk and sticky pop filled the air.

"This is disgusting," Asa cringed as her feet momentarily stuck to the ground with each step.

"Oh sorry, your majesty," Vala turned to the girls. She transformed mid swing. "We'll do our best to make sure you don't break a nail while you're saving the world."

Asa opened her mouth to quip, but withdrew it. Sighed, "Point."

"So," Mei Ling held Flea up. "How does this work?"

"Yeah…" Asa shifted her weight as she let go of Nither. "Does it hurt?"

"No, I wouldn't really worry about it." Vala shook her head. Ran her hand up and down her side. "Everything feels natural once you're in."

"Kay," Mei Ling drew in a deep breath. "Let's do this."

"Yeah," Asa shifted her weight while kicking her head towards Nither. "Totally stoked."

Mei Ling closed her eyes. Steadied her breath. "Okay, now what?"

Suddenly, a flash. Flea's shards parted as he tackled Mei Ling in the chest. His chains engulfed her being. Her eyes shot open as a surge of energy ran through her body head to toe. Her brown eyes slit to mimic a fox's as her skin smoothed out her acne and repaired any scars.

Her clothes burnt off as golden chains wrapped around her feet, torso and arms. When the light dimmed to reveal her armour, it appeared to be identical to Vala's aside from her colours. Black shoulders, arms and skirt. Her torso and heels a grey.

"Whoa," Mei Ling stumbled forward.

At the same time, Asa was tackled by Nither. Lightning sparked along her bare skin as her soul irrupted energy through her entire body.

"Jesus!" Vala brought up her arms in defense as a beam of lightning cracked the brick wall next to her.

Dust filled the alleyway. Slowly it parted as the light faded to reveal Asa in the same armour but orange shoulders arms and skirt. Her torso and heels a yellow.

"Holy." Asa stared down at her hands. Flexed them as sparks danced all around her skin. After a moment, the electricity dissipated. "That was intense."

"No kidding," Vala looked over at Rift with a raised eyebrow. "Did I do that?"

"No," Rift bobbed around Asa. "She's a Valkyrie, that's why."

"What? I'm a what?" Asa perked up. "What's that?"

"An Angel," Mei Ling cut Rift off. Her voice was low as she studied herself. She had never felt as at home as she did in this very moment. Some new memories of the Echo Army came to her. "Valkyrie we're a group of Angels who used a ritual to attach their cores to strings connected directly to the end of the universe. It works like an artificial soul...

Unlike Angels, when they die, Valkyrie have a second life. But it isn't heaven... it's to protect everything at the end of all time. They're intense warriors," Mei Ling looked over to Rift. "How do I know this?"

"Sweet." Asa nodded with a high chin over to Vala.

"Not bad," Vala bumped fists with Asa. "Could use an all-star on the time—team" She shook her head as she stumbled through her words. "What the hell was I saying... anyways," shrugged, "all I can do is jump over things and heal other things."

"Well," Rift bobbed. "Mei Ling, you are a Kitsune. Perhaps it is a part of the reincarnation process? Your people did create the armour."

"Yeah," Mei Ling closed her eyes and released a heavy breath. "I'm a Kitsune. Scholars, engineers and blacksmiths. We are apparently super smart."

"Explains why you know everything that ever happened," Vala grinned as she referenced an old joke. "Ever-er"

"Shut up," Mei Ling smirked.

Mei Ling jerked her head to the side as if she had just been struck. Her eyes crushed as tears fell. "Jesus Christ," She stumbled, both girls reached out to her but not in time, her face collided with cement. Trails of black and grey flowed in the wind as she was returned to her normal clothes.

"What the hell!" Asa fell to Mei Ling's side.

"Oh crap," Vala joined Asa, with a low brow and smirk, "you're next buddy."

"Wait… what?" Asa jerked towards Vala, her eyes filled with horror and confusion. "What the hell just happened?"

"She is fine," Vala shifted Mei Ling's head to the side. Placed a glowing hand to a cut in her forehead. Vala wove the wound closed. "She's just tired. It'll take a few tries before you're—"

Gravity suddenly grasped Asa by the shoulders and yanked her down. Her eyes rolled in the back of her head as she collapsed over top Mei Ling. Trails of orange and yellow flowed through the air as her normal clothes were returned to her.

Both Lights rolled out from the girls.

"Weird." Vala sat up. Looked over her shoulder to Rift, "I got tired, but these two are knocked out."

"Yes," Rift studied the two. "Mei Ling makes sense… Kitsune are a weaker species. This will always be a bit more taxing on her soul to maintain form. Which of course will affect how easy it is for her body to maintain it."

"And Asa?" Vala looked over Asa for any injuries. She was fine.

"She is an Angel, like yourself." Rift rested over Vala's shoulder. "She shouldn't be having any more issues than you. Spiritually you should be about the same in strength… perhaps her human body is weaker? She may have adopted some kind of human disease that is affecting the armour."

"Great," Vala took in a deep breath. "Guess we just sit around til they wake up then…"

"Yes," Rift fell to the ground in his cat form. Batted both Lights over to better see their unlit orbs. "Their Lights fused with them upon transforming. That's different from you and I. Perhaps related to how much quicker they lost their energy."

"Hopefully they can get that together before we need'em," Vala returned to her everyday clothes as she stood.

"I'm sure they will be fine." Rift returned to his Light form and swayed around Vala. "I hope they wake up soon. We want to be home early, your father wanted you to practice driving."

"Pffft. The road test isn't for another week." Vala folded her arms as she slammed her back against the brick wall. Leaned on the tip of her heels with her toes pointed upwards. She kept inching forward to test how far she could go before she would slide down. "Kind of have more important things going on right now, saving the world and all."

"Perhaps." Rift twirled his shards. "However shouldn't a hero of mankind be able to parallel park?"

"*Ugh!*" Vala batted Rift away. "I hate everything you stand for." She slid down the wall.

CHAPTER SIX: GOOD AND BROKEN

April 17th, 06:15

The sun's light had just began to dance along the edges of the low moon, pushing back what remained of the night. The always present Saskatchewan winds caught up a tumbleweed of Regina litter. Grocery bags tumbled along the student parking lot of Wade W. Wilson Collegiate. The plastic bags would rise but the dust they had collected along their journey always kept a portion of them to the ground, oddly swaying them left and right just before the wind would die down. Flatten during the break of wind only to be kicked back up and tumble all over again.

The back part of the school had crumbled red tile that outlined the chipped sidewalks. Everything vandalized by Mother Nature's constant melting of snow, the sudden cold drops to expand what found its way into cracks. The ice pushed asphalt and concrete to its limits, breaking everything down, adding to the prairie dust.

Sitting on a brown steel bench, next to the handicap stalls, were Asa and Mei Ling.

"She's late." Asa swung herself forward, caught her chin in palms that shot her elbows into her thighs. She sat just on the edge of the steel bench so her exposed legs wouldn't send shivers up her body from the cold metal.

Mei Ling sat against the bench with her arms thrown over the back. "She's always late." She didn't bother to remove her ear buds as her eyes stared upwards through tinted lenses. The pinks, orange and red were greyed by her sunglasses.

"No she isn't," Asa glared towards Mei Ling, who clearly wasn't listening.

"If she isn't ever late, then why the hell are we always so early?" Mei Ling rolled her neck over to glare at Asa. When there was no reaction, she realized her eyes were concealed by blackened lenses. Frowning, Mei Ling returned her attention to the sky.

"It's just weird, is all I mean." Asa sighed, rolled her face over a knuckle while her one arm fell free. "I want to get this shit going. I still can't jump over a house."

"So yesterday I was at this pawn shop for video games," Mei Ling took out the earbud between the two. "This guy bought a sealed copy of Earthbound for like 350 bucks."

Asa looked around as if she were being pranked. "Why would I even care about that?"

"Because," Mei Ling drew out her sentence as she tilted her head towards Asa. "It's probably the greatest RPG ever."

"I don't play video games." Asa rolled her eyes.

"Man," Mei Ling stretched while yawning. "Aside from being superheroes, we don't have anything in common."

"Nope," the word scraped its way out of Asa's mouth. With sludge in her veins, she trudged over to a handicap sign. Spun around it with the assistance of a single arm.

"Why would he want a sealed copy of a game?" Mei Ling ran her hand over her music library, trying to find a new song. "Like what's the point, how can you enjoy it?"

"Same reason men spend money on anything." Asa fell against the sign, with her back towards Mei Ling.

With a raised eyebrow and tilted shades Mei Ling looked up at Asa, "Which is?"

Asa raised her entire brow as she gave a grin. "He wants to pop its cherry, Mei Ling."

Mei Ling paused from cycling through her library, "Ew."

"Yep," Asa rolled her eyes, as she shifted into folded arms. "What time is it?"

"Seriously?" Mei Ling held up her iPod and her cellphone. "I can also roll down my sleeve, if you want. How do you not own a watch?"

Asa shrugged, made no effort to face Mei Ling.

"Well, it's…"

Kinetic force from a grey massive cloud, a combination of cement and steel and asphalt, sent Asa off her feet. Gravity tore her to the ground. Friction scraped her skin and shot a canine tooth into flesh.

The compression against her temple, the blood flooding her mouth and the lack of vision, brought on by the storm, dumbfounded the girl.

Her legs were liquid as she attempted to stand up, though she wasn't quite sure why she was bothering.

A haggard cough came to her ears. Asa crawled towards the cough.

It was Mei Ling, who had been tossed off her bench and onto her back. The air forced from her lungs had called upon the immediate need to fill themselves. The inhale had only brought on crusher dust and the coughing began.

"Mei Ling!" Asa shoved a fist into Mei Ling's chest.

"Fuck!" Mei Ling curled to her side. Caught her breath. Glared upwards to her assaulter. "*What the fuck!*"

"S-sorry," Asa found it difficult to breathe in the tornado of dust.

"Jesus," Mei Ling took Asa's hand, as the girls helped each other to their feet.

The dust had found the ground. Ahead—where the woodworking room had been—was a large hole in the side of the school.

"Holy shit!" Asa tripped over herself, as she had attempted to near the disaster. "What the hell was that?"

"A bomb?" Mei Ling back pedaled, ran into a trash can. With heart in her throat, she white knuckled the tin.

The temperature dropped. The scent of sulphur in the air. Both girls slowly looked towards one another, the colour out of their face, then back to the explosion.

From under Mei Ling's bunny hug came Flea. Her eyes widened as the quakes began in her person. "Do we gear up?"

"What?" Asa jerked her head to Mei Ling, her voice cracked several pitches higher than normal, "Are you insane?"

"Yeah," Mei Ling nodded nervously, as she took a few steps towards the explosion. "Probably, yeah."

Swallowing sanity, dismissing self-preservation, for maybe once in her life, Mei Ling brought honour to her family. Trembling hands reached outwards to Flea. A blinding light overtook the two and a frightened girl was replaced with a proud knight.

Flea expanded into thousands of grey and black threads. The cloth was tight. It cut off all circulation, but Mei Ling could feel every bit of her energy pulsate through her person. Everything felt more solid, more purposeful. A surge of adrenaline rushed up her spine and widened her irises. The armour had taken hold, and it knew what it wanted to do. In turn, Mei Ling found her calling.

"Let's go save the world," Mei Ling turned to Asa with a wide smile.

"Jesus Christ," Asa almost pulled out her hair with one hand while she tossed out Nither. "You're enjoying this too much."

Nither expanded into thousands of orange and yellow threads. They reached to lace themselves around Asa. Tightened and became one.

The surge of energy that had ignited focus within Mei Ling simply started a wildfire within Asa. Everything became hot, pulled in all the wrong directions and before she could warn Mei Ling—

Bolts of lightning scorched the ground as they slashed out violently like whips of raw energy. The hood of a car compressed in on itself, brick dust filled the air and a handicap sign was shot skyward.

"Whoa," Mei Ling brought up her arms defensively. "Spaz, much?"

"Sorry." Asa curled over her knees, as she tried to stop her body from turning into an explosive. "Been practicing…" Asa finally stood, now somewhat confident in her ability to control the energy. "You should see my garage."

"Here," Mei Ling offered her hand. "I have an idea."

The energy convulsed through every part of Asa, randomly jerking her in various directions as another bolt of lightning lashed out to the world. The bolt crossed Mei Ling. She didn't react as her reflexes were too slow, but it left a cool imagery as if she were a mountain that couldn't be moved. Asa knew Mei Ling was *this* close to soiling herself from the bolt, but she decided to retain the badass image instead.

They took each other's hands. The magic between the suits coarsed through one another. Asa felt ice creep up her arm, through the chakra channels in her body and seep deep within the warmth of her chest.

It was as if Mei Ling's armour was speaking into Asa's, giving it some sort of information that it currently didn't have. In a brief moment the lightning composed itself.

"Whoa." Asa gulped. "Thanks. How did you know that'd work?"

"Didn't," Mei Ling shrugged. "I got the idea from the Wu Xing. It's the study of the Chinese elements. They seem to have some truth to them, probably based on our powers? In it they have five elements and each has their own representative colours. We seem to reflect that. Yellow and orange is Earth, grey and black is Water."

Mei Ling turned towards the school. "I'll get into the history lesson later, but I sort of followed the lead down the rabbit hole and came across Chakra. The life force in the human body. Which lead me to acupuncture... Wikipedia can be a real addiction. Then I sort of just put it all together myself." Mei Ling laughed. "Just now, I really hadn't spent too much time on it."

*   *   *

Black tar dripped from the edge of the hole. As the tar gooped down it made the opening in the side of the school look like a demon's mouth with jagged teeth. Inside the school had been perverted into a black toned cavern.

An unnatural darkness consumed everything inside, as if it had all been painted over with a pure black shadow. The shadow fought to escape the school, as if rays of light expanding as far as their origin point would allow.

The smell of sulphur overwhelmed the girls, the acid kicked up in their gut. It wasn't long before the armour controlled the situation, removing the annoyance of nausea.

Inside they stepped. First Mei Ling, who swung a leg widely over twisted metal and bent low to dodge the goop. Groaned when she failed and some made its way into her hair. It hardened instantly, but she was able to drag it out with her hands.

Two deep breaths were taken, before Asa was able to kick off the lead that had manifested itself in her veins. With great mental strain, she trudged forward into the darkness. The tar didn't bother her, in fact she didn't give it notice.

The cold spots caught Asa's attention. She brought up her arms to catch her elbows. Something supernatural prevented her armour from properly regulating body heat. Small moments of normality crept in, but failed shortly after. The constant flux of heat to chill was more frightening than the cold itself. Asa wished it would end, but it wouldn't.

The darkness was strange, Mei Ling thought. The shadow seemed to layer itself on top of everything in sight. She could make out objects and their colour, but the details of the object became blurred to the mind. She stared at a turned over chair for several minutes before she gave up on trying to figure out what it was.

Like a word on the tip of your tongue, nothing in the shadow was recognizable. Above was a light, which glowed but it still was faded and consumed by darkness so Mei Ling wasn't quite sure what it was.

My hands… Mei Ling looked down at her palms. Her entire body was visible, she confirmed that Asa was as well, then continued to scan the room. On the other side were glass doors, past them, plants kept in the entrance hall of the school.

Trees!

She was able to make out the plants. The darkness layered non-organic objects, but the living was out of its reach.

"What is that thing?" Asa pointed to the chair.

In that moment Mei Ling made a bet with herself. Returned to the chair that she didn't recognized, reached out and touched it. A trail of light held to the steel legs as her hand walked along towards the plastic seat. "It's a chair." By the time she stood back up she couldn't tell what the object was, other than by memory.

"Weird," Asa copied what Mei Ling had done.

"Yeah," Mei Ling turned towards the exit. "Fuck this."

The two weren't more than three steps from being out of the school when fright was replaced by an egotistical right of might. They paused as their minds tried to understand why they felt so righteous in that moment, but then it didn't matter.

With purpose, fuelled by the adrenaline of the armour, they headed back into the school.

Deeper they went. Down the hallways until they reached the cafeteria. Though she had to squint to see anything, Mei Ling noticed a large hole in the floor about halfway down the hallway. By some miracle she still had a grasp of what missing space was.

Pretending she knew what hand signals military operators used, Mei Ling signaled to Asa to be quiet and to slowly follow.

"Huh?" Asa jerked her head back in confusion. She still trailed, and even with Mei Ling to steady her armour, it was not 100% and didn't cloud out all of her fear.

"Ugh," Mei Ling rolled her eyes before following it up with a stern glare. "Shut up and follow me."

"What crawled up your butt?" Asa took a deep breath, before she stepped out from the hallway,

"I'll show you if you don't *shut the hell up,*" Mei Ling hissed as she pointed to the hole in the ground. *"Something very big made that!"*

Asa gritted her teeth into a mixture of 'up yours' and 'my bad'.

With an exaggerated exhale of breath, Mei Ling turned back to the hole. Took a second to collect herself before falling through it. Black and grey threads expanded from her heels to soften the landing and void it of sound.

The darkness inside was thicker. Mei Ling could feel the tar claw its way down her windpipe. She coughed into her arm to silence herself. In doing so, she realized the light around her person was beginning to grey itself out, slowly matching the shadow around her.

Great, Mei Ling turned towards Asa who had just fallen. *We can't be down here very long.* Though Asa couldn't read her mind, it was clear what Mei Ling was saying through her eyes alone.

Asa coughed into the back of her knuckle. *Great.*

The girls weren't sure where they were; it was impossible to get bearings in a place when your mind was unable to tell what the objects in the room were. Twice they ran into tables before realizing how to walk around them.

It infuriated Mei Ling to be so detached from her brilliant mind. Which was good, as the anger consumed her every thought and pushed out the fear that she logically should have been feeling.

Her anger-driven steps were cut short by the sound of something metal hitting the ground. Both girls froze as they slowly shifted their eyes to line up. A chill ran down their spines as they swore the sulphur smell intensified ten fold.

Swallowing fear, they both gulped and turned towards the sound. It came from within, and something was moving around that must have had been just as blind as the girls, as it was making a lot of noise.

A man turned the corner, Mei Ling grabbed Asa and crouched. She wasn't sure what she was hiding behind, but prayed that the man wasn't quite sure what it was either.

Though she had no way of knowing it, David walked past the two. Both raised their eyebrows to the sight of a man in a cane scuffing through the darkness.

"I'll open the gate. You load up." David called over his shoulder, but did not look. If he had, he surely would have had seen the girls sitting in the middle of nowhere. *Like idiots,* Mei Ling thought.

A flash of cyan and blue strings ignited the air into a pulse of energy. Neither girl could make out what they were looking at, as the shadow over took it the moment the spark fizzled out.

All they knew was the man was now missing.

Mei Ling pushed her finger to her mouth, to stop Asa from asking what had happened. With a bit of improv hand gestures, Mei Ling attempted to communicate with Asa.

Let's go see what they're moving. None of this made its way through to Asa.

What? Asa raised her eyebrows and waved her hands.

Mei Ling suppressed her need to shout, instead laying out a palm facing upwards, using her other hand to move two sets of fingers along as if someone were walking. *Let's walk.* Took on the expression of taking a dump while holding her hands as if gripping something. *To see what their hauling.*

Asa almost laughed, thumbed up that she understood.

The two slid along the walls, as they carefully made their way down the hallway. Mei Ling made sure to gently wave her hand outwards, to make contact with objects in a more controlled environment.

It took several minutes for them to cross a short distance but it had been worth the effort. The girls arrived to an opening, only able to tell that the doorway existed thanks to the cyan light that trimmed it.

Mei Ling held up her hand to tell Asa to wait here. She then peered around the corner to try to find a light source.

The room was empty, no one was inside, save barrels of silver that glowed cyan.

"What are those?" Asa kept her words low; she physically crouched as if it would help keep her words softer.

"No idea." Mei Ling reached out to study one.

The barrel was a couple hundred kilograms but Mei Ling didn't find it too heavy with her armour. From a closer look, the metal was made out of similar shards as the Lights. These shards were firmly stuck together by a means Mei Ling wasn't quite sure of, as they had no indication of being welded.

As her hands ran across the metal, Mei Ling's mind was busy at work figuring out what exactly these were. They gave off light, and unlike the strange sparks from the man, these did not vanish.

Her eyes transformed into that of a Kitsune, fox-like slits. This allowed her the ability to scan the barrels and draw memories from them.

"Okay," Mei Ling had confirmed her suspicion. "These things are for storing energy from souls. They siphon off nearby humans. Side effects include depression and anger. Either way… bad.

"It's pretty clever. Hiding these in a high school. I mean how many teenagers fit that description?" Mei Ling put the barrel down.

"Sure," Asa slowly nodded her head. "How do you figure?"

"I'm not sure," Mei Ling shrugged as her eyes returned to normal. "I just looked at them and kind of remembered, but it's all foggy. They glow, and just like us being the only light in this place, I would take that as confirmation of whatever they are as being organic on some level."

The cyan light swayed along the room, like a wave in the ocean. Both girls looked towards the barrels to see whatever they contained to be moving, ever so slightly. Before their minds could connect the dots, the ground started to tremble.

The tremble wasn't long before it was a quake. The barrels themselves now vibrated, their metal pressing into each other as they moved along the floor. The wave of light became more violent.

Something big is coming!

They didn't waste time to confirm with each other. Both turned towards the door to haul ass back out the way they came.

Light blocked their way, much like the light of the girls but at the same time an entirely different source of light. This light towered over the girls, it crouched and a snort suggested it was well aware the two were in the barrel room before it had even entered. Two hands pulled the door frame open. The walls crumbled with little resistance, as red glowing eyes pierced Mei Ling and Asa.

"Fuck off," Mei Ling tried to gulp, but her throat was too dry.

One of the mighty hands reached towards her, but Mei Ling rolled to the side. Without waiting to confirm if Asa was in sync with her mindset or not, she barrelled past the shadow and down the hall. She had no intention of fighting something so large in such an enclosed place, especially with invisible surroundings.

The invisible surroundings didn't waste time getting in her way. In haste, Mei Ling kept bouncing off of things, stumbling over things and crashing through other things.

She didn't look back, until she had jumped through the hole and was back in the parking lot.

A chilling scream came to her ears. Mei Ling slid into the light of day and turned back to search for Asa. Heart raced as she realized she had left her friend alone. There wasn't enough time to dwell on her carelessness, as her gut curled over her knees, as she was lifted off the ground and Mei Ling was thrown into the front of a parked car.

Asa rolled from on top of Mei Ling to the ground. With a grunt, Mei Ling rolled over her side and fell off the car. Words weren't exchanged as the freshly thrown Asa stumbled to her feet.

Brown eyes quaked as they took one last look at the darkness before deciding to sprint away from danger. Asa's mind ran wild as fear overtook her. The armour's best efforts could not halt her.

No mind was given to Asa as Mei Ling gathered herself. Stood tall as the warmth in her chest fuelled white knuckles and gritted teeth. Her soul beckoned her forward, with great loads of regret and dread, Mei Ling did this. By her third step in, her mind was no longer doubting the decision.

Mei Ling eyed up the shadow. It stood twelve feet tall with a four foot shoulder span at the edge of the darkness. Large jagged spikes tore through every joint. His grey rotting skin flaked from the breeze. The shadow was so horrifying, all Mei ling could think of was how he looked like a demon. His disgusting nature made her thoughts fall back on her native tongue: *mogwai!*

Then there was Mei Ling. Five feet and four inches even. No ounce of muscle on her 140 pound frame with a jab reach very shy of anybody's envy.

So this is it. Mei Ling let a grin cross her face. *This is how being a superhero feels.*

Mogwai stared at the frightened girl, his nostrils flared. On exhale, a white mist escaped.

"I am going to peel your skin back before I rip out your beating heart." Mogwai words were deep, distorted and echoed through Mei Ling's entire being.

"You always this charming?" Mei Ling forged the grin into a flat expression. Attempted to come across indifferent about Mogwai's statement.

The spike came quick, almost too quick. Blood trailed from a fresh opening in the side of Mei Ling's bicep. The wound was deep enough to break skin, not catching anything important. The demon had ripped a spear of bone out of himself, which instantly had been replaced, then hurtled it at the young knight.

Mogwai did not waste time with his follow up. Gravity, more than skill, took Mei Ling's back into a sharp arc as she fell. Her knees instinctively buckled. Her body as flat as possible.

The spike grazed over her torso. Grey flickers of light skipped across the fabric of her armour, leaving Mei Ling unharmed. The spike crashed into the side of a building across the street.

Mei Ling rose to her feet. Heavy breath. A sweat on her brow. Eyes tight. Teeth gritted. Regret that she never was one for the gym.

Another spike came from Mogwai. Time seemed to slow down as Mei Ling took everything in.

Her forehead was wet, but it wasn't sweat, it was water. Not water that exerted from her pores, but water drawn from the air around her. The grey light that saved her torso from being torn apart had been ice that she had instinctively pulled from the air.

Water. It was everywhere. The air. The grass below. On her skin, in her skin and beneath it. Throughout every living thing.

Mei Ling brought up her right arm. A wave of water wrapped around her fist and ran down her forearm. Using her new weapon she landed an upper-cut to Mogwai's spike.

As the bone was thrown to the side, Mei Ling looked over her fist. How the water had balled and fell. Thousands of tiny black and grey threads retreated into the spade of cloth that ran from her wrist to loop around her middle finger.

The armour seemed in infinite supply of material. From her wrists tiny threads shot into the air to latch onto reality around her. Using these threads the armour allowed Mei Ling to manipulate her environment. To break down an element, in her case water, then weave it back into whatever she could imagine.

Quickly her eyes danced along her arm as she debated what else was possible.

With both fists balled, Mei Ling pulled water inwards, by slamming the two together. Some splashed away while most stayed on her knuckles.

The water boiled. Steam flowed from her knuckles and down past her forearms. The heat was unnoticed to her skin, but certainly wouldn't be to her target's flesh!

Mogwai swiped. Mei Ling fell to her knees to slide right under his reactive attack. Dug her heel into the soil and launched herself up towards Mogwai.

Smashed a closed fist into Mogwai's rib cage. Mei Ling couldn't help but grin. Mogwai skin bubbled and pussed almost on contact. Mei Ling followed up with a right punch to the chest.

Swinging over her right shoulder, Mei Ling followed her entire body into a punch. Moving at full force, Mei Ling crushed Mogwai's testicals under the might of her fist.

Mogwai screamed. The distortion pierced Mei Ling's ears. As the beast fell to his knees, so did Mei Ling.

Covering her ears, Mei Ling cursed. It felt like her eardrums had just imploded.

Ahead of Mei Ling was Mogwai, whom currently was curled over himself. Whimpering. The impact had moved him four metres.

"Peel those off," Mei Ling fought to stand, shook the entire way up. Ears rung. Mei Ling could hardly hear herself speak. It was difficult to balance "Okay asshat. Walk it off."

A grunt came from Mogwai. He slowly arched his neck back so he could look across to Mei Ling. "I will devour the souls of your entire blood line." His breath slow and steady. Eyes bloodshot.

"Please." Mei Ling pretended to dust her sleeves off. "The only one's bloodline whose continuing after today, is mine." She took a boxer's stance. "Bet you never bust again."

From Mei Ling's heels came a thick mist, an effortless manoeuvre that quickly took over the entire parking lot. Reducing Mogwai's visibility but kept hers quite natural.

It was now time for jagged razor to meet fresh flesh. Mogwai ran at a speed which seemed impossible for his bulk size.

God I'm stupid. Mei Ling ran to meet Mogwai head on. During her sprint, she extended her fingertips to summon water around her forearms, then ran each hand over the opposite forearm to harden the water and stretch it out into wrist blades.

She fell on her knee, as Mogwai swiped at her, spun and cut into his outer thigh with each blade. Came to her feet and jabbed forward several times to stab his lower back. He cried again, the piercing scream caused Mei Ling to back pedal. Before she could recover, he had turned and reached for her.

Mei Ling brought both arms up in a cross. Clutched her hands into fists. A thick wave of water came up with the arms and the closed fists commanded the wave into a thick ice shield.

Mogwai's massive hand wrapped around the shield. It only took a second for it to splinter then shatter.

The shards cut into Mei Ling's skin. She shrieked. Thin red slits were left all over her exposed skin. Face, legs and hands. The rest clashed against her protective armour and fell harmlessly.

Mogwai backhanded Mei Ling's side. Caught her left arm and crushed it into her rib cage. Mei Ling ragdolled across the parking lot. Crashed into a steel post that held up the batter's cage to a baseball diamond that sat next to the parking lot.

The moment left Mei Ling as darkness flowed over her.

The mist vanished. Asa became wide eyed from the horrific scene ahead of her.

Mei Ling's mangled body tossed aside. Mogwai struggled to keep balance while he laughed, wincing in pain.

Horrified and confused, Asa stood at the edge of the dissipating mist. Fear too great to allow herself to plunge into it and return to Mei Ling's side. Her eyes now busily darting from friend to demon.

Mogwai slowly drew one of his spikes out from his shoulder. Twirled it along his fingertips as he begun a slow and steady walk towards Mei Ling.

"Mei Ling!" Red faced and wide eyes, Asa sprinted to get between the two. Her friendship overcame her fear.

Through a blacked eye, Mei Ling struggled to make sense of her surroundings. Everything was blurry. Brown ground was easy enough to make out. The blue blotchy part above, clearly sky. However there was a big grey smudge slowly growing that was squeezed between brown and blue. The impact had loosened her optical nerve. A sharp pain burned at the back of her left eye, and the burning caused the right to blur with tears.

For some reason Mei Ling felt she should know the smudge. A large looming presence illuminated from it. However, something was wrong with Mei Ling's brain. She couldn't connect the smudge to her short-term memory. All there was was blinding pain and a sickening feeling in the pit of her stomach as she eyed a slightly smaller spinning smudge.

Mogwai raised his spike. The smaller smudge no longer spun. Light caught the bone's tip which glistened from Mogwai's black oily blood. Blues, yellows and red made the blood hypnotic to Mei Ling's confused mind.

Mogwai grinned ear to ear. His jagged teeth clenched so hard in excitement they caused his gums to bleed. Mogwai tightened his grip on the spike. "I will devour everything you've ever witnessed." His rewound laughter frightened Mei Ling as memory seeped into the moment.

Though confusion was still at the reigns of her mind, Mei Ling connected to his laugher. The demonic aura that Mogwai cast off with each breath was impossible to misinterpret.

Without focusing thought or vision on the little smudge, Mei Ling didn't need to realize what the spike was. In the back of her mind one thing was certain above all other things.

Mei Ling was going to die.

There would never be a reveal to what exactly a Kitsune was. Mei Ling would never play out her role in all of this. She would never kiss a boy. Drive a car. Drink until her bowels expelled out of the reverse orifice. But all of things she would miss out on, Mei Ling was saddest that she would never played in a band.

The spike charged downwards. Gravity didn't bother assisting the bone to contact with Mei Ling's flesh. The air parted, sending an outward shock wave from the shear force of Mogwai and creating a sonic boom. Asa, who had been sprinting fast enough to blush a gold medallist, was thrown to her back.

The sonic boom emptied Asa's lungs. Eyes went wide in horror as Asa witnessed the world in slow motion. She attempted to reach outwards as her body was torn away from the scene. As her back cracked against a fence's steel post, all Asa could think about was how her second friend at this school was now her first friend to ever die.

The blow to Asa's skull brought the world to a cold darkness. She slid down the post. Limp. Her unconscious body fell forward into the dirt.

Before Asa had felt the shockwaves impact, however, two amazing things occurred. Happening with perfect timing as to only be chalked up as miracles.

A thunderous sound cut through the air several times as each miracle rocketed down to the earth. A fiery trail behind each meteor. On contact with the earth, the entire block shook.

The first miracle connected to the spike. Snapping it in half was not a justified description. The force tore the spike apart, preventing it from reaching Mei Ling.

The second miracle came shortly after. The rock was larger than the first one that sniped the spike mid-air, aimed at Mogwai's head and a great deal of rage and precision was behind its accuracy.

Mogwai's forehead caved in. His neck bone crumbled into hundreds of shards. The rock tore skin and before it exited out the back of his skull. Its heat melted the beast's entire brain.

The lifeless brute fell backwards into the crater caused by the second meteor. Mogwai was dead. Asa and Mei Ling alive, but horribly injured. The sniper had a grin on her face.

A sigh of relief escaped Dawn's lips, which had quickly curled into a grin. It had been at least five years of practice without ever using a live target, besides a gopher or that one time a spider crept into her bed when she was thirteen. It was a great feeling.

Dawn stood 5'7". Pale skin, blonde hair that fell to her shoulder blades and green sea eyes. At this moment her chest extended and hands confidently rested on her hips.

A bit of a shame lingered, as Dawn realized she was more proud of her first confirmed kill—as a sniper—and not at saving Mei Ling's life. Though that may have been, Dawn thought, because Mei Ling was a stranger and she knew damn well who Mogwai was—had been.

Above Dawn's shoulder hovered a Light of her own. The device went by the name of Ozazi. The two stood on top of the school, using the height of the building to get a better angle.

Dawn leapt to the ground. Flipped mid-air for show, not that anyone was around to see it. Landed softly next to Mei Ling. Silver and white threads escaped under her heels as Dawn touched the ground.

"These two look pretty green," Ozazi sighed as he bobbed up and down. He attempted to angle its eye to the ground, as a sign of lowering its head in disappointment.

"I'll take green," Dawn knelt down to check on Mei Ling whom had felt the sonic boom directly. Dawn held no expression as she checked for a pulse.

"Looks like her armour is keeping her alive." Dawn stood. Tapped Ozazi's butt with a finger to tilt him out of his sad expression. "If she hadn't been so green, she may have fought better but she'd have used up all her magic and died."

"Then I suppose we are lucky." Ozazi bounced around in glee as he spun around Dawn. "Her left over magic reserve is keeping her alive?"

"Hardly." Dawn walked towards Asa. Still no expression. No urgency in her step. "If we don't find ourselves a healer she might need a government grant to afford someone to wipe her ass."

"I do enjoy your humour, Dawn." Ozazi barrel rolled.

Dawn allowed herself to smile, but only for a short second.

It only took a moment for Dawn to finish checking on Asa's injuries. As she did, her eyes turned a milky white so she could scan Asa fully. Dawn almost broke into laughter.

"Seriously?" Dawn shook her head, her eyes returned to normal. The lack of expression back on her face. "This one is running a full tank. Cracked skull, internal bleeding, her spinal fluid is leaking all over her internal organs, and she'll be left with nothing more than a migraine in an hour."

"Terrific!" Ozazi bounced as he spun around Dawn, for a second time.

"Yeah." Dawn rubbed her temples. "This one is so green we'd be better off referring to diarrhea than grass."

"Oh dear." Ozazi beeped red as he tilted his vision upwards.

Vala landed between Dawn and Asa. Dawn back stepped, lost her military pose, caught off by the sudden appearance of Vala. This was quickly corrected even before Vala looked up from her crouching position.

Not missing a beat of the heart, Vala sprung forward with a glowing fist towards Dawn. With little effort, Dawn brought her hand forward and under Vala's elbow then pushed it outwards to avoid the light all together. Spun around the disoriented Vala to grab her shoulder and elbow then kicked out her footing.

Dawn slammed Vala's face into the cement.

"Who are you?" Vala's teeth grinded as she shifted her face so her cheek dragged along the cement. Her eyes darted from Mogwai's broken body and Mei Ling's motionless body. "What did you do?"

Dawn sighed. "I'm on your side, Vala." Released her pin on Vala. "I saved your ass the other day, remember?"

Vala rolled onto her back, ready to spring up and attack once more, but caught Dawn's face this time. "Oh..." Vala's light vanished as she did remember Dawn. Her heart still raced as her mind tripped over itself in confusion. "What... what's going on?"

"I just saved these two from Zwart." Dawn jerked her thumb over her shoulder to Mogwai. "Heal your friends, and we can catch up."

"Right." Vala ran the back of her glowing fist across the edge of her mouth to both heal the cut inside her cheek and remove the blood that was escaping the corners of her lips.

It only took a second to heal Asa. Vala had improved her healing and, with Asa not expelling any of her own magic, Vala was able to reroute that flow of energy into what she needed. Mei Ling took *much* longer.

Muscle and organ had to be repaired, sometimes rebuilt, bones put back into place, among the many other things. It took Vala about ten minutes to finish healing Mei Ling, everything made more difficult from her lack of magic. Vala wove her own energy into Mei Ling, but she had to be careful. Pushing her own magic into another's body at an accelerated rate could mutate the cells.

Once both were healed, Vala stood. Both girls still unconscious, but stable. "So." Vala turned to Dawn. "Who are you... who's this?" She waved over Mogwai, "And why did he almost kill my friends?"

"Zwart." Dawn walked over to Vala with purpose, slightly annoyed that she had to repeat herself. "He is one of the few of the Dragon's Queen Army that she wastes Distance on sending to the Garden."

"Okay, sure." Vala nodded with a glare permanently planted on her face. "And how the *hell* do you know that?"

Dawn didn't feel inclined to answer Vala and chose to ignore her. Before Vala could open her mouth to say something offensive, Rift appeared. He had followed in Light form but his floating was much slower than Vala's jumping, now that she was getting better at it.

"Ozazi." Rift bounced in place. "It has been ages, hasn't it?"

"At least three thousand generations." Ozazi barrel rolled at his own joke. It had fallen flat with everyone else. The girls did not laugh and Rift did not roll. "Where are the other Lights?" Ozazi sought to stray attention away from his poor humour.

"For some reason the girls need them to fuse during transformation." Rift swayed. "We never had much opportunity to test run the armour. Apparently there are some complications."

"Interesting." Ozazi quickly scanned the two girls. "The Kitsune I understand. We always thought that their souls were too human to support the transformation one-hundred percent, but the Valkyrie's should be able to transform without her Light."

"Thank goodness." Rift bounced. Barrel rolled out of excitement. "Your scanners are in full function!"

Ozazi swayed back to his peer. "Why would it not?"

"Well..." Rift tilted downwards. "Neither I nor the others can. Our scanners seem to have malfunctioned."

"You think that may have been caused from long hibernation?" Dawn tried to get a few words in.

"Oh sure," Vala swung her arms up while turning the opposite direction. "Talk to them. Whatever."

"No. It was only a few years longer than I. We've been hibernating for millions of years." Ozazi was stilled a moment, rare for him. Turned back to Asa. "Still. Even with the Lights malfunctioning, that one should be able to transform."

"I have a theory on that." Rift nodded. "The string that connects to Ragnarok likely is syphoning too much energy..." Rift eyed up Dawn. "Seems this Angel is able to transform on her own."

"I thought—" Ozazi begun.

"It was a guess," Rift barrel rolled.

"You're an Angel?" Vala went wide eyed as she turned back to Dawn. "Do they still spell that a-n-g-e-l, or was I confused and has it been replaced by b-i-t-c-h?"

"Yes, I am." Dawn was quick to answer. Face still blank, but her voice held a slight annoyance. Dawn was much more interested in listening to Rift and Ozazi; she didn't even bother to make eye contact with Vala.

Cunt. Vala folded her arms as Rift swayed in front of her in a gesture she took to keep her thoughts to herself. *Dick.*

"Dawn hasn't ever had to use me to transform." Ozazi bounced. "I was awoken by Dawn on her fourth birthday. We have been training ever since. I believe Dawn awoke earlier, as being an Angel, she is much more connected to the sensitivity of the awakening."

"Yes." Rift allowed himself a bounce. "That is splendid news. Dawn should be the strongest of the girls then."

"Perhaps." Ozazi eyed Vala. Bounced. Scanned. Then swayed a moment as he thought to himself. Turned to Rift. "What did you manage to drag out of hiding over here, anyways?"

"I'm right here, you know." Vala tightened her folded arms as she looked away. "Rude."

"I'm not sure." Rift swayed. "As I said, my scanners aren't quite working. Perhaps she is a human soul that collided with our awakening stream? We aren't designed to scan Atoms of God. It would explain how she has a much weaker magic source. Though even with that she is capable of seeing strings."

"Rift!" Vala glared. "The hell, man?" Vala shivered in disgust. "Don't talk about my body to complete strangers."

"No. Not Human." Ozazi started to buzz. "But something... something we weren't expecting to find so quickly, perhaps?"

"What do you mean?" Dawn went wide eyed. Her attempt to hide what her mind had concluded was wasted.

"You are not suggesting…" Rift slowly reed backwards. Very slowly, he tilted himself towards his knight. "Vala, couldn't possibly…"

"What?" Vala took a step back while darting eyes among the crowd. "What am I? What the hell is going on?"

"Vala," Ozazi placed himself between the others and Vala. "You are the Echo that originally formed this army."

"Shut up," Vala broke into a nervous laughter.

Dawn lunged through Ozazi, which pushed him several feet to the side, and grabbed Vala by the shoulders. Shook her three times in excitement with a wide grin across her face. "You're her!"

"Aaaaah!" Vala cried throughout the vibration. "Please stop."

"Sorry," Dawn let go. Cleared her throat as she recomposed her stature.

"Yeah, it's cool," Vala pretended to dust off the areas Dawn had touched. "Miss Popular now that you know I'm your boss, eh?"

Without paying attention to Vala, Dawn turned to the Lights for consulting. "So now what?"

"Dude," Vala threw a hand in the air. "What is your deal?"

Everyone thought it best to ignore Vala and continued their conversation without her.

"We should give these two the day off." Ozazi looked over to the other two knights. "I have been jamming the emergency calls to avoid interference, now that we are done here I'll allow them to go through. Dawn can take Asa home while Vala may take Mei Ling. We will met to speak about this later."

"How does everyone know my name?" Vala raised an eyebrow as she returned to the familiarity of folded arms. "Could I be ever so graced with an introduction?"

"I believe my name has been said," Dawn picked up Asa before leaping in the air, without another word.

"Are you fricken serious?" Vala cuffed both hands around her mouth to emphasize her shout. Turned to Rift with grinding teeth, "I don't like that girl."

"You don't need to like them, Vala." Rift began his way to Mei Ling. "But you do need to get along, she may be our strongest ally."

"I can't believe you rubbed shoulders with them like they're everyday chums," Vala almost spat her words. "They've clearly been spying on us this entire time. They know our names, she even saved my life the other day—"

Eyes widened as they quaked a moment. Vala stopped moving as her brain caught up with her words. She replayed the night Maggie had died.

"What's wrong?" Rift turned to Vala. "Are you okay?"

"She…" Vala bit her thumb before balling her fists. "She should have helped me save Chelsea… and—"

Rift watched Vala's body shake with anger. He debated about saying something, but before he reached that moment the sounds of sirens came. Vala let her hands fall in defeat as she let out a heavy sigh.

CHAPTER SEVEN: DAWN ON ICE

April 17th, 20:30

The Tanaka household was an eggshell white bungalow, with brown trim, a well-kept yard and a mid-renovated basement. A detached garage connected to the house with a wooden arch way that one would have to pass under to get to the front door.

The kitchen full of dirty cutlery, pots and pans intensely soaking in a nearly overflowing sink. Bent heads and cupped hands were in the dining room. Words danced out of Chika's lips of thanks and grace. Proper and rehearsed pitches and tones on each syllable.

At the end of the prayer her two sisters and parents 'amen-ed' along with her. A warmth buzzed around the table as the peaceful display was cut through with manic action. Potatoes passed, corn binged and turkey torn; Chika let her lips curl.

Events of the other day slipped away. The twisted demon, the strange girls and the news of the unlucky boy. The news talked briefly about the event but with no photo evidence, all of it was hearsay. Some speculated a cougar had snuck into the city, and people were over exaggerating from the state of shock brought on by witnessing a man torn apart.

Dinner was quick. Chika hardly noticed her mask that night. Though at this point in her life it was less a mask and more of a pressure that built over time at the base of her skull, only surfacing during stressful times. Chika would go weeks without the pressure presenting itself; she had no idea where it came from.

After dinner Chika cleaned the dishes, as she did every Tuesday night. Then would come an hour of family TV watching, before Chika would retire upstairs to work on assignments.

Night was swift. In a moment it was eleven o'clock and Chika started to yawn. Typically she would sleep around ten to wake up at six for lane swimming just before school.

As the weight of a drawn out day begun to take hold, Chika stripped the day's clothes for a set of purple pyjamas with farm animals. It was embarrassing, but Chika loved them. They had been the last gift her late grandmother had given her. Chika had taken up swimming to avoid horizontally outgrowing the present.

A tap came at her window. With veins that felt of sludge, Chika looked over her shoulder to the dark glass. In the window floated a Light, accented on its trim with her bedroom light, the rest of it nearly invisible.

Chika stumbled in a contorted mess. Her groggy mind relied on her eyes for information, which faced the window; however, when her body attempted to backpedal from the window, her half awake mind closed the gap between her and the danger. Caught up in an alarmed confusion as she moved closer to the frightening object, Chika turned her ankles awkwardly and lost her footing.

The bedroom carpet came fast and hard. Chika twirled twice on the way down.

Jagged tooth split Chika's inner cheek. Copper filled her mouth in a sinking sensation. Chika used a finger to fish around to investigate the damage, but hardly any blood had been spilled.

"Chika honey. Are you alright in there?" Chika's mother called from the hallway.

A second tap brought Chika's eyes up from blood and towards the dark window. Slowly Chika rose; first her torso and then one knee at a time. While still knelt, Chika tilted her head with a raised eyebrow.

The device in the window seemed to be bobbing in delight. Every third bob it would pause, allowing its many silver plates to spin around its centrepiece.

A second call filled with more alarm, followed with footsteps.

"Yeah." Chika made what she assumed was eye contact with the ruby centrepiece. "Just tripped."

Chika stumbled to her feet, but caught herself with the aid of a nightstand.

Subject of her own adolescent ignorance of mortality, Chika was beckoned forward.

Quivering fingers almost danced with a childlike electricity along the window latch. The crank of the window creaked from years of neglect. Chika had to push the last bit open as the crank stopped working.

The Light bobbed through the opening. Chika's eyes traced the outline the silver plates gave off in her dim room. They were almost as reflective as a mirror.

"What—" Chika's voice masked her excited curiosity, but wide joyful eyes hide nothing. "—are you?"

"I am the fourth forged Light." The device twirled its plates. "I don't have any name that you'd be able to pronounce without a split tongue."

Chika narrowed her eyes in a brief state of confusion.

"That being said," the device bobbed around the room to study Chika's life. It studied Chika's pictures of Bible camp, the Bible on the nightstand and the chore trophies on displayed. "I believe your Bible was originally written in Hebrew." His ruby flashed as he scanned Chika. "You may call me Esh. The Hebrew word for fire."

"Fire?" Chika cocked an eyebrow. "Why fire?"

"Reasons." Esh laughed—twirled.

"Okay." Chika fished for the desk chair which resided behind her person. "Esh. What are you and why are you here?"

As Chika sat her shirt rode up, she tugged it down and when it wouldn't stay, she kept a hand in front to hide her stomach from her guest; no amount of swimming could avoid vertical growth.

"I am a device referred to as a Light. We were forged by the Echo, who deemed the Atoms of God to be salvageable." Esh hesitated a moment. "To be saved. Protected. Corrected. Cured." He danced along on several words for another minute before growing bored of the English language. "The First Language is very basic. I find English to be so fun—fulfilling. Enjoyable. Exciting..." he continued a moment more before realizing what he was doing and stopped.

Esh bobbed a bit more then continued. "Think of the universe as a womb for the successor of the Voice. When the Voice created everything it was a mathematical equation to, over the course of trillions of years, birth its child."

Esh continued his story with several interruptions with his affection for English. Chika followed along with a tilted head, cocked eyebrow and low jaw. Rubbed her temple once it was all complete.

Chika's voice was low and mostly kept to herself, "This all sounds like something I already know. Every time you're speaking, I get two sentences of information ahead of you." Chika felt that pressure at the base of her neck.

"So." Chika rose from her seat, clasped her hand tightly and began massaging to manage the annoyance. "I am one of the knights." Flashes of another life time sped forth. A warmth inside her chest, like nothing she had ever felt before, ignited. Strange threads expanded past her on the horizon beyond her room and pulled in countless flashes of another world.

The threads tightened on the last image, a woman wielding a blade of fire, before they snapped. The world retracted back into itself and Chika was left in her room. "I can shoot fire!" Chika looked down at her shaking hands, with a grin ear to ear. A warmth in her chest extended to every part of her being. She laughed, "Reasons… that's funny, Esh."

"Thank you." Esh bobbed. "It makes sense that you are filling in the spaces yourself. You were designed to be superior to all other forms of life. It is to be expected that you are absorbing everything as well as you are."

"Designed?" Chika felt the room spin. Thought rolled through the images once more, this time standing still on a dark figure. One she couldn't quite make out. She could tell it was red, but a shadow laid over top it and for whatever reason, her mind couldn't identify it. "By whom?"

Chika fell to her knees. Used one hand to brace her weight against the dresser to slow her descent. Another hand fished around the dresser for the garbage can.

Chika puked.

An unforgiving reality piled on the pressure in her skull as years of family gatherings and community rushed invisibly by her ears.

"The Dragon." Esh answered Chika's question. "You are a Dragonborn."

Chika used the back of her fist to whip the corners of her mouth. She knew in the furthest depths of her soul that Esh was not lying. Brown eyes looked up pathetically to a cross on the wall.

Tears fell as Chika embraced her own truth; she was a blasphemous abomination.

*   *   *

Weights, a treadmill, a bench and pull up bar were all sandwiched in the tiny living room. In a corner a stack of novels laid for entertainment. The kitchen was kept perfectly organized. A mattress acted as a divider of the two 'rooms'.

Dawn yawned her way through the entrance. A thick layer of dust clung to her pale skin. Cement chips hardened around her torn jeans and white bunny hug. She tossed her work gloves to the side, and kicked off her steel toed boots.

Dawn threw her keys on a heap of unfolded clothes. Ozazi escaped the safety of her bunny hug as Dawn stripped, revealing herself in a full bodied mirror. Her eighteen-year-old frame held the body of a lightweight MMA champion. Though the suit enhanced her abilities beyond human limitations, Dawn was obsessed with keeping her six pack and toned limbs. A statement of commitment more than anything else.

A strong chill flowed along her naked body. The fair hairs on her back stood up in alarm as goose bumps ran rampant along her.

The window to the apartment was smashed.

"Shit." Dawn quickly put on her bunny hug. Slowly, she made her way to the only room with a closed door, the washroom.

Expectation turned into a relieving confusion, as the hooligan light buzzed on; the washroom was empty.

"No axe wielding rapist here," Dawn leaned against the door frame while she flicked the light on and off in a state of boredom. "Really felt like breaking someone."

Ozazi twirled. "Perhaps something was taken?"

"No." Dawn flared her nostrils. Even with the layer of cement dust plugging her nose, the apartment reeked from her sweaty gym equipment. "I have nothing worth stealing. Not unless they want a hundred year old stove or my used thongs—" Dawn paused on the thought. "Oh dear lord."

"Don't worry." Ozazi swayed. "We don't have a mid-aged pervert on our hands."

"Oh?" Dawn used her foot to rummage through her clothes. "Some asshat kid with one too many rocks?"

"I sort of wish." Ozazi circled the kitchen table. His voice hissed on a word Dawn couldn't pronounce and hardly understood.

"It activated." Dawn was wide eyed. "How is that even possible?"

"Well, we are crafted from the metals of the River." Ozazi broke the encryption of Dawn's neighbour's wireless network, and deployed a copy of his latest worm to computers across the world. "Perhaps the Dragonborns extra sensitivity latched onto our network. Subconsciously activated our spare Light."

"Ugh." Dawn shivered from the tips of her toes to the frayed ends of her hair. "I'm trying to imagine the scaly acne girl in a mini skirt. Defiantly wanting to sit this one out."

"I enjoy this side of you, Dawn." Ozazi used video streams from corner store security cameras to triangulate a location. "When your walls are down and you allow yourself to accept the fact that you are a teenager."

Dawn didn't waste time transforming when she realized Ozazi was purposely delaying. Her voice became very stern. "Where?"

"I have an estimation. About half a mile from here." Ozazi joined Dawn by following over her shoulder.

$$*\qquad*\qquad*$$

"You need to go back." Chika shoved her index finger into Esh's face. She sat on her bed, with legs and arms wrapped around a pulled up body pillow.

"I cannot take it back, Chika." Esh swayed while tilting his nose down. "You decided this in your previous life."

"Well this has to be a mistake." Chika bit on her thumb nail. Her head began to shake shortly but quickly and repetitively. "There is no way my parents would accept it." She took a moment to curse in Japanese. Swearing was uncharacteristic of her and came across as unnatural even to Esh, who had just met her.

Esh studied the pictures and books on the walls. "Chika. Your world has hundreds of religions. How could you possibly think yours is one-hundred percent true?"

"Hey!" Chika swung an arm. "Watch your—" brown eyes darted over Esh, "*mouth?*"

"Every faith has something right that the others do not, while also having elements that are wrong." Esh shifted his metal plates in a shrugging motion. "Why would you let this bother you? You've spent your entire life enjoying something with your family. If it makes you and them happy, why push that away? Even adults still have fun with Santa when they're the ones on the side that realize he is no longer real."

"I..." Chika hesitated as memories flashed through her mind's eye. She knew it was all real, but accepting an entire new outlook on life in a moment came with its complications. "I can't accept that it's all a lie, Esh."

Her stomach tightened as her mind swayed a moment. Chika pulled tighter on the pillow. Buried her face deep into the feather dew. Screamed.

Esh uneasily swayed over Chika's shoulder. "Chika. You don't have to accept my story or your memories as truth. Maybe it is all a lie, how would I know? I'm just a robot programmed to think whatever my programmer thought that I should."

"How is that supposed to make me feel better?" Chika muffled from her pillow.

"Yesterday you saw a demon. That's how I was activated. You are Dragonborn. My metals were forged from the River. You and I are more connected than any other knight will be to their Light. I can sense your memories as you can sense mine. As such I also have the greatest empathy as your memories allow me to produce emotion." Esh brushed Chika's cheek to force her face to be lifted. He then swung into her centre view. "Why don't we ignore the history lesson, and just go be a superhero?"

Chika stared at Esh for a moment.

*　　*　　*

"This is it?" Dawn sank her hands deep into her windbreaker. Dawn admired the well-kept home, to her it was something that belonged on the front page of a Christmas catalogue.

"Well Ozazi," Dawn spoke down the neck of her jacket. "Let's go get Mrs Silver Spoon."

"What makes you so sure it's a girl?" Ozazi buzzed.

Dawn perked up with eyes upwards diagonally. "*Caaaaan* boys be knights?" Dawn pictured hairy legs in a skirt which caused her to debate if the scales would have been better.

"It's a possibility. The armies were all female, but souls don't have sexes so there is a chance."

"Gross." Dawn pushed the image out of her mind. Dawn started to walk up to the front door. It's perfectly painted white wood felt warm. "Think the armour would be the same?"

"The Kitsune designed the armour and only their women are warriors; so I assume they never felt the need to design male modelled armour."

Dawn knocked. "Can you fill me in on names?"

A buzz came as Ozazi quickly searched social media. "Sora, age nineteen; Chika, age fourteen; and Hitomi, age ten. If it's the mother, could be Sakura, but she is forty-five and I doubt the rebirth would be that far off."

"So Sora or Chika?" Dawn danced over the options as voices neared the door. "Guess I'll just go with whichever one doesn't answer the door."

"Sora would be my guess. If she was able to activate her Light on her own, I would assume that she is quite mature."

"Good. Twirl if Sora and sway if Chika." Dawn made sure her zipper was tight so Ozazi wasn't visible."

The door opened. A man in his early fifties towered at the entrance. His pale skin threw Dawn off. "May I help you?"

"Um." Dawn shifted her weight. "Is Sora home?"

The man studied Dawn for a moment. "She is. May I ask who's asking for my daughter at such an hour?"

"My name is Dawn, sir." Dawn tried to look helpless but it came off as a nervous smile. Which left the man feeling awkward instead of sympathetic. After a long pause, Dawn added, "Cyr. Dawn Cyr."

"Dawn, huh?" The corner of the man's frown began to twitch into a curl. Dawn tilted her head with a cocked brow as he burst into laughter. "Sorry kid. I'm just messing with ya. Had you going, huh?"

"Yeah—" Dawn shifted her weight into a shrug. "Sorry to bother you, but—"

A hand was brought up to halt Dawn. "Don't say another word. Sora helps a lot of girls out from the church. I know it gets personal. It's between you and her." The man stepped aside to widen the doors opening. "Come in, Miss Cyr."

"Thanks." Dawn smiled. "Seriously." Dawn stepped in.

"My name is Henry." The two shook hands before Henry closed the door. "I need to apologize, but I don't recognize you. Been busy at the firehall last few months. Do you know the way?" Henry gestured for her jacket.

"Uh." Dawn pretended to admire the living room's leather seats, massage chair, and awards on the banister; but really she was slipping Ozazi into cupped hands while removing her jacket. "Down the hall right?"

Henry chuckled while hanging up Dawn's jacket. Dawn slowly spun, dragging Ozazi out of line of sight to her back. Rolled up her shirt and put him under it. "Basement. Here. I'll show you."

"So you're a firefighter?" Dawn didn't need to fake her interest. "I want to be one of those, one day."

"Well if you don't mind me saying, Dawn." Henry led Dawn through the kitchen to the basement door. "You look more built than most of the boys at the hall. I'm sure you'd do a fine job."

"Thanks." Dawn smiled.

The stairs soothed the feet as they rumbled from the dryer in a room located underneath. The basement was split down the middle by the staircase. To the left was a door with no frame outlining it, to the right an exposed entertainment room that held leaned over drywall and various tools.

His knock was a gentle, yet powerful one.

"Yes?" A soft voice came from within.

Dawn collected her game face. Distant and depressed.

"Honey. Dawn's here to see you?" Henry smiled at Dawn's contorted face. It broke her disguise, for a moment.

The sound of a keyboard followed by some shuffling. A minute past before the door creaked open. An asian girl with pigtails, glasses slid to the tip of her nose and clothed in torn jeans and a spaghetti top. "Who?"

"Dawn." Henry repeated, not overly fond of his daughter's choice in wardrobe.

"Hi." Dawn tried to act innocent, but she wasn't very convincing. Dawn felt exposed and was sure she blew it. "From the church?"

With an extended index finger Sora pushed her glasses over her eyes. "Oh. I didn't recognize you." Sora smiled at her father. "We're good. Thanks, Dad."

The room was dark, only lit by a television shoved in the corner of the room on top an expensive oak desk. Even in the dim lighting Dawn could tell it was a perfectly kept room. Sora softly closed the door.

"Sorry." Sora tossed herself into her chair, spun around to her desk. "Was just doing Towards the Future. Give me a second."

"Towards what?" Dawn pulled back with a raised brow.

"We're on Ultimate Dark Falz and I'm a HUcast. No one really wanted me in there to begin with." Sora shut off the TV, which left the room in complete darkness aside from the red numbers from her alarm clock. "No one's going to miss me." Without standing Sora slid across the room to turn on the lights.

"Oh. Well." Dawn looked around for the missing Light. "You could have kept playing. I can wait."

"Nah." Sora yawned. "Games are games. Life is life. I assume if you're here it's more important than that over hyped scape doll."

"Well, I don't know about that." Dawn sat on the bed. "I'm sorry I'm here, but I didn't have anywhere else to go." Dawn placed her eyes in the opposite direction of Sora. Well aware she wasn't a good actor.

"It's fine." Sora sat up. "I'll grab you a toothbrush and a sleeping bag." Before Dawn could say a word, Sora was gone.

"Okay." Dawn awkwardly rose. Unsure what to think of the situation, she began her search.

Under the bed were neat stacks of school books, while half the room was a display of fantasy titles of all eras. Dawn wasn't sure what to think of the arrangement, but she took the time to pull each one aside to make sure nothing was hiding behind it.

"What are you doing?" A hoarse voice came from the door.

A mental sigh of relief came over Dawn as she thanked God that she had been caught looking at books and not in an underwear draw. She looked over her shoulder to find Chika.

Stuffed nose and red eyed, Chika stood in the door frame. A part of Dawn remembered that look; being young, scared and alone with the weight of the world on her shoulders.

Dawn glanced at the novels in her own hands. "Looking for something to read?" Dawn cocked a grin.

"Oh." Chika sniffed. "Where's my sister?"

"Grabbing me a sleeping bag." Dawn noticed a silver ball in Chika's hands. "What's that?"

"Oh." Chika shrugged, then pocketed the device. "Just something I wanted to talk to Sora about."

"Cool." Dawn stepped passed Chika to gently close the door.

Dawn's proximity caused Chika to become wide eye, arch her back away from Dawn's body and hold her breath until Dawn finished pulling away.

"You know it's not cool for superheroes to cry," Dawn tossed the book aside.

A shiver ran up Chika. "W-what?" She backed up. "I'm not a—"

Ozazi swayed out from under Dawns shirt. "Hello!" Ozazi bobbed. "Pleasure to meet you, Chika."

Chika attempted to speak, but volume fell short though thought certainly ran rampant with suggestions of what to say.

"Hey. Relax." Dawn smiled. "It's a pretty sweet gig. Sure there's no dental, but we get to punch stuff."

"I—" Chika attempted to make words.

"You and I," Dawn grabbed Chika by the wrist and led her out.

The girls swiftly and quietly made their way up the stairs. Chika did little to stop Dawn leading her out the side door and into the darkness of midnight.

The backyard was almost designed for someone to secretly sneak out of. No major windows faced this direction, the detached garage, large trees in the back yard and the tall fence hid all possible angles of curiosity.

Chika cringed as her bare feet touched the icy pavement.

Dawn turned to Chika. "Ready, soldier?" Striked her serious stance.

"No." Chika embarrassedly snorted back her stuffy nose. Dawn broke her stance with wide eyes and curled lips. Chika blushed from Dawn's taken back reaction.

Ozazi hissed Esh's true name, "Some assistance please."

Esh twirled around Chika. "You'll enjoy this. I'm told it's quite the rush... thrill... adventure..."

"Blast?" Chika tried to add to Esh's ramble but was interrupted by him crashing into her chest.

Golden chains overtook Chika as red and purple threads erupted around her. For the first time in her life, Chika realized the emptiness in her chest cavity as a warmth filled the hollowed region. Her soul shot a surge of strength, purpose and endorphins, unfelt by Chika before.

"Whoa." Chika looked herself over. She smiled to see her favourite colour, purple, take over her arms and skirt while red made up her torso and heels.

The same sensation as when Esh explained the origins of the universe, came to Chika. She felt like she knew what the armour was just as she was about to ask the question.

Blinding silver and white light caused Chika to bring up her hands. When she brought them down, Dawn was in her own set of armour, with Ozazi over her shoulder.

"You're that girl!" Chika shrieked, reactively covered her mouth realizing she should be quit. "The one that saved that other girl!"

"I am?" Dawn cocked an eyebrow to Ozazi. "I save a lot of people, you'll have to narrow it down a bit."

"The bus. The other girl with," Chika ran her hands up and down herself, "this."

"Oh," Dawn nodded as she recalled yesterday's encounter. "That was me."

Chika twisted around looking for Esh. "Where is Esh?"

"Yeah," Dawn scratched her face. "Bit of a glitch in the system. Turns out only Angels are powerful enough to borrow from their Lights. Where Dragonborns, Kitsune and Valkyries need a complete merge."

"You're an Angel?" Chika looked Dawn over head to toe. It wasn't hard for Chika to believe her. Dawn's thick long hair, bright green eyes, flawless pale skin, long legs and toned body were desirable.

Reality came back and crashed. Chika lowered her head in shame. "And I'm a child of Satan."

An awkward chill ran down Dawn. She exchanged a cocked eye with Ozazi before guilt took over. She sighed before closing the gap between the two.

Dawn pushed Chika's shoulder, this caused Chika to back step and look up at Dawn. "I know your family is super religious, but the Dragon created the Dragonborn. Just like the Voice created Humans. Your ability to be a good person is just as likely as a Human to be evil."

Chika's expression did not change. Dawn mentally rolled her eyes. "I want to show you something."

*   *   *

In the centre of the city was the fourth largest urban park in Canada. The waters of Wascana Park were still, a rare occurrence in Regina. The crescent moon sparkled a brilliant white over top the water.

Elm and poplar trees ran along the coast on both sides, blocking out most of the lamps to blacken the dirt path that looped the lake. Darkness masked the thousands of goose droppings that were landmines to anyone's feet.

Thanks to their ability to leap the distance of a football field in a single bound, it hadn't taken the girls much time to make it to the park.

Crouched under a tree, Dawn and Chika watched a man stumble through the dark. He wore a torn toque, ripped windbreaker and the ankles of his jeans were frayed. His complexion purposely chosen to draw in racist onlookers. The empty bottle in his hand to compliment the facade, everything else an aid to his act.

"Watch," Dawn whispered over Chika's ear. Chika pulled forward, a bit conscious about her personal space.

"For?" Chika spoke too softly, overcompensating due to her nervousness. Luckily Dawn had intended to continue her thought with or without a reply from her student.

"You'll pick up on it after some time." Dawn slowly crept around to Chika's side, used a branch as a crutch to move up and over a bush. "You just need to get a vibe for it. The wrenching in your stomach, the smell of sulphur in the air, the random hot and cold spots in the area."

"Are we," Chika twisted her mouth in a fit of confusion. "Hunting ghosts?"

"And you think that's weird?" Dawn laughed. "You literally just jumped your way across the city."

"Point." Chika stood up, her thighs killing her from crouching. "So, we fight it?"

"That thing isn't a ghost, more like a demon." Dawn pulled on Chika's shoulder to force her back to a crouch. "The Dragon's Queen manifest these creatures. I don't know how. They mimic us. Seek out humans and steal their souls. From what Ozazi can gather they infest humans. It is more economical to send to our realm when you are only sending a spirit and not an actual body."

"Their souls?" Chika went wide eyed.

"Yes. They're real," Dawn looked around as she heard a car driving by.

"I know they're real." Chika glared. "I'm Catholic."

"Whatever," Dawn shrugged it off. "I'm told that warmth in your chest is you finally connecting to it. It's the source of your power."

145

"Where does yours come from?" Chika spoke a bit louder than she should have. Curiously got the best of her, but thankfully the man didn't notice.

"That's complicated." Dawn looked to Chika and ran her hand out front of her body up and down. "This is my soul. Hopefully it doesn't come up, but I'm more durable than you. I just don't get a round two."

"Round two?" Chika raised an eyebrow.

"Yeah." Dawn turned back to the man. "I don't get a heaven. Angels are immortal so I'll never get sick or die from old age. But if I die, I don't have anything after this life."

The man's attempt at appearing drunk had worked. A patrol car had noticed the man, the police pulled over.

Dawn watched the interaction. "These things are collecting human souls. The idea is they can be converted into energy that can bend the fabric of time and space..."

"Insane. Like what?" Chika fell forward, to her hands and knees, to catch a look at Dawn's face. Her hand snapped a twig; the conversation between police and the man was too loud for it to be heard, but Dawn shot her a look all the same.

"Their goal is to build a bridge from the River to the Garden so the Dragon can enslave us." Dawn leaned forward, played with her ring. "Each soul they collect fuels their base stationed in the Between. They use it to move supplies from the River to here."

"So…" Chika began a new question.

"Hey." Dawn cut her off. "By the way, when you're confused why you're not pissing yourself, its cause the armour makes ya man up." Without much else Dawn took off across the street, kept to the small crevice of darkness between the light of the street lamps.

"Wait, what?" Chika perked up, but Dawn was already across the street. "Crap," she mimicked Dawn to the best of her ability.

The drunk stumbled out of the light. His voice replaced his slur with a distorted reversal of words. Both officers reached for their side arms. Red eyes froze the men in place. An eerie unearthly sight that sent shivers down spines and burrowed deep into their souls.

The man's right hand morphed into a three talon claw. His jaw dislocated for two more rows of teeth to protrude; each tooth no shorter than five centimetres; his face a demented abomination.

The man rushed the officers. Dawn got between the two parties, swung around her left to his right. She grabbed the talon by the wrist with one hand while she shot her free palm upwards into his locked elbow.

The bone snapped. His voice howled. Dawn let him go. He stumbled in a state of pain and confusion. Freedom from Dawn's grasp let him end his tumbling fit onto his back.

From the ground, he arched his back so his stomach was skyward. His shriek ear deafening. He grasped the wound.

"Okay," Dawn dusted off her hands. "You're up to bat, champ."

"What?" Chika emerged from the shadows with wide eyes. For a reason she couldn't explain, the man didn't shock her, but Dawn's summon to arms was startling.

Everything felt natural to her. Chika would never be able to put it into words but nothing would feel more natural than being in armour. There was a calm that came over her person when she should be freaking out.

"I'm a big baseball fan," Dawn shrugged. "It's an American thing."

"You're American?" Chika turned, like a rookie, away from the man to face Dawn.

"Whoa!" Dawn grabbed Chika by the shoulders and in one fluid motion twisted her around, hard. "Green bean. Keep your eyes on the enemy."

"Huh?" Chika's eyes trailed over her shoulder, still focused on Dawn. They rolled to face ahead just in time to see the man.

He had stopped flailing around on the ground. Rushed her. Chika brought up her arms in defence. Dawn rolled her eyes, followed by shoving Chika towards confrontation.

Chika stumbled forward. Back arched and arms pulled back; on her third step in the damp grass, everything clicked.

Wide eyes had found a fist aimed square for her nose. Tight eyes took over and forced Chika into fourth gear. She grabbed his wrist.

Everything stood still for a minute, or so Chika thought, but in reality it was a few heartbeats. Unsure what to do, now that she had her opponent by the wrist, Chika did the only thing that came to mind.

She yanked his arm towards her; low then with great force, aimed for his face.

Still having his wrist in hand, Chika punched the man in his face with his own fist. Twice. Then four more times until his legs buckled.

Three more on the way down, with a final one for good measure. Teeth were scattered around both his chest and the grass.

With a warmth in her chest and an ear to ear grin, Chika stood up.

"Holy shit!" Dawn slapped Chika on the butt so hard she was briefly lifted off her feet. "That was insane. And hilarious!" Dawn looked over the mangled mess with a grin crossing ear to ear.

She crouched to get a better look. "Oh man, do you see his nose? It's so busted it's an innie!" Dawn grabbed the man's chin to turn his face over to get a better look. "Man, his jaw's broken in like seven places."

"Thanks," Chika walked up to Dawn's side, rubbing her rear end.

Rubber peeled and exhaust filled the air. Both girls looked up to see the police car racing off.

"Timmy's must be closing soon," Dawn laughed as she rose to her feet. Realized it was a Canadian thing to do and added, "Eh?"

Chika gave Dawn a cocked eyebrow then shook it off. "Shouldn't we stop them?" Chika turned back to the red headlights that were just fading from sight.

"And do what?" Dawn jerked a thumb to the mangled body. "You want to do this to some cops? Man you're hardcore."

"No," Chika went wide eyed and brought up her hands in defence. "I would never—"

"Chill," Dawn placed a friendly hand on Chika's shoulder. "I'm joking."

"Oh," Chika blushed, tilted her head to the ground. One arm fell while the other looped hair over her ear. "Sorry."

Dawn turned to the body. "No one's reporting this. No one would believe them. Best case they say he was on bath salts."

"Is that a drug?" Chika inspected her work. "He isn't human, right?"

"Not in the least." Dawn crouched behind the man's head. Looped her arms under his armpits. "Once these things get inside of you, you're done. They'll lie and tell you the persons still alive, but they aren't. Killing them detaches them from the soul, frees the host. Never feel guilty for what you do to these things. The only thing they have in common with us is they're a sack of meat... We should ditch the body all the same."

Chika took the man by the legs. It wasn't necessary, as Dawn could support the weight herself, but Chika wanted to be polite. "I feel like we are in The Godfather."

With a blank face and low jaw, Dawn tilted her head as she looked over Chika's shoulder to the lake. Chika jerked back in confusion as she too, turned towards the water.

A fog had come in over the lake, thick in the background to block the other end but thin enough to make out most of the middle and all of the coast between it and the girls. In the centre of the lake was a man with arms extended outwards with fog coming from his palms.

His strides were short, his head tilted forwards as he made his way to the girls. Each step he took froze the water below him. Slowly the ice expanded past his steps until the entire lake was frozen over. The closer he came to them, the easier it was to notice his contorted face and hear his backwards laughter.

"Whoa..." Chika let go of the body. Her back pedal was stopped by Dawn's gentle, but firm, hand to her shoulder blades.

"You got this," Dawn grinned as she changed her gentle touch to a forceful shove. Chika stumbled a few steps before stopping herself. She turned back to look at Dawn with puppy dog eyes. "Chika, you can shoot fire. Come on." Dawn glared.

"Oh," Chika turned to the man then looked down at her own hands. "Right."

The armour revved up as it fuelled Chika with the rush that she needed. Swallowed her fear, took into a sprint across the park, leapt off the shore line and came down on the man.

Chika cupped her hands together and came down with a stream of fire.

The man didn't have time to defend himself as the flame engulfed him. Chika fell to the ice. Cutting her flame in time to not thin the ice too much but her heels still dug into slush.

"Whoa," Chika eyed her hands. Slowly stood up as a silly grin crossed her face. She turned laughing and waved to Dawn.

Five demons fell to surround Chika. Grey dried skin stretched so tight around their muscles that pink flesh was exposed in series of gashes. They towered over the knight by several feet. Pupil-less golden eyes sat on the outside of their skull, bobbed with the slightest movement.

The lake shook with their weight, which caused Chika to lose her balance. One demon shoved his weight into Chika's side, she stumbled into a full collapse. She shrieked as one demon plucked her out of the decent, then pulled her inwards.

Dawn tightened her eyes from across the lake.

Dawn rushed the lake. One demon sprinted to meet her. She jumped up and over it, slammed her palms on the base of its skull. Used the momentum to flip over top of it and into a spinning twirl. The force sent the creature through the ice.

Dawn came down, hard. Slammed a fist into a demon's jaw, it tore right through flesh. While bone skipped along the ice, Dawn caught the fist of an attacker. Grabbed the wrist with on hand, led the demon downwards and she grabbed his shoulder with her free hand. Pulled as hard as she could, tearing the arm apart at the elbow.

Swung around to smash her new weapon into the face of a demon on her six. Let go of the arm, continued with the momentum to catch another demon in the side of the face with a kick.

Before finishing falling to the ice, Dawn had already leapt to the others. Came down left fist first. The demon attempted to duck the attack but failed and Dawn's knuckle met the base of his skull. Her force so great she followed through him and into the ice. Four large cracks shot outwards along the lake.

Her heels touched the ice, she pivoted to her right and caught a demon with the back of her fist to crush its windpipe.

Dawn turned to the final demon, the one holding Chika, with a glare bathed in the blood of her enemies. Leaned forward, shot off and slammed a fist into the shoulder of the demon with such force the arm was torn free.

Chika screamed as blood splattered her face. Instinctively, she crouched while bringing up her arms to block the splatter but it was too late. Still with momentum, Dawn spun around and kicked with both feet into the demon's chest. She could have done it hard enough to crush its chest cavity and end it all right then, but chose to finish with flare.

Still mid flip, Dawn lined up her ring's crosshair with its torso. A thunderous sound came with a blink of her eye.

A shockwave filled the entire city. The meteor decimated the demon. A geyser of water erupted. The force of impact shattered the ice. Chunks of it were tossed into the air. Remains filled the night with a chilled mist.

Dawn spun, took Chika in her arms, and jumped backwards to land on a chunk of ice as the ground beneath them crumbled. Shifted her body weight to prevent the chunk from tipping itself over, Dawn rode it like a board as she steadied it.

"Holy," Chika looked up at Dawn. Breath heavy, heart racing and face flush. Adrenaline still fueled her with fear of death. Slowly the suit reached into her and pulled that fear away. "Holy shit."

"You kiss your mother with that mouth?" Dawn grinned as she placed Chika on her feet, making sure to not rock the chunk of ice too much.

"That." Chika ignored the blood across her face as she made eye contact with Dawn. "That was amazing, Dawn. Thank you. Thank you so much!"

"No problem," Dawn ran her hand to push a loose strand of hair. Smirked as she realized her forehead was still dry; not an ounce of sweat had been spent.

White mist kicked up as hard chunks collided all over the girls. The impact caught the knights off guard. Quick to find stable ground, Dawn pushed Chika who struggled to hold her balance.

At first the shove caused Chika to stumble, but after several hops along sinking chunks of ice, she managed to leap to the shore line.

Still airborne, as her leap was more arced than straightforward, Chika looked towards her ally. White powder filled the air. Through the entanglement of the miniature blizzard, Chika realized her fortune was founded by sacrifice.

When the ice had gave, Dawn instinctively pushed the person she was responsible for to the side. There had been no time to put up a proper defence. Mighty claws wrapped tightly around her person.

The chill came fast. Like knives against her skin the subzero water penetrated all the heat from her body.

Dawn struggled to kick the beast off of her, but couldn't contort herself to catch a piece of him. Her arms buckled before the lake floor came.

Air rushed out of her lungs as the demons arms closed further. Instinctively she gasped for air, but was only rewarded with mouthfuls of ice water. Green eyes widened in horror as the mind numbed, lungs burned and heart quickened.

An insane amount of pressure came across her skull as the defences of the armour weakened. With magic focused on the structural support of her skeletal system, Dawn was no longer safe from the pressure of the deep water.

The muscles in her throat worked overtime, but only cold water filled their efforts. Limbs convulsed as they violently fought for freedom.

The darkness crept in, phasing out the white light of the moon and only catching glimpses of the final raising bubbles.

"*Dawn!*" Chika leaned into a leap but was cut off by Ozazi. The silver shards in her peripherals caused her to take a double take, stumble to a stop.

Ozazi shot upwards, then dove at a sharp angle through an opening in the ice.

With energy depleted, Dawn's struggle dimmed into a flail. The demon grabbed her by the back of the skull in one of his mighty hands. Shoved her face into the lake floor. Dust clouded the two as the impact kicked up the base of the lake. Though she continued to fight, Dawn no longer strained the demon.

The hand came off Dawn. The demon jerked to the side. Ozazi swayed through the liquid, confused of his environment after the collision with the demon's temple.

Dawn rolled to her shoulder. With the last stage of darkness overthrowing consciousness, Dawn lined up her crosshair.

The sky was littered with water, ice and dirt as five meteors crashed throughout the lake.

The geysers reached outwards, caught Chika in their splash zone. She didn't blink as she became soaked head to toe by the cold water. She didn't feel its cold penetrate her skin. Her mind only knew the spectacle.

Dawn had no time to aim. Had used as much magic as she could muster to fire as many times as she could before the blackout. Lady luck had been present, and one tore the demon in half.

The power was beautiful. Chika didn't wait to absorb the art and leapt into the water.

Ozazi shined a flashlight overtop the limp Dawn. Chika found her quickly. With little effort, both thanks to the last year of lane swimming and her armour's enhancements, Chika brought Dawn safely to shore.

Energy from Dawn's armour surged through her. A gasp for air turned into a cough that spouted water. Chika looked towards Ozazi for advice, but the Light had none. By the fifth cough, Dawn had her breathing under control.

"Ow," Her lungs were on fire, in a constant state of expansion and collapse. Dawn ran her hand over her face, leaving a trail of mud. "Ugh. Goddamn it!"

Unsure what to do, Chika broke out into hysterical laughter. Ozazi joined her with a twirl.

"What's so funny?" Dawn pushed herself up to her elbows. Her lungs beginning to remember how to normally control the flow of oxygen.

"I thought you were going to die," Chika tried to steady herself but it proved difficult.

"And that is funny?" Dawn raised an eyebrow towards Ozazi. "And *you!*"

"Sorry," Chika cleared a tear from her eye. "You look ridiculous."

"Oh yeah?" Dawn shot a stink eye. "You think it's funny?" Slung mud at the two.

*　　*　　*

At a choke point in the middle of the lake was a white stone bridge with two driving lanes and walk paths on either side. Its thick stone railing made perfect seats for the two girls to hang their legs over the lake.

A river of pink, orange and red swam across the sky to consume the fading darkness of night. The girls leaned forward with bottles in hand and wearing normal clothes while the morning commuters drove behind them.

"Thanks, Dawn." Chika stared down at her yellow drink.

"No problem." Dawn turned to Chika. "For what?"

"Everything, mostly." Chika shrugged. "This whole thing sort of rocked my world. You said some things that turned this around."

"Please." Dawn grinned. "You just enjoyed kicking some ass."

"Well. I do like saving your butt." Chika giggled as she sipped on her drink.

"You did good." Dawn tossed her bottle cap into the river. "Not too bad for a greenie."

"Yeah." Chika blushed as she smiled. "Better than that moron who nearly got me killed."

"Who?" Dawn raised an eyebrow.

"Girl from the bus. Long hair. White." Chika realized she described Dawn. "Not you."

"Clearly." Dawn laughed. "You saying we all look alike?"

"What!" Chika tensed. "No! My dad's white."

"I'm kidding." Dawn tossed a playful punch towards Chika's bicep.

"Oh." Chika crushed her eyes to fight the embarrassment.

Dawn took a long swig of her drink. "Vala isn't perfect, but she's not terrible."

"Are you kidding?" Chika almost went cross eyed. "That moron almost got me killed. Me and the others on the bus. Who the hell brings a demon into a public area?"

"I don't disagree with you." Dawn emptied her bottle. "But to be fair. Vala was a one man army at that point. Plus I snipe with comets. That's insanely awesome. You throw fireballs which is okay, I guess."

"Hey!" Chika hipped a fist.

"Vala shoots rays of healing light. The *only* reason she didn't die that day is because I showed up." Dawn tightened her eyes.

"I guess." Chika sipped, looked away to avoid common ground. "I'm still not cutting her any slack."

"Oh," Dawn laughed. "For sure. None of us gets off easy. Seven billion lives are banking on it. I just think if no one dies then why judge the methods."

"Pffft." Chika rolled her eyes. "You're too soft on her."

This caught Dawn off guard. "Yeah well..." Dawn bit on her lip. "You're a butt head." Dawn stood up on the bridge railing.

"I'm a what?" Chika jerked her head upwards.

"Hey." Silver and white threads shot outwards from Dawn as she transformed. "We better get you home." Two cars slammed on their brakes as they gawked in the brilliant light.

"Oh shit." Chika dropped her bottle as the sound of the cars colliding came to her ears. Turned over her shoulder to see the drivers *very* upset, but not much damage done. "Esh!" Chika reached for her Light, red and purple threads came as she transformed.

Dawn laughed as the two men came out of the cars to yell at the girls. "We better get going before you have to punch someone else."

"I hope Sora didn't rat on me." Chika twisted her face.

"Do sisters do that?" Dawn jerked back a bit with a raised brow.

"Oh." Chika rolled her eyes. Brought up both palms in a 'backup' expression. "You have no idea how petty women can be till you live with three of them."

"I bet."

The girls cut off the angry slurs with a leap across the water. As they vanished behind the rooftops of the houses that lined the lake, both men dropped their arms in defeat. They shared confused expressions as both of them questioned life choices.

CHAPTER EIGHT: MIDNIGHT STRIKES

April 18th, 07:00

The wind was crisp. A light fog sat over the city as an unwanted early spring snowfall trickled over the landscape in a thin white blanket. By midday it'd be a mixture of slush and pools of water.

Half asleep, a fourth cranky and a fourth awake, Vala waited for her bagel to pop. The three minutes felt like a lifetime.

The six-grain bagel had its reputation as a healthy alternative tarnished by a thick layer of cream cheese. Vala didn't stop til there was enough that when the top was placed the cheese would escape both its sides and holes.

On her way out of the porch screen door, Vala licked her thumb free of cheese while fishing for sandals with her toes.

The sandals were a faded baby blue, the sole too thin to provide much defence against the cold of the ground. Luckily Vala's Saskatchewan-bred skin had a high tolerance.

Like most girls her age she wore a thick bunny hug to combat the chills, but with infinite wisdom still wore shorts.

The wind was low, a Saskatchewan treat, as Vala made her way across the wooden deck. A rotting board creaked as she crossed to the railing.

The brown paint was chipped, three years overdue for a new layer. The backyard had an old tree house from her childhood and a strong smell of poop from her rundown neighbour's yard.

Four dogs, no ownership of a scooper. Vala was used to it so she didn't much mind it. Sat down on the steps.

Her bottom's heat instantly melted the thin layer of snow, leaving her shorts damp.

She tore into her bagel. Cream cheese flooded her mouth and found its way around the outside of her lips. The back of her forearm was used to clean the mess, leaving a questionable stain along her arm.

Vala ate her bagel and checked social media with one hand. A smirk crossed her face when she found a video of herself leaping across the city. The clip was short, maybe ten seconds and with the low quality cellphone camera everything was pixelated. No one would be able to identify her.

But, to keep up appearances, Vala commented on the post. *Faaaaake!!!!1!*

Bagel devoured and celebrity tabs kept up on, Vala pulled out her flip phone. No new messages, not a surprise given she only had her parents, the knights and someone who made no effort to reach out to her.

Not that she blamed Chelsea—who would have kept tabs with their mother's murderer?

With a heavy sigh, she glanced towards the phone's clock. There was still a half-hour til they were to meet, the park only ten minutes away. To kill time, the laptop returned to her focus and many flash videos were pulled up.

"We should get going," Rift stood on the railing. He was looking over to the barking dogs in the neighbouring yard. "Those animals don't much care for me."

"Yeah." Vala licked her lips clean on the way up. Wiped her bottom free of the slush. "Dogs hate cats." She offered Rift her arm.

"Why?" Rift climbed up to sit on her shoulder.

"Dogs are just species-ist," Vala shrugged.

Rift glared at the dogs as they slowly vanished as Vala descended down the deck steps. "I find it difficult to believe they even possess an I.Q. high enough to form opinions."

"Yeah," Vala fought with the rusted gate lock. "I use to think that too, but my aunt has a dog that barks to tell you when to hit play on your PVR."

"Your world baffles me," Rift swapped shoulders. "A new bewilderment each day. It is confounding."

"You know people who use big words usually aren't as smart as they presume themselves to be." Vala kicked up her shoulder to cause Rift to shift to the other side. She prefered him on her right.

"Excuse me," Rift hissed as he passed her ear.

The sudden burst of air caused Vala to pinch her ear and shoulder together, followed by laughter. "Don't do that!"

A buzz came to Vala's pocket. She pulled out her phone in a panic. Sighed when it was an unknown number. "Pffft," Vala denied it.

Her phone wasn't back in her pocket before it rang again. Vala sighed and looked again to see the same number. Curiosity set in, and she shared a cocked eyebrow with Rift as she took the call.

"H-hello?" Vala cleared her throat.

"What's your name?" The voice snapped like a whip, and ended in a heavy puff of air from flared nostrils. "You should always answer the phone by giving your name!"

"What?" Vala veered back. "You called me."

"Yes. I did." The nostrils flared again. "Are you open?"

"Uh," Vala shifted her eyes to look down the block. "Yes. Yes I am."

"Really? Its early. I didn't think you would be."

"We," Vala smirked to Rift, "are always open this early. New policy."

"Good." Nostrils flared again. "I'm going to talk to your manager when I get there. You have an attitude."

Nostrils hung up. Vala stared at her phone with wide eyes. Snapped it shut, "That was fucking weird."

"I am curious to meet this fifth member," Rift purred.

"Oh yeah?" Vala shoved her phone into her pocket with her left hand while playfully pushing Rift with her right. "Is five the magic number so you can ditch me? I am the Echo after all."

"Oh," Rift dodged the second assault. Batted Vala's hand away. "If only such a miracle were to bless me."

"I hope it's a dude," Vala chuckled at the image of a oversized man in armour with hairy legs.

She froze as it dawned on her that she hadn't actually considered a boy could be a knight. "Hey… can guys be knights?"

"Yes, why wouldn't they?" Rift tilted his head in confusion.

"Ew," Vala shivered as the image became more vivid. "They get different armour right?"

"I'm not sure," Rift shrugged. "Doubt it."

Vala swore she could taste her breakfast kick back up into her throat as she turned onto the park path. Gravel crunched under each step. Ahead was a play structure just behind a row of mix-matched fences.

"Hey," Asa nodded. She sat on the swings, alone. "You're late."

"You're actually early," Vala fell into the free swing. Rift ran down her leg and to the edge of the sandbox.

"Details," Asa shrugged as she planted her feet in the sand, tilted her hips side to side.

"So…" Vala took a few steps back in her swing, until she was forced to her tip toes. "You're the first one here, eh?"

"Oh?" Asa looked around. "God help me."

"What?" Vala fell to Asa's height, her voice cut and eyes tight.

"Dude," Asa rolled her head over to Vala. "You're elevator talking me."

"I…" Vala twisted her face while debating on the next course of action. "Hate you." *Nailed it.*

Twisting her swing so she faced Vala, Asa laughed it off by booting Vala in the side.

"Hey!" Vala stumbled off her swing with hand on hip. "Dick, that hurt."

"Aw muffin," Asa rolled her eyes. "We're superheroes, suck it up."

"I," Vala ran daggers over Asa, "will never regret giving you a diet soda."

Unsure if that was an insult or compliment, Asa smiled. "You think this new knight could be a dude? Like imagine his legs in our skirts."

"Right?" Vala swung her arms out and low towards Rift. "These are the questions."

"It isn't very likely it'd be a male," Flea's voice came from behind Asa.

The girls turned to see Mei Ling steps away from the sandbox. She looked like death. Her face was pale, nose crusted with snot and the bags under her eyes had their own bags. Mei Ling held Flea, in his dog form, in her hands.

"Dude," Asa drew back in her twisted swing as if scared she'd catch whatever Mei Ling had.

"You look like crap," Vala laughed.

"Blow me," Mei Ling sniffed heavily.

"Maybe after dinner, or at least a movie," Asa laughed at her own joke. Realized the twisted faces the others were using, and her smile faded.

"Ew," Vala and Mei Ling pulled back in unison.

"They're late," Mei Ling frowned through muffled words. Her eyes tightened on the display of her cell phone. It read 8:15 am.

"Well," Vala rubbed her arms. "I'm cold. Mind providing us with some cover, so we can gear up?"

"Sure," Mei Ling snorted back more snot. Ran her crusted sleeve under her runny nose. "Give me a sec."

The trek to the play structure felt like a mile. Mei Ling leaned against the damp wood. Her head pounded, the density between her temples faded and her throat was on fire. Wanting to capitalize on the fact she now knew that there was a heaven, Mei Ling debated about ending it all right then and there. Save herself the weeks of half breaths and hacking up a lung every few minutes.

With a groan that came from the deepest recesses of her gut, Mei Ling allowed herself to slip around the wooden pole to be hidden under the play structure. Using the slide, a net ladder and whatever those yellow X's and O's were; Mei Ling transformed.

Suddenly the clouds parted and light from the heavens shone down onto the planet to place Mei Ling in the spotlight of bless. Her nostrils flared and were no longer met with coarse snot, but soothing oxygen, nitrogen, argon, carbon dioxide, methane and many more elements of air; she welcomed them all.

She felt a numbness over take her throat as a chill crept in to dampen the fires. The sensation expanded her lungs which sent oxygen throughout her body. Her parting thoughts hardened into the genius brain that it once had been. In her glory, Mei Ling smiled.

Taken inspiration from the soothing chill that ran through her person, Mei Ling wove a thick fog by reaching towards the clouds above and pulling down the water in them. She thickened the cloud around the entire park before she returned to the girls, made sure to keep the swings free of the fog.

"My god," Vala's eyes widened and her jaw hung, both quaked. She trembled as she pulled herself back a step. "It… it's alive!"

"What?" Mei Ling jerked back.

"Dear God," Asa leaned forward to mimic Vala's gaping mouth. "You have colour in your face."

As much as Mei Ling enjoyed her restored complexion, she complimented her frown with folded arms. "Little advice, colds go away while in armour."

Asa pulled up Nither, in his rabbit form, by his armpits. Her eyes tightened as they shot daggers into his. "You have failed me in controlling my powers, but you better cure cramps." Yellow and orange threads wove around Asa.

"That'd be sweet," Mei Ling smiled at the thought.

Involuntarily, Vala shifted her eyes and pulled her body in on itself. She hadn't meant to give attention to herself, but the other two were quick to pick up on the knee jerk.

"You okay?" Mei Ling cocked an eyebrow, took a step forward. Vala wasn't aware of it, but water was forming around her eyes.

"Yeah," Vala felt her body vibrate along with the words. Her eyes hurt for some reason, but she didn't notice as she stepped back. She grabbed the elbow of a limp arm as her eyes hit the dirt. Her voice hoarse, "I don't get those anymore."

"Oh," Mei Ling took a step back and her hand followed. She looked over her shoulder to Asa; neither of them were sure what to do with the information.

The silence felt longer than it was but shorter than it probably should have been. Vala started to laugh to herself. "Who wants to change dirty diapers anyways, right?" She pressed her thumb and index finger into her eyes to block out the world, tried to focus on the tremors that coursed through her being, and still them.

"Yeah…" Mei Ling pulled her eyes to the side. Her teeth pulled over top themselves as she tensed up her shoulders. Her mind felt clouded again, much worse than her cold had mucked thought. Her chest, the warmth inside that connected them all, pulled towards Vala, and she wanted to desperately reach out and comfort her friend, but her feet were cemented to the ground. Her entire body a statue frozen in time as her mind blanked.

"Sorry. I didn't know." Asa cleared her throat then shifted her weight. The motion was awkward, but brought Mei Ling back. She silently thanked Asa with the look in her eyes.

"It's cool—" Vala's sentence choked, and she balled a hand around her mouth, leaned into it with hard pressed eyes. Her face flushed and she stopped breathing. She fought to steady her heart, in hopes that her voice may follow suit. "It's no big deal."

"When did it happen?" Mei Ling attempted to pretend to be herself by moving her hands through the air. However her arms didn't leave the side of her torso, and the awkwardness was highlighted by her slouching.

"Year ago now, I guess." Vala drew in a deep breath, still had her eyes closed. The cold air from Mei Ling's fog filled her lungs and made everything seem to stop swelling up inside. With a half smile, she opened her eyes. "I'm better now. Just can't have kids."

Asa dug her tongue in her lower lip while she twirled the swing chain around her fingers. "I still feel shitty. Sorry."

"Asa," Vala almost laughed. Caught herself by holding her breath, but her cheeks blushed from the awkward attention. Then she did laugh. It was all over, it didn't make sense for her to dwell on it any longer than she already had. "It's fine. I'm not embarrassed about it around you guys. I'd just prefer not talking about it."

"Cool," Asa nodded her head as she freed her hand from the chain. Her eyes dropped to her feet as she clung to the upset pit in her stomach. She felt she had to focus on the guilt, as she deserved it, afraid the armour would kick in and wash out the feeling with a flood of endorphins. "This might sound stupid, but can't you just heal yourself?"

"It's not stupid," Vala shook her head, pulled her hair behind her head with both hands, then sighed. "The way my magic works is if I heal something that huge, and it's been in place for awhile, I risk mutating the cells too much. I could end up with cancer or something."

"So," unable to handle the murky tone, Mei Ling shifted her weight, then the tone of conversation. Turned to Asa with the most forced smile of her lifetime, "They gone?"

"Oh god," Asa sighed with relief. Fell back into the swing as the weight of guilt left her. "Yes. I might not go back to civ clothes for the next week."

"Week?" Mei Ling went wide eyed. "Jesus. Mine's only three days."

"I hate you." A flurry of rage inspired thoughts, fuelled Asa's glare. "One of my bitches doesn't get em, and the other hardly deals with em." She kicked the sand. "Great."

Vala and Mei Ling exchanged grins as they laughed a moment to themselves.

"So," Mei Ling almost sung her words. "We're using the B word now, huh?"

Vala had wanted to point it out herself, but a hint of guilt kept her from joining in. When she closed her eyes she saw Chelsea.

"Yeah," Asa shrugged. "Figure we may as well go steady."

*　　　*　　　*

Two flickers of light came from the East. The girls turned to see Dawn and Chika, freshly transformed, making their way through the fog.

An overwhelming heat came to the tip of Vala's ears as a furious pressure fought to escape her skull. Her eyes remembered Chika, and in a fit of disbelief they darted all over her body.

"You're kidding me," Vala folded her arms and converted the darts into a stern focused glare. "Seriously?"

"Yes," Dawn displayed her boredom of the groups immaturity with her steady voice, spine in perfect posture, chin slightly tilted upwards. Chika, who stood a step behind Dawn, tilted herself forward just a bit to catch a glimpse. Cocked a grin at the foreign mannerisms that Dawn was now displaying.

"Yeah," Chika tore her tilted head away from inspecting Dawn to face Vala. A juvenile grin crossed her face when she took a good look at Vala, *it is the girl from the bus!* She matched Vala's disapproving folded arms with her own self aware, cocky, folded arms.

"Didn't know they let twelve-year-olds enlist," Asa grinned as she pushed her way between Mei Ling and Vala. Offered a fist for Chika to bump. Not realizing she was supposed to bump it, Chika raised an eyebrow. With a unsure pace, Chika connected their knuckles. "I'm Asa. Welcome to the family."

"Thanks." Chika still spoke to Asa, but shot a sly grin to Vala, knowing it was eating her up inside. "Dawn told me you're our go-to."

"Pffft," Asa rolled her eyes. "Yeah, if she was being sarcastic."

Not quite sure what was going on, Mei Ling swapped the attention of her eyes between Chika and Vala. Ended with a relaxed glare on Chika. "What can you do?" The purple and red colours suggested: *Fire.*

"This," Chika waved her hand and from it bursts of fire puffed into existence. To show off, she ended the small shot with a stream outwards from the group. The flame thrower singed the tips of the grass, and almost caught the slide Mei Ling had hid under on fire. "Tadah!"

"Whoa," Mei Ling abandoned false annoyance with bewilderment. "I totally got jewed on my powers."

"*Hey!*" Vala shot a glare, tossed a fist into Mei Ling's bicep. "I don't make Asian jokes."

"*What?*" Mei Ling almost snorted. "Yesterday you told me my boobs were too big to be Asian!"

"Oh yeah," Vala couldn't hold back her laughter. Rolled her eyes as she fist bumped Chika. "Welcome."

"Thanks," Chika gave a half-hearted smile.

"Now that the introductions are complete," Dawn folded her arms as the others relaxed their pose. She commanded their attention with both her intimidating stance and deep voice. "We should probably make sure everyone is on the same page."

The girls exchanged nods.

Dawn turned her attention to Vala. Her sharp eyes made goosebumps run rampant all over Vala's skin. "Did you let everyone in on that you're the Echo?"

Wide eyes crossed Asa and Mei Ling, then went sharp as they twisted their necks to glare at Vala. Each surprised then upset that this was kept from them.

"Did now," Vala shrugged through a grin. "Surprise," extended jazz hands.

"Kind of important, don't you think?" Asa shook her head with a smile. She actually found it more funny, and very Vala, than anything else.

"Yeah," Vala laughed while shifting her weight uncomfortably. "Kind of... forgot, actually." Tried to dig her hands into her pockets, but her armour had none.

"You," Chika rolled her eyes, then ended in a glare, "forgot... that you are the entire reason, for all of this." Chika used her hand to wave over everyone's armour.

"Yes." Vala almost spat back. "I did. I happen to live a very unconventional life."

"Good lord," Chika turned away and walked ten paces. Took a deep breath to collect herself.

"Okay," Mei Ling cocked an eyebrow at Chika. "Temper tantrums aside..."

Mei Ling extended a finger. "First, totally a Vala thing to do. It's fine."

"Thanks." Vala's smile sat comfortably on her face as she folded her arms in content and topped it off with a satisfied nod. *Someone gets it.*

"Second," Mei Ling turned back to Dawn. "I actually don't have a second, so please continue." Asa laughed, while Vala facepalmed.

"If we're done joking," Dawn stepped into the middle of the group to make sure she took centre stage. Ozazi swung over her shoulder. "Now that we know that Vala is the Echo that checks off one of our goals off of the list of things to do."

"Glad I could assist," Vala piped in, Dawn's eyes caused her to swallow her words.

"Continuing…" Dawn sighed before she took her serious stance to its next level. She folded her arms behind her back and stood wide legged. "The most important thing we need to consider is Vala's identity and protection. If they get her, we lose."

"How's that?" Mei Ling waved her arm from folded arms. Her face was twisted and her words matched that, she did not hide the fact that she wasn't a fan of Dawn's attitude. *She has a stick up her ass, for sure. I am not a goddamn child.*

"The sad thing is we don't really know what they're planning." Dawn made eye contact with Mei Ling. "We know their objective is to complete construction on the Bridge so the Dragon and his army can invade the Garden. That's about it. We don't know exactly how they plan to convert Atoms of God into Distance, but I am assuming the power of an Echo matches or exceeds that of an Atom of God. They're practically gods as is. So if they know who Vala is, we lose."

"Yes," Rift swayed in Light form just above Vala's shoulder. "Vala is also what happens to power your armour. Though we get the power from the part of her still within the Womb, that actual part is the Echo. We could possibly lose that connection if Vala isn't here."

"Yeah," Vala lifted up her brightest golden string. It was invisible to the other girls, but even though they couldn't see it, they each somehow knew what she was doing. "I have a string for my family and close friends," then glared at Dawn and Chika, "and you guys as well. Then there is this string. I think it might be some kind of anchor for my soul or something...?"

"That is a possibility," Dawn nodded. "So we should talk combat. First off we can't babysit Vala or they're going to know exactly what we are doing and likely catch onto who and what she is to us."

"So we just let her up front and centre?" Chika raised an eyebrow. Her voice was back to normal, her temper in check.

"Yes." Dawn nodded. "We should have her upfront to lead us in. I think it establishes her as a threat and that we aren't necessarily concerned if she lives or dies."

"Thanks," Vala tossed a hand in the air with rolled eyes. "I'm excited to be a part of this plan."

"You know what I mean," Dawn shook her head. "But we do need to keep an eye on her. She not only has the ability to heal and recharge our armour, but she very possibly is the entire reason we can even summon them. She goes, we go, then the Earth goes."

"Lovely," Mei Ling punched Vala in the bicep.

"Ow," Vala rubbed it. It didn't really hurt, but she felt she needed to play along to lighten things up.

"Don't die." Mei Ling smiled. "Us and Earth aside, it would totally suck."

"Oh?" Vala nodded with ducked lips while looking upwards. "I think we're on the same page with that one."

"Cute." Dawn mentally rubbed her temples with her hands, but kept her stance. "You probably won't be in that much danger anyways. If they think you are our big gun then they may just focus on us small fries. Easier to kill us then take you on one on one."

"I don't like that that is an assumption," Vala shook her head to herself as she pictured all the ways this wasn't going to go right.

"It'll be fine," Dawn tried to make herself seem even more serious, but didn't know how. "They can't send all that much at us. As long as we stay on this side of the remaining strands of Distance, than we should stand a fighting chance. If they send too many or anything too big then they risk cutting themselves off forever."

"How do you know this?" The girls weren't quite sure who had asked it, but they all had had it on their minds.

"Fine. I'll come clean." Dawn sighed. Her stance didn't break composure, but her tone lined itself with a bit of doubt. "There is a cult that follows the Dragon. Established hundreds, if not thousands of years ago.

"Because the strands of Distance are so weak from the River, they converted humans into their order. The cult doesn't have a name. It isn't written in any textbook. I doubt anyone has any idea it exists.

"It's only purpose is to train humans to fight for the Dragon. They give the cult tools that can tap into the power of the soul to fuel powerful weapons. People from the cult aren't superhuman so for the most part they shouldn't pose a threat, but their swords can cut through even the strongest of magic.

"Those barrels you found the other day were given to the cult to collect. They drain energy from Atoms of Gods and it is what they use to fuel teleporting from their base to the Garden.

"I know all of this, because I was one." Dawn waited for the others to say something.

But no one did.

"I was one," Dawn repeated herself as if to drive it home. "When I was very young I awoke to my powers and left the cult. Left my family."

"Jesus," Mei Ling looked over to Vala who took a step forward.

"So you're fighting against your family?" Vala tried to make sense of it.

"No." Dawn glared.

"She is fighting for them," Chika studied Dawn. "If she saves the world, she saves them. Even if she is miserable for doing so, she wants what is best for them. In the end. So they don't become slaves."

Dawn felt her face heat up from the attention. Her gut twisted, as it all made her want to gag. "Let's learn to throw a punch."

"Punch?" Mei Ling jerked a thumb to Chika. "Some of us are above that pay grade."

"Sure," Dawn grinded her teeth a moment, then corrected to her stillness. "And when she's exhausted too much energy for fire or is around something explosive? Or hey, imagine this, maybe she comes across someone her element is weak to."

"If she can't—" Mei Ling grinned into another joke.

"Let's just get to it," Asa cut Mei Ling off. "Vala can't attack and I haven't unlocked my powers yet. We need this."

"Fine," Mei Ling rolled her eyes. "I'll save my wit for a more receptive audience."

"Good." Dawn turned away from the girls. "I've seen Vala use her leaping properly and I've shown Chika a few things. Let's start by getting Asa and Mei Ling caught up. Once we have movement down we can work onto punching."

"Cool." Asa followed. "I like hitting things."

"For what it's worth," Vala showed an elbow into Mei Ling's back. "I think you're a hoot."

"What are you, eighty?" Mei Ling shook her head with a grin. "*Hoot?*"

"I happen to look young for my age, yes." Vala nodded. "It helps to exfoliate."

"Stop." Dawn shot daggers at the two jokers. "Stop joking. This is serious. We could all be dead. Soon. Followed by seven billion lives."

"Bu-" Vala started.

"Children. Infants. Everyone." Dawn took a step towards Vala to line her up. "Every single life that is on this planet, or will ever be. We need to get serious. Right now, right here. For them."

"Oh come on," Mei Ling hipped one of her hands. "The hell could possibly happen?"

*   *   *

Frayed ends of cyan fell around David, as they pulled back into a nothingness, he adjusted his tie and checked his cuffs. The iron room that he found himself in was bare, save two guards by a two door entrance that curved upwards where they met. The room was large, kept empty to allow for transportation via the Bridge.

Everything in the castle was crafted from iron. The walls, ceiling, floors, doors and no decour. No engravings. Art was not a concept the Dragonborn embraced, which left the large castle feeling flat, empty and lifeless for a human.

David greeted the guards with a grin. "Gentlemen." They did not move from their posts until he took a step forward and only then to open the doors wide enough for David to pass through.

As quickly as the doors were to open, they closed. David frowned as the door clipped the back of one of his heels. In any other circumstance he would have felt the need to speak his mind, but it was dangerous for a human to overstep their boundaries in this place, even if they were as far up the food chain as David was.

A young human boy with dark skin, cold eyes and ten centimetres of height over David stood waiting for him. He was built strong, though most of it was hidden under his expensive suit. Only recently had the young man earned his promotion to be David's assistant.

"How was your trip?" The boy handed David a cane.

David took the cane with a bit of indifference. Sure the cane was his typical dark oak, which he loved, but his original, the one he was forced to leave on Earth, hid his Brand. The blade could ignore the protection of magic and cut through just about anything, so David understood why this may not be the best thing to bring near a Queen. That being said, David still disliked not having it at his ready.

"Great." David grabbed the cane with annoyance. He had nothing against his part bodyguard, part secretary, but still had fumes over his mistreatment by the guards. It was easier to shove around a fellow human. "Do you have any updates for me, Sky?"

"Some," Sky held out a file folder. "We've managed to use a computer algorithm to search for their faces via social media. Once we found who they were, we dug a bit deeper into government accounts. We have names, blood types, birthdates, and locations."

"Blood types?" David raised an eyebrow as he took the folder.

"We were extensive. Once we had their names we stole their medical records." Sky began to follow David down the hallway. "We were hoping that we may find that they've been reborn with some kind of allergy or defect that we could exploit. Sadly, no such luck, sir."

"Great." David tucked the folder under his armpit as he sped up his pace. "Does she know?"

"No," Sky informed.

"Good. Lets keep it that way, for now—"

"Dunkel has the information though." Sky took into a light jog to beat David to a door so he could open it. "I believe he plans to inform her shortly."

David froze. Sky awkwardly held the door open as David stood alone in thought for a moment.

"Fuck." David turned around to head the opposite direction down the hall. His pace was the quickest he could muster with his limp.

"Is something wrong, sir?" Sky ran to catch up to David.

"I just don't want us to look foolish." David took a deep breath. "They look down on us. We need to make sure she knows who's doing what around here, so we don't lose our place when this war is over."

"Yes sir," Sky nodded in agreement.

*   *   *

The Throne Room of the Dragon's Queen, like the rest of her castle, was iron. The walls were bare with no decor, the floor perfectly smoothed and cleaned.

The entrance was dual doors that ran the full height of the room. It took many servants a full minute to push and pull the doors.

Each a Dragonborn, the servants appeared very human save their reptilian irises. They each wore red robes with purple trimming. Hoods fell over their heads to shadow their faces, but with the right angle their eyes would leave a frightening image when reflecting the room's light.

At the end of the throne room was a giant glass window that held the River in its centre of frame. The red and purple planet hung in the starless sky just above the peaks of deep blue mountains.

At the base of the window sat a two sided throne. The Queen typically looked towards her husband's kingdom, the other half only used when she had an audience.

David and Sky had managed to get themselves through the doors before they closed behind Dunkel. The three lined themselves up several metres away from the throne. Each of them patiently awaited the Dragon's Queen to move to their side of the throne. No words were exchanged and no one dared to complain, not even in their mind's eye.

The Dragon's Queen appeared to be in her late twenties. Stood at six foot eleven. Short cut black hair kept tied back. Green reptile eyes. Her skin tattooed purple with red lines detailing scales. The red lines outlined her eyes, nose, lips and jawline but did not scale her face. She was the picture of beauty for the people of the River.

A black dress draped over her muscular body. Sides of her legs exposed by slits. Navel and cleavage by a cut in the dress running from her pelvis arching up to either shoulder. Arms wrapped in various straps.

Her throne crafted from the bones of various animals of her kingdom. Each dipped in iron at the chair's core to hold in place, but from a distance it appeared she sat on the bones. A soft red pillow for her bottom.

"Where are we on the Echo Army?" the Dragon's Queen held a stern voice. Every word well pronounced. She spoke in her freshly learned English to boast to the lesser beings of her superiority.

"I've tracked their location." David held up the folder with a grin across his face. The Dragon's Queen's choice of English had delayed Dunkel's ability to speak first, as it took a moment for his mind to work its way around the words. "Names and addresses. Took a while but I used a computer program to match their faces with pictures on social media accounts."

Dunkel, human in appearance save his grey lizard eyes, frowned. In his mind's eye he pictured removing David's head from his shoulders.

"Hmm." the Dragon's Queen curled her lip. "You humans seem too readily expose yourselves."

David knew better than to correct her confusing grammar. He was her third agent in the last year. Silence was the wisdom of a man who wished to continue breathing.

"Give the files to Dunkel. He and Sky can form an attack." The Dragon's Queen waved in disappointment. She didn't need a reason to justify killing David; a line of power hungry men were readily able to replace him. However it had become a game to the queen. David knew it, and that is what made it so fun. She would test him and he would have to find a way to not give reason to be destroyed.

With a bit of resistance, but not enough for it to be noticed from her throne, David handed the folder over.

"Would you rather kill their family first?" Dunkel shuffled the papers.

"I think a statement needs to be made." The Dragon's Queen leaned forward. "Soon the Dragon will eclipse their sun with his mighty wings. The site may prompt nuclear weapons. Why don't you and Sky slaughter their people and those knights? Have them broadcast it to their entire planet. Let's try to make them submissive. Protect my husband's new realm as much as possible."

"Great." Dunkel grinned. "I was hoping you'd want a bloodbath."

David remained still and polite but inside, his mind ran wild. Sky remained still in both body and mind.

"I can arrange camera crews," David finally spoke after his thoughts had finished gathering.

"Good. Now go!" the Dragon's Queen relieved them with a wave.

Dunkel turned first with a grunt and a grin. Sky paused to be the last. David followed two strides behind Dunkel.

Once the trio was through the exit, David picked up his pace to match Dunkel. Withdrew a picture of Dawn from his inner jacket pocket.

"Dunkel." David adjusted his cuffs. "Their biggest threat is Metal. She can snipe with comets. Tore through Zwart in a single shot."

"Please," Dunkel chuckled, "I'm not Zwart."

"You aren't." David nodded, in his mind he rolled his eyes. "I'm aware. I just thought if I scratch your back, you could scratch mine."

The group stopped at a small door. Inside minions had prepared five humans. Each kneeling on the ground. Gagged and bound by ankles and wrists. Each in rags of either purple, white, grey, green, or yellow; representing each element.

"Fresh pickings," David waved over the group. "We've upgraded the possession method. Storing a ghost in a human host body saved on resources, but loses the durability of your race. Our new method is the reverse." David handed Dunkel a gauntlet to wear.

Five set of eyes widened in horror as Dunkel's grin grew. With one mighty hand Dunkel reached out to a woman in purple rags. He grabbed the base of her neck. Pulled her in. Shoved his gauntlet fist into her chest cavity.

Though gagged, her scream was still deafening as she thrashed in pain. Dunkel fished around, found the Atom of God within, grasped it in his mighty hand.

Red and purple threads flashed along the dark room. Minions tightened their grip to keep the other slaves from running. Sky looked away. David looked, but his eyes held boredom.

Slowly Dunkel retrieved an orb out of the slave. Frayed ends trailed off the orb to dim into nothingness. The slave fell lifeless. In Dunkel's hand, a blinding light in the shape of an orb sparked violently.

His smooth pale skin began to twist and bubble. Muscles grew rapidly all over Dunkel until he shadowed those ahead of him. His left arm a cannon and his right a three digit claw. No fingers just serrated blades.

Dunkel placed the orb into the cannon. His skin glowed a bright purple then crackled into streaks of red. His body fused with the fire spirit within the human. In a moment his own Dragonborn soul devoured the human soul. His eyes glowed a bright red before fading into a deep crimson.

DISTANCE BETWEEN ECHOES

*   *   *

In the heart of downtown, a small park cut its way into the gridlock formation. In the centre a large white stone structure with stone paths spread out like a spider's web in every direction. Large trees polluted the grassy field.

Those coming and going to the various shops or parking metres that outlined the park were busy keeping their nose to the ground, ignoring the panhandlers and their weather-worn cardboard signs.

Sparks of cyan and blue ignited as frayed threads rolled into one another to create a knot. The strings weaved in and out of each other, through and over each other. From the centre unfolded a man and his oak cane.

Onlookers slowed their pace to slack jaw at the singularity. Some took a moment to remove their shades and squint.

David stepped out of the knot. The fall caused him to stumble, but he was able to use his cane as a brace to keep balance. With a heavy sigh and a fix of the tie, he collected his composure and ignored the onlookers.

David didn't waste time as he dialed his phone to begin getting a news crew to the site.

The knot unfolded a large mass, Dunkel, which prompted ear deafening screams. David sighed, unamused, he plugged his ear with a finger. Attempted to speak over top the panicked public, which wasted no time sprinting in every direction.

Dunkel's distorted laughter only hastened the fleeing crowd. The beast strolled over to a tree, and in one hand, pulled out the large poplar along with its roots. As the trunk was raised up and over Dunkel, some earth fell free onto David's shoulders.

David continued his conversation, but took the time to shoot the back of Dunkel with a glare. Gently brushed the dirt free of his expensive suit.

"I feel like a child again." Dunkel laughed as the tree impaled itself into a corner shop. The weight fell free and swung out into traffic, sending a car head over heels onto its back.

As he walked to investigate what damage he had brought, he rolled his laugh up a notch. "I've missed having playthings."

"I bet." David hung up his phone. "Not that I needed to, but I set things in motion. Crews should be here soon. Try not to kill anyone until they arrive." David frowned towards the crumpled car. "This is a small city. Their crews aren't used to being in actual danger."

"Wouldn't want them to get cold feet." Dunkel lit a tree on fire with the aid of his cannon, before tossing it into the street.

"Glad you're getting it," David glanced around as he pocketed his phone. "Where's the kid?"

As if on command, Sky stepped out of the portal. The fall did not bother him in the least.

"Oh." David clapped his hands together. "Good. Kid. Get up some place high. Dunkel's our bait. You're the hook. The Echo is the fish. Let's reel us in a contender, shall we?"

"Sure." Sky let his eyes dart around the city. It was his first time in Canada, he expected more snow than this. Shrugged off the thought before he rushed towards a hiding place.

"Alright." David took a few drawn out steps to reach Dunkel. "I'm not bulletproof, so I'm going to get going. I trust you'll be fine without me."

Dunkel glared down at the little man, the picture of removing David's head returned to his mind.

David smirked. "Okay. I'll leave you at it."

*   *   *

A buzz of a cellphone cut the training in half. The girls slid to a stop as each turned to Mei Ling with cocked eyes.

"What?" Mei Ling jerked her head back. "Don't get mad because I thought to place *mine* aside before transforming so it's still around."

Vala attempted to say something funny but fell on her butt in exhaustion. Her mind blanked a moment and she forgot what Mei Ling had said. Folded her arms in defeat as she was sure she could have said something humorous.

"Put it away," Dawn frowned with an extended palm. "Or give it to me."

Mei Ling's jaw was low and eyes wide as the cellphone was so close it illuminated her face. "Okay," She looked up with a glare. "First off you aren't my mother, Dawn. Second—" She turned the phone to face the girls "—there is a monster downtown."

"Oh," Dawn shifted her weight. "Let's go do something about that, then."

"Yeah." Mei Ling nodded as she dematerialized her armour to pocket her phone before transforming again. "Let's do that."

CHAPTER NINE: IN THE AFTERNOON

April 18th

Mouldy coffee cups rolled along cracked sidewalks. Cardboard signs with thick black marker of all varieties left behind from pan handlers. Crumpled parking tickets skipped down empty narrow one way streets. A modern, stylized tower rose twenty stories high at the corner of park.

The all glass building had a slanted triangular cut that ran all the way down the corner that faced the park. A sky bridge connected the building to its neighbouring twin. Five figures landed on the top of the tower.

"There he is." Dawn tightened her eyes. Below, she watched the purple and red mass of muscle and bone pluck a tree out of the ground as if it were a weed. "Great. He's got a fire element."

"So?" Chika raised an eyebrow as she weaved a small flame into existence.

"Fire," Dawn shot Chika a look, "hurts a fucking lot."

"So." Mei Ling stepped to Dawn's right. "Doesn't look like anything special. Asa and I can punch it."

Asa gave an unconvinced grin. "Yay," One hand grasped her other elbow.

Vala made her way to the front of the pack, a drawn out breath steadied her heart as she walked towards centre stage, her armour doing its best to drive her nervousness out. She placed a gentle hand on Asa's shoulder as she passed by. The two shared half a second of reinsurance through touch alone; Vala didn't look over her shoulder to make eye contact.

Her eyes were busy looking forward. The glistening irises locked on the edge of the building. With each step she took, they fell lower and lower. Until she saw Dunkel.

He was huge. Larger than anything she had gone up against. Vala had seen Zwart but the titan was in the dirt before she had even arrived on the scene. This would be her first fight against something so large—and something intelligent.

"This could be something big. They haven't made a public display on this level before," Dawn straightened up into her usual stature as she made her way to the edge. "Everyone follow me."

"Hey," Vala placed the back of her open hand against Dawn's naval. Gently she pulled it back. Dawn took the hint and stepped backwards. Vala stepped on the edge of the tower, the tips of her toes snuck over. "Don't be stealing my thunder… we had a plan, remember?"

"Alright" Dawn's lips curled into a grin but she quickly corrected it. "We'll stick to the plan."

"Yeah…" Vala watched Dunkel peel apart an SUV as if it were tin foil. "Time to kick some ass." Forced the clot in her throat down into her stomach.

Chika looked upwards with a low brow towards Dawn, who shrugged the look off. Mei Ling grinned towards Asa, who looked like she was about to lose her lunch.

"Hey," Mei Ling elbowed Asa. "Just pretend he's one of those goth chicks you like punching so much."

"Oh," Asa nodded nervously. "He has the body type. Shouldn't be hard."

"See," Mei Ling slapped Asa's back. "Joking already, you got this."

Vala walked on the edge of the building, across the cut in its corner. Imagined herself sliding down on a toboggan. *I bet I could survive it.*

Once she reached the end of the cut in the building, Vala let herself fall to the bridge. Spun in her decent so, when she landed, she would be facing Dunkel. Slowly she rose up, twisted her face as she thought of the coolest thing for her to say in that moment.

"Hey, limp dick!" Vala shouted. *Success.* In full confidence, she stomped a foot forward in an attempt at an intimidating stance. Elbows in, legs locked, fists balled and brown eyes turned daggers.

Dunkel turned just in time to see the girls synergize as they each fell perfectly around Vala, two on each side.

"Get the hell off of my planet," Vala rolled her neck before ending it in a glare.

"Excellent." Dunkel dropped the car in his hands. A man, who had soiled his pants, unbuckled himself, fished for the latch on his door, fell out of the car, and ran on all fours for the first metre before getting to his feet.

"You're all assembled. Lined up like the good little Angels you are." Dunkel flexed his muscles. Each spike grew, tearing skin to reveal crimson streams that flowed down the cracks in his skin. "Let me pluck you."

"Whoa," Mei Ling went wide eyed. "Guy's got his grammar in check. This one's gonna be a lot smarter."

"We'll still kill him," Chika nodded.

"Oh." Asa drew a three second breath. "Totally."

"Hey," Mei Ling grabbed Asa's by the hand. The touch allowed their armour to connect. "We got this."

Asa's armour used the information it needed to still her racing heart. With a smile, Asa whispered, "Thanks Mei Ling."

"For what?" Mei Ling pulled her hand away before anyone noticed what the two had done.

"Guys." Vala looked over her shoulder with a glare. "Seriously? I'm trying to do something right now."

"Sorry," The three bit their tongues, tried to take serious stances, but the moment had passed.

"Okay then," Vala shook her head as she turned her attention back to Dunkel.

"This is the part where I ask you to surrender." Vala wove green orbs of blinding energy in the palms of her hand. A flare from the light caused Dunkel to squint. "Please. Refuse my offer."

Before Dunkel could retort, Vala dragged her teeth over themselves. "Dawn. Do it."

With her hand cocked like a gun, Dawn took a step forward, swung her arm over and around Asa's shoulder. Brought down her index finger. Blinked. A thunderous sound rippled through the city as a rock fell out of orbit.

In one fluid motion, Dunkel demonstrated his agility for a creature his size, diving out of the way of the meteorite. As the space rock tore through dirt, it kicked up cement, hurled asphalt free and parking metres imploded into the point of impact.

Still in motion, Dunkel scooped up a tree to hurl horizontally at the bridge.

Not interested in waiting her turn, Chika hurled a fireball. At the same time, Asa and Mei Ling took a leisured step off the bridge. Angled during their descent to kick off the ground like rockets towards the demon.

Chika's fire caught the tree, breaking it in halves that spread wide around the girls. Dunkel hadn't stopped moving, he punched a tree in half and tossed it towards the girls with a spin.

Dawn and Chika leapt off the bridge as the trunk crashed horizontally into its side. Glass spilled into the air. Vala watched through the shattered razor blades as they trailed harmlessly along the outlines of her eyes.

Mei Ling wove the water in the air into a trail of ice. Slid on her knees while she weaved her wrist blades. Dunkel swung but Mei Ling shifted her weight on the ice to get around his fist. Dug a blade into his side, caught bone. The sudden resistance mixed with her forward momentum, muddled together, and sent Mei Ling spinning like a top off to the side.

"Shit!" Mei Ling slammed her back against a tree.

She fell forward a few steps. Mei Ling's armour protected her from most of the impact, but her mind still fought to adjust to what had just happened. Before she could gather her thoughts, a fist came her way, cut short by Asa.

From the side swung Asa, her fist sent Dunkel off balance. She bobbed in and out of several jabs to get under his reach. Slammed a knuckle into his distracted jaw. Dunkel back pedaled from the impact. Asa followed through.

"That's my girl!" Mei Ling cheered.

With a grin across her face, Asa took into a crouched run. Threw fist after fist into the chest of Dunkel, propelling him backwards as she kept charging forward.

A disgruntled Dunkel swung blindly. Asa let herself fall backwards to dodge the large appendage. A spike from his arm skipped along her cheekbone, leaving a thin trail of red. Asa didn't seem to mind, didn't even notice, didn't even care if she had noticed. All she knew was a satisfying sting crossed her chin as she used her core strength to spring back up to implant a fist into Dunkel's hip bone.

Mei Ling pole-vaulted off of Asa, planted her hands onto Dunkels free arm, and as she slid along his body she coated his arm in ice. Shards burst into the air as he flexed his arm upwards, snapping the ice, grabbed Mei Ling by the torso. She screamed as the vice, that was Dunkels hand, shoved everything into itself. He tossed her aside. She flew, wrapped around a street post and fell to the ground.

"Ow," Mei Ling's eyes rolled around her skull.

Her jaw cracked against the brick street. Kicked up a tooth into her cheek to free blood. Mei Ling spat as she rose to her feet.

Dunkel dispatched Asa, whose concerned eyes had followed her friend, with his fist. Buried the young knight into the dirt. He charged Mei Ling, who managed to weave a shield of ice just in time. The ice cracked as she was tossed off her feet.

Mei Ling crashed into the hood of a parked car, slid up and over, ricocheted off the front of an SUV. Landed on the ground. Grunted as she spat up.

Thunder rattled the city, Dunkel side stepped the meteor as he raised his cannon towards Asa. From the muzzle spewed a wide spray of molten lava. Cars and parking metres melted into twisted metal. Asa rolled off her back, her right side stung from the intense heat.

"Can't let him do *that* again," Dawn lined up another shot. Dunkel dodged just in time for the meteorite to tear into the ground.

Cement littered the air; Asa took the brunt of it in the gut and face. "Dude! Hit something." Asa looked up to be backhanded by Dunkel. She flew out of the park and imploded into a car which toppled over until it collided with a lamp post.

"You," Dunkel charged Dawn, "won't be doing that again."

"Unless I want to," Dawn dropped to the ground, leaned forward to launch herself towards Dunkel.

Dawn swung her fist over her shoulder to generate as much power as she could. Their knuckles met. A shock wave shot outwards, lifted cars around them by a few inches, cracked glass of nearby objects and kicked up dirt and grass.

Without the need of a plan and relying on the connection between the team, Dawn collapsed to her knees as fire roared over her. Dunkel stumbled backwards. Dawn shot two fists into the gut of Dunkel before back flipping, catching his jaw in the process.

Dunkel spun several times in the air. Dawn, still airborne, lined up her sights, drew out the shot until their eyes met, winked.

Thunder. Dawn landed on her knee, brought up her arm as she turned the opposite direction. Blood erupted outwards from the origin point. Flesh and bone skipped along the dirt, over cars and into the windows of nearby buildings.

With a crimson soaked armour, Dawn cracked a smile. As Dunkel's blood and flesh rained down onto the ground, Chika landed.

"*Grooooss,*" Chika cringed as droppings fell onto her shoulders.

"Thanks for the flame thrower," Dawn tried to mimic her team mates, "eh?" Fist bumped a confused Chika.

A flicker of red and purple light escaped the cracks throughout the entire street. The Atom of God within fuelled the beast, and before the girls could react, the beast was through the asphalt.

Dirt and asphalt exploded from below. Dunkel gave no attention to Chika, as he charged through her and into Dawn. Dawn took the time to pluck Chika out of the air by her heel and whipped her around to safety. During the spin, Dawn brought up her other hand to get another shot off. As she closed her eye just before she summoned a rock out of the depths of space, Dunkel swatted Dawn's hand to the side.

His fist cracked her skull as it threw her off her feet. The pain shot through her entirety. A high pitched ring took over the sound of the world. Her neck muscles tensed, and without the strength of her magic, her skull would have skipped freely along the street.

But as Dawn flew through the air, she ignored the pain as her eyes were wide in horror at what she had done.

In the trail of the thunder, came the echo of shattering glass. It sounded like a heavy rain as sixteen floors worth of glass exploded outwards. The soul shaking sound of thousands of pounds of metal beams buckling under their own weight rushed through the streets.

Mei Ling rose to all fours form the noise. She watched the building implode in on the entry point.

DISTANCE BETWEEN ECHOES

Flickers of eighth grade assemblies swooped through Mei Ling. She dug her feet into the ground as she launched herself forward. The cold memory of the news feeds filled her mind, which fed her strength. Like a virus, the armour infected Mei Ling with the eye widening horror of when the newscaster advised the falling debris were people. With the flashes of her brother's face in the back of her mind, the stitched wings on her back ignited in gold light.

Mei Ling dug a heel into the ground as she brought up her arms in unison. With the weight of the world in her hands, Mei Ling wove. Metal pipes below snapped as the city's entire water source was ripped out of the mains.

What remained of the windows were pushed inwards as a hurricane wrapped itself up the building. Red face, divulged of oxygen, led Mei Ling through the motions as she slammed her fists into each other. The black and grey strings entangled along her fingers solidified the hurricane into an ice cyclone.

The icy prison held the tower together. Mei Ling fell to a knee as the world shattered into a nothingness. Her armour unwrapped itself from her person as she fell face first into the dirt.

Vala slid to Mei Ling's side, scooped her off the ground as she spun to a stop. Ignoring the world, Vala looked over her friend. Mei Ling's eyes were closed, breath slowed as if sleeping, and all the colour remained in her face; other than her street clothes, she seemed fine.

Unconvinced, Vala wove green light around Mei Ling. She used its energy to penetrate Mei Ling's exterior and hunt for damages. But nothing was wrong with her body. Her magic in her armour wasn't depleted, and for all Vala could tell, Mei Ling shouldn't have collapsed in on herself.

Then something tugged at the light in her hands. The gold string that connected the two girls, knotted itself around the green string and pulled Vala's consciousness along for the ride. The world unwove as Vala plunged into the nothingness that was Mei Ling's mind.

Years of reality rewound itself as strings rebuilt a library.

*   *   *

Dust clung to the hundreds of textbooks and novels. Rough, short, grey carpet. Yellow faded walls. The only sound, the buzz of a television. Hundreds of children crammed into the elementary school room.

"Where?" Vala felt her gut twist in on itself. She fell forwards as her mind lost its density. Blanked of thought, she stumbled around in the darkness of her own mind. Tightened her eyes and teeth as she fought to find herself.

The news feed cut in. Vala was snapped upwards. Her mind clung to the sound, brought her back in on herself. She turned to face the kids, but no one had any faces.

The image shook her. Vala stumbled a moment as she tried to fight for balance. Fell forward, caught herself on a chair. Her lungs fought for air as threads of brown and green loosened off of her. She returned to street clothes. A heat ran over her as gold and pink threads melted off of her. Layers fell and fell.

Vala screamed as she watched her eyes fall off of her, and forward to the floor in swirls of thread. Vision never dissolved as her eyes were constantly weaved together from behind her sockets. The hypnotic visual didn't hurt. When it stopped, Vala was twelve years old again.

The threads below vanished and she was left alone in the room, crouched over the chair she had been grasping. With a deep breath, Vala looked upwards to see the only faced person in the room.

A tear drenched Mei Ling. Over and over the tears rewound up her cheeks then out again. The colour in her face came back then left again. Her jaw loosened then tightened into full exertion again and again. Time looped itself as her mind fixated itself on the moment.

DISTANCE BETWEEN ECHOES

Vala clasped her jaw as she swallowed emotion. Her entire body shook as she stumbled through the crowd of suspended children. Fell to her knees as she wrapped her arms around twelve year old Mei Ling. "It's okay. This isn't real." Vala swallowed. Heat rose up her throat and poured behind her eyes. She had to close them once it burned too much. Tears fell. "It was. But it's over now, you don't need to be here anymore. He isn't coming back. God I am so sorry, Mei Ling. I am so sorry that your brother is gone, but we need you right now. Okay?"

*   *   *

Dawn rose to her feet, but a fist brought her back down. Her brain rattled around in her skull; Dawn swore it had freed itself. She couldn't put thought into action, as there was nothing to call upon. Her mind was blank as the fists kept coming.

Finally the world came back to her, but not of her own fruition. Dunkel dragged the rag doll out of the soil by her left arm. His teeth widened into a smile. As the edge of his lips curled into wrinkles, his wrist jerked itself to the side.

Dawn screamed. As the bone in her forearm parted from itself, pierced skin and tore freely, her mind shot back to the moment.

Dawn scissored her legs around Dunkel, twisted herself, dug a fist into the ground and pulled herself down wards as her back snapped the opposite direction.

Dunkel was hurled away from the tower. Dawn stumbled to her feet. Chika landed, "You okay?" Dawn didn't reply.

She tucked her limp arm into her armpit and charged the beast. Chika followed.

*   *   *

"Shit. Shit. Shit. Shit.," Asa sprinted out of the park, leapt. Arced herself through a window and landed. Slid along the ice, caught herself by grabbing an open door. Her mind raced as she darted her eyes around the building. The entire building had been drenched in water and then frozen. From what Asa could see, there wasn't a speck that wasn't ice.

With her armour in overdrive, Asa relied on its adrenaline to push further into the building. Stomping as she went to snap the ice for traction. At top speed she searched the floors. It wasn't long to find a room of cowering people.

A dozen people were low to the ground. Each shivering, sobbing and praying. "Whoa," Asa marveled at how the ice had perfectly traced the people, keeping them safe.

"Okay," Asa ran her tongue along the inside of her mouth. It was dry. She tried to think, but it was hard to hold onto something. "Fuck it," Asa stomped through the room, grabbed two people and leapt out an open window.

Mid air she spun the screaming people around themselves. She landed into a crouch to cushion them. Dropped the two, and without a word, returned to the building.

*   *   *

"Hey," Vala clasped a hand on her friend.

Mei Ling's eyes were on fire, lungs convulsed as they fought for air, her neck muscles tightened as she wrapped her arms around Vala. Everything was so real. Everything had pulled her back to that moment years ago. Her nails dug deep into the back of Vala's neck as she fought to burry her face even deeper into her friend's chest.

Her suit had found what it had needed, and abused it. Reached deep into the back of Mei Ling's mind. To a memory she had drowned out with guitar strings and graffiti art. The armour consumed her entire mind with the thought.

Now, in the present and back to reality, Mei Ling still felt her thoughts consumed with the smell, touch, scent and sounds of that moment. As she tightened her grasp around Vala, all she could feel was the cold steel of the chair legs she had been gripping when she saw the second tower hit.

Unsure what to do, Vala wrapped her arms around her friend. Drew her in as close as she could. Pushed her face up against hers. "I'm here."

"He..." Mei Ling gasped for air. "He's gone. I... I don't have a brother, Vala. I. I don't have a brother anymore. He's dead. He's gone. He is dead, and I don't have a brother anymore! He died. Vala. He died. Just now. I. My brother. I don't have a brother!"

Vala clenched her teeth together as her entire body shook. Fire ate at the back of her eyes as she pulled back on her tears. She wasn't sure if she should join Mei Ling in crying or hold back and be strong for her. Was it right to bring Mei Ling back to the moment, or did she need to follow this through?

What had the armour done to her? What was left of her? What was Vala supposed to do?

Nothing. Yet everything.

Vala choked on her breaths as she looked upwards to the flickers of fire and the sonic booms of the battle ahead. She didn't pay mind to those rushing by her from Asa's rescue. Her mind saw past all of that and focused on the horizon as she tightened her arms around Mei Ling.

A pit in her stomach rotted her core, before Vala had even brought her hands around from Mei Ling's back and into her chest. "I am so sorry to do this," Vala closed her eyes. Green light threaded into the golden string between the two.

A warmth rushed over Mei Ling as the tears suspended in time. Her eyes slowly opened, didn't quake. Her breath steady. The red in her cheeks was withdrawing. "What." Mei Ling looked over her hands as her armour returned to her person. "What did you just do to me?" Her eyes looked up with a hurt, that cut deep into Vala's very soul.

"I," Vala choked down oxygen. "I needed to. We need to."

Knowing that she should be mad, knowing that she should still be sad, knowing that the world was out of balance and that Mei Ling shouldn't be okay with all of this; she was. She was okay with everything as she rose to her feet. The magic in her armour over taking insanity that it had originally knotted her state of mind into, and poured rationality into every crevice of Mei Ling's mind.

Without a word, Mei Ling joined Asa in retrieving people from the building.

"Hey," Vala reached out next time Asa landed.

"Holy shit," Asa looked Vala up and down. Vala's face was pale, and her eyes looked through Asa. "You look like shit, what happened?"

"Go," Vala jerked her thumb over her shoulder as she swallowed her guilt. "Mei Ling and I can empty the building. You help Chika and Dawn."

"Sure," Asa nodded, before leaping towards the two.

*   *   *

The girls had driven Dunkel into the third story of a building. Chika came down on the giant with three quick jabs before he spun out of the assault, catching her with his backhand. Chika fell into, then through, a plastered wall.

Dawn leapt off the floor, spun mid air to kick off the ceiling and drive her good fist into Dunkel. The impact sent the two through the floor, and then the next one, and into the basement. Dunkel rolled his shoulder. Dawn slid off of it, through debris, twisted on her heels and with a wide grin boasted, "Come on!" Dawn tucked her arm back into her elbow. "I'm getting bored."

Dunkels only reply was a glare.

Dawn rushed the beast. Leapt and swung several kicks towards Dunkel, but he effortly shifted his main mass from each blow, reached forward.

Dawn grabbed exposed rebar wire from the main floor, used it to pull her legs up and over Dunkels attack. Ran up his arm as she held onto the metal, tearing it out of the ceiling as she went.

She ran up and over his arm. Caught the warped rebar under his chin, fell behind his back and dragged him to the ground. The entire floor shook under his mass. Dunkel had managed to stop himself from a full fall by spinning in the descent hands-first. As he began to lift himself off of the ground, Dawn wrapped her legs around his neck. Reaching over his skull, she dug her hand into his eye socket. Grabbed the top of the bone and pulled back with all of her might.

At first he grunted through the pain, until she managed to get more leverage to increase the pull. His teeth widened as his distorted screams consumed the room.

Before he was able to reach behind his person, Dawn had already rolled off of his back and to a safe distance. Chika fell in front of him, and before his mind could change his initial account, she had woven flames into a high powered jet.

The building's siding exploded as Dunkel was thrown into the street. Dawn and Chika leapt after him, landing just outside the building. Asa joined them.

"Hey." Asa awkwardly smiled as she looked over the blooddrenched Dawn, and followed the trial to Dunkel. "You've been busy."

With purpose, Dunkel shifted himself upwards, his blood soaked eye staring deep into Dawn. His frown wrinkled his nose as steam escaped his nostrils. Dawn smiled, then frowned as his lips curled upwards.

With a flash of red and purple, Dunkel drew on his Atom of God once more. To call his speed a blur would have been an injustice. The wind kicked Chika and Asa up off their feet and to the side as his mighty hand engulfed Dawn and rocketed forward with her.

Through the building they had just been fighting in and into its neighbouring one. Dunkel dragged Dawn through the ground the entire way. The heavy cement cracking along the top of her skull as she was constantly reminded about her injuries the entire journey.

As they left the second building and back into the street, Dawn grabbed his wrist with her only working hand pulled herself up so her back would absorb some momentum to slow them down.

Now able to, she dug her feet into the ground. Threads of white and silver kicked up at her heels. Using the same magic she used to cushion her falls, Dawn brought the two to a stop.

Before Dawn could adjust herself to throw a fist into Dunkel, many had found their way into her face. Her legs buckled as she fell backwards from the force. Each impact dug her deeper into the earth.

Chika came first, a fist to the side of Dunkel's skull, but he wouldn't be moved off of Dawn. Chika slid past the two along the street, curled her back towards Dunkel as she continued to move away from them and wove flames towards Dunkel.

Dunkel couldn't be bothered to block the flames as he continued to bury Dawn.

Asa came from the same side that Chika had. The heat had forced Dunkel's vision away from the flames, and even though he still punched Dawn repeatedly, he didn't need to look at her to do so. Dunkel saw Asa coming a mile away, pulled back off of Dawn to let the flames catch the rocketing Asa.

She screamed as the fire consumed her, but her cries were cut short as Dunkel caught his fist into her back. Chika cut the flame as Asa ricocheted off of her. Chika was thrown to the ground in a spin. Asa was tossed through the corner of a shop, passing through two sheets of glass before sliding along the street.

Without full control over her armour like the others, she was exposed after the blinding shot to her back. The glass had cut deep into her flesh and trails of blood mapped out the pattern her body had made as it had been tossed along the pavement.

Dunkel turned to look at his handy work.

Below him, Dawn rolled her eyes around her skull. Her nose pushed in on itself. Her cracked cheekbone shoved upwards, pinching her eye in its socket. Blood fell out her mouth. Several teeth collected in the back of her throat.

The air was heavy. With it came rivers of blood. She coughed to dislodge her air way. Dawn's mind swayed.

Her head fell to the side. The cold soil felt like a cloud against her burning skin. She couldn't find herself. She didn't understand who she was, or where she was, or what had happened to her.

With a mind distanced from reality, Dawn's eyes wandered. They found the blue sky. She smiled at the white fluffy clouds that skipped over themselves in the strangest designs. The heavy prairie winds kept them busy, so she laughed.

When she did, her head tilted to the side. Looked upwards to the large mass above.

Everything came back. Years of training fuelled her legs pulling up to her chest, the push off of her shoulders, the vice she created around his hips, the core strength that raised her off the dirt and the fist that found Dunkel's face.

Thrown off guard, Dunkel backpedaled. Dawn followed through, flipped over him to kick him in the base of the skull. Dunkel stumbled forward, turned to be met with another kick.

Dawn followed the kick with another, then a punch. Led Dunkel in a tango of ruthless, unrelenting blows to every part of his body that she could muster a hit on. She didn't care where the blows landed. She didn't care how effective they were. She didn't care how much they hurt. She just cared that they *did* hurt!

The two danced through a building, then another, as Dawn kept up the case. Fighting wildly through the blinding pain that rushed through her body. She knew that if she stopped the pain would truly seep in and she wouldn't be able to continue fighting.

Dawn swung hard, sending Dunkel down a street. He turned mid-air to toss several cars towards Dawn. With eyes dead locked onto him, Dawn slid up and over each car as if it were second nature to do so.

Dawn spun around his skull and scissored her legs around his neck to bring him to the ground. Dawn slid in and out of his reach as he flailed about. White hot flames came over her shoulders as Chika joined her side.

The two caught their breath as Dunkel rolled over top of himself. Desperately trying to smother the flames that were melting his flesh.

"Thanks," Dawn curled over her knee as she fought for air.

Chika cupped hands over her face. Blood fell from Dawn's eye socket, out her ear drums, down her twisted nose and between her lips. "Are… are you okay?"

"I told you, I'm an Angel. We're durable as hell," Dawn fought to her feet. "I think—" her legs buckled in on themselves. She tightened her eyes, which increased the pain in her one eye. Did her best to ignore the pain thriving throughout her being, as she stood. Holding herself someplace between standing and a crouch. "I think we are tiring him out."

Chika's armour pushed her mind past Dawn's appearance. "Starting to think that Vala isn't the only moron on the team." Chika playfully pushed Dawn.

"What?" Dawn first looked up at Chika, saw the flickers of red and purple dance along her cheekbones, then turned towards Dunkel. Once again he drew from the Atom of God within. "Shit."

*　　　*　　　*

Sirens echoed throughout the street. The winds were cold and low. The streets empty save for a single little girl, who laid limp in a labyrinth of blood soaked streets.

Vala lifted Asa's limp body up into her lap. The trail left by the melee had not been a hard one to follow. Vala and Mei Ling had finished removing everyone from the building before rejoining the girls.

A deafening thunder filled the streets. Vala looked up to see a tidal wave of crusher dust. She pulled Asa's face into her chest, and bent over her. Protecting her airway from filling with toxins.

The tower had fallen. It's dust and debris peeked over the rooftops of buildings, pushed through their windows and doorways, and seeped through the alleyways; the girls were near the edge of its reach.

The dust clung to the air, fading everything in a coat of brown. Vala didn't pay it any mind. There was a hole through Asa's stomach where her kidney should be. A spike in Dunkels arm had caught her. Gashes all over her body poured out blood where flesh had been torn back from the glass windows. Vala's eyes danced down each stream sporadically in a panic.

"Asa." Vala's hands tightened around her friend. "Don't die on me." Sniffed back her tears as she gently placed Asa down and got to work.

Mei Ling knelt down to get a better look. "She's dying. Fast. We need to heal her."

"I can see that." Vala felt dizzy, but she managed to grind her teeth through her words. The world spun around her and her powers seemed to be dragged along with it, getting further away with each passing second.

"Shouldn't be too hard. She isn't nearly as beat up as your ass was," Vala took in a deep breath, her tone didn't hide her nervousness.

"Yeah," Mei Ling tightened her eyes on Vala. Her tone was stern, and her tense body reflected an anger her armour wouldn't actually allow her to feel, but her mind was wise enough to fight through all of it and know what she should be feeling. "Easy, right?"

"The easiest." Vala gulped through terrified eyes, not picking up on Mei Ling's tone.

An explosion came. Mei Ling jerked upwards, then quickly shuffled to her feet. "They need me." She looked down at Vala. Her eyes swelled up to match Vala's plea. It told Vala that Mei Ling knew what she had done had been necessary, though in the back of her mind Mei Ling wasn't quite sure how she sat with all of it. Once her armour was removed, she supposed she'd have her mind back to herself to decide.

"Hey," Mei Ling's words were soft, "get the bench warmer back out there, will ya?"

"Mei Ling." Vala looked up to her friend, tears in her eyes. Mei Ling refused to continue eye contact. "Don't die."

"Don't tell me what to do..." Mei Ling took in what was possibly her largest breath of her life, then leapt towards the chaos.

"Okay. This isn't too bad, huh Asa?" Vala's eyes darted over Asa. Wove light over her hands and much like she had with Mei Ling, she searched for what was the matter. "Worse case I mess up, and you die. Easy, right?"

Unlike with Mei Ling, there was a lot wrong with Asa. Most of her blood was spilled out onto the street. The magic levels in her armour though great, were drastically depleting to fight for survival.

Rift's warning fuelled her intention as Vala tried to decide the best course of action. If she simply rushed her healing aura into Asa she could mutate the cells and give her cancer. The only option was to refocus Asa's magic into herself to help stabilize, but that wasn't an option either.

Asa had it the hardest among the girls to connect with her magic. Vala didn't think it was possible to allow the armour to heal itself when it was met with so much resistance.

So what was left?

A golden glisten broke Vala out of her thoughts. From her chest, down into Asa's chest, was a golden string. Her body shuttered at the thought of reliving what she had just gone through with Mei Ling, but no other option seemed possible.

But something was strange. Mei Ling's soul had reached up and out of her person to clasp Vala tightly and draw her along. Had it been Mei Ling's armour which seemed to have much more control over its host, or was it Mei Ling herself asking for help when her armour was betraying her?

Whatever it had been, in no way, shape or form was that happening now. Asa was still. Her flow of magic was still. Her armour was non-responsive. The only thing was the golden string and its strange glisten.

Vala tilted her head in a moment of confusion, until her eyes focused beyond her tears. Two golden strings expanded out from Asa's chest, which was unlike the other girls who only had the one. The first string connected Vala, and Asa, as did the other girls strings. The golden strings were their connection to the Echo portion of Vala still within the Womb. The source of their power.

So what was this other string? Vala leaned forward, not with her body but her soul. She used the string that connected the two together to see further into the second string of Asa. The string seemed to disappear into a nothingness for Vala's eyes, but her soul could seek past that.

Through the endlessly knotting of the golden thread came a cyan portal so tiny an atom was large in comparison. Beyond the wormhole was a strange warmth. A pleasantry followed by a chill of the end. The end of everything.

"Ragnarok!" Vala pulled herself away from Asa, and with that her soul snapped back into her body. With the action Vala dragged along a knowledge that she rarely had control of. "The Valkyrie are warrior Angels. Unlike our legends, they don't take warriors to Ragnorok they—"

Vala studied the golden string. It was knotted in an endless loop. She closed her eyes to mentally weave the warmth in her chest outwards and down to Asa. Through her friend and into the string that led to the end of all things. As her soul traveled down the string it unknotted it.

"Angels don't get an afterlife. Their bodies are their souls, a balancing out of their immortality is they don't get reincarnation. But what makes the Valkyrie so much stronger than a normal Angel is the bypass. The loophole. They get both worlds, they are bound to an afterlife. Their souls are knotted with the end of existence. When they die, their soul is ripped out of their body, which is their entire body, towards the end of the universe. They're reshaped and allowed one last battle before they're met with nothingness."

The burning sensation of her tears vanished as golden light took over her eyes. Vala felt the universe's energy flow through her person as the wings on her back glowed. She reached into the portal and found the final knot in the tunnel of time and space. Vala corrected it. Surging energy with herself and the end of all of existence.

Slowly the light faded out of her eyes as her wings returned to their normal green. Golden strings escaped Asa's wounds then tightened before retracting into her body to seal the wound without consequence.

Vala waited a moment to take in all that had happened. Once she was convinced she would never truly understand her brief moment of clarity, she used the lamp post as an aid to stand.

"It's not 100%." Vala smiled down at Asa. "But it's all I can do. Rest is on you." Vala turned to the battle.

*   *   *

Brown eyes rolled upwards from the back of Asa's skull. Loud banging about two blocks away rattled her mind, making her nauseous. Her head pounded and every part of her body hurt. She cringed every time she heard the banging. Mind numb of the present situation, Asa slowly rolled to her side.

One hand at a time, she grabbed the lamp post. With all her upper strength she pulled her torso off the ground, then with the aid of quaking legs she managed to stand upright.

Taking a moment to gather some energy, Asa leaned her limp body against the lamp post. Noticed a strange sensation at her lower right hip.

Pressed her eyes as memory of her wound returned. Asa attempted to gather thought but that *damn* noise kept distracting her mind. She let herself stay leaning against the post as her mind absorbed the noises. Slowly they stopped rattling her skull and became sounds she recognized.

Cement being pulverized, metal scraping bone and high, rapid explosions. Like a drum, they started to beat in the back of her mind. Her trailed thought followed each beat as she pulled herself away from the post.

Her eyes shifted to the side as her mind tried to organize the drum beat; something was playing just below it. It took a minute to figure out what it was, but soon the sound of moans and grunts were unmistakable.

Asa stumbled further into the street, catching herself several times. Her ears led her towards the vicious battle from the sounds of the underlying noises.

It clicked. The noise was her friends, and they were losing. A part of her wanted to collapse. Have her legs give out from the weight of the world that she felt on her shoulders. Curl into a ball to cry until everything faded into nothingness.

But something was new. Unfamiliar and powerful. A warmth inside of her chest cavity pulsed throughout her entire body. She could feel every crevice the power dug into. Lightning hurled itself through her veins, and it felt more natural than the breath which filled her lungs.

For the first time in her life, Asa felt in control. Sparks of electricity danced along her skin, no longer as sporadic chaos, but because she willed it to. Small pockets of lightning popped and ran jagged lines over various limbs. She took a moment to play with the lightning, to move it from hand to hand, to confirm its complete obedience.

The power of a past life. The strength of a Valkyrie. The instinct of a warrior. The rage of an avenger. The fury of a storm. *The ferocity of Asa Larson!*

With a deep breath, Asa let her eyes close again. Though she had its complete control, Asa wasn't interested in taming the lightning. Instead she focused the energy deep within. Burrowed it as far as it would go into the emptiness within. Pushed it to the edge of eruption.

Eyes opened. Asa took three long strides before leaping up and over the street. She cleared a three story building. Down below, on the other side, were her friends.

As Asa came up and over the building, her mind focused on what was happening below. The world felt like it came to a crawl as her eyes darted along the battle, taking everything in.

Thick smoke filled the air, flares of energy being tossed about littered the scenery. Chika was in mid windup of a fireball. Dawn caught in a flip over a spew of lava. Mei Ling's arms were weaving an ice barrier to protect herself from shrapnel of an exploding car. Dunkel cocked his cannon for another assault. Vala collapsed to her knees, exhausted.

Asa landed on the street. No word was given. No moment wasted. As her toes touched down, she had already begun her sprint. She rolled her shoulder as she side swept the fireball from behind. She followed the flames to use them as camouflage.

She didn't need to ask for permission, or send a series of commands; there was no need for anyone to even know she was there. There was no need for anyone to be there. Asa didn't need any of them. She only needed a victim.

As Dunkel swatted the fireball to the side, Asa made her presence known.

She weaved the caged energy out of her core, behind her person, through her arms and into her hands.

Asa leapt. Wrapped her legs around Dunkel's throat. Buried her thumbs into his eye sockets. Poured lightning through her and into Dunkel's skull. His distorted howl echoed throughout the street.

Dunkel flailed. Asa gritted her teeth as she tightened her legs' grip, then plunged deeper into Dunkel. *"Go to hell!"*

The beast thrashed. Back stepped and whipped Asa around, but she wouldn't be moved.

His claw came up and around. Pierced Asa's back. She tossed herself backwards as she screamed, but her hands and legs tightened. Though in excruciating pain, Asa refused to fail. Her teeth grinded over each other even harder as she swung back into the assault.

With electricity cooking the inside of his skull, Dunkel succeeded on the last tug at the Valkyrie. This time she loosened. Streams of blood trailed behind Asa as she soared down the street.

Shifting her weight in mid air, she twisted her body about so her feet faced the forward momentum. She landed on the side of a truck. Orange and yellow threads sparked to soften the blow. With white knuckles, clenched teeth and tight eyes, she aimed towards her target before rocketing forward. Even with the safety of her magic, the metal imploded from the force of the sonic boom generated by her sheer might.

Asa had angled herself towards the building behind the stumbling Dunkel. Shoved a heel into the siding to grip and sprint upwards, firing lightning out of one hand as she rose. The force of the lightning helped Asa propel herself up the building. The entire time she seared the back of Dunkel's skin. He stumbled under the heat.

When Asa reached the height of her arc, she condensed lightning into her left hand. She flipped so her hands faced the building. Allowed the condensed energy to erupt. The explosion sent Asa soaring into the air.

She flew higher than she would have ever been able to jump. Twisted her body so her hands were now skywards. Slammed them together. An explosion blackened the sky. Asa rocketed to the ground.

Dunkel curled over a knee as he tried to gather himself. His entire body covered in burns. He took in a deep breath before standing up to charge the girls who stood in awe at Asa's assault.

Before he could put thought into motion, 160 pounds moving at Mach speed caved in his skull. Asa's knee cap tore through his bone as if it were made of putty.

The girls exchanged looks of confusion as Asa took a bold stance over Dunkel by resting her foot on his back while hipping her fists.

Asa gave a sly grin, "Didn't we have some kind of monster to deal with?"

Before Asa could bring up her arms in defence, Vala had attacked her. Arms wrapped so tightly in a triumphant embrace. She made a point to make it the tightest hug she had ever given anybody in her entire life; having super powers helped.

"Holy shit!" Vala laughed as she dug her face into Asa's chest. "You're like the coolest fucking thing ever made ever!"

"Dude," Asa looked around the ground as blush ran rampant. "You're embarrassing me."

"Hey!" Vala fell free from Asa, still laughing. "What kind of girl can't hug her bitch in public?"

"Don't answer that," Mei Ling fist bumped Asa. "Glad to see you didn't die."

"Yeah," Asa rubbed her sides. "Not for Vala's lack of trying."

"Dude, you're so messed up back here." Vala wove her light into the open wounds along Asa's back.

"Oh man, that feels *amazing!*" Asa rolled her neck. "Thanks for saving me, by the way."

"Well I need you around," Vala used an arm to wipe sweat from her forehead. "You're the only one a size bigger than me. It'd be embarrassing to be the fat friend."

Asa tightened her eyes, but couldn't stay mad. The three girls burst into laughter.

"You weren't bad out there," Dawn smiled.

"Didn't see you out there," Asa grinned. "Were you even doing anything?"

"Alright girls," Dawn smiled at Asa's joke. "Not bad for our first team battle."

"Asa died." Chika pointed out.

"We levelled half the city," Vala spoke from behind Asa.

"Dawn, you broke your arm." Mei Ling went wide eye.

"What?" Vala tilted to see round Asa. Dawn had no colour left in her face and her stance wobbled. "Holy shit man, how did you... weren't you like kicking and punching and... holy shit."

Dawn smiled through the pain. It was forced, but she did truly feel as happy as she attempted to present. "Hey any time you kick some ass without breaking a nail, am I right?"

"Oh good." Mei Ling playfully tapped Asa on the chest with the back of her hand. "It jokes."

"When it can." Dawn turned to Vala. "Hey Vala, mind spotting me some of that healing?"

"Hope so," Vala looked down at her hands. She strained to make them softly glow. "Might be running low on batteries."

"Great," Dawn sighed.

Two bright beams slid over Vala's shoulders and under her chin. She instinctively pulled back from their enormous heat. Now that she was opened, the blades vanished as the two hilts fell down. Sky's arms came under her armpits, he ignited the hilts as quickly as he caught them. Red and purple blades roared millimetres off Vala's skin. Sky held the brands with perfect precision.

Vala strained her neck even further, but Sky followed her neck with a blade.

The reactions amongst the girls were varied. Most of their brains, still exhausted from the previous events, were riddled with confusion as they attempted to process what was going on in front of them. None of them had ever seen a brand and had no idea what to make of Sky, let alone his swords running over the skin of their friend. But Dawn tightened her eyes on the man. His uniform and his weapons reminding her of home.

The only sound was the revving of Sky's blades, the silence broken only by Vala. Her eyes pushed tight, and voice strained as her neck reddened from the heat. "D-Dawn."

Dawn felt the hairs on her back raise as the tips of her ears reddened. Hearing Vala ask for her help lit a furious fire within her chest. "Let. Her. Go." Dawn's teeth grinded so hard it was heard through every word.

"Don't follow us," with cold eyes and steady words, Sky began to step backwards with Vala.

"Don't!" Instinctively Mei Ling took a short step and reached out, but the cold dart of Sky's eyes commanded her to stay in place. "Don't hurt her, please."

His only reply were threads of cyan and blue escaping from the nothingness. The strings wove themselves into a sphere. The knot peeled itself back as Sky took Vala into the portal.

It collapsed leaving the girls alone in the street.

"*Fuck!*" Dawn slammed her leg into the nearest object. The metal of the car caved in on itself from her might. "*Goddamnit!*" She tossed her right fist into its windshield.

"Whoa!" Chika back pedalled from Dawn. "It's okay, we will get her back." She turned to the others," Right?"

Asa shrugged, slowly turned to Mei Ling who was the closest to the portal. Her body was very still but if you looked hard enough, there was a very slight tremble.

Dawn slid down the car. Leaned her head against its cold metal as tears fell from the pain of letting her arm fall limp. Slowly she brought her left arm up to her chest with her right hand and cradled it there.

She didn't reply to Chika.

CHAPTER TEN: DAPPLED SHADE

April 18th, 19:05

The temperature had risen. White powder melted into brown slush. Human sized treads dragged along cement, over the layers of crusted carpet and onto slippery tile.

Cars littered the front entrance of the hospital. Pushed bumper to bumper to side door. No reason to their collective manner. Vehicles as tightly as they could get before the bodies would rush out and through the automated doors.

Sirens echoed throughout the streets. They came to, as fast as they came from. Every ambulance, fire truck and police cruiser zippered through traffic. The low dust's orange and pink bleeding through thick smoke from burning buildings and into the darkness of night.

"Jesus Christ," Mei Ling led the group down the sidewalk. They were back in civilian cloths. They slowly made their way around a car that had claimed it as a parking spot. "What the hell did we do?"

She slowed her pace as she spun around to take it in. Raked her hand through her hair before running into the entrance of the hospital.

Dawn dragged her feet. The colour in her face completely vanished. Her mind washed of reason, craving for the blood that could inspire thought. Asa carried most of the weight, while Chika held onto Dawn's other side. The two guided Dawn through their causality.

Mei Ling ran in. The place a congested entanglement of human misery, people's elbows into others stomachs and toes into heels. Everyone shoved so close to each other you could smell the combined body heat. Cries from children caked in crusher dust. Moans from bruised elderly. Shouting and teeth dragging from panicked adults. Mei Ling's gut twisted and dragged itself down; she had to physically hold it to relieve the pain.

She tapped someone's shoulder. "Is this for emergency?"

The man had the darkest complexion that Mei Ling had ever seen, but he was white as a ghost. His blue eyes stared through her. His jaw slack. He tilted his head, trying to fathom what he had been asked.

Mei Ling gulped into a back step. Bumped into someone in scrubs. "Hey!" Mei Ling grabbed the woman's elbow.

The nurse shot daggers, first at Mei Ling's grip, and then into her eyes. *"What?"*

"My friend. She's hurt." Mei Ling wrapped her tongue behind her lower lips, trying to moisten her mouth. "Real bad."

The nurse looked around. "Who the hell isn't?" Tossed a shrug before returning to Mei Ling's eyesight. Twisted her face at Mei Ling, who stared through her and towards Dawn. The nurse turned to meet the remains of Dawn.

Blood covered the right side of Dawn's face. Her nose contorted and shoved up into her right eye. Skin swelled overtop of her eye and bruises were rampant across her face.

Wide eyed, the nurse reached out wards to Dawn.

The nurse tilted up Dawn's chin. "Follow my light," Dawn looked up but her eye didn't track the nurses flash light. "How long has she been…" the nurse looked around. Shook her head then snapped her fingers at Mei Ling. "Grab a chart from over there."

The nurse relieved Chika of her duties. "Follow me," The nurse led the girls through the labyrinth of people.

"What happened to her?" The nurse was moving as fast as she could. Her head darting at each door, searching for an open room.

"We were caught in a building," Chika spoke up as she tried to keep up with the group. Her legs too tired from carrying Dawn's weight. "It came down and something… something heavy fell onto her."

"On her face?" The nurse darted into a room.

Curtains sectioned the already cramped room into six areas due to the infestation of new patients. Thousands of new bodies shoved into every nook and cranny. The four girls had elbows into each other, claustrophobia induced shifting feet as they each struggled for more room, but none was to be had.

Asa and the nurse got Dawn onto the bed. Chika sat next to Dawn to help keep her up while the nurse searched through a cabinet for supplies.

"I'm going to check your vitals. Are you allergic to anything? We're going to have to give you painkillers before we get you cleaned up," the nurse did her best to smile.

Void of expression, Dawn stared not at her mangled arm, but through it. Replayed the events in her mind, as the nurse then spoke to Chika.

"I… I don't think so." Chika clawed air down her throat; it kicked the entire way down. She leaned into her friend, to catch her eyes. "Dawn, are you allergic to any medicine?"

Dawn didn't speak, she only very slightly shook her head.

"Okay," Chika turned to a nurse with a nervous smile. "I think we're a go on meds."

"Hope so," the nurse cringed with a shrug. She turned to Asa and jerked her head to the door. "We need more room, hun."

"Right," Asa nodded. "Chika, I'll be outside, okay?"

Chika looked up with wide eyes that quaked with a silent plea to stay.

"I'll be right out here," Asa clamped her hand around the door frame as she shifted into the hallway, so that Chika knew she was still standing there.

The atmosphere was drenched with a lemon and vinegar cocktail. The entire hospital walls and floor were damp with an ocean of fruit and chemical.

Asa twisted her nose before she bore it into her bunny hug. Her sleeves were pulled over her balled hands, an attempt to create a barrier between her and the germs. Her grandfather had sold janitorial products for a living, her temporary germaphobia brought on by the masking of actual cleaning, twisted her gut.

A weight crushed her shoulders as far down as they could slouch. Asa couldn't figure out why her thoughts were consumed by the cleanliness of the facilities. Images of Vala being taken, the sound of the nurse checking Dawn's vitals and the hollowed feeling in her chest from the crushed walls she knew were just beyond the doors of the hospital.

"Hey," Mei Ling pressed her back to the wall as she flipped through the various forms. "Do you know Dawn's last name?"

"No," Asa's voice muffled by her gas mask.

"Date of birth?" Mei Ling fidgeted with the pen.

"No."

"Do you know if she is Canadian? Shit. Does she have a health card?"

"No."

"Any idea if heart disease or cancer or diabetes runs in the family?"

"No."

"How about—"

"*Mei Ling!*" Asa swung her hand down. "Stop it. Please. For the love of God. Shut. Up."

Mei Ling left the wall with a low brow. She didn't look back at Asa as she made her way to the waiting room.

"Oh goddamnit," Asa pinched the bridge of her nose, germs be damned.

*   *   *

Moans of the injured echoed off the walls. Dawn was now dressed in a white gown and had an IV stuck in her arm. Blood cleaned from her face, stitches laced her right eye, bandages wrapped around both eye and nose, and her arm in a sling.

The girls had been moved to a new room to await a CAT scan or a MRI; no one remembered which was first. Dawn's eye had been treated, to save it, but her arm would have to wait.

Chika and Dawn sat on the edge of a row of seats, while Mei Ling and Asa stood with their backs to the hallway.

Chika sat forward with cupped hands dug into her forehead. The words of the doctor, that had finally come in, echoed in her head. *We need to check for brain damage, and prep her for surgery to rebuild the eye socket.*

The space in her chest cavity felt void of warmth. A nothingness was deep and dark within Chika and she didn't know how to fill the hole. She reached out, in old habits, to God, praying for Dawn over and over.

Dawn's mind looped over and over, filled with images of purple and red sparks. The rise and fall of Dunkel mucked in with ash that replaced walls that had once made up the city. Disappointment radiated throughout every cell in her brain, and for the moment, physical pain receded into a mental knot of guilt, nausea and pain killers.

She had been tasked to guard the Echo. It was Dawn's duty, the sole reason she left her family and their cult. She saw herself as the self-appointed person to save the world.

Someone, in a hurry, bumped Dawn's IV stand.

"Ow," Dawn dulled her tone. She looked over to her teammates and saw her own defeat reflected on all of their faces.

Not needing to acknowledge the situation, Dawn turned her attention towards her mangled hand.

"Can you move your fingers?" Chika dug tears out of her eyes with the back of her wrists.

"Yeah, it's fine." Dawn winced as she folded her thumb in, followed by her index finger and partly shook her ring and pinky as she attempted to flip Chika the bird. It failed, but the message got across.

"Dawn!" Chika snorted into a laughter. The shaking hurt her eyes, and she slowly stopped.

"Fine." Dawn looked ahead of her, towards the hundreds of injured people. Dawn touched her forehead as the room momentarily went dizzy. The bandage blocked out most of the light in her right eye, but she was still thrown off by the displacement of her eyeball. The double vision was nauseating.

"Place is swarmed," Mei Ling muttered as she leaned her back to the wall. A mini stroke ignited as the wall gave. Luckily, Asa grabbed her by the elbow, just in time.

"Stand much?" Asa managed a smile.

"Forgot there wasn't a wall," Mei Ling broke into laughter when their eyes met. The kind that rolls in your tummy until it bursts up your throat and out your mouth. There was no stopping it. She rode the nervous reaction out.

Many looked. Some understood. Most didn't. Some were too busy to give it any thought.

"I don't think there's anything funny about this." Chika glared towards Mei Ling.

Mei Ling cleared her throat. Not being one to apologize, "Out of context, certainly was." Her voice was hoarse, and her swelled eyes coupled a stuffed nose.

"Whatever," Chika rolled her eyes. She reached out to Dawn's right arm. "Does it hurt?"

Chika's concerned touch shot up Dawn. She was stunned, tried to free herself from empathy by pulling back. "I'm—" she had to clear her throat. "It's fine. I'm fine. Hardly feel it. Drugs."

"Oh." Chika sat up, pocketed her hands between her legs.

Trying to ignore Chika's withdrawal, Dawn faced Mei Ling. "How do we get her back?"

Mei Ling tensed, pulled back and flushed her cheeks. "Why are you asking me?"

"I'm not," Dawn did her best to pass her annoyance on through her tone. "It's an open mic."

"No idea," Asa was the first to admit defeat.

"Seconded," Chika sighed as she turned her attention elsewhere in the room, towards two bandaged children that couldn't have been older than ten. Their faces were stained with dried blood that hadn't fully washed off. Bandages littered their bodies. A mother did her best to cradle them both but she kept finding injured areas. The pressure at the base of Chika's skull, something she hadn't felt in weeks, came back to her.

"Ditto," Mei Ling shrugged.

"Well isn't this *fucking* fantastic," Dawn instinctively balled her good hand, pain shot through her. "Goddamnit." Dawn grinded her teeth as she keep her volume in check.

"*Hey!*" Mei Ling hissed as she closed the space between her and Dawn. "Check yourself. You're the know-it-all, why do you think we'd know what to do?"

"I don't." Dawn pushed herself as close to Mei Ling as she could get.

"Then get over yourself," Mei Ling ran her teeth over themselves.

"Get over yourself! I can't be expected to do everything!" Dawn debated about slugging Mei Ling in the face; even with her shattered bone, it would've been worth it.

"So what are we?" Mei Ling swung her arms out. "Benchwarmers!?"

"Sometimes," Dawn tightened her eyes. "Yeah."

216

"Go fuck yourself! You think your shit don't stink, because you're an Angel? You're just a girl—"

"I'm not needed here." Chika stood up, unnaturally quick. Everyone in the room stared at her, as most had already been staring at the argument. It took a moment for Chika to swallow the heat in her throat. "I don't know what we can do. Having a childish argument isn't going to change that. I know first aid, maybe I can help the staff."

With that, she disappeared out into the hallway, leaving the rest to marinate in their own stupidity.

"Thanks," Dawn leaned towards the empty seat next to her.

"For what?" Mei Ling looked to Asa for support. "This isn't on me."

"Nope," Asa pocketed her hands. "You're both retards. She's like twelve, just went through world war three in her own back yard, and your bickering like a divorced couple in front of their children."

"We—" Mei Ling began.

"Let's stop measuring dicks," Asa sighed. "Let's be constructive."

Mei Ling melded the thought before folding her arms. "She's fourteen."

"Who?" Asa raised a brow.

"Chika. You keep saying she's twelve. She's fourteen." Mei Ling muttered as she eyed the ground.

"The fuck does that matter?" Asa dug her fingers into the side of her face. She trembled and wanted to shout, just like the rest, but she kept her tone and volume under control.

"Mei Ling is a Kitsune," Dawn sighed through closed eyes.

"So it's all back to me, then?" Mei Ling blew some hair out of her eyes.

"No," Dawn turned to make eye contact. "You're smart. Know things that you shouldn't."

"She's not wrong," Asa punched Mei Ling's bicep. "Use that brain."

"Well, okay," Mei Ling sighed. "I don't know, but let's talk."

"Talk?" The two exchanged confusion.

"I don't think. I know. It's hard to explain, but we need the right question for me to answer." Mei Ling hooked her foot to pull the empty seat out, and around Dawn—who was forced to lift and angle her IV in one hand. "Sort of, anyways. It's random. Confusing. Works on a jump start." Mei Ling sat. "So, talk."

"Uh," Asa shrugged. "How's the arm?"

"It's fine." Dawn lied.

"Why don't you suit up? Your armour can heal it, right?" Asa squatted to be at the same eye level as Dawn.

"They heal minor things," Dawn balled her healthy hand. "They can't do big stuff. Bone or major organs. They can sustain us, and speed up healing, as long as our tanks aren't dry. But they can't repair something like this."

"Why'd you take out that building?" Mei Ling fought to keep her tone normal; flashes of the towers bled into the back of her eye.

"I didn't," Dawn collapsed forward. "He swatted me aside, like I was nothing. I would do anything to save this rock but I would never endanger anyone, not on that scale. Not like that." She looked across the room to a little girl. A bandage was tied where a kneecap used to be. Dawn purposely balled her arm to fuel the pain she deserved. "I could *never* do this."

"When the tower fell you stopped it," Asa looked over to Mei Ling. "How?"

"Luck," Mei Ling shrugged. "My shoulder blades were on fire, then I had this surge of energy. Like when we transform and connect to the Echo. But, it wasn't a flash, it held. I wove more water than I could have had imagined possible."

"Was pretty incredible," Asa grinned.

"Thanks," Mei Ling looked to Dawn, who turned away. "Your sleeve. Why is it blue? It was the same colour as that portal that guy took Vala through."

Dawn shrugged.

"Thanks," Mei Ling leaned back in the chair so the front legs lifted off the ground, and hooked her feet under Dawn's seat to anchor herself in place. "Colour seems to mean a lot with our powers. White and silver for Metal, red and purple for Fire, yellow and orange for Earth, grey and black for Water, and green and brown for Tree. Blue doesn't fit into any of that. You don't weave anything do you?"

"Weave?" Dawn rose a brow.

"It's what I'm calling it. How we manipulate the elements. Bend them to our will. Did you ever notice the threads that expand from our armour?" Mei Ling looked back and forth, both girls seemed clueless.

"Just comets." Dawn shrugged a shoulder.

"Meteorites," Mei Ling corrected with an invisible pen.

Dawn rolled her eyes. "I know the difference. Comets sound more badass."

"True." Mei Ling fell forward. The slam made the two girls cringe, and the rest of the room scowled their way. "We are limited by moving our elements. All of us, 'sides you. Well, Asa and Vala seem to twist the rules a bit by drawing from internal energy. The behaviour is the same, though. Even when I went super—"

"We aren't naming it," Dawn frowned. "This isn't some anime."

"Fine," Mei Ling shrugged. "When I 'drove' the Echoes power, instead of being taken along for a ride, I still wove. I didn't summon the water out of nothing. Drained half the city's water supply, probably."

"Unlike my comets," Dawn nodded.

"No," Mei Ling shot. "You can't magically—" laughed "—make something out of nothing. That's impossible. Matter can not be created, nor destroyed."

"So where—"

"If you were weaving your 'comets', they would be satellites or space debris. It's rock. It's coming from some place. You aren't weaving, you're summoning. Probably not even relying on the metal element of your armour." Mei Ling sat up to think it over.

"You think I can do more than just comets?" Dawn perked up.

"Have you ever tried?" Mei Ling did her best to emphasize how stupid she thought Dawn was.

"Why would I? I can shoot fricken space rocks at people," Dawn looked around to confirm that that was truly the coolest option. Everyone showed their agreement, with a nod.

"While you're learning how to write right-handed, you should look into that."

"Okay," Dawn dragged the word out, then followed it into a grin. "You have a plan, don't you?"

"If some glow stick wielding jerk-off can manipulate time and space, so can we." Mei Ling stood. "We are going to ride a wormhole into space. Using the same technique Dawn uses to summon her 'comets'."

"Great." Dawn frowned, "How?"

"With your—" Mei Ling noticed Dawn's raised arm. "You can't summon the sleeve."

"Nope." Dawn lowered her arm. "Plan B?"

"Plan B." Mei Ling nodded.

"We have a plan B?" Asa cocked an eyebrow.

"Nope." Mei Ling's smile spread even wider.

"Then what's with the goofy smile?" Asa fought with herself to understand what was going through Mei Ling's mind.

"I've never felt this way before," Mei Ling laughed a bit.

"Felt like what?"

"Stupid, like you." Mei Ling playfully poked Asa's forehead. "I'm excited to explore this new sensation."

"Thanks," Asa batted Mei Ling's hand down. "If you need any advice, come my way."

"Thanks, bud," Mei Ling tapped her chin. "So when I count on my hands, do I go up to ten, or use one hand as a place holder to remember what to multiply with once I roll over?"

"Dude," Asa slowly shook her head. "What?"

*　　*　　*

Chika stepped into the hallway. Right away shouldered by a nurse, then someone off to find a loved one. She sighed as she took in the suffering around her.

We did this, Chika had a knot in her gut, felt the need to clench it with a hand.

After a few seconds of feeling sorry for herself, she grabbed one of the nurses before she could be shouldered again.

"What!?" The nurse's nostrils flared.

"Sorry," Chika fought to smile. "I know first aid. Can I help in any way?"

*　　*　　*

"Hey, Mei Ling," Asa drew in a deep breath. "You think she's going to be okay?"

"We'll get her back," Mei Ling played with a hand sanitizer dispenser. "If they wanted to kill her, they'd have done it right in front of us. They need her for something. This whole thing. Sending demons to our world… we thought we were sleeper agents finally showing up to the war. Stopping them from gathering Atoms of God. They did all of this to wake us up. They need more than seven billion souls to do whatever it is they're doing. They need us, or rather, Vala."

"Yeah," Dawn stood, regretted the decision almost immediately, but refused to sit back down. "We've got time, then."

"What?" Asa swapped her attention from Mei Ling to Dawn back to Mei Ling. "How can you be so sure, how do you know this, how long do we have?"

"Long," Mei Ling smirked. "I've never met the guy, but I'm guessing this Dragon has quite the ego, right? I'm also betting that whatever they're doing involved Vala being an Echo. There are only two left in the universe, right? One's too proud and one was hidden amongst the masses."

Mei Ling held up her hand to fist bump a confused Asa. "They may have an idea of what they want to do, but no way they've done this before. They have product testing on their hands. Research and development. We might not have a lot of time, but I'll figure out how the hell to teleport to the Bridge."

"Then we go kick some ass," with a contorting face attempting to swallow feelings, Asa fist bumped Mei Ling.

"Yeah," Dawn shrugged. "Why not."

*   *   *

"You look nervous," Sky glanced over to David. Both stood in the human quarters of the Dragon's Queen's castle.

They were tiny, no bigger than a hotel room with six double beds shoved into each one. No TV. No books. No art. A shared washroom down the hall.

They were to stay inside the hallway, which was shoved some place in the basement, until called upon. No mingling in the hall, having to bite one's tongue if you ventured out of a room.

The only luxury, a balcony in one of the rooms. David often occupied it alone, as if it were a private office. He stood here, both hands on the railing, overlooking his home.

Earth was so beautiful, in all its vast blues and light green shades.

"I am nervous," David motioned for his cane.

"Why?" Sky handed the oak piece over.

"Do you know why the order exists?" David faced his second hand.

"To serve the Dragon, of course." Sky nodded.

"No. That's what we feed the low ranks, and tell the Dragon's Queen. Our real reason is to preserve mankind." David glanced over to the Earth. "These creatures out class us in every way. It'd take longer without our aid, but they were always going to win. We few, we who serve the Dragon, will be what remain of the human race."

"We will be rewarded."

"We will be pets. At the very best."

"And the worse?"

"Cattle. But we will be alive, some of us. Briefly."

CHAPTER ELEVEN: DISTANCE

May 3rd, 0830

Morning sunlight crept through once white, now stained yellow, vertical-running plastic blinds. A few blades were missing. The heat register swayed the rest to reveal a jagged split in the window. Beyond, an overgrown lawn, and farther than that, an unkempt neighbourhood.

Barefoot, long shorts and a tank top; Mei Ling's dulled mind fumbled with the plastic lighter. Liquid almost absent. Three flicks before a flame raised out of its tip.

Daily ritual had become numbed from a warrior's spirit; still necessary, if not redundant. She slid the incense through the flame. Elbowed the lighter as she waved out the fire, to allow ash to engulf her nostrils.

She twisted her face from the smell. She placed the incense properly in the shrine, which held a dark framed picture of her older brother. A deep breath bore down any raising heat in her lungs.

Mei Ling smothered the ache inside with a mind determined to forgo mourning.

She put the lighter away in the kitchen before she fished in the fridge.

It was strange. She wasn't sure why, but every day she did this ritual. Every day it had become purposeful, like everyone else in the family. But since Vala's abduction, she almost felt like she couldn't be bothered by any of it. It ate at her.

Shing was gone. She had grown to accept the fact she never would see him, but now souls were real. She knew this to be factual. She shouldn't be dulled to the thought of her brothers death. Mei Ling should feel more connected to him than ever, but—

She grabbed a cold can of pop. Pushed the thoughts out of her mind.

"I've read that that stuff is very bad for the human body," Flea waved around Mei Ling's shoulders. "It's an acid. If you pour it on the paint of a car, it wrecks the paint."

"Oh yeah?" Mei Ling used her tongue to fish out soda trapped in the cans edging.

The kitchen had faded brown cabinets, worn white tiles torn through to the floor board, a pulled out dishwasher with last nights' drying dishes and a fridge with an ice dispenser that no longer worked.

Mei Ling grabbed a pink letter H from the door of the fridge, "I hear magnets are bad for computers."

"Are you threatening me?" Flea swirled backwards.

"Yup." Mei Ling used her hip to close the fridge door. She grabbed a cup of freshly poured coffee before playfully ducking under Flea to make her way to her bedroom.

The room was a claustrophobic nightmare. A desk shoved in the corner which prevented the door from opening all the way. Her bed so large that the closet doors had been removed years ago. Posters of anime and musicians did their best to hide the faded walls.

Mei Ling slipped on slippers before making her way to the closet. She struggled to push her clothes to the side; they hardly budged from the over congested closet. With an arms length of an opening, Mei Ling leaned in as the clothes sprung back into her sides. She swore less from pain and more out of spite.

After a moment of digging around, Mei Ling returned with a notebook. Pushed her desks chair into the hallway, then closed the door. Sipped on her pop as she used one hand to flip her notebook open. Descended, slowly.

She knew every word in the book, but it had become ritual to re-read its basic notes. Each page a new discovery in her efforts. A manual, of sorts. Mei Ling prayed that she could pass it around, save her the trouble of tutoring the others.

Mei Ling's legs bent up and over each other. She focused her eyes on Flea, who floated ahead of her.

"Let's try not to be disappointments today," Mei Ling very slowly and purposely took a drawn out swig of her pop and hid it under her desk.

For the last few weeks, everyday had been the same for Mei Ling. Wake up, make an appearance in first period in time for attendance, slip home to spend the day learning Distance manipulation, eat supper, band practice from six to eight, more Distance training, shower, bed. Repeat. On more days than she'd care to admit, showering had become optional.

Weekends offered less deception and more time plucking chords, but it all felt the same. Mei Ling had entered a bit of a haze. The concept of time was lost in most cases.

Flea's shards expanded to unravel black and grey threads which crept in and around Mei Ling. A shiver ran down her spine as she fought the thought to banish the armour back into the nothing. With thoughts of being infected again at the front of her mind, Mei Ling's stomach twisted as she transformed into her armour. Every day it was a brief distaste that she had to push aside.

DISTANCE BETWEEN ECHOES

By focusing her mind's eye, Mei Ling went through a series of mental gymnastics. Pictured the sleeve. The inners of which was a complex circulatory system of energy. It took a moment to get her thoughts to flow along with the energy and make a strong connection.

Each day it took less and less time. Her record was three hours, but many days turned up nothing.

Both music and food helped keep her spirits up, but with each passing day, the weight built itself up. At any moment, the Dragon's Queen's army could complete their bridge, then everything would be lost. This fuelled frustration, which put Mei Ling into an indescribable state of exhaustion.

On the fifth hour, Mei Ling finished the connection. She sighed. Plunged two sets of fingers into her temple. Her head throbbed.

Cyan and blue threads escaped the fabric of reality. Extended into the physical world. Wound around her arm and collar. Tightened.

Now connected, Mei Ling reached out to the material. A surge of energy ran through her body and into her soul. Navigating the energy was much like solving a Rubik's Cube blindfolded, with broken thumbs and every square was a smaller more complex cube with its own cubed squares. You had absolutely no frame of reference, save the acknowledgement of another party.

An odd congestion flowed through Mei Ling. Her veins felt like they were replaced with maple syrup. Oxygen felt distant as the room slowly spun. Only every third breath felt like it was working. All of her senses vibrated information to her brain. The taste of sugar on her mouth pushed and pulled in intensities, as if her body was indecisive about whether she indeed had anything in her mouth at all.

White hot light flickered behind her eyelids. The room steadied itself, as her Kitsune eyes came into focus. Ahead of Mei Ling, where she had once seen Flea, she now saw herself. Her true self. Her first body, mind and spirit; and it was beautiful.

The reflection's eyes were brighter, with longer and thicker eyelashes. Its face seemed paler, didn't have the scars of recent zits, and most importantly, it didn't have the nose that she didn't quite enjoy. The reflection's hair was just as thick and black, but it was woven in a maze of braids that must have taken hours and many sets of hands to craft.

Like a child first discovering its reflection in a mirror, Mei Ling was transfixed on her appearance. It clouded her mind for several minutes during each connection. Everything about her body had always felt so fake, so wrong. Finally truth and perfection were in sight.

Now over the reflection, Mei Ling dove deeper. Used her mind's eye to focus on the thoughts within the reflection. Shifted through a lifetime of knowledge to pinpoint Distance.

Searching her past mind was easier than establishing the connection; it was almost reflexive. The first few times the connection had been severed from the sudden feedback of thought. The complicated matter of reading your own mind meant you were reading your own thoughts, about wanting to read your thoughts, about wanting to read your thoughts, about reading your—

With a deep breath, Mei Ling focused both of her minds on one task: the manipulation of Distance. Once in awhile, she would cringe as her focus would waver and a feedback, much like a microphone held up to a speaker, would spike through her being.

The technique involved connecting one's soul with the energy of the sun. Stars housed all seven elements and were directly connected to the Voice's original power. However, the Distance was much too far to establish a connection directly.

Using the reflective light from the moon, the Kitsune could focus Distance and open portals to the different dimensions, traveling along what thin strands of Distance remained.

With a sigh, Mei Ling disconnected from her past. Crushed her eyes and rubbed her temples. She fell backwards, to sprawl out on the cold hardwood floor. The AC from the heat register blew up her hair into a frizz—it felt *amazing!*

In her relaxed state, her armour vanished. Flea swayed from above. "Were you successful?"

"Yeah." Mei Ling relaxed her eyes, but kept them closed. Fished in her pocket for her cell phone.

Without looking, she dialed Chika's phone number.

After a countless set of rings, it went to voicemail.

Mei Ling brought her legs up, then swung them to propel herself into a sitting position. "Seven billion lives and you're on silent? Are you *fucking* kidding me?" Mei Ling hung up.

It took Asa five rings to pick up her phone. "I'm in class. Had to duck out. Sup?"

"Chika won't pick up. Her cells on silent or something. Can you believe that?" Mei Ling furiously ran a hand through her hair. Nails clawed her scalp so violently she swore they were about to split her skull wide open.

"Ugh…" Asa drawled. "Maybe she's just taking a dump?"

"Ew." Mei Ling cocked back. "That's gross."

"Well, I don't know what to tell you." Asa sighed. "We good?"

"Totally." Mei Ling let an arm fall to her thigh, bent it as she leaned forward with three pumps. "Though I'm a little freaked that we might end up in the wrong place and die. I'm basically mentally manipulating raw energy, to convert matter into a state of energy, use that energy, which is now us, to punch a hole into reality, then propel us across time and space, to rematerialize said energy into matter. During all of which, I am hoping, I can still have a grasp of my own consciousness to do all of this."

A very uncomfortable pause came.

"Fuck it," Asa finally weighed the subject. "Not like you can practice."

"Yeah, exactly." Mei Ling playfully pushed Flea away, who was attempting to listen in. "We either die tonight or when the Dragon's Queen shows up."

"Yup." Asa shuffled the phone around. "Let's hero up."

"Thanks." Mei Ling laughed. Looked at the calendar on the back of her door. "Actually... tomorrow is a full moon."

"Ugh." Asa's hard pressed eyes came through her tone. "Now I'm sick to my stomach. I'm totally going to wig if it's that much of a wait."

"Yup." Mei Ling grinned. "See yeah, Asa."

"Seriously. Can't tonight?" Asa's voice was comically shaky.

"Ha. Get over it." Mei Ling ended the call. With a smile she looked up Dawn's number.

Asa looked down at her cell. Alone in the hallway, she sighed heavily as she pocketed the phone. Her head turned to look back to the class, but stopped mid-turn. Brown eyes danced along the lines of the orange tiles of the school. When they came to a greyed chip, she stopped.

Asa left her belongings in class. Exited the school.

*   *   *

The sun was warm and the sky cloudless. Summer weather had crept into the Prairies and removed the snow from the city. The sounds of jackhammers and reversing gravel trucks filled Victoria Park. Dawn and Chika sat at the park bench, sipping bubble tea.

Esh sat on Chika's shoulder disguised as an Atlantic Canary, getting a lot of attention but no one the wiser. Ozazi sat in Dawn's jacket pocket, refusing to transform.

Dawn's right eye still patched to hide the two sets of surgeries she had had. Her nose back to normal, save the very slight bend, where it had healed funny. Due to short supplies Dawn had been stuck with a pink cast, which she rested on the table; to Mei Ling's dismay, and Dawn's delight, Chika was the only name signed.

"Dude." Dawn gagged on a tapioca ball. "These pearls are as hazardous as the calories in the shake. You Asians are intense."

Chika laughed as she played with her straw between pinched fingers. Swirled the tapioca that rested at the bottom of the bubble tea. She glanced quickly over Dawn. "Guess you never drink this stuff, huh?"

"Nope." Dawn placed her tea on the table. Her right hand rubbed her cheek to both cool down her face and warm up her numb hand. "I haven't had artificial sugar in years. Juice and supplements. Once I turned sixteen I dropped out of high school and took training pretty seriously."

"Wow. That's a mouthful of exposition." Chika swapped hands as her left had become numb. "It's so cool that you're that dedicated. Did you get your GED?."

"Nah. No point." Dawn looked over to Victoria Park. An outdoor play was being put on on a temporary stage. Children laughed and danced along with the youth group. If you kept focus on the stage, and didn't let your peripherals catch the construction, you'd never had guessed Dunkel had attempted to wage war less than a month ago. "I sort of accepted that my life wasn't mine to live. Too much is riding on us being ready."

"And we're not." Chika put down her tea. She tilted her head down, but looked upwards to Dawn with raised eyebrows.

"Nope." Dawn shrugged. "But we'll get the job done." Sipped on the drink.

"How can you be so sure?" Chika tried to catch an angle to see on the other side of Dawn's sunglasses. It was difficult to tell, but she believed there was joy in Dawn's eyes as she watched the kids at play.

"I wouldn't be risking drinking this if we weren't fine." In a lapse of judgement, Dawn attempted to use her left hand to pick up her bubble tea. The cup toppled and Chika caught it. "Thanks."

"No problem." Chika smiled.

Dawn kept looking at the play as she fished for the drink blindly.

"It's a good thing we have you, Dawn." Chika pinched the straw again. "You're an Angel after all."

"I guess." Dawn simultaneously turned to Chika while putting her straw back in her mouth. Spoke through sips. "Angels were caretakers. I don't remember my life before any of this, but I was likely a glorified janitor."

"You mean past life?" Chika corrected with a smirk.

"No." Dawn shook her head. "Asa and I are still on the one. The transferring into the womb more or less gave us amnesia. Angels don't have souls. We might not age or get sick, but if we die, we die." Dawn shifted her lips around her face. "I guess now that I have a human body, I don't even have those other perks going for me."

"Oh." Chika withdrew. "So what's that say about Dragonborns—"

Dawn slammed a fist on the table. Heads turned. Chika jumped in her seat. Dawn waited for people's attention to be drawn back to the play. "Stop feeling sorry for yourself. You're a Dragonborn. Get over it. You aren't evil or unholy. Your soul is a copycat of Atoms of God, but from something with less power. You're no different than Mei Ling. At least your body has a soul, real or not. Asa and I are more like—well, I don't know a metaphor."

Dawn realized she hadn't handled the situation well, so she changed the subject. "Asa's our real MVP. If she can keep her head out of her ass. Valkyries were straight up warriors. A few dozen of them took on the Dragon. They're the real deal. Without them, we wouldn't have the scale that was used for our armour."

Dawn paused, realizing Chika had been told all of this before. She made sure her head was tilted to hide her rolled eyes. Babysitting didn't sit well on her face.

"There are five of us though." Chika's gut twisted. "How can we stop the Dragon if thirty-six Valkyries couldn't?"

"We can't. Not head on." Dawn was glad Chika changed the subject, but was still annoyed at the pessimism. "But we don't have to. We kill his Queen and we win. She's only a Dragonborn. Nothing too difficult."

"Unless the Dragon was smart enough to give her a scale." Chika literally pointed the obvious out with an extended index finger. "Then she could make her own armour."

"Oh, probably does." Dawn smirked. "Chances are she has an entire scale or two on her own."

"Than…" Chika studied Dawn. "Why are you smiling?"

"The Kitsune designed our armour," Dawn softened her voice as she watched the play. "If the Dragonborn were as smart as the Kitsune, this war wouldn't have been cold for the last million years."

"Or they're using all his scales to make a super army." Chika decided to finally smile.

"There you go." Dawn finished her tea. "I seriously don't get these things. The pearls just get in the way. Why not just have a milkshake instead?"

"I don't know." Chika chomped on three pearls in a go. "They're favourite part." Chika twisted her lips as she realized her blunder, "They're *my* favourite part."

"Are you kidding?" Dawn cocked a brow. "Gross, Chika."

"Well—" Chika was cut off by the ringing of Dawn's cell phone.

"Hello," Dawn answered more than questioned. Her eyes went glazed, voice stern and her posture straightened. She knew who it was without looking; only three people had her number; one had no business requesting a chit-chat, the other was sitting with her, and the last one was, "Mei Ling. When are we going?"

"Um." Mei Ling was thrown off. "This must be Dawn, only she could look so hot and sound like a forty year old man."

"Hilarious." Dawn rolled her eyes, masked it with her tone. "Are we set?"

"Jesus," Mei Ling rolled her eyes, purposely let the expression come through her tone. "I'm the one lifting all the weight here. You're the one dragging her feet and being pointless."

Dawn knew this to be true. A heavy sigh. "Sorry."

"Wow." Mei Ling blinked twice in disbelief. "I didn't realize your vocabulary was so extensive."

Dawn rubbed her temple, unimpressed. "Mei Ling."

"Yes. Sorry." Mei Ling cleared her throat. "Tomorrow night is a full moon. Meetup, say, five? I want a pizza before we die."

"Sure." Dawn turned to Chika. "Tomorrow at 5:00 PM we are heading out."

"Got ya." Chika fired off a gun gesture.

"Who are you talking to?" Mei Ling raised an eyebrow, as she slowed her voice in a legit state of curiosity.

"Chika," Dawn realized exactly what Mei Ling was getting at, she smiled at Chika. "We're out having bubble tea."

"Are. You. Kidding. Me?" Mei Ling grinded teeth, tightened eyes, imagined bashed in skulls and smears of blood over cement. "Why the hell is her phone on silent? What if there was an attack or—wait. Why wasn't I invited? I love bubble tea!"

"We'll see you tomorrow night." Dawn ended the call.

"Was she mad?" Chika emptied her drink. Did her best to pretend she didn't care.

"She was," Dawn searched for the words, "Mei Ling."
Chika laughed.

*   *   *

Night was on its way. The twilight cast across the Saskatchewan sky in an ocean of orange and pink. The magnificent clouds captivated Asa's easily distracted mind.

Dressed in a worn green bunny hug, jean shorts and sandals, Asa rested her shoulder against the Smith Street bus stop. She held Nither in her folded arm, in his rabbit form. Most nights she waited for her mom at this stop.

The bus rolled up. Asa politely waved at the driver, who waved back. The door slowly creaked open as Asa bounced on her heels, with hands stuffed in her pockets, in a nervous mess.

"Hey, girl." A sugar sweet voice touched Asa's ears. Asa looked up to her mom. With bleach blonde hair, a spray tan and green contacts, the thirty-two year-old smiled. She held the height and body frame of a twelve year old. Asa, embarrassingly, was mistaken to be her mother's older sister. Asa's tall frame matched her late father and only the colour of hair and eyes resembled her mom, though vanity products disconnected the two.

"Hey, Mom," Asa let Nither drop to the ground before she stepped up the first step to help her mother with her walker.

"You brought the rabbit?" Dennette cocked an eyebrow. Asa simply nodded.

Dennette, Asa's mother, had fallen down the stairs when the rails had given out. Asa had spent ages four to twelve being cared by her grandparents while Dennette healed from head trauma.

The two now lived alone in a small two bedroom split. Asa's mother worked minimum wage, so the upstairs was rented to generate some money. They had been there a year last month. Asa had recently been forced to transfer high schools due to a school location bylaw that came into effect in the fall.

"How was work?" Asa grinned as she took her mother's purse. With a slouch, Asa squelched the height difference.

"Fine." Dennette smiled. "Alex asked me out." A too familiar glow was in her eyes.

Asa loved her mom and respected her strength and ability to overcome her accident and raise a child as a single mother. However, her mom had a weakness for men. Any man. Every man.

"Mom." Asa was stern. "No sleep overs. The Jeffersons said they'd move out if—" Asa shivered from her head to her toes. "—you know."

"I can keep quiet." Dennett's smile was uncomfortably large.

"No. You cannot." Asa crushed her eyes in between her finger and thumb, while punching the pedestrian light.

"There are ways," Dennette winked.

"Oh god. Mom. Gross." Asa covered her ears, as Dennette laughed.

"I'm kidding, you know." Dennette sighed as she struggled down the curb of the sidewalk.

"I don't believe you." Asa rubbed the goose bumps off her arms. "Seriously."

The two entered the house through the side door. The door was too small for the walker, so it was left behind. Asa helped her mother down the narrow flight of stairs to their basement door. Unlocked the second door.

Asa led her mother into the kitchen/living room to a chair. Afterwards, she went back upstairs to fight with the walker, to fish it around the narrow door frame. Locked the main door. To her side, a whiteboard with magnets and a diagram told the household who was in and out. Moved their names to the "in", but as the Jeffersons were out, she left the deadbolt unlocked.

Food was ready, sitting on a pan on the stove. Asa warmed up the oven so they could reheat it. The microwave had died two weeks ago.

"How was school?" Dennette patted her knees to summon Nither onto her lap.

The table was just big enough to get one set of elbows on either side. White chip paint on top with metal silver trimming that was falling loose, leaving dangerously exposed edges.

Asa shrugged. She played with the settings of the oven. At first four, but that felt too low, so she went five… rethought and landed on four.

"Asa?" Dennette tightened her eyes a moment. "That isn't like you."

"Mom." Asa dug her hands deep into her bunny hug. "We need to talk."

"Oh no." Dennett went wide eyed. "You're pregnant?"

"Wha—" Asa glared at her mom, but then burst into laughter as she sat down at the table.

"Why are you laughing?" Dennette joined the laughter.

"Because once I tell you what is going on, you are going to wish I was knocked up." Asa felt the laughter trail, but her smile stayed. Dennett's did not. "I'm going to be blunt, Mom. I'm pretty much a superhero."

"Like one of those girls from those fake internet videos?" Dennette tried to laugh, but it was forced. She didn't understand the joke. "Don't tease me."

Asa sighed as she reached over and cupped her mother's hands in her own. "I'm serious."

*   *   *

The house was beginning to buzz to life. Mei Ling swiftly, but quietly, slipped on her bunny hug and grabbed her guitar. Slipped out the side door with Flea on her heels. She had zero interest on being picked on.

Mei Ling and her pug made their way down a main arterial road. Past the dying strip mall, the high school, church and finally the movie theatre. The twenty minute walk led Mei Ling into a bay.

The road was patched with different shades of black from the many years of quick patch jobs to the corroding Saskatchewan road. Three houses into the bay was a house with an open garage door. Two seventeen-year-old boys just on the inside, and a third boy in the back.

"You bring your guitar?" A tall boy, by Mei Ling's standards and no one else's, stood at the edge of the garage. His thick brown hair hadn't been cut in six months and fell wherever it wanted. His goggle-thick glasses slid on the end of his nose, the arm twisted from roughhousing.

The boy called Flea over and rubbed his head so fiercely that Mei Ling swore it was tittering on the edge of tearing the skin free. It was a friendly gesture though, and Flea didn't seem to mind it in the least.

The boy's name was Morgan, and if Mei Ling had anything to say about it, his name would be "babe". However, having never been kissed, Mei Ling always felt on edge about pushing the subject. Though she did enjoy how his eyes tended to dance along the edges of her curves.

"Yeah." Mei Ling plopped down on a bench just inside the garage. Disappointment in her voice as she set up her blue guitar. Still sitting, she leaned over to jack its extension into a free amp, to the point she almost toppled over. "Your ass needs to learn it, so I can use my bass."

"No way," Morgan shook his head. "We suck ass and we need my bass playing to keep us that way."

"Whatever." Mei Ling rolled her eyes.

"You can strum my bass anytime, Mei," another voice came from Morgan's side.

Mei Ling shivered. The way he shortened her name made her taste acid in the back of her throat. The boy had a pizza face and an extra twenty pounds. Hair hadn't been washed in days and his clothes stained with what Mei Ling hoped was toothpaste drippings.

"That doesn't even make sense," Mei Ling avoided looking up at Jared. She only tolerated him because he was best friends with Morgan.

Jared shrugged off Mei Ling's attitude.

Curiosity had Mei Ling dart her eyes up to see the new member. The unknown man was in his later twenties. Sat at the drum set spinning his sticks. His hair was long, probably fell to his shoulder blades, but it was held up in series of thick spikes by half a day's salary of hair products. His skin was white as rice, but his hair dyed black as night. Mei Ling thought he looked like a tool.

The band had just lost their drummer, so Mei Ling asked a stupid question. "Is he our new drummer?"

"Yup. Works with me at the leisure centre," Morgan jerked a thumb over his shoulder to the newbie. "His name is Zeke."

"Hi." Zeke nodded, scratched his bare chest. The only thing he wore were worn out jeans and a serious of rubble multi-coloured straps around his left forearm.

"You any good?" Mei Ling swung her strap over her neck as she stood up. She was ready to play. Why wasn't anyone playing?

"Show her." Morgan grinned.

Zeke cracked his neck. Twirled his drumsticks. Jammed into the Pokémon battle music.

"Whoa." Mei Ling went wide eyed. When Zeke had finished she added, "You single too?" Zeke laughed, a bit of blush to his cheeks.

"Hey!" Morgan glared. "No dating within the band."

"Dude, chill." Mei Ling shook her head. "He is like twelve years older than me."

"Well I—" Morgan shifted his weight. "Okay." Turned away from Mei Ling and to his mic stand. "Whatever."

"Cool." Mei Ling slightly tilted her head, as she cocked an eyebrow. "You okay?"

"Yeah. Fine. Whatever." Morgan blushed. Lied through his teeth, which he didn't part as he spoke; his native accent was difficult to hide when he was upset. "I'm just nervous about our first gig. Breaking Melody is gonna rock."

"I still hate our name," Jared rolled his eyes." The first one was way better."

"Shut up, Jared." Mei Ling and Morgan said in unison.

"Ah come on, guys." Jared picked up his own guitar. "Peek at Chu was an amazing name."

"Yeah. Right." Mei Ling turned to join Morgan's direction. The band faced outside the garage to mimic facing a crowd. "Clever use of my last name, I get it."

"You're such a ball buster," Jared ran his hands down his guitar. "Let's just play before the princess tries to cut me down anymore."

*   *   *

The Tanaka table buzzed about with chatter of Sora leaving on a missionary quest. She was to lead a small group to build an orphanage in Africa. The flight would be leaving two days from now.

Chika couldn't help feel that it was odd that both daughters were departing the same weekend, although no one else knew this but her.

In Tanaka fashion, a grand event meant turkey, mountains of mashed potatoes, and oceans of gravy. Vegetables were only included if they were marinated in butter and coated with salt; if you could taste the vegetable itself, then the chef had failed.

Everyone was proud of Sora for taking her big next step, so a feast had to be held. The dining table was between two other tables to hold the entire extended family. Dawn had no idea the Tanakas owned so many tables. She had spent the last few weeks over frequently, explored every room in the house for one reason or another, but had failed to ever find these two extra tables.

The monstrous table led from the kitchen into the living room. Twenty seven chairs surrounded it. The chairs were a mixture of dining chairs wrapped in leather, old wooden ones from the basement, and a few bar stools. Lastly, a high chair for the newest addition of the family, Alexander.

Chika sat next to Alexander. She enjoyed making faces at the six-month-old; he, on the other hand, found them less than amusing. It only took a few minutes for his outburst to become earth shattering. Chika kept to herself after that.

Dawn found herself squeezed between Chika and Sora. The three of them were the bar stool musketeers, according to some uncle who was less funny than he thought. It had been brought up at least seven times before the food had even touched the table.

To keep up appearances, Dawn had to continue to lie to Sora and the family. Dawn had been placed by chance next to Chika. Most nights the family only sat six to the table, and Dawn shared a side with Sora every time. The odd time she was lucky enough to be across from Chika, so they could make some conversation, but even then it was kept to a few sentences every five minutes. Dawn felt odd having a friendship with someone so much younger than herself and hoped no one else shared that thought; to keep the thought from arising, Dawn just tried to ignore Chika as much as possible when the parents were around.

A few judgmental eyes passed Dawn from the extended family. It was no secret why she was here, even if it was a lie. Everyone knew if Sora had a friend at the table, they were going through a rough patch. The cast and bandaged face only fed the gossip, the most popular being an abusive boyfriend.

"So." Chika's grandfather clapped his hands together. "Who'd like to say grace?"

People shifted weight in their chairs as a few people were nominated. No one jumped at the chance to do it themselves. Finally Sora sighed, and spoke up. "I think it's Chika's turn."

With a set of tight eyes and stern upper lip, Chika accepted. She made mental note to give Sora the dagger eyes once Dawn was no longer blocking vision between the two. Even with Dawn there, Chika knew Sora was smirking to herself.

Before beginning the prayer, Chika relaxed herself. Let the anger wash over her. Let the frustration of Alexander's cries, while being burped, fade out. Soon she, and the family, were alone in a silence brought on by the unity they shared. Anyone making sounds to themselves were no longer irritating and no one gave it much mind.

"Amen." Everyone said once Chika had finished.

The moment grace was over, the room exploded with chatter and the passing of food. Dawn's inexperience did not go unnoticed. She caused a backup of food transferring three dishes deep. She attempted to juggle unloading dishes onto her plate, transferring the unnaturally hot bowls of food and answering the probing questions from the aunts and cousins.

Do you have a boyfriend? "No."

Why not? "Too busy, I guess."

Oh, are you in post-secondary? "No."

If it isn't boys or school, than what is it that you are busy with? "I train, a lot."

For? "Mixed martial arts."

The lie sparked interest from the men. Soon they were asking Dawn the questions, which she much preferred. Dawn assumed that the men had a general interest, while the women were attempting to find seeds of gossip.

How long have you trained for? "All my life… or so it feels like it."

How many hours a day? "Six or Eight. Depends."

How much can you bench? "Three hundred."

A pause. After a moment a cousin asked, "Is that good?"

Private conversations began as they debated on her response. Dawn laughed after a few minutes. "Yes." She finally replied. "It is."

Is that how you hurt your arm? "*No.*"

With the awkwardness too high for anyone to continue the topic, an aunt cut in. Any siblings? "No."

Do you live alone? "Yes."

Where in the city? "The East End. Near Prince of Wales."

"Sorry." Chika whispered out the edge of her mouth.

"It's fine." Dawn shrugged.

*   *   *

"So, you're an Angel?" Dennett awkwardly shifted her weight. The tiny chair made it difficult to manoeuvre.

"I think so," Asa shrugged from the entrance of the kitchen. Hands dug in her bunny hug's pouch when she leaned against the doorframe. "Like a specific race of Angel, a Valkyrie."

"What's the difference?" Dennette used her walker as a brace to lean forward.

"Not really sure. Other than we are warriors." Asa joined her mother at the table. Fell softly to her seat. Took a drawn out breath. "But I don't really feel like one."

"Shut up." Dennette playfully punched Asa in the forearm. "You're a Larson. We are born fighters."

"Sure." Asa rolled her eyes. "Against a hundred and twenty pound girl with daddy issues, but not against an army of Dragons."

"Pffft." Dennette waved her hand. "I'm not letting you short change yourself, Asa. You've gotten more pounds of muscle than I ever had on me and a few feet. You are a beast."

Asa raised her brow. "Thanks?"

"Look." Dennette placed a steady hand over her daughter's shaking hands. "The hardest thing I have ever done in my life was recovering from my fall. Years of physio kicking my ass so that I could take care of my most precious possession: you."

Asa gave a half smile. "Mom, I'm not you. I'm not a machine."

"Asa," Dennette tightened her eyes. "I was only able to get through all of that because I had you to lean on. Only eight and helping her mother eat and bathe and wipe—well you helped when you were a child. When you should have been playing with dollies or—I guess in your case, cars. You are my inspiration."

Asa drew back, but kept their hands tangled. "I didn't know you remembered that." Asa squeezed her mother's hands.

"I don't remember much," Dennette smiled. "But I would never be able to forget the love of my daughter."

"Jesus." A heat rose in the back of Asa's eyes. She used the back of her wrist to claw away tears. "You're making me cry."

Dennette frowned. "Don't be such a baby."

The heat drained down from her eyes and into a warmth in her cheeks. Asa laughed. "Thanks Mom."

They smiled at each other. Then an itch she couldn't quite scratch caused Dennette to ask. "Dragons... seriously?"

*   *   *

Mei Ling stood outside her younger sister's bedroom door. The hallway was pitch black as everyone had receded to their rooms for the night. The low hums of television and other electronics bled into the hallway; enough to get an understanding, but too muffled to paint a picture.

Hesitation was a modest word to describe Mei Ling's indecisiveness to knock. She had been sitting in her own room a moment ago. Trying to get to bed when she felt the need to walk over here.

Two years ago, her best friend in the whole world lived behind this door. They watched anime together, played the latest Pokémon, and of course gossiped about the girls in each other's clique. They never studied together, which hurt Mei Ling the most when school had been the thing to sever their connection.

After Mei Ling turned down her full ride, everything fell apart. The scholarship had meant so much to Mei Ling's parents and in turn the rest of the family. Jia Li, her sister, lost respect for Mei Ling's choices. Her parents lost their love for a prodigal daughter.

Mei Ling couldn't blame either party. One lost a role model that could do no wrong, and the other lost a perfect child for a sudden disobedient one; but Mei Ling just wanted to be normal. Enjoy life as a kid before adulthood crashed in.

It had been the biggest mistake of her life. Mei Ling's stubbornness prevented her from fixing the relationships in such a manner. She would stick down the path she had chosen and hoped one day the family would open up to it.

Mei Ling drew in a slow breath. "Jia Li?" Mei Ling knocked. The instant the back of her knuckle lifted from the oak, her heart began to beat a hundred times a second.

Mei Ling swore she could hear her own heart beating. In an attempt to squelch the sound, she held her breath, nervous that her sister would sense her fear and not open the door.

A minute passed before the hum in Jia Li's room silenced, though it felt like an hour for Mei Ling. From inside Mei Ling could hear Jia Li cross her twenty-year-old mattress. Hop barefoot to the hardwood floor. Each step a sticky echo in the nerve wracking silence.

The knob shook. A sigh and a curse as Jia Li realized that she had locked it. A quick turn of the latch and the door swung open.

Jia Li stood in the door frame. The spitting image of Mei Ling, save being three inches shorter and the waist length hair. Jia Li was eleven, so one day the height would even out and the two would pass as twins; Mei Ling smiled at the thought.

"What do you want, Jeh?" Jia Li had low eyes that reeked of sleep deprivation. A pen in her ear and a notebook in hand.

Mei Ling froze, she had forgotten why she knocked.

"Jeh Je?" Jia Li repeated the Cantonese word for older sister.

"Uh." Mei Ling shifted her weight as she grabbed both elbows. "Wanna hang?"

Jia Li went wide eyed in disbelief. "You want to watch anime, or something?"

"Yeah. Sure." Mei Ling gave a soft smile. "That'd be awesome."

"Okay," Jia Li drew out the word with tight eyes. Studied her sister as she backpedalled into her room to sit on her bed.

Mei Ling carefully closed the door before following. She held her breath, afraid too much noise may alert their parents; that they may intervene so that Mei Ling didn't poison their only remaining child.

Jia Li's room was half the size of Mei Ling's, but held just as many objects in it. A tube TV was squeezed next to a misshaped desk of box crates and plywood. Doors removed from the closet. A single-sized bed that was probably older than the girls combined. Notebooks littered the mattress of the bed. Pens, a cellphone, and a few plush animals were squeezed between the books.

"Were you studying?" Mei Ling lifted a text book. She recognized it as her own.

"Well some of us have to, Jeh Je." Jia Ling self-consciously snatched the book out of Mei Ling's hands.

"Oh." Mei Ling took a step back. She reverted into wide eyes and grabbed her elbows. "Sorry I—"

"Oh." Jia Li realized the confusion, but could only think to do a ten second tidy of the bed. "I didn't mean—Jeh Je, sorry." Jia Li sighed as she hung her head in shame. "I meant that it takes a lot of effort for me to get good grades. I need to ace my finals so I can get into a better high school. Mom and Dad can't afford to pay for private."

Mei Ling broke into a historical laughter. Jia Li glared. Mei Ling whipped a tear from her eye, overwhelmed by relief. "It's okay, Muih Mui." It didn't feel as awkward to say as Mei Ling thought it would. The two hadn't talked in what seemed like forever, but it was very apparent that Jia Li never stopped using the word 'sister' even if Mei Ling had.

"I wanted to apologize." Mei Ling sighed as she fell next to her sister. Mei Ling played with her fingers as she gathered thought.

"For what?" Jia Li pushed the hair away from the left side of her face to get a better look at her sister.

"Everything." Mei Ling shook her head as her chest became hollow. Squeezed her eyes as they began to burn and tear. Sobbed as her throat collapsed in on itself.

"Jeh Je?" Jia Li's voice quaked in rhythm with her watering eyes. Hoarse voice scraped through every word. "Why are you crying?"

Mei Ling violently shook her head. Used the back of both wrists to drag back the tears. The remaining mess were crimson eyes puffed in a manner that looked almost allergic. "I don't know, Muih Mui. Probably because I'm an asshat."

"What?" Jia Li sniffled. Rubbed out her tears, but they wouldn't stop. Jia Li had always been known for crying and it caused Mei Ling to burst into laughter. "Why," *sob*, "are you laughing?"

"You're such a baby, Muih Mui." Mei Ling bear hugged her sister. Dragged Jia Li over top her and the two fell to the floor. The impact jammed Mei Ling's elbow and she swore.

Now it was Jia Li's turn to laugh at Mei Ling. "Hey!" Mei Ling failed at preventing her eyes from watering. "That really hurts."

"Now who's the baby?" Jia Li punched Mei Ling in the chest with jest. "Huh, Jeh Je?"

"Ah, what the hell, Muih Mui?" Mei Ling broke the bear hug with a roll out. "That freakin hurt."

"Oh." Jia Li leaned against her bed with her head fallen backwards. She stared up at the fan in her room. "We haven't laughed like this in a while, huh Jeh Je?"

"No," Mei Ling sluggishly rose. Rubbed her wound the whole way up. "I'm remembering why, though."

"Pffft." Jai Li rolled her eyes while rosebudding the air. Suddenly her eyes glazed and face went blank. "Are you doing okay?"

"Oh," Mei Ling rubbed the base of her neck. "Nothing I can't handle—"

"Mom and Dad fight a lot," Jia Li followed the blades in a trace. "You're not around much, but it's always about you."

Mei Ling hunched over to pick at her toes. "Yeah."

"Why don't you seem to care?" Jai Li shut her eyes.

"Look, Muih Mui." Mei Ling turned to attempt eye contact. "I'm not who or even what you think I am."

Before her sister could speak up, Mei Ling continued. "I'm going to tell you something, about me. Something important. It's heavy and you aren't going to be able to stop me from doing it. You can't tell mom or dad or anyone else..."

*   *   *

"That's a lot of stuff for one night." Dawn stared down at Chika's two stuff backpacks. "Why do you need this?" Dawn held up one up with a raised brow.

"I figure I may as well not forget anything." Chika slid on long jeans and a bunny hug. "Might get caught sneaking back in."

"Yeah." Dawn threw the bag at Chika's gut. Reflexes were slack and Chika curled over the denim on impact. "You're such a ninja."

Too afraid to properly swear, Chika mouthed 'vacuum'. Dawn rolled her eyes.

"I still don't get why you want to stay at my place." Dawn tossed the other bag over her shoulder. Fought to open the bedroom window. "It's kind of smelly and we'll have to share the bed."

"Oh." Chika drew her bag into her face. "I'll just smother my face so I don't smell your BO."

Dawn glared. *Well, it's sort of true...* Dawn relaxed.

She helped push Chika up and over the open window seal. Dawn joined her after. The two made sure to move slowly and precisely along the twig-riddled concrete path way. Once they were down the driveway, they picked up the pace to make some distance.

"So what do you want to do tomorrow?" Chika dug her chin into her pillow as they walked. The girls had kept quiet until they were a block's distance from the Tanaka residence.

"I'm not sure," Dawn dug her hands deep into the pockets of her windbreaker. "Not bubble tea."

"You're lame," Chika used the tag of her pillow to scratch an itch under her chin. "Want to catch a movie?"

"Sure." Dawn shrugged. Hit the crosswalk button with the back of her fist. Looked both ways when it took too long to change over. Jaywalked the empty street. Chika looked both ways in a panic. Fought the urge to wait and with a deep breath followed Dawn. "What's playing?"

"Uh." Chika juggled her pillow and phone while nervously looking for cars. She had taken a picture of the newspaper before their grand escape. "You into horror movies?"

"Not overly." Dawn took Chika's pillow for her. "When you've actually fought Demons, some makeup and lighting doesn't do it anymore."

"Okay." Chika twisted her face. Dawn noticed the phone's display gave an eerie glow over her face. Dawn laughed. "How about something with explosions?"

"I can summon comets." Dawn grinned at her own joke. "CGI robots and smoke aren't exactly thrilling."

Chika frowned. "Well if you're down with tempting fate there is a movie about demons and hell."

"Hmm." Dawn tapped her chin. "I do miss Jersey... sure why the heck not."

"Deal." Chika snapped her phone shut. "4:20 pm."

"Great. Our last movie is going to be a fifty-year-old man putting on layers of makeup to play make-believe." Dawn shook her head with a grin. "Wonderful."

"Don't have a stroke," Chika adjusted her backpack. Almost dropped her phone while putting it back into her pocket. "Do you actually think we aren't coming back?"

"Be a bit naive if I thought it'd be easy." Dawn twisted her hands within her windbreaker. A habit she still had from her early childhood. The twist caused the jacket to roll up a bit up front. Part of the inside lining visible. "But I have every bit of confidence that we'll win."

"Yeah." Chika slid her lower lip under and across her top row of teeth. "You think Vala's still alive?"

"Oh yeah." Dawn dragged the words out. Twisted her jacket to a second roll then unraveled it all. "Definitely."

"How can you be so confident in that?" Chika sped up so she could see Dawn's face, needing both an audio and visual assurance.

"She's an Echo. and they know that now." Dawn pulled out her keys. "Whatever they are planning requires an Echo. The Dragon, right? Well, he's trapped. Vala isn't. They either want to know why, or they'll use her as she's closer to us to do whatever they're planning."

"Any idea what they're planning?" Chika didn't feel assured—at all.

"With Vala? No idea." Dawn tossed and caught her keys with the same hand. "They need a bridge to get here. Something big, like what Mei Ling is about to do but times… a lot. Past that, I have no clue."

"Oh." Chika looked at her toes as they walked.

"Why the sudden interest? We just had this conversation." Dawn turned to eye up Chika. "You've never asked about Vala. I didn't think you even cared."

"How can you say that?" Chika's face flashed red. Voice clawed up her throat, "Of course I care."

"Chill." Dawn playfully punched Chika. The lightweight tripped from the attack. "I'm just joshing ya."

"Oh," Chika's crimson rage dissipated into a rosy blush. "Sorry."

"Stop acting so weird," Dawn pushed open her door.

CHAPTER TWELVE: MIASMIC EDEN

May 4th, 23:00

Dull yellow orbs did their best to penetrate the darkness. Light from faded street lamps crept around the edges of the park. The breeze went almost unnoticed. Four girls stood in the field.

The moon's silver light trimmed their armour. Mei Ling drew in a deep breath as the clouds blocking the full moon crept away. Once the white ball was completely in view, she glanced over her shoulder to her friends.

Three sets of nods assured her it was time. With a smirk, Mei ling raised her right arm. The blue sleeve pulsed as her mind focused on the empty field ahead.

She focused her mind as she bore deep into herself. Found that warmth inside, called to the full moon, and, using it as the Kitsune referred to as 'the sun mirror', Mei Ling connected to the origin of the universe.

Siphoned the blueprints of reality. Harnessed the secrets left behind from the Echo. Focused them and wove them to her will.

She poured the warmth inside her chest up and through her arm into the blue threads that wove themselves around her collar, down her shoulder, past the bicep, and knotted in the palm of her hand. The energy buzzed in her arm, pulling her forward, but she dug her heels into the dirt to ground herself. The sleeve was powerful. It was heavy. It was hers.

Thunder cracked with no dark cloud in the sky. The energy in her arm lashed out on the world with a powerful burst of energy. The wind from it rattled the trees. Its power seeped into the night. Clouds closed in on the night. Thickened. Twisted. Deepened. Electricity snapped the air. The energy danced along the clouds. Every star blocked out of the sky, leaving only the moon in focus.

Her execution was raw. Untrained. Too much energy was being spent and relapsing into the area around her focal point, and Mei Ling knew this. She tightened her mind. Tried to focus her armour, much the same as she had used chakra to tame Asa's armour. The power quaked through her and numbed her joints. She bit down as she pushed forward.

"Whoa," Asa marveled as every light vanished in the night. The power had gone out.

"It's a lot different than when *he* did it," Chika stepped to the side, hoping to use Dawn as human shield.

"It is." Mei Ling grinded her teeth. She struggled to pull the threads for the portal out from the many strings of creation. "They were teleporting to an Inbetween. A reality between the realms. We," threads began to protrude from her palm, "are going to an entire new plain of existence. Eden."

"The Garden?" Chika looked up at Dawn.

"Eden," Dawn smiled. "We are in the Garden." She shrugged, "A bit of a misconception."

"Like... *the* Eden?" Chika was wide eyed.

"No. Don't get too excited." Dawn rubbed Chika's skull. "We aren't going to be tourists. It's just a pit stop." Chika pulled away, annoyed.

The threads slowly wove into each other. Overlapped. In and out, Mei Ling struggled to knot the Distance into a portal. *Shit.*

Asa placed her hand on Mei Ling's shoulder blade. Mei Ling looked towards her friend with a cocked brow. "What... what are you doing?"

"Helping. Ugh, Chinese element?" Asa smiled.

"You don't know what you're doing," Mei Ling's laughter vibrated from the energy in her arm.

Asa shrugged. "Is the big baby okay?"

"Peachy," Mei Ling balled her fist. Snapped the threads of Distance into each other. They broke, then sewed and finally knotted. "Just peachy."

"The peachiest." Asa slapped Mei Ling's back as hard as she could while still being in the realm of play.

"Okay," Mei Ling clenched her sleeve with a free hand. An earthquake in her arm, she felt her right arm numb and, using her left hand, attempted to hold it together. "Who's up first?"

"I'll go," Dawn looked down at her cast for a moment. It had taken a great deal of concentration but she had managed to bypass it dematerializing. Her face freed of stitches and bandages. The magic of her armour effortlessly held the wound closed and kept her eye in its current state. It was blurry, exposed to the world and not ready. She kept it closed half the time to avoid double vision.

But that didn't matter, so with a grin, Dawn looked over her shoulder to Ozazi. "You follow me, then the rest, okay?"

Ozazi tilted into a nod, but Dawn hadn't waited. She was the leader, they'd do what she had told them to. Confirmation was not a necessity.

She traced the threads of the portal with her eyes. They were in a constant state of motion. Though knotted together, the threads seemed to keep rotating over each other, as if not bound. Dawn felt her mind quake, became dizzy, as she tried to comprehend what she was looking at. "Jesus," She touched her temple to ground herself.

"Try not to think about it," Mei Ling shouldered Dawn to continue moving. "It doesn't make sense. It isn't supposed to. That's the point. The way you manipulate the laws of reality is you ignore them. Our minds are a part of reality. Your soul isn't. It reaches over and beyond it. Use that warmth like a light and hurl yourself into that tunnel." She smiled, "Don't screw up, though, or you'll die."

"Right," Dawn smirked, figured Mei Ling was talking out of her ass.

As she reached out towards the portal, the threads seemed to loosen and unfold themselves. Dawn gulped as she pushed forward. The threads wove back around her. She vanished.

"*Dawn!*" Chika covered her mouth, felt foolish for the outburst.

"She's fine," Mei Ling softly laughed.

Dawn couldn't understand what she was seeing. An endless ocean of cyan and blue strings was the best her mind could come up with. It took a minute. Her brain pounded. She felt a dampness from within her skull which she didn't understand. But the warmth. Her soul was along for the ride, and guided her as if it knew where to go.

*　　*　　*

The girls were thrown through the portal. Each landed on their knees. The strings of both portal and Mei Ling's sleeve, unwove into the nothingness. The girls fought to rise, their legs felt void of energy, but each managed to control themselves once standing.

Their minds took a moment to ground themselves as their brains coped with being torn down. Broken to the basic building blocks of the universe to only be tossed back together. Once they were able to conceive what happened, they noticed the darkness around them.

It wasn't long until they realized the eternal darkness was only the beginning of the gloom of the woods. Large tree trunks, the size of skyscrapers, littered the woods. The massive trees expanded so high upwards that their branches and tops meshed into a green and brown sky. It was impossible to tell if it was night or day.

The brief life of the light, left by the strings, allowed Asa's eyes to zero in on silver silk which danced along the maze of branches, all thanks to her fear of spiders.

"Shit." Asa was glad the darkness of the forest masked the horror across her face.

"What?" Dawn darted her eyes as she readied a stance. "What did you see, Asa?"

Asa shifted her weight. "Oh." She grabbed both her elbows. Tightened her grip so hard it felt like someone were hugging her, making her feel safer.

"Spiders." Asa gagged on the word. The thought of black hair, red eyes and creepy legs filled Asa's inner eye. The lack of true sight only intensified the vision. The picture of the gigantic spiders so vivid that Asa felt her skin crawl with their imaginary legs. She curled over her arm. The safety net failed.

Vomit poured out of Asa's lips. The sounds of the splashing caused the other girls to backpedal.

"Disgusting." Chika covered her face with cupped hands. Though she knew Asa couldn't see her, she still glared out of spite.

Instinct brought Asa's face up. The two sets of eyes locked in the darkness. Before the second spewing came a raised fist sporting a single digit; it quickly collapsed into a knuckle as the second release of bile left Asa's lips. "Up yours," she coughed through convulsions. Prayed for her armour to take control of her mind and pour the warrior spirit she so desperately wished for, but it wouldn't. It couldn't.

Like a revving car struggling to start in a cold winter's day, Asa could feel the threads of her armour verberate energy into and out of her. It couldn't focus. The atmosphere interfering with its complexity.

"Charming." Chika rolled her eyes. Chika straightened her leg and slowly waved it in the dark to search for a root. When she found one, she sat.

"You okay?" Mei Ling gently swayed her arms out in an attempt to find Asa, but had no such luck.

"Enough of this." Training dammed Dawn's flight response. Her voice held a strength that each girl grasped to in the darkness. "Chika. You control fire. Use. It."

There was a long awkward silence as Chika blushed in shock of her own stupidity. Asa let out a chuckle, which Mei Ling joined in its contagious manner.

"Ugh." The laugher fuelled Chika into action. Flames escaped her skyward palm. She brought the hand in front of her and, with aid of a second, she fuelled the flame to twice the size, using two hands to contain the fire in a safe orb of light.

Something was off. Different. Chika couldn't focus in on what, but her connection to her armour and abilities were clouded. When the orb felt large enough, she frowned as if she had everything in check. "Here."

The light was enough to bring a safe sense of bearing to the girls, even if the flickering flames produced stretched shadows into the makings of nightmares. Each girl found themselves twisting their neck to check on shadow people in the corner of their eyes.

Mei Ling offered Asa a hand, and with both a groan and a smile, Asa took it, "Thanks."

"This place has seen better days," Ozazi swayed apart from the group.

He continued, "Without the caretakers, a darkness has spread. This was once a beautiful place."

"Okay." Dawn darted her green eyes from tree, to silk, to girls. "Asa keep both lunch and vision down. Everyone else put your eyes up high. That's a ton of webbing, far too thick to be Earth sized."

"How big do you—" Asa cuffed her mouth. Every ounce of will spent on controlling her stomach. "How big are they, Mei?" Asa's voice felt it belonged to a child in that moment.

"Well," Mei Ling ignored her name being shortened and eyed the sky. "Using my degree in biology and years of study on animals that don't actually exist..." Mei Ling cracked a smirk. "Big."

Tremors ran through Asa. She crushed her eyes with index and thumb, in an attempt to steady her nerves.

"Asa." With patience depleted, Dawn dug her index finger into her temple. "You can shoot lightning bolts out of your goddamn fingertips. Chika is a fricken human flamethrower and Mei Ling is... Mei Ling..."

"Oh," Mei Ling folded her arms. "Thanks buddy, love you too." She pressed her lips to the air.

As empathically as possible, Dawn rested her hand on Asa's shoulder. It came off fake, but Dawn wasn't acting; just out of practice. "When your mom used to tell you that they're more scared of you then you are of them, she was talking about right here. Right now."

"Kay." Asa strained a smile. Locked hands with Mei Ling for emotional support. "I'll be fine. Let's go."

*   *   *

Mei Ling's eyes shifted into her Kitsune state. The pupil flattened into a fox-like presence and her brown irises turned blue. All around her, invisible to the others, were magnetic pulls. Mei Ling was able to track them, and in a moment found the flow spiralling down a path way between the trees.

She had learned about the pull when reading her past self's mind. The Kitsune set up artificial magnetic pulls all around the forest. It allowed their lost to find their way home.

Ozazi turned on his scanner, then drifted off from the group to scout.

Without having the means to light the way farther than a few metres, the girls had to walk. Leaping would only risk cracking one's skull against stern bark.

After a couple of hours, the ground tremored. Soon, the darkness that danced just outside Chika's flicking light became lit. Black replaced itself with a series of red glowing dots. Two large at the bottom and the rest trailed in an arc above and outwards from the set's centre point.

Hundreds. Asa's arachnophobia drove the estimate into millions of eyes watching from the deep black. Their bodies still a mystery, thanks to the darkness, were the size of a lion. The spiders made a strong shuffle sound over the roots and trunks of the trees. Shivers shot up each girl; instinctively, they brought up their arms.

"Back to back." Dawn's attempt to make an unwavering command was a complete failure. Her voice shook through every word. "Face outward."

Her green eyes darted along the sets in the darkness. Heart violently pounded. Her mind spun out into the mindless pits of fear. Dawn attempted to stay in control, but without her ability to summon a meteorite…

"Mei Ling!" Dawn suddenly remembered her allies.

"Y-yes," Mei Ling shivered sporadically through her words. "Got any plans?"

"Just one." Dawn kept her eyes towards the masses, while she blindly fished through the darkness for Chika's wrist.

Dawn's unexpected touch startled Chika. Her hand was jerked to the side and with it her flames were extinguished. The light died. The eyes flooded inwards.

"Mei Ling, put up a shield around us, now!" Dawn yanked Chika off of her feet and planted her in front of Dawn. Without asking for comfort zone permissions, Dawn broke any personal bubble Chika might have wished for. Dawn quickly positioned Chika's hips to get the body in the right direction, then grabbed both elbows and pushed them forward.

"Chika. Fire!" Dawn screamed in Chika's ear. *"Now!"*

Fire erupted from a confused and startled Chika. Flames shot forward violently with more ferocity than Chika had ever mustered before.

As the heat scorched both spider and tree, Mei Ling wove her ice shield.

The orb was thinner than what would sit in the realm of satisfactory, but Mei Ling aimed for speed over quality. The shield forced Asa to suck in between the backs of Mei Ling and Dawn. The only opening had Chika's flamethrower roaring out of it.

Knees bent and arms locked, Mei Ling fought to maintain the integrity of the shield. Body after body of the spiders collided with the orb, followed by a scampering of claws as each one attempted to get out of the way of their brethren. Boney spikes tearing into and out of each other, sometimes clipping the ice, as they stained the orb crimson.

The ice rumbled with each impact. With every dozen bodies thrown at the shield came a split. Mei Ling cringed with each one, her gut twisted as she prepared for the shield to give. She did everything she could do to maintain the orb, but something inside of her had a disconnection from the element.

"Dawn," Asa did her best not to bump into any of the girls. She stood in an awkward pose as she fought for head room under the dome and footing among the roots. "Mei Ling isn't going to last."

"Swell," Dawn spoke through grinding teeth. Her eyes focused on Chika's dimming flame. It would give out soon, as well.

Dawn looked over her shoulder. "Asa," Her confident voice had somehow found its way back to her lips.

When eye contact was made through the faint orange glow of Chika's flame, Dawn continued. "On the count of three, I need you to send out a shock wave. As powerful as you've ever imagined. Can you do that?"

"S-sure," Asa nodded. She couldn't explain it, but her legs were trembling mentally. How she was managing to stay in control of her body, Asa had no idea. "I won't puss out."

"Good," Dawn grinned. *"Three!"*

Asa went wide eyed. "What?" Control suddenly stripped from her.

Dawn fell backwards. Hooked her cast under Chika's armpit, swore, barely managed to drag Chika downward. As red heels slipped, flames arced towards the heavens slowly dissipating into the night.

Mid descent, Dawn reached out for Mei Ling, but the pain in her arm had delayed thought and messed with her timing.

As her rib cage cracked against the root of the tree, she let out a gasp for air but didn't miss a beat. Looked upwards for her target. *Found it!*

With her arm pinned between her body and a root, Dawn managed the strongest jab she could muster towards Mei Ling's thigh. The charlie horse caused Mei Ling's legs to buckle underneath her own weight.

As she caved, so did her orb. A mist fell over the girls as the ice vanished. In seconds, the only evidence of their defence would be droplets of dew on their bodies.

The splash of water woke up Asa. Gathered thought and a deep breath brought dancing lightning along her body. The beasts closed in. A claw only centimetres from her face. Its talon reached outwards. The tip outlined her smooth skin.

With a blood curdling war cry, Asa shot out lightning as far as the eye could see. The shock wave cut through bark and ignited parts of the wood, if only for a moment.

Dawn struggled to draw Mei Ling between the roots, while tightening her grip on Chika, so both girls didn't move and get themselves electrified.

She pinned them until the light vanished. No fire, no sets of eyes, and no lightning. Darkness came fast and left each girl with a hollow feeling. For a moment they each questioned if they were alive, or not.

"Did we die?" Mei Ling laid on her back. Too afraid to reach over and soothe her charlie horse with a firm rub. Her eyes kept skyward, hoping to catch a strand of light to prove her existence.

"I didn't," Chika curled over Dawn's good arm. Her entire body shivered.

"Same," Asa collapsed to her knees. The high of living through her worst nightmare was so great that she ignored the pain of hitting the roots with such force. "Though I'm overly confident in the fact that I just shaved ten years off my lifespan."

Mei Ling managed a sarcastic laugh as she sat up. Reached for her thigh and rubbed the pain out. "So. Who's betting the light attracted them?"

"Pretty sure that's unanimous," Dawn groaned. With Chika still clinging to her good arm, Dawn sat up and dragged the cowering knight with her. "So we keep to the darkness."

"Awesome," Asa sighed. "Nothing like shuffling around in the dark like a moron."

"As long as there's no Lego to step on," Mei Ling stood. "Then I'm okay with it."

Dawn cradled her cast as she stood. Chika slid off of her, never wanting to leave the safety of the roots. Dawn tried to rub the pain out in her arm but the cast prevented any real massage. After a moment, she gave up on it ever feeling normal again and pulled Chika to her feet by the back of the neck.

"Okay," Dawn rubbed the back of her neck. "Footnotes. First thing, our armour is fucked."

"Agreed," Mei Ling nodded as she attempted to weave water out of the air. It took longer than she had expected, even with her newfound low standards.

"Chika could hardly control her fire. Mei Ling should have kept that shield up." Dawn rubbed her rib cage. "I can fall off a skyscraper. Be pushed through buildings. But my ribs are killing me from falling maybe a few feet."

Dawn turned to Asa, though in the darkness it didn't serve any purpose. "MVP to Asa though." She shrugged, "Sorry for the startle but I needed you jump-started to get you going."

"Sure," Asa shrugged. "We're good."

Dawn looked around, then shrugged. "Guess this direction's good as any."

Suddenly, Dawn's ankle cranked to the left as her foot had fallen into a sling. The hunting trap, specially designed to not make a sound, retracted Dawn into the branches above. Before Dawn could shout, she had been swarmed with endless threads of silk that covered most of her face, forcing her voice to stay concealed, as well as her entire body from the neck down.

The only sound to suggest anything had gone on at all, was the thud created when the back of Dawn's skull collided with a root from the sudden loss of footing.

Arms came up as human instinct told each girl to defend themselves. After several seconds passed with no attack, the girls caught on that it wasn't a spider.

"Um…" Mei Ling broke the silence. "What was that?"

A pause.

"Dunno," Asa knelt down to try to feel around for whatever might have fallen. Her hand found Chika's ankle.

Chika screamed. She back pedalled away from Asa's grip. Stumbled, but ran into a tree trunk to keep her balance.

"Oops," Asa laughed. "Sorry." She couldn't stop laughing.

"Don't do that!" Chika screamed. Suddenly remembered the spiders, took a deep breath to steady her racing heart and control her volume. "Scared me half to death."

A pause.

"Weird." Mei Ling's voice trailed upwards. Though her eyebrows' raising wasn't seen in the pitch black, with the tone of her voice they all imagined her doing so.

"What is?" Asa gave up on her hunt and stood.

"This should be the time Dawn would pull rank and whip us into shape." Mei Ling's voice was slow. Her mind twisted with thoughts she did not like to imagine. "Think she fell?"

"You can't be serious." Asa fell back to her knees. "She must be KO-ed."

"Oh my…" Chika's voice danced along the line of silence and a whisper. Her words quaked as her heart ached. She pressed her eyes shut in an attempt to smother the worst of thoughts. *There is no way she's…*

"We need to look for her!" Chika attempted to weave fire for a light source, but it only fizzled. She was out of juice.

Heat rose in her as frustration deepened. She had hardly used any magic, and she was out!

"We will." Asa tried to look towards Chika. Hoped her voice would be comforting, but it wasn't as steady as she had attempted it to be. It fooled no one. She was just as worried as Chika.

A snap of a twig came to three sets of ears. Each girl perked up in the darkness. Became very still as they waited for another sound to follow.

Seconds passed, but no second sound. Whatever had caused it had either gone away, or it had been a mistake that wouldn't be repeated. With impatience fueling stupidity, Mei Ling stood.

"Who's there!" Mei Ling slowly ran her hands over top themselves, having to triple the normal time to manifest the blades. She serrated them.

With a deep breath, Asa let lightning dance along her body. She focused it into the palms of her hands and stood. Her heart steadied. Reality sunk into the back of her mind as her brown eyes danced along the darkness, and let fantasy take over the possibility of what could be coming next.

Her legs quaked. Her throat was dry. The tears stopped. Mind grounded in the possibility within the darkness. With clarity, Chika managed to find a little energy hidden within to ignite her hands.

As the sparks came to open hands, a strange swirl of wind came to her ears. Before the fire could fully ignite around her fists to unleash hell onto the world, her body was lifted and jerked to the side.

For a moment Chika wasn't quite sure what had happened. By the time she hit the ground, finished biting the inside of her cheek and rolled to her side, she knew that she had been entangled in some kind of rope.

Asa turned to the side. Without a reference point, she had no idea where anything was. The air cracked as she wove a stream of lightning blindly into the darkness.

Trees, roots, the face of a wide eyed Mei Ling, and dead bodies of spiders were brought to sight as the lightning flew through the air. The bolt crashed into the trunk of a tree. A chunk fell to the side as sparks of flame briefly existed before burning out a moment later.

Caught off by how close Asa had hurled certain death to her person, Mei Ling didn't notice the swirl of wind until it was too late. Her forehead slammed into root as her neck cranked backwards and the rest of her body fell.

Her neck didn't snap but the whiplash was quite devastating. Thought left Mei Ling as she blacked out.

Now alone in the darkness, Asa stood as still as humanly possible. Every thought told her to run. To side step. Move in anyway, shape, or form. She knew that they knew where she was, and that she knew that they knew.

Darkness was one thing. Spiders with their eight red empty eyes, eight gross hairy legs, two disgusting jaws that leaked sickening, thick acid and thousands of curled hairs was another thing. But being alone was everything else…

… and it was nothing. All worry was soon disposed of as a swirl hit Asa. She was thrown to the side.

A sudden heat escaped her chest and ran all across her body. Something deep inside of Asa came out. Something mighty. Something powerful. Something swift. Something pissed.

The forest became as clear as day as plasma hurled itself in every direction. Cracks of lightning clashed against root and trunk. Chunks scattered around the air. The bindings on Asa caught fire, vanishing from existence.

Asa twisted her hips and dragged her heels along the ground while using an arm as a brace. Turned herself to where the sling had come from. Spat to the side. Stood. Ran.

The light was gone, but Asa had caught a glimpse of what she needed. She leapt through the air. Brought both arms behind her as massive amounts of lightning scorched the very air around her.

She fell on top of something. Asa wasn't sure what, but it was living, and her heel quickly found its jugular. Pinned the squirming body to the ground as she tossed one bolt of lightning to her right and then another to her left.

The first scream, from her victim below, was more of a gargle followed by a gag. The next two were shrieks as electricity coursed into their chests, through their circulatory system, and out the backs of two bodies. They danced in a spastic fidget as they flew through the air, crashed into trunks and slide down to the ground.

Three sets of footsteps came. Asa spun, on the heel planted into the throat of her victim, to face the noise. Wove lightning and shot it forward. It hit one of the attackers. She curled over the bolt as it slammed into her stomach, tore most of her armour and sent her flying in the opposite direction. Her spine collided with a tree. She rolled down it motionless.

One girl dodged to the side. Swore in a language that Asa didn't understand. The girl looked up horrified, but Asa didn't have time to take that part in.

The final set of feet had leapt up and over both lightning and Asa. Landed behind the young Valkyrie, and without the need to turn around, shoved an elbow over her shoulder.

The impact hit Asa at the base of her skull. The world swirled as she fell to the ground. Thought gone as she was knocked out.

The two remaining women took a moment to sigh. Their hearts raced from an adrenaline rush they hadn't felt in centuries.

"What the hell was that thing?" The girl that had dodged spoke an ancient tongue. Rubbed her eyes, blinked twice, as the lightning from Asa had unadjusted them from the darkness.

"Not a thing." The one that had knocked Asa spoke. She stood over top Asa, her eyes were seasoned and had no issue readjusting to the pitch black of the forest. Her purple eyes ran along Asa's armour. "An endangered species of sorts."

"What does that even mean?" The girl kept blinking. "I can't see anything!"

"Ginseng." Her voice was stern. "We're going home. We are taking these three with us."

"What about…" Ginseng gave up blinking. It wasn't going to happen. She would have to rely on her basic training and memory of the forest floor.

"They'll live." The girl looked over her shoulder at the two that had taken it the worse. "Might not be battle ready ever again, but we'll tend to that when we need to." She reached down and picked up the girl who had been victim to Asa's heel.

"Whatever they are," the girl's voice was hoarse and she coughed through every syllable, "They're heavy as hell."

*   *   *

As the venom wore off, copper was the first piece of the world that came back. Dawn's cheek cut from her teeth dragging along the inner pink flesh of her mouth during the impact of the fall. It would pass in a while, but enough had pooled to warrant a spit up.

Try as she might, the silk wrapped around her jaw too tightly to open it. Dawn swallowed the blood to relieve herself of the annoying taste.

Green eyes rolled around Dawn's skull. Back to front, up and down and then rotated around. Everything was dark. It took her several blinks before thought came back to remind her she wasn't suddenly blind.

Memory was fragmented at first. Dawn remembered the forest and the girls, but not why. She attempted to free herself; with stupidity or forgetfulness, she favoured her left arm.

Pain ran through her. Up her arm, past the shoulder, through the spine and into her mind. Everything was jump started into a focused thought.

Dawn swore a muffled curse. Tightened her right hand into a fist and put all her might into breaking the silk. It took a very long time. The fabric kept stretching along with her, never tightening to a point where she could begin to push it beyond its limits.

After several failed attempts, she tried to pull the silk as far as she could, while pulling her feet upwards to her chest. The silk clung to her body and wouldn't detach itself. She struggled to get any leverage.

Defeated, Dawn gave up for a moment. Attempted to gather thought for a new course of action, but before she could figure out what thought could accomplish over brawn, she was freed of her trap.

An arrow cut through the air and broke the webbing. Confusion ran through her mind, but years of training allowed Dawn to maintain enough focus to adjust her body so she didn't land head first on the ground.

The forest spun around Dawn. The webbing fell lose enough she could tear it off her person. Now at her feet, she swayed from the head rush from standing up too quickly.

With the rub of her temples, Dawn was able to still the forest. Hard pressed eyes helped to steady the mind. A deep breath helped to steady it further.

She tried to look around for whoever had freed her but her eyes may as well have been none existent.

"Oh," Dawn danced on her tiptoes for a moment. "Really could use a flashlight right now."

A twig snapped.

Dawn turned towards it. Before her eyes could find the intruder, she felt a cold pierce her right chest just below her collarbone. A sharp pain followed.

The arrow was deep, but somehow missed anything important. Before Dawn could either take in the relief of that, or look upwards for her attacker, another arrow hit her.

This time in her left bicep. Steps of something large, but swift, pounded with such might that Dawn shook along with each of its steps.

She looked up in time to catch the butt of a bow in her chin. The force lifted Dawn off her feet. She toppled backwards.

She rolled down hill. Toppled over roots. Cracked her body against the mighty bumps. Her journey ended as her back collided with a root raised out of the ground.

Air was forced out her lungs. As she panicked to fill them, more steps came.

Dawn looked up in time to see a large beast with a jagged blade. Still breathless, Dawn rose and swung.

* * *

Asa woke up. Her body fatigued from the enormous amount of power that had escaped her body. While her brown eyes rolled around the back of her skull, Asa felt a strange chill all over her body.

Similar to how each girl had discovered the warmth of their soul, Asa was now discovering that she had always had energy flowing through her entire being; with her reserves on empty, everything felt hollow.

Her hands were ice cold. She ran them all over her body but with the lack of energy, she found them to be clumsy. She typically ran hot, but it seemed that had been a part of the devastating power that flowed within. Now that she had drained that power, Asa felt frozen.

"Hey," Chika gave a sarcastic grin. Wrists cuffed together she sat against a tree trunk to Asa's left. "Asa's awake."

Asa blinked at the strange sight of Chika's restraints, then she noticed her own. It explained why her dexterity was so clumsy. "Shit."

"Yup." Mei Ling watched the girls that had captured them. They grouped around a campfire; three on their feet, three laid on their backs.

The women looked almost human, save fox ears out the top of their heads and tails from their spines. Two of the ones awake had two tails, while one of them, five.

Her words were more serious than normal, "I think they're Kitsune." Her eyes looked on the woman she believed to be the leader, the five tailed one.

"Great," Asa closed her eyes. She attempted to rub gunk from them but the restraints made it too awkward to continue. "We show up for help and the cavalry wants to put us in the dirt."

"Doubt that," Mei Ling rolled her neck over to Asa. It ached, a lot. Nothing seemed to get the soreness out. "We were all out for quite awhile. They could have easily ended us then."

"Maybe we're prisoners." Chika spoke funny. It caused both girls to look in her direction.

Chika had her tongue shoved into her right cheek. It pressed against her wound and ran along the cut from the inside. Chika couldn't help it, as it was the only thing relieving her from the pain.

Then it dawned on Asa, as her hands fell to her jeans, they had been de-armoured! She looked around for Nither, but couldn't find him anywhere.

Chika's words were soft as she continued. Attempting to keep her words hidden from her captives. "They didn't find Dawn. Maybe they think we're bargaining chips."

"Great. We're relying on a cripple," Mei Ling hung her head. The pain spiked. She quickly brought her head back up followed by a groan. "Ugh! My freakin neck."

Her raised voice didn't go unnoticed. The leader turned her attention to the three girls. Walked over to Mei ling.

Mei Ling tried to stay still, to show she wasn't intimidated, but it was a lie. For every centimetre the woman took, Mei Ling shifted a millimetre away.

The woman noticed Mei Ling's quaking eyes. She whispered softly to Mei Ling in a strange language, which Mei Ling understood, though she wasn't sure how.

"You're injured." The woman placed her hand on the base of Mei Ling's neck. A thick cream was spread over the injury. Mei Ling didn't bother questioning the good faith as the relief to her pain was amazing.

A grin crossed Mei Ling's face as she began rolling her neck, enjoying the freedom of normality.

"Oh, my God. Yes," Mei Ling closed her eyes to forget the pain. "You definitely have the touch."

The woman laughed. "So why don't you tell me who you three are and why you've hospitalized my people before I slit your throats." Her firm massage turned into a death grip on the back of Mei Ling's neck.

Yellow painted claws clasped so tightly that Mei Ling was positive they were teetering just before full penetration.

Mei Ling squirmed. Panic overtook as her thyroid pulsed against the woman's ring finger.

"Whoa!" Asa lunged forward, but fell back on her butt. She hadn't noticed she had been tied at the waist to the trunk of the tree. "We're knights, of the Echo Army. We are here to meet the Kitsune because we need help."

Asa wasn't sure if she was surprised or disappointed with how quickly she spilled the beans.

The woman looked over her shoulder, to her allies; they shared a moment of disbelief. Then she turned back to Asa "So, it's time for our cold war to heat up a little?"

"What the..." Asa shook her head. "I don't understand a damn word you're saying. Just.... please... let go of Mei Ling."

The woman removed her hand. Cleared her mind then spoke perfect English. "We'll take you to our camp." She felt it would be redundant to repeat her original piece.

"Really?" Chika went wide eyed. "Just like that?"

"Dude," Asa stood once her binding had been cut. "I'm just stoked that we aren't getting gutted."

"Throats slit." Mei Ling rose once free. She glared at the woman during her ascent. "She threatened to cut our throats."

Chika grabbed her neck as she silently repeated the words to herself.

"Awesome," Asa gave a defeated grin.

"My name is Mad Dog," The woman spoke. "I'll take you to our home."

"You trust us, just like that?" Mei Ling's eyes were tight with distrust while her lips rubbed together in disbelief.

"No," Mad Dog's smile revealed her teeth. It unintentionally came off more eerie than friendly. "I don't believe you are what you say you are. Pretending to be mythical warriors. But your Valkyrie is depleted of her powers. I think we'll be fine."

"We also got these guys," Ginseng spoke up from the fire pit. She hadn't bothered to unbind the girls. In her hand she held up a blue stone. Strange electricity of various colours laced around silver plates.

The girls went wide eyed. Inside the lightning prison were their Lights. Esh, Nither, Flee and Ozazi all bound in a prison. Their orbs colourless...

"Are they—did you!" Mei Ling instinctively took a step towards Mad Dog.

A smile simply met Mei Ling's attempt at intimidation. Mad Dog shook her head slowly. "They are fine. Once your magic drained, these fell out. I assume they're devices to weave armour. Another reason we trust you: we have these. We'll take good care of them until we figure things out."

"Thanks," Chika glared.

"How do you know what I am?" Asa raised an eyebrow.

"I'd like to know how you know English," Mei Ling looked back and forth from each party. Chika and Asa were confused, as Mei Ling still spoke Kitsune. "And how do I know this language?"

"Many Kitsune study languages. That's how you know our language," Mad Dog then turned to wave over her injured, "and that's how I know she is a Valkyrie. At the very least, an Angel."

CHAPTER THIRTEEN: WHITTLED NOVEL

Black clouds began pulling themselves apart, so that silver light could penetrate the thinner areas of the forest and reach its floor. The rays had the tint of moonlight but intensity of a sun. The rays gave a strange wave effect from rattling branches. Enough light to see small details of objects ahead, and if close enough, even facial features.

Several hours into the knights and their captors walk, they came to a part of the forest that had been purposely thinned. Jaws dropped as the moon revealed itself. A tri-ring of silver light burned, too bright to stare at.

The Kitsune village came into view. Logs ran upright, bound by large ropes and snug too tight side-by-side so that no light escaped. The wall ran the full length of the village, and seemed to disappear into the woods on either side. Two large doors rested in the centre, with a pulley system designed to lift things up and over the wall.

The village had grown awkwardly over the years. The wall had to be built up, over, and around various large roots. Most of the inside of the village was bare of the mighty roots but a few crept in from the edges.

A heart didn't beat before the girls had bows drawn on them. A few warriors leapt over the wall to rush to the wounded. Several more behind them, taking positions to aim into the darkness.

A warrior each took the girls by the back of their clothes, and ignoring the village gates, the group jumped over the wall. The injured followed, being held by two warriors each.

On landing, Mei Ling couldn't help but ask, "Why even have a door?"

Mad Dog shrugged. "I'm not an architect. How would I know?"

"Good point." Mei Ling looked over her shoulders to Asa, so they could exchange shrugs.

"Not really," Chika kept her voice low, mostly to herself. Her eyes glared at the prison Ginseng held.

Weeds and flowers littered the soil of the village. Most houses were single story but a few grew taller. A large white building tucked itself in the back. A stone dome took up the centre of the village.

Much like humans, the Kitsune ranged in all walks of life. Different haircuts, clothes, and races. The women wore long sleeves down to their wrists, with skirts, dresses or leggings that didn't dip lower than the knee cap. Men had their legs covered, with their sleeves rolled up to their elbows; the elderly to their wrists. Each Kitsune held a different set of tails; the children lacked any, those that looked to be teenagers held one, and the number of tails went up from there, each tail representing a century of life.

The girls each gave uneasy waves to greet the curious crowd that had gathered. Most Kitsune were still and unsure what was appropriate. Only the odd child returned the gesture.

Eyes stayed on the knights as the crowd parted to let in an elder of the tribe, the only one amongst the entire village to hold nine tails. She chanted and waved her hand to bless each injured warrior before they were taken off to be tended to.

Once the injured were removed, she gracefully walked to the girls. "And who are these?" The woman spoke English. She offered the question as a friendly gesture more than a necessity. It was easy to tell the three didn't belong amongst their ranks.

"They claim to be a part of the Echo Army." Mad Dog jerked a thumb to the girls. "Either they're telling the truth or the Dragonborn figured out how to forge Dragon scales."

"Yes," the woman spoke softly but powerfully. Her eyes danced over Mei Ling, then the other two. A swirl of thought muddled into daydreams of the events of the past few days in each girl's mind. "They're telling the truth."

"How do—" Mei Ling began.

"They need to travel to the Bridge." She watched Mei Ling's reaction. Curled a smile when she confirmed her assumption. "The Kitsune may study with me. Take the Valkyrie and Dragonborn to the barracks. Also, return their Lights."

"Why?" Mad Dog raised an eyebrow, the question out of confusion, and held no disrespect.

Ginseng powered down the prison. The Lights each sprung to life.

Flea swung over Mei Ling's shoulder. Mei Ling extended a fist, which Flea vied his entire body to return the gesture.

"Hello, Chika," Esh flew into Chika's extended fingertips. She cradled him down next to her. "It's good to see you. A pleasure. Great. Amazing. Joyful!" He continued for some time...

Nither fell into Asa's in his rabbit form. "Hey, buddy," Asa gave him an extra tight squeeze.

Ozazi looked puzzled.

"They have a friend they left out in the woods. Take them and teach them what you can, so they don't die when they reach their destination." The elder pointed for Ozazi.

Following instruction, Ozazi joined Asa and Chika. He swayed about as he leaned towards them, "You two will have to fill me in."

"Yeah, for sure," Asa hugged Nither.

The Elder took Mei Ling's hand. "I knew you, sister. In your past life, and in one of my many. Come."

"Uh… okay?" Mei Ling looked at the other two. "How did you know that we had a friend missing?"

"Better question, why didn't you tell us when we were around her location?" Mad Dog seemed more irritated than curious.

"Uh," Asa shifted her weight, as she got the dagger eyes from Mad Dog.

"We didn't tell you because," Mei Ling gave an awkward grin, "we kind of thought—"

"We thought you might slit our throats," Chika folded her arms. "We don't trust you."

"Didn't," Asa corrected. "We do now."

"Whatever," Chika rolled her eyes.

"Hey," Mei Ling glared at Chika. "Stop being an ass."

Chika opened her mouth for a response, but stopped herself.

"It's fine. We understand," The elder woman gestured to Mad Dog with a wave of the hand.

"Yup." Mad Dog lead Asa and Chika to the white building. "She's going to be hard to find if she's on the move."

"Mei Ling," The woman brought Mei Ling back to facing her.

Mei Ling raised an eyebrow. "How did you know my name?"

"I can read thoughts," The woman removed her hand from Mei Ling to wave her fingers in view. "From a distance it's more foggy. Leaves a sensation of daydreaming on the target. But with touch I can find everything that I need in a moment and without a trace of my mind to theirs."

"Rude," Mei Ling ran her hand forward and back along her bunny hug to 'clean' it.

"Excuse the intrusion, but it's the quickest way to isolate what you know, what you don't know and what you think you know about Distance." The woman smiled. "You're smart, even by our standards. I can see why you were chosen to aid the Echo. However, your means of weaving Distance is crude, but we can correct this."

"Sure." Mei Ling was dragged by the woman in the direction of the dome. "Just…" she freed herself, "stop reading my mind. It's creepy."

"Ah," The woman nodded. "It seems mankind has taught you to fear the intimacy of the mind."

"Yes," Mei Ling trailed a safe distance. "Yes it did."

"Perhaps by the end of the day we can correct this, too." The woman paused her steps a moment to turn back to Mei Ling. "My name is Verga."

"Nice to meet you, Verga, I'm Mei Ling," Mei Ling tried to offer a smile. "I would offer to shake your hand, but I'm afraid you'd mentally molest me again."

Verga frowned.

"Hey, so," Mei Ling matched pace with Verga. "I was wondering, after you teach me how to fling us through time and space… could we maybe borrow a few warriors? Could use them."

"No." Verga shook her head. "This is your war, not ours."

"What?" Mei Ling swung her arms out. "But if we can't stop the Dragon—"

Verga stopped. Her glare tightened onto Mei Ling. Her words were low and powerful. "If you fail, and I believe that you will, I will disconnect Eden from the Garden. Bits of Distance cling between the Garden and the River. No such thing connects us to the River. Once we shatter the sun mirror, the Dragon can not reach us."

*   *   *

The interior of the stone dome was laced with trees tangled with one another. They grew upwards in hopes of reaching the sunlight that came from the series of small openings above. Knee high grass made up the flooring. It was lush, even the parts void of sunlight.

In the centre was a stone fountain, raised a couple of metres off the ground by a hexagon stone foundation, made up of many steps that split in every direction. At each point in the hexagon, a pillar raised; thin and tall, they reached a few metres before vines escaped from within the poles, via their tops, to give the fountain a ceiling.

The fountain had small spouts of water that danced in a rhythm. In its centre, an arched tree with hundreds of thin branches. Every leaf in all stages of life; patches of green, orange, yellow, red, and brown. No sign of any fallen leaves.

"Tell me, Mei Ling." Verga crouched so she could run her hand along the tips of the grass. "Has your species finished their studies on quantum physics?"

"Nope," Mei Ling spun around to take in the sight. "Pretty cool, eh Flea?"

"Yes." Flea swung low and closer to her. "I have memories of this place, though it was much different."

"Yeah?" Mei Ling stomped around the grass a moment. "Did they use to have a lawn mower?"

Verga ignored the two's private conversation. "Do you know about calculus? Have you learned this yet?"

"What? Yes." Mei Ling's face twisted, but quickly corrected itself. "When I was three. I taught myself."

"I see." Verga hummed between her sentences. "Are you sure? Have you been taught anything in your life? Did you actually have to bother teaching yourself?"

"I've known everything my whole life. I guess, I 'tried' math when I was three and just knew it." Mei Ling scratched the base of her neck while she ran through various memories. "Well, actually I needed guitar lessons."

Verga stopped as she straightened her spine and twisted to face Mei Ling. "What is a ... guitar?"

"It's a musical instrument." Mei Ling felt her smile reach her ears while the pitch in her voice increased. "Traditionally wooden. A string instrument with a hollowed base. The strings run from the base and up the neck—like a shaft. You strum the strings with your fingers or a small object called a pick." Mei Ling played her air guitar as she gave the explanation.

Verga eyed the fountain's tree. "Interesting." She then returned her gaze to Mei Ling. "We don't have instruments here. Music, when enjoyed loudly, attracts the shadows of the forest. We simply hum."

"That sounds horrible." Mei Ling dropped her imaginary guitar. "Makes sense, but sucks."

"Yes." Verga smiled. "But we do what we must."

"I have a question," Mei Ling danced on the thought a moment. "How come I can understand you? How come you can understand me? How do you know our words for things but don't know what they are?"

"Did you ever wonder why every language has certain patterns? Every one of them has vowels and consonants. We just need a reference; the armour does the rest." Verga pointed towards Flea. "You understand me now because you have the knowledge of a past life. I understand you but I once wore the armor, and its magic still flows through my veins, even if only a little. The magic itself corrects our language so that we make sense to one another, but we don't. You see my mouth flapping along with English words, but it isn't. When I speak English, the magic is changing our thoughts. We think we are hearing and seeing a language that we know, but we aren't."

"The fuck?" Mei Ling cocked a brow to Flea.

Verga pointed to the tree. "Do you know why you're so smart, Mei Ling?"

Mei Ling shrugged. "Good genes?"

"Yes." Verga laughed. "The Kitsune are wise. Your spirit is that of our people. Like I said, some of its knowledge has seeped into the shell of your body."

"I figured they were related." Mei Ling eyed the tree. Her narrowed eyes studied its white bark that almost looked plastic. "Don't tell me. We're smart from eating apples?"

"Apples?" Verga simply smiled.

The two walked up the steps to the base of the tree. Here, Verga reached under a lump of leaves to fish around. A moment and she removed her hand, grasping a rectangle fruit with smooth edges, red in colour with grey thin stripes.

Verga bit into the fruit. As she chewed her eyes rolled back, heart raced, and skin flushed. After swallowing, her eyes glowed blinding white for a moment.

"Here." Verga handed the fruit to Mei Ling. "Focus your thought on portals. The fruit will do the rest."

"Okay." Mei Ling shrugged. "What the hell, right?"

The world unwove into golden threads as Mei Ling bit into the fruit. From the depths of nothing came strings of black and grey to weave her armour. Before thought could manifest, a warmth overwhelmed her entire body; gravity jolted from behind, the pull so intense her bones rattled violently.

She fell forward to her knees as years of study crammed itself into the back of her skull. It burnt as the cells in her mind were rewritten with this new information. Blood trickled down her nose as tears flowed from her eyes.

Her limbs buckled as her mind went blank. Mei Ling's entire body flared from the surge of energy poured into her being. Then it collapsed to the ground.

*   *   *

The barracks stretched across half the village and towered over any other structure. Chika was wide eyed in amazement as she took in the incredible architecture. The floor and walls were carved out of a single mould of white marble. Try as she might, she couldn't find a seam.

The ceiling from inside was a series of logs. On the outside—Chika paused as she realized she hadn't even looked to see what it was.

"Is the ceiling tiled?" Chika asked Asa.

"Huh?" Asa cocked an eyebrow. She had been busy admiring the wooden shelves that lined the entire east wall displaying weapons of all varieties. Ladders, like those found in old libraries, ran along the shelves to allow Kitsune to travel up and down them.

"The ceiling... ugh, roof." Chika jerked her head skyward. "I didn't catch if it was tile or just wood." She looked to see the ceiling painted white. *Is that tile or wood or...* She squinted.

"I honestly was too busy watching six metre tall marble doors being cranked open to care." Asa's words trailed near the end of her sentence. Her eyes were transfixed on warriors drilling.

"Hmp." Chika folded her arms as she twisted her lips and rolled her eyes. In doing so, something caught her eye and she stilled her legs.

She let Asa walk ahead, as her attention eyed the warriors suiting up. Each was at the peak of physical condition. Muscular, yet agile, and many had the scars to show their years of service.

Asa continued along. Her eyes darted to catch the different exercises at play. Close quarters grapples, disarming weapons, acrobatics, among others.

She stopped when she reached Mad Dog, who stood among three others. Asa noticed the other three had simple loops of string running from their wrist to their middle finger where Mad Dog, like Asa and her friends, had a spade connecting the two.

Mad Dog looked over her shoulder to smile at Asa's curiosity. "Our ranks are displayed by our hands. If I'm familiar with your Earth terms these are Privates. You're a Lieutenant?"

"Sweet." Even without her armour, Asa ran her hands together as she took a moment to take in what the spades represented. Suddenly, Asa realized she only knew one thing about the military, which was thanks to Hollywood. "How do we salute?"

"Like so." Mad Dog placed her extended index and middle finger over her pulse in her neck. "Like this."

"Looks like you're checking your pulse." Asa mimicked it.

"That's because we are." One of the three spoke. She was blonde, pale, tall, and had broad shoulders. The girl had been amongst those that brought them in, Ginseng. Asa envied her reach. "If you're alive, you can take another order." She saluted Asa.

"Intense." Asa smiled, saluted to relieve the Kitsune. "My name is Asa Larson... ugh, Lt. Larson?"

"We call it Lacus." Mad Dog corrected, then jerked a thumb to the trio. "They're Brachium. We also don't address ourselves by rank. Just because your job is to make sure somebody else is doing theirs doesn't make you any more important."

"I'll do my best to remember that." Asa grinned. "I want to do my best to respect your—our culture, but I'll admit that I'm no linguist."

"It's fine." Ginseng smirked while she gave the brunette to her left a friendly jab of her elbow. "Guarana here can't speak any English and she's like four hundred years old." She then translated herself to mock Guarana, who replied with a glare. "Sometimes the magic doesn't connect right to the brain. Our armour isn't the same as yours, as it has limitations to how much it can take control. We can hardly jump a few metres. Heard you can do much more than that. Still amplifies our powers, but not as much as yours."

"It was harder to use our power here," Asa pointed out.

"The atmosphere is lacking magic. When the Womb was moved away from Eden the planets spirit was never replaced. Our world is dying, but we get by," Mad Dog made sure to point out.

"The Womb?" Asa raised a brow.

"The collective of Atoms of God. Where a human soul goes when it dies," Mad Dog smiled.

Guarana saluted Asa as she spoke in Kitsune. Mad Dog translated for Asa. "She says she heard you can manipulate lightning. She's very excited to fight by you."

"Thanks." Asa took in the entire group. They each wore the same orange and yellow as she did. "We're all Earth elements?"

"Yes." Mad Dog nodded. "But we can't all do what you do. Each element has many potential abilities."

Mad Dog pointed. "Guarana," Guarana had flat brown hair, was slim and short, with dark skin. "Can manipulate fine dusts and sands."

Mad Dog pointed to the Ginseng. "Ginseng can weave smoke."

Mad Dog pointed to the third. Who was dark skinned, had shoulder length hair, and held a build that mirrored Asa. "Taurine can move rock."

"And you?" Asa asked while she finished saluting Taurine.

"I make big things fall down." Mad Dog grinned, as did the others.

"Sorry. Got... distracted." Chika's eyes still trailed a moment while she joined the group; her eyes were quick to dart across each grin. "What'd I miss?"

"Nothing." Asa saluted Chika. "This is how they salute. Pretty cool, eh?"

Chika mimicked it. "At ease, soldier." The two shared their first laugh together.

Mad Dog cocked an eyebrow to her trio. "Alright ladies. Let's get to it." Mad Dog tossed both Asa and Chika a spear.

Asa and Chika exchanged looks. The weapons weren't anything special. Wood shaft, with a stone tip. Basic.

"We are actually using these?" Chika held the object as if it was fragile. At any moment she was afraid it would fall apart. "I'm a living flame-thrower and Asa is—fricken awesome."

"I am," Asa ran her hand under her upwards tilted chin.

"I bet." Ginseng chimed in.

"You're a living moron," Mad Dog turned to the door with the trio on her heels.

"Hey!" Chika tightened her eyes as she took a step forward. Asa put out an arm to ground her.

"We are in a forest," Mad Dog rolled her eyes, "and you want to start fires."

"Oh…" Chika let her eyes fall, as she reflected on the events earlier in the dark. "Oops."

"Oops." Asa laughed as she punched Chika in the arm. "I'm still awesome though." Lifted up her spear. "So you can use mine too."

"I. Hate. Your. Soul." Chika pushed past the spear.

Asa was left hanging. "Ah, come on, Chika." She couldn't stop laughing.

"So," Ginseng eyed up the girls, "you have interesting choices in battle gear."

"Do you not have any armour?" Mad Dog gestured towards the warriors changing. "We should get you some, before we leave."

"Nah," Asa tossed her spear to Ginseng. The rest starred as Asa closed her eyes, took in a deep breath, found that warmth inside. Electricity sparked along her body as orange and yellow threads reached outwards from Nither to weave her armour. "I'm good," Asa grabbed the spear from Ginseng.

"Wow." Ginseng was wide eyed; the other's jaws dropped.

"What?" Asa smirked.

"We've never seen someone transform before," Ginseng turned to Mad Dog. "Guess they are who they say they are."

"Yeah…" Mad Dog frowned.

"Wait. What." Chika stepped in. "Didn't you suspect something was amiss when our armour vanished on its own?"

"No." Ginseng played with the material of Asa's armour, testing if it felt the same. "We put our armour on like clothes. They aren't as powerful but still, our armour falls apart when we die or are knocked unconscious. To prevent someone studying it. We assumed they were the same."

Gaundra spoke, Mad Dog translated. "Why aren't you transforming?"

"I uh," Chika flushed. "I'm not in the mood."

"You're not in the mood?" Ginseng raised a brow.

"I'm just tired, that's all." Chika folded her arms.

With empty reserves of magic, Chika was given Kitsune armour. Once Chika was geared up, they grouped up outside.

Mad Dog spoke to the squad, "Typically we travel in groups of six. No chatting to draw attention to ourselves. If she is an Angel, she has likely freed herself by now. Because we need to call out to find Dawn, we have planned to meet up with another group. Once we do, we will begin to search."

"Question," Chika put up her hand as if in class. "What exactly is out there? We saw spiders, sure, but we handled it." Esh nodded while floating over her shoulder.

"I'd like to know as well," Ozazi nodded. "I believe I am feeling… concerned, for Dawn's well being."

"Yeah." Asa nervously fidgeted at the reminder. "Isn't this place supposed to be all heavenly? Why is it so… spooky?"

"Spooky?" Ginseng raised an eyebrow.

"Yeah. Way to put it mildly." Mad Dog shook her head. "This was a great place before the Dragon poisoned it. Kitsune were caretakers to the Atoms of God. Angels were the caretakers of the land. When they left, we fell behind. It's hell out there.

Heaven doesn't exist. Not here. Not for Kitsune or Dragonborn." Mad Dog turned to Asa. "We reincarnate at best. Angels have no afterlife. You'd be best to remember that."

"Sure," Asa shifted her weight while she ran her hand over her arm

The squad pushed ahead to the entrance of the village. In the woods, Chika and Asa trailed. Watched and mimicked.

*　　*　　*

Hours passed. Judging by her sore calves and ankles, Chika assumed it had been at least five hours but it had only been about three. Walking up and over the roots the entire journey had been a chore but not the cause of the pain. It was the longest amount of time Chika had stayed in armour and she still hadn't had the best rest in the world, although pride wouldn't allow herself to admit to the others.

Their armour didn't have full access to the knight power. Without the connection to the Echo, they were less durable and couldn't jump great distances. Chika could feel the suit behaving more like it was drawing from a depleting battery rather than drawing from a direct power source. The fire she wove at camp, to test the armour, was limited and felt foreign. Even though it was a cheap imitation, it still strained her body.

Without relying on their magical jumps, the heels were impractical for long distance. While Chika wondered why the Kitsune bothered to use heels in the first place, Asa was busy studying Ginseng.

Her form was perfect. Every movement felt deliberate, yet effortless. The others were just as well trained, but something about Ginseng caught Asa's eye. She had presence of cockiness that Asa admired.

Mad Dog's hand raised in a split V. The squad halted. Asa and Chika, a pace later, with Ozazi and Esh swooping low to hide. Chika looked from Asa back to Mad Dog in confusion. Asa tightened her eyes ahead.

Mad Dog had been leading the entire way without concern. Now she demanded a halt, *why?*

Her hand pointed twice to the right, the first time using index and middle finger the second included her ring finger. Taurine and Guarana went right. Mad Dog then pointed left once using every finger then went in that direction. Ginseng turned to the girls. Signaled for them to stay. Then she joined Mad Dog's direction.

Chika swore the only sound in the forest in that moment was her own breath. Her heart raced and soon she swore she could hear that as well. Without her real armour she was just a child in the dark. She prayed for her armour, even if it's connection was limited by the strange planet's atmosphere.

Asa felt more relaxed as her eyes attempted to see through the darkness to catch a hint of the Kitsune. Something pulled at Asa, a feeling of clairvoyance so true she acted without having to be told.

"Asa!" Ginseng called, but Asa had already woven a lightning bolt into the air.

The beast was deer-like but its mouth and eyes were in its chest cavity. Antlers protruding from its shoulder blades, looped and knotted with crimson tips. It's midnight purple skin singed black from the lightning.

The half tonne beast fell in front of Chika. Her shriek was not ignored by the squad, as they emerged from the forest. They didn't bother attempting to hide their laughter.

Ginseng punched Asa's arm in jest to mimic the Earth gesture she had witnessed earlier. "Perfect. Didn't expect anything less."

"Thanks." Asa shifted her weight.

"Not bad." Ginseng turned over the deer. "We call it a Tep. They have an organ about the size of your head that produces sugar. It's insanity." She drove a dagger into the breast of the beast.

"The rest tastes like ass," Mad Dog smiled at Asa. "We don't eat em. Poison the body and hope something big and nasty eats it."

"I have heard it is delicious." Ozazi piped in.

"Tasty. Delectable. Yummy," Esh hummed along.

The Kitsune shared looks of annoyance for Esh's ongoings. Chika smiled towards Esh, "Zestful." She successfully silenced his ramble with a shared laugh.

Mad Dog held up a red organ. It was a sphere with laced indents and thousands of tiny bumps throughout. The still-beating basketball shaped organ oozed around her fingers. "The organ produces sugar that they excrete through their hooves. They'll find a predator trail and connect it to another. Letting them kill each other, or at least come back to clean up whatever there is for leftovers."

She tossed it to Taurine who began to slice up pieces for everyone.

"You need to eat it raw." Mad Dog licked the blood off her finger tips.

"No wonder they call you Mad Dog," Chika was disguised by the entire display.

"Call me, what?" Mad Dog cocked an eyebrow. Her confused look was exchanged with her trio.

"Mad Dog. In English it means a crazy or angry animal. Dogs are like little hairy things." Asa tried to explain, but failed.

"Oh." Mad Dog rose. "My name isn't Mad, Dog. It's Maauhd Auhg. You're not saying it right."

"Oh." Chika blushed. "Sorry."

"It's fine." Maauhd Auhg leaned her back on a tree, smirked to her team. "Kind of cool though."

"Hey! What's my name mean?" Ginseng grinned.

"No idea." Asa shrugged. "Chika, you're Japanese. Help me out here."

"What?" Chika jerked to Asa. "It's not Japanese, racist."

Slices were passed around. Asa stared down at what looked to be a ten ounce slice of raw steak with white sugar crystal oozing from the blood; her heart sank just about as deep as her teeth.

The texture was loose like raw meat, but fell apart like a juicy melon. As Asa chewed, she could feel the sugar crystals grind across her teeth. The sweet treat tasted like an explosive mixture of watermelon and strawberry.

It wiggled all the way down.

"Ah," Chika watched Asa's reaction. The strange dance as she swallowed the meat made Chika distance herself from the bonding moment. "No."

She tossed the meat back to Ginseng. "I'm good," Chika ran the back and front of her hand over the grass. Her attempt to remove all the juices was in vain.

"Seriously?" Ginseng raised an eyebrow, followed up with a shrug, just before taking it all in one bite. Her full mouth sprayed as she attempted to multitask eating with speaking. "Your loss."

"Nope." Chika stood back up. "It's really not."

"You should have tried it." Asa licked her fingers. "Pretty good."

Chika shook her head. "Nope." Played with her sticky fingers by pressing them together then stretching them apart.

"I do not blame you," Esh whispered into Chika's ear. "I've never been fond of sweets, myself."

Guarana fixed the Tep into a trap. She poured a vial of poison into the chest cavity where the organ had once been. She then propped the beast up into a sleeping position.

"Won't fool anything with a decent I.Q." Maauhd Auhg patted Guarana on the back.

"Yeah. But those aren't what we're after, right?" Asa did her best to fit into the group. She attempted to mimic their posture. "Big, dumb, and ugly."

"Exactly." Maauhd Auhg ignored Asa's awkward pose. "Let's continue finding Dawn."

*   *   *

"*Fuck!*" Dawn grasped her cast. Teeth grinded and back arched as her forearm was shattered once again. She swore uncontrollably out of her lock jaw.

Dawn stumbled back two strides before buckling under the pain. Collapsed over bent knees. Everything was at a standstill.

Reality meant nothing. The only thing Dawn had mental capacity to spare for was the throbbing that ran up her arm and through her entire body. Whatever had been left of her bone felt as if it had just been crushed into a fine dust.

Though wincing, Dawn managed to finally look up at the assaulter. The creature had been pushed back about a foot, which was unimpressive for the Angel, considering she could Hail Mary a sedan.

The beast stood hunched with muscles so large for its frame its spine couldn't straighten, which looked as if it would collapse in on itself at any moment. A mixture of jet black and ash grey feathers covered its entire body. A long, dry, black beak covered in white slashes and chips from years of struggle. The only thing not horrifying about the creature were the brown human like eyes.

In its hands, the creature held a twelve foot long bow. Thanks to a decade of practice, the bow was perfectly hand crafted. Both its hood and quiver made from a leather crafted from a creature that Dawn didn't recognize.

"What are you?" Dawn's jaw quaked as her teeth cut into each other. Still fighting the pain, Dawn found it difficult to speak. Her green eyes studied the beast, but it was difficult to tell its expression without seeing its face muscles or lips, but through his eyes, Dawn believed it to be astonished by her might.

The truth couldn't have been further from Dawn's guess. The Tengu was captivated by the softness of her voice, a beauty his battleborn ears had never witnessed. Years of isolation left him only to imagine what a Kitsune's voice may have sounded like.

Tengus had the ability to mimic any voice they heard. Kitsune warriors were trained to keep their voices low when in Tengu territory to avoid giving them something to replicate and trap future Kitsune. This had left the young Tengu with no concept of their voices, and it was much more beautiful than anything he had imagined. Due to the Kitsune ferocity in combat, the Tengu had imagined the voice to be more stern and deeper.

The Tengu brushed a tear from his eye with his elbow; never letting go of his weapon.

"Where are your tails?" The Tengu spoke in the first language as he relaxed his grip on his bow. His voice was a distorted echo of itself. "Were they removed? You couldn't possible be—I've never seen a child outside the wall."

"I'm no Kitsune." Dawn hissed as she tucked her left arm into her right arm pit. With tight eyes and trembling legs, Dawn attempted to stand.

The pain was too great, and Dawn fell forward. With two mighty strides, the Tengu was able to catch Dawn's limp body. He gently brought her to the soft soil. Turned her over and studied the wound.

Dawn's eyes rolled up into the back of her skull as the world blurred into darkness.

*　　*　　*

A beast swooped through the air. A humanoid with reversed knees, gigantic hands and arms covered in muscle. Its face eyeless, wrinkled, and pulled back like that of a bat's. A chilling scream, designed for echolocation, had warned Chika and Asa. The girls leapt to the side. The beast's large wings were not agile enough to turn towards them.

It ran into the boulder next to them, its rib cage taking the brunt of the blow as it had attempted to redirect mid air, but failed. With its mighty claws, the beast relieved its frustration by crushing the boulder.

Asa's eyes were wide and her jaw low. "Holy shit." Electricity danced along her finger tips.

Chika brought up her spear, but Maauhd Auhg's hand gently lowered it. Maauhd Auhg had a grin as she walked towards the beast.

"I'll put this guy down." Maauhd Auhg ran her left hand over her balled right. Sparks ignited and a white hot light engulfed her right hand.

Maauhd Auhg swiped her left hand to straighten the lightning into a blade. Hums and crackles came to the jagged blade as she held the bolt of lightning like a sword.

She twirled the sword to bring the blade behind her person before rushing forward into a charge. Brought the blade upwards to meet the beast.

The beast tried to block the blade. Maauhd Auhg poured her shoulder into the shove. The beast stumbled and she brought the sword around. Leapt forward to catch up to its back pedal. Split the beast in half as both his arms couldn't come up quick enough.

The trees rustled and soon many more were upon the group. Maauhd Auhg fell to her knee as she finished the original beast. Looked up to the oncoming traffic with a grin.

The next beast came while she was still crouched. Maauhd Auhg stood up, tilted her body so it became thinner to dodge a claw. On her way up, she had swung the sword in an arc to cut the beast clean in half. Hip to hip.

Still in motion, Maauhd Auhg spun with her momentum into a low run. Three were on her in a group, so close their shoulders pushed together. Their claws reached and their jaws snapped.

Maauhd Auhg ran to her left as they came down. She aimed her sword to the sky. It took out the right arm of one beast and the left of another. She punched the third beast with her sword hand. It fell to its knees and grabbed its broken nose. Maauhd Auhg spun around cutting through the beast's hands and skull.

Mid spin, to her surprise, Maauhd Auhg caught another beast that she had not seen. The blade ran clean through its chest cavity.

This confusion caused Maauhd Auhg to take a breath to regain her bearings. Stopped her legs and darted her eyes. A pack of beasts were skyward. They did not dive on the first fly by. Betting they'd come down on their second fly by, Maauhd Auhg readjusted herself to face where the beasts would appear between the trees.

She condensed a large amount of energy into her left arm.

The energy exploded and Maauhd Auhg road the blast into the air. Soared over the group of girls, who were dispatching the two disarmed beasts.

With jaws slack in disbelief of Maauhd Auhg's speed and ferocity, Asa and Chika arched their vision to follow her ascent.

The beasts did come back around. As Maauhd Auhg road the blast she noticed these were of a slightly different species. Their eyes honed in on her. She grinned as a thought crossed her mind.

Maauhd Auhg turned her body so she flew horizontally over the head of a diving beast. Split her free hand's fingers to bore her digits into the eye sockets of the creature.

The beast howled in its high pitch bat scream as the heat of her hand cauterized its face around her fist.

Drove her blade into the side of a tree, twisted in the air to plant her heels into the bark, so she now stood horizontally, facing the ground.

Still holding the creature's skull, she swung her hand back so violently it snapped its neck, ending its howling. Brought her hand back around to bat away a beast dive bombing her.

She brought the beast back again with more ruthlessness as the cauterized wound tore free from her grip. On release, the beast flew across the sky into another, causing it to spin out of control to connect with another, grounding them both.

The two beasts fell to the ground, to be met by Ginseng and Guarana. Ginseng punched her fist through one's snarling jaw, opened her palm in its throat. Poured smoke into the beast until its lungs filled. Trails of smoke escaped its nostrils. Ginseng let it fall.

Guarana had her hands to her side as she ran. She brought them up to weave thick streams of sand from the forest floor. Clapped her hands over the beast's ears. The sand drilled through his ear drums and buried deep into its brain. The beast convulsed as she let go.

Maauhd Auhg, still up high, turned her attention to more beasts. Leapt towards one. Brought her sword up its chest cavity and out of its rib cage.

As it fell, she roundhouse kicked another beast in its temple. Her heel pierced the soft skin, blood streamed through the air, as the beast lost its sense of flight, and fell.

Taurine waited below with two floating stones to crush the beast's skull.

A beast dove at the airborne Maauhd Auhg. She reached out and grabbed it by the snout, jerked its vision down and ran up the back. Her blade trailed behind, splitting the creature.

She jumped off of it. Her left hand burned bright once again. Twisted to find a target. Tossed her sword like a javelin to pierce its throat.

Her hand exploded in the face of another demon. It launched her to the final creature. She slammed her white hot fist into its throat. Crushed its windpipe.

Maauhd Auhg fell between Asa and Chika. The two girls darted their eyes all over her in a state of confusion.

The beast fell next to Asa. It desperately grasped for air, but none was found. Its wings attempted to get airborne again, but it hadn't the energy

With a deep breath, Asa mimicked Maauhd Auhg's lightning sword. Her's was less solid and flowed like a whip as she walked. However, it became stiff when Asa brought it up and then back down for the kill.

The severed head rolled along the roots.

"That," Chika held her spread hands to her temple, "was amazing!"

"Thanks." Maauhd Auhg smiled. Joined Asa who had just released her sword. "You learn quick."

"That's the first time I've ever been accused of that," Asa stared down at her open hand. It still vibrated from the intensity of the lightning sword. "Thanks though."

"Sure," Maauhd Auhg placed a friendly hand on Asa's shoulder. "Maybe I can teach you two a few things before you go."

"Heck yes!" Chika ran to join the two with balled fists and wide eyes.

"Maauhd Auhg," Ginseng called from up ahead, just in the line of sight. She was almost invisible on the edge of darkness, but even at the distance it was easy to see her horrified face.

"Wait. Here." Maauhd Auhg ordered Asa and Chika.

The two exchanged looks but didn't disobey. Maauhd Auhg and Ginseng were gone for about five minutes before returning.

"Taurine," Maauhd Auhg jerked a thumb to where they had been. "Looks like these things hit the hunting group before us. Bury our dead."

Taurine nodded.

Maauhd Auhg faced Asa and Chika. "This is life as a hunter. Happens more often than we'd like."

"I'm sorry for your loss," Chika locked her eyes on the tips of her toes, as she fought back swelling water around her eyes.

"Why? You didn't kill them." Maauhd Auhg jerked her head back in confusion.

"It's an Earth expression," Asa placed a reassuring hand on Chika.

"Oh," Maauhd Auhg tried to understand it, but failed. "It's fine… we'll have to look for Dawn without them."

*   *   *

Hours had passed before Dawn awoke. A strange incense lingered with a scent she couldn't place. With a groan, she sat up. Eyes fluttered to gain focus, but there was no light source to retain information from.

In a state of confusion, Dawn realized she was dehydrated. Forgetting the moments before the darkness, she decided to lick the back ends of her mouth in an attempt to moisten it, giving herself time to gather thought.

"Are you thirsty?" The Tengu's voice seemed to come from every direction at the same time.

Wide eyes came over Dawn, as she tried to scamper backwards, but ran into a trunk. Cracked her head hard. Cuffed the back of her head as she fell forward, pushing her chest into her bent knees. De-armoured, the pain went undampened.

The voice came again. It came from everywhere. Blind, unable to pinpoint the direction of sound and the pain rushing through her body, left Dawn with an emotion that she hadn't felt in some time: fear.

"Are you thirsty?" The voice came back.

"No," Dawn rubbed her hand against the back of her head. The pain had gone as quickly as it had come, but confusion held as Dawn wondered why it had hurt to begin with.

As if on command, silver light penetrated the branches. The rays made the web and branches as clear as day but left the forest floor still draped mostly in darkness. However, there was enough light to realize she was in everyday clothes.

"The venom in the webbing drains magic," The Tengu answered a question Dawn hadn't thought to ask just yet. "Your armour vanished shortly after I had attacked you."

"Yeah," Dawn gulped. "About that, how did you hurt me with an arrow?"

"The trees repel magic. They lose the quality quickly, so I have to make new arrows each day."

"Explains why it hurt so bad when I fell on my ribs," Dawn touched her side a moment; then ran her hands over her chest. Where the arrows had entered, there were metal loops. "Did... did you stitch me?"

"I apologize, but with Kitsune you either attack them or they slay you, I did my best to repair what damage I caused." The Tengu played with a strange wooden contraption that had smoke coming from it. "I made this incense as an apology. It is an airborne painkiller."

"That explains that," Dawn touched her arm, remembering having slammed it against the Tengu. It was badly bruised, exposed, and in a homemade splint. The way part of it bulged turned her stomach. "Look, I..."

Looking around Dawn noticed that the parting of the clouds had revealed a sight so grand, Dawn lost herself in the moment.

The gigantic trees were cut free of their branches from root upwards of seventy feet. The bark cleaned, save for small remaining jagged pieces of bark.

The symbols were palm sized and about a couple hundred wrapped around each lap of the trunk. It only took a moment for Dawn to clue in.

She was surrounded by a novel. Each tree a page of a book. Each lap of symbols a paragraph. The trees went on in every direction Dawn turned.

"What the fuck?" Dawn began to walk to a tree.

She ran her hand along one of the symbols near the base. They were crude, but there was a sense of pride behind each symbol. She felt that each one was a stroke of paint in the expansive canvas.

Her green eyes ran along each symbol as she back pedaled to see the top.

Unconsciously, Dawn transformed. A shimmer crossed over Dawn's eye, leaving a milky appearance. Though unaware of this change, Dawn did notice its effect.

Each symbol now a word. A soft language that Dawn's inner voice played back to her.

The story was about two lovers. The woman a fair skinned, soft spoken, but powerful Kitsune. The man a creature of the dark, a murderous beast with the heart of a poet, a Tengu.

Dawn was forced to take long strafes in clockwise fashion around the tree in order to follow the story. She had started deep into the tale, so elements were confusing, however she did notice the pages were numbered. At the top, four larger symbols indicated the page. Dawn did her best to follow along.

"This is about you?" Dawn turned to the Tengu.

He had been watching her read his novel from afar. He slowly shook his head. "Not me, but like me."

"Okay," Dawn looked back at the story. Placed a hand along one of the symbols.

An explosion cut through the air. The Tengu gathered his bow and rushed towards it without missing a beat of the heart. Dawn was just as quick to begin, but after several strides stopped, her transformation faded into silver and white threads, her magic depleted.

"Damn," Dawn balled her hands. A small sting ran up her left arm as she realized she had moved too far from the incense while reading.

Before she could begin walking towards the painkiller, the Tengu returned.

"Your allies have returned for you," He handed her a strange wooden stick with leaves wrapped around it tightly. "This is a flare. Make some distance before you signal your friends. I do not want them to discover my home. They will kill me."

"Sure," Dawn pocketed the device. She began running in the direction, then stopped to turn around. "Thanks."

Dawn ran as far as her legs would carry her. Stumbled to take a rest and popped the flare. It took about half an hour before the team descended around her.

"Dawn!" Chika sprinted to Dawn and picked her up in an embrace.

"*Fuck!*" Dawn swore as pain shot up her arm.

"Sorry," Chika let go.

"Jesus," Dawn grabbed her arm. "Can't a girl catch a fricken break?"

"I didn't mean to—" Chika brought up her hands as she backpedaled.

"Shut up," Dawn laughed as she reached around and pulled Chika in, to finish the hug. "Who are these guys?" Dawn jerked her head towards the Kitsune.

"They're Kitsune hunters, helped us find you," Chika couldn't contain her smile. "I'm super excited you didn't die."

"Makes two of us." Dawn nodded. "Hi, Ozazi."

"Hello," Ozazi swung low. Kept a professional distance.

"Where is your armour?" Asa cocked an eyebrow.

Dawn shrugged. "I got caught in a hunter's trap. Drained my reserves."

"Tengu," Ginseng spat with disgust.

Dawn hide her distaste for Ginseng as she made her way to Maauhd Auhg. She could tell by the way Maauhd Auhg carried herself that she was the leader. "Thanks," Dawn offered a hand.

"No problem," Maauhd Auhg shook hands. "We should get you to camp to rest before you head to the bridge."

"We got that figured out?" Dawn turned to the girls, who both nodded.

"Mei Ling is learning how get us a portal," Asa took a few steps closer. "Hopefully we can get there before anything bad happens."

CHAPTER FOURTEEN: THE BRIDGE

May 7th

Cyan desert spread out for miles in either direction. To the west and east they ended in sharp deep blue mountains that protruded upwards to twelve kilometres. Each mountain rose and dropped with dramatically sharp jagged rocks, filled with cracks and layers of the desert sands that had been blown upwards.

The desert seemed to continue to the south forever, disappearing from sight as the horizon caught up. The path seemed to lead towards a floating green and blue planet, Earth. The small amount of light, which seemed to come from no visible source, outlined the planet. It left a crescent glow around the edging, leaving most of the blue rock eclipsed in darkness.

Several kilometres towards the north, two ridges left either side of the mountain ranges. On top of each cliff sat a single castle that stretched over the opening between them. Iron beams were built into the mountain range and into the castle to support the weight.

DISTANCE BETWEEN ECHOES

The castle was built from three wings with the drawbridge leading into the southeast corner. Spiralling marble dragons ran up either side of the bridge. Men walked the upper parts of the exterior with weapons of all sorts. A tower sat in the centre of the wall, which seemed impossibly narrow for how tall it was. On top of the tower was the Dragons Queen's throne which extended out from the tower, then looped upwards to create a glass dome. Just behind the dome sat a fully lit River.

The River was a red planet large enough to engulf Earth three times over. The surface of the planet etched with deep water filled canyons, curving too precisely to be natural formations around the planet in a corkscrew fashion. From the Bridge, the oceans, all of which were connected, seemed to be purple strips around the crimson ball.

Though it was impossible for someone on the Bridge to notice with just a glance, the River did not spin. The planet was forever locked in its orbit with one side stuck in perpetual daylight with boiling rivers, while the other side held glaciers of ice over top its oceans. Only a thin band along the planet, where day turned to night, was suitable for any sane creature to call home. There, a horde of Dragonborn, dwelling in cities carved of bone, rock, and steel, awaited orders from their King.

Threads of cyan and blue ignited into a furious spiral of energy that steadied into a knot. The crudely formed portal stood a few centimetres off the ground, giving off a strange gravitational push that caused the loose sand below to ripple along the desert floor like tiny waves.

From the portal came Dawn and Ozazi, followed by Chika and Esh, then Asa and finally Mei Ling. An aftermath of being sent between dimensions left an intense rush from the deconstruction of their atoms and the instant recompiling that strained body, mind, and soul. As they were hurled into the soft sands, each took a moment to collect themselves before realizing that they were fully conscious, not in a spiralling dream.

"Where," Asa pinched the bridge of her nose in attempt to combat her numb mind and the spinning environment, "are we?"

"We're here," Dawn attempted her military stance but the nausea of the portal made the charade quite obvious. She stumbled twice while trying to get her balance.

Curled over her knees, with hands on either side of her rib cage, Mei Ling attempted to steady her thoughts as she also fought to combat the nausea coursing through her body. This second portal had been much more stressful on the young Kitsune. Unlike the trip to Eden, this jump was to an artificial reality that reeked of the supernatural. The back of her throat stained with the scent of sulphur.

Her brown eyes quaked as she heard her very bones vibrate several times. Her armour silently worked to keep everything in order while her mind relayed confused messages to all senses. A moment passed before she even realized she had been staring at the sand below with great interest.

She cupped a handful of dust and slowly let it trickle from her curled hand. The cyan fell, clumping into gel-like crystals during the descent, and by the time they met the sand, it was impossible to tell where one grain of cyan had started and the other ended. On impact to the ground, tiny ripples ran over the clump where it would fall apart into a fine dust. The entire process was so quick that Mei Ling tried it three times before she totally understood its behaviour.

"Is this Distance?" Mei Ling slowly rose to her knees. Looked from the Earth over to the tower, the strip of land that seemed to go further. "They manipulated the element into a physical form. It's literally a bridge. I know we called it that but I never imagined... I just... thought. Jesus, it's a *fucking* bridge." Her breaths were short, as her mind twisted to remember how to speak.

"Well," Chika arched her back while applying both hands to her lower spine to relieve a blinding pain that had come with the travel through the portal. Her pause had been much longer than originally intended as she tried to push the pain from her back. Finally giving up, she pointed to a narrow point vacant of mountain. "It isn't finished."

Mei Ling disagreed but her strained body kept her quip internal. She believed that the mountains to the west and east were simply walls to contain most of the Distance. Though she couldn't quite get her mind around the idea in her current frame of thought, she believed this was much like their armour. The mountains were the physical representation of a container housing the precious material. The south and north were open because the distance was intended to openly interact with the two planets that sat on either end.

"Okay, ladies," Dawn mentally pushed the sickness out. "We've got quite the hike ahead of us." She flexed her left fist to test her Kitsune cast as she imagined driving her knuckles square into something ugly. It hurt, but she didn't care. "Chika, weave something."

Chika nodded. Ran her hands over top of themselves. The fire balled, expanded into a disc, then shrank into pressed palms. "I have full control." Chika still wore the armour gifted to her by the Kitsune. The forest had dampened her ability to recharge her magic.

Esh floated over her shoulder. Next to him, Ozazi. Both Lights studied the River ahead. Sank into themselves. They had never been programmed to be in such an environment. Each exchanged a nod before following their knight.

"Good," Dawn smiled as Ozazi found his place next to her. She whispered to her friend. "Everything okay?"

"I never imagined coming to such a place. Not without the Echo, at least."

Dawn shrugged. "Let's get to it."

"Yes sir," Mei Ling mocked with a salute as Dawn passed her. She immediately regretted the disrespect for authority, as her body sank into itself.

"Looks like you're going to get use to those heels," Asa slapped Mei Ling on the back as she walked passed.

"Ugh." Mei Ling groaned as her face returned to looking at her knees. *So, this is my life now?* Mei Ling paused a moment as she accepted her reality, but a warm push from her chest cavity beckoned for the castle. "We seriously need to look at unionizing."

She waved her arm about to dismiss her sleeve and the portal in one motion. Mei Ling fished her arms around to find something to use as a booster. Without hesitation, Chika hooked her arms under Mei Ling's armpits and pulled her to her feet.

"Thanks," Mei Ling ran her hand across her forehead. She swore she had a fever but her hand felt nothing abnormal. "Be a good Christian, would you, and let me lean on you?"

"Sure." Chika simply smiled as she helped Mei Ling along.

The girls trekked for an hour. They kept to a slow pace to give themselves time to recover, but had to move in case any patrols came by to investigate the cyan spark that may have been noticed in the night.

Mei Ling's mind drifted in and out, but with the aid of Chika, she managed. Chika herself felt similar effects but, thanks to her Dragonborn soul, she felt a warmth inside her chest heating up with every step she took. The closer she neared the River, the stronger and more connected to her past life's power she seemed to be getting.

The ground slowly drooped into something the girls considered to be a valley. Strange blue stones were littered around in all shapes and sizes. They were large enough and far enough from each other that the girls easily kept in a straight line, only once or twice having to slightly navigate around one.

"The dust seems thicker here." Mei Ling dragged her feet as the girls walked. Smiling at the trail she left. The dust was deep enough that it was almost like walking on a beach with the way it wrapped around your feet.

"You won't be able to get that out of your shoes." Chika glared at Mei Ling's feet.

"Pffft." Mei Ling rolled her eyes. "It'll remove itself when my heels de-materialize."

"Whatever." Chika let Mei Ling stand on her own. This sudden disconnection almost caused Mei Ling to faceplant.

"Hey!" Mei Ling caught herself on her second step, glared with a stern frown. "The hell, man!"

"If you have energy to fool around," Chika took a moment to glare over her shoulder, their eyes shot daggers that cut deep. "Then you have the energy to walk on your own."

Dawn shot Chika a glare. Chika's eyes fell to the ground, with her face away from Mei Ling, she masked her shame.

"Jeez." Mei Ling shook her head and exchanged a smirk with Asa.

"Bitch, eh?" Asa spoke under her breath as she stayed back with Mei Ling, letting the other two move ahead without them.

"Yeah." Mei Ling removed her heels. In one hand she swung them over her shoulder. "No kidding."

"Ugh!" Asa retracted from Mei Ling. "What the hell died? Your feet reek."

"Hey!" Mei Ling shock an index finger in Asa's face. "I've been teleporting us all over creation, haven't showered in half a week and just walked a few miles. What'd you expect?"

"How about some common courtesy?" Asa pinched her nose as she walked ahead. "You realize that if we get into a fight, you can't jump or land without those." Mei Ling smiled at Asa's distorted voice.

"I'll manage. I have two Angels and a bitc— Dragonborn. You guys don't need a measly Kitsune—"

The air in their lungs was replaced with cyan dust. The debris kicked them off their feet and onto their back. The girls rose as the world fell, then they were slammed into it several metres away. Shoulder over shoulder, they skipped along the ground like rocks on a lake.

The pressure had swept both Lights out of the air. They were forced into each other. Richocated. Slammed into the dirt and buried.

Dust lashed outwards. Swarmed along touchless winds. Sulphur bleached the air. Cyan sands spun into bodies; bodies became a horde.

The beasts were tall. Towered over the girls. Thick shouldered and big limbed. Humanoid without expression. Rock like skin of blue and cyan, built of Distance. The shriek of blackened demon souls consumed the sands. Distorted and reversed screams ignited life into the Draugar.

Mei Ling swatted at her loosened heels. Missed. Slid to a stop too far from them. Looked upwards to see a Draugar. Its scream pushed her hair back, pulled the skin around her eyes tight, burnt her throat and filled her lungs.

Copper filled her mouth. Mei Ling fell over herself. Lungs choked on the gas. Eyes stung. Throat condensed. Limbs convulsed. Chattering teeth fought to make words.

A flash of light skimmed Mei Ling's head, singeing her hairs as it went. Asa had cleaved the Draugar with her lightning blade. The beast fell in half. Asa scooped Mei Ling in one arm, used her blade to block a fist. Leapt backwards to her allies.

The team had distance on the Draugar. The creatures moved slowly, until they didn't. Less than a metre from a victim brought on lightning reflexes. They became blurs as they lunged superhumanly fast towards the girls.

"Will she be okay?" Chika fell to Mei Ling. Hands all over, she fought to find what was wrong.

Mei Ling's face was red. Breaths heavy. Eyes wide. Tears drenched her face. Nails dug into her sides as she struggled to find herself.

"Asa." Dawn took off, Asa at her heels. A blink of an eye and Asa was ahead of her. Leapt into the crowd. Swung twice through four bodies, rolled and blocked, then kicked off a Draugar, tossed her sword like a javelin.

Fell. Wove a new blade. Slashed another as heat fled over her shoulder from the explosion of her first javelin. Asa kneed a beast in the throat, spun to come down on another with her blade.

Dawn repeatedly plunged her fist in a Draugar, each time dragging more rocky innards. Each fist met new sandy flesh. The sands pulled themselves back together just as quickly as they were being torn apart. She turned to tell Asa.

"Asa—" A swipe caught her arm. Dawn lifted off her feet. Soared. Fell into the grasp of another. A bear hug collapsed over her. Sand dug into flesh. Condensed. Like razors, the grains sped along every inch. She struggled, strained her neck, fought to keep lips free and breath frequent.

A Draugar advanced on the two. Chika fought to weave fire. Flickers illuminated her hands, nothing else. "Come on!" Chika swung under an arm, spun to grab Mei Ling by the wrist, dug her heel into the ground, and pulled her friend free.

Tossed Mei Ling aside, away. Chika caught a jab in the jaw. Stumbled. Ducked. Wove fire, it was extinguished by an interrupting reach. Chika rolled out of it, leapt free. Fell to Mei Ling's side.

Again she fought to weave flame. It wouldn't stay lit. "Screw it." Chika spat to the side. Swung her vision towards the River. Forced her mind to find the warmth. Sought through the chaos within, past it, and to her power. Dragged it out kicking and screaming. Turned back to her assaulters. Reached her arm to the side where she knew Esh had been buried. "*Esh!*"

A blinding light penetrated the sands. Red and purple threads trashed about. Wove around Chika. Built armour over top the Kitsune armour. A surge in her chest tore through her like a kick to the gut. She fell to a knee.

Chika came up to block three lightning fast swipes. Swung out of a fourth. Wove a sword of flame. Cut the Draugar. Rolled to another and slit it vertical. Kicked off another to land by Mei Ling's heels. Rolled. Slashed. Wove a flamethrower towards Dawn's capture. Rocketed back to Mei Ling. Slashed three more.

Her suit was back. It was in control. It drove her like the warrior she was!

Dawn fell out of the Draugar's grip as the flames tore its top half apart. She rolled, leapt, and landed knee first on a Draugar.

Mei Ling found herself. Her armour forced the pain out. Whatever the gas had been, it was suppressed. Mei Ling scooped up her heels without waiting for a heartbeat. Chika disarmed more Draugar as Mei Ling rolled out of one's reach. Two clicks and the straps were tight, her heels on.

Wove water into an orb around her to blocked an attack. Pushed the water outward. The water forced every Draugar it caught off their feet. Wove around Chika and dissipated.

"Nice," Chika grinned.

Mei Ling's Kitsune eyes watched the Draugar pull themselves back together. Magnetic waves infested each square centimetre of the valley. "They're pulling themselves back together. Some kind of magnetic field."

"How do we stop it?" Dawn shouted as she punched through a Draugar. Leapt off its reforming body into, through, and out of another. Spun and took down another with the back of her heel. Kicked its skull into the gut of another. Caved in its face with her fist.

"I don't know," Mei Ling darted her eyes along the bodies. Her head spun. A spinning Draugar crashed into her. The world tiled, then shock and finally straightened as her back laid flat to the ground.

Flame caught the Draugar's defensive fist as Chika pushed the Draugar backwards. "Thanks," Mei Ling fell to her knee as Chika pushed into the rest.

Mei Ling's breath was short. The suit was failing. Was it the gas? Or was it something else… her mind couldn't focus. Couldn't decide. Her head pounded over and over. Lower back strained. Every atom in her being was on fire. Worse, her tank was on E.

Asa wove lightning throughout the horde. Pushed hundreds to the side. Punched another. Cut more. Frowned as everything put itself together as if she hadn't done a thing.

"I'm not getting anywhere." Asa's breath was heavy. Sweat flooded out of her pores. She shrugged into a deep breath then rushed back into the horde.

A Draugar lunged toward Dawn. Its fist flattened, straightened, and it receded down to its bicep. It repeated a stabbing motion with its newly morphed spear.

Dawn rolled over it, pushed out of it, and took the arm off with a low spin and the back of her heel. The freed spear caught flesh. Split bone. Gushed blood. Lifted a hundred pounds into the air. Took it across the landscape. Generated a deafening scream.

Dawn turned. The red in her face faded into ghost white. Eyes wide. Jaw dropped.

The scream was petrifying. It made Dawn's world feel like it had been peeled back entirely, leaving only her in a pitch black existence with only one light source ahead outlining the frame of a fourteen year old girl.

Chika curled backwards as the spear penetrated just above her right shoulder blade. The force forced her off her feet and through the air. By the time she came down and slid in a spiral to a stop, she was unconscious as shock had taken over.

"*Chika!*" Dawn reached outwards as she screamed.

Realizing her stupidity, Dawn began to stand but was forced to the ground. Her chin scraped the sharp dust below as the Draugar smashed its foot down on her spine. Its entire weight on her back, Dawn felt every organ pushed out of place as her spine strained to prevent snapping. Air rushed from her lungs as the force had winded her.

Tight eyes fought to block the pain as gasping lips attempted to fill her lungs. Dawn dug her knees into the dust and brought her forearms in wards. With every ounce of strength she forced herself up.

Now up on her arms and knees still with the foot pressing down, Dawn grinded her teeth as she tried to find the strength to push even further. Her arms quaked as they began to buckle under the weight.

The Draugar was displeased that Dawn had forced it to bend its leg, so it attempted to straighten it. The Draugar brought up its foot and before Dawn could scamper free from underneath, it brought its foot back down on her.

The tonne of force caused her to collapse back to the ground. As she fell, her face was jerked to the side, and cyan poured into the open wound on her chin. The grains scorched her at a cellular level, like a chain reaction spreading throughout her blood stream.

She chose to ignore the burning but couldn't over look the second stomp. Dawn fell slightly, turned so her right arm was tucked under her body. She no longer would be able to rely on it to prop herself back up.

The deafening scream echoed through Dawn's mind. Stuck on replay, she kept catching flashes of Chika's curled body with strands of crimson following her rag doll body across the surface of the Bridge. Her chest quaked in a hollow spasm that made Dawn feel like vomiting over herself.

With hard pressed eyes, flush cheeks, and grinding teeth, Dawn found something inside of herself as she heaved her chest with a deep breath followed by a powerful grunt. The wing pattern on her back glowed a bright gold as she slammed her left fist into the ground below her.

Pain erupted up her broken arm and into the base of her skull. Any normal person would have passed out from the pain of their own arm slowly crumbling away as the bones fell apart but Dawn was beyond that at this point.

With a strength she had never felt before, the golden light exploded from her shoulder blades. Expanded in a split second into a hundred foot wing span of pure energy. The wings pushed the Draugar off her back—freely passed by a confused Asa and Mei Ling—they continued to topple over any other being Dawn thought of as foe.

The wings lasted but a moment. Retracted in a blink of an eye but with energy still surging through Dawn, she spun around on the spot with blind rage and reached into the chest of the Draugar that had been crushing her.

The light on her back ran down her arm from within her body. Repaired both bone and muscle. Dawn used her healed arm to rip the core of the Draugar torso and with the same motion, brought her fingers together so hard they touched, leaving the stone a fine dust in the wind.

Pink trails of her cast fell to the ground. "They have cores inside. Find them. End them."

The light faded back into silver cloth as Dawn felt light headed. She fell forward into the sand. Caught herself with her arms and legs but remained crouched. The world was heavy. The burning in her veins left her and, with it, all of her energy. Somehow the armour had diverted and fed off the sensation.

With a foggy mind, Dawn reached towards the sands in confusion—

A Draugar came after Dawn but a blade of lightning tore through it. With blade still in hand, Asa slid to Dawn, put her arm under Dawn's stomach, and leapt to Chika's side.

Asa dropped Dawn next to Chika and turned back to fend off the army as Mei Ling fell next to the group. Her arms pulled back as she wove water over the team into an ice orb on the heels of Asa.

Mei Ling stood overtop Chika and Dawn. Dawn had her eyes closed. Her skin tight and pale as she cringed with each heavy breath she took. Mei Ling could only relate it to watching someone on their deathbed. Though she couldn't actually see it, Mei Ling knew Dawn's energy tank was as close to zero as one could be without being quite there.

It took every ounce of her being to move her eyes over to Chika but Mei Ling did it. Her heart sank into her stomach as she knelt down over the young Dragonborn. Her face drained of all colour, breath short and slow, blood oozing out the wound around the lodged spear.

"Okay, okay," Mei Ling knelt as low to Chika as she could get. Her voice a soft whisper as she kept speaking to herself while trying to figure out what to do. "Okay... okay. Okay, maybe if I remove the spike..."

Slowly she grasped the spear. Took in a long drawn out breath as she used both hands to slowly lift the spear free of Chika's back. Her gut wrenched as the spear got caught on something she only assumed was bone. Mei Ling almost threw up as she jerked the spear free and tossed it to the side.

A chunk had broken free from the tip. Mei Ling reached for it, but the wound instantly healed over itself. "The fuck?" Mei Ling jerked back up. Looked around for anyone who could explain what had happened. "Can we even do that?"

"Is she okay?" Dawn's voice was faint and had to draw a breath between each word. The world spun, she had no sense of belonging, but thought clung to the scream. To Chika curling over that spear.

"Oh thank God," Mei Ling turned to Dawn with a strained smile. "I thought you were dead."

"Nope," Dawn managed a smile but it was lost quickly.

"I don't know what I did," Mei Ling turned back to Chika in bewilderment. "She just healed herself."

"How?" Dawn slowly rolled over to her side. Used her elbows to keep upright. "What did you do?"

"Nothing. Just removed the spike. But she's alive." Mei Ling rolled Chika onto her back. Made sure her air flow was clear. Pushed sweat from her brow. "Asa's out there. Alone."

"Nah." Dawn watched the flashes of light dance across the ice. She knew every flash was another victim Asa's sword met. "Girl's a beast."

"Maybe." Mei Ling sighed. Bent over her knees and pressed her palms hard on her thighs. With a bit of strain, she stood. "I should probably die alongside her."

"I'll come," Dawn struggled to stand but her limbs slipped underneath her. They were completely drained of energy. The world still spun.

"No." Mei Ling turned, in mid spin wove two swirls of water, flicked both to Dawn's wrists. Balled her fists so the ice pinned Dawn to the ground.

"Hey!" Dawn spat as she struggled but was too tired to break free.

"I don't need some cripple holding me back." Mei Ling turned back to the outer wall of her shield. She rubbed her temple, the strain was returning. "For God's sake, Dawn. You're going to get everyone killed."

Mei Ling spun her hand to create an opening in the orb, leaving Dawn dumbfounded as the ice sealed behind her. Dawn turned to look over at Chika, sighed, then allowed herself to fall against the sand to rest.

Her eyes darted along the battlefield to find Asa. Flickers of light came with each strike of her mighty sword. Mei Ling grinned as she leapt over to Asa. Put her arms in the air and while still in flight swirled them to weave the water out of the air.

She landed next to Asa who was crouching low in exhaustion, bruises covered her body from strikes that had made their way past her blade. Mei Ling ran back to back as she pulled down her arms and pushed them forwards, spinning around a confused Asa as she did so. The stream of water formed a whip that brought every Draugar it hit off its feet and backwards into another.

"Thanks." Asa smiled as Mei Ling bent down, grabbed her bicep, and braced her back. In a sequenced effort the two pulled Asa to her feet.

Able to keep herself on her feet, Asa pulled away from Mei Ling. The sudden displacement caused Mei Ling to collapse to her knees. "Dammit." Mei Ling heaved her chest. "I was using *you* for support."

Asa laughed while she wiped her running nose with the back of her wrist. "Yeah. I'm tired too." Snorted.

"I can see their bodies." Mei Ling pressed her palms on her thighs and bent over them. A pounding in her chest was growing. A mixture of teleporting, the gas, and using her abilities was too taxing. "They have cores. Distance is being drawn in with magnetic forces. Take out the stone in their torso to kill them."

"I have been—"

"No." Mei Ling groaned as she ran her hand over top her beating heart, it felt frightening fast. "You haven't been."

"Oh." Asa sanked her eyes for a moment before realizing the Draugar were making their way back to them. "You good to go?"

"Sure," Mei Ling rose to her feet to share a fist bump with Asa. "Why not," her breath very forced.

CHAPTER FIFTEEN: LIMITED REALIZATION

April 18th

Vala stood in the centre of the throne room. Her eyes couldn't adjust to anything. A dark layer ran over everything. She knew her hands were bound, but when she looked at the strange metal, her mind couldn't place what it was.

Sulphur seeped down her nostrils and deep into her lungs. When Vala looked upwards she saw the glow of a biological creature. The Dragon's Queen rose from her throne chair. A supernatural curl to the witch's lips.

"Welcome to my home," the Dragon's Queen had a tone of friendship which made the entire situation that much more nerve wracking.

"Thanks for the hospitality," Vala tightened her eyes.

"I offer a momentary friendship," the Dragon's Queen embraced Vala.

Vala felt the acid in the back of her throat kick up.

"If you promise to aid me in transforming the Atoms of God into Distance, I will allow you to live," the Dragon's Queen smiled. "As my servant, of course."

"Oh," Vala nodded while shifting her weight. "I'd love to, but, no."

Sharp eyes followed by a tight grasp to Vala's throat came from the angered Dragon's Queen. "Look. Here. You will do as I say so that I may return to my husband's side."

Red ran over Vala's face as she struggled to gasp for oxygen. "What do you want me to do?"

"I need your powers to fuel a machine my men have built." The Dragon's Queen let go of Vala.

"Sure thing," Vala smirked as she tried to use her bound hands to soothe her throat. Threads of brown and green unraveled her armour. "Not."

With a deep breath, the Dragon's Queen returned to her throne. From behind it she retrieved a darkened layered cage, and within it floated something. Vala struggled to see what it was, and only could because it was held in front of the glowing Dragon's Queen.

Then it spoke. The voice stuttered Vala's heart. Widened her eyes. Dried her mouth. Rift's words reached her ears, "Vala. Don't worry."

Vala's entire body shook as the hairs rose. In a rarity, Vala held her tongue.

The Dragon's Queen removed Rift from the cage before placing the prison on her throne. Walked over to Vala and used her hand to force Vala's chin up for eye contact. "I will have my men use the full extent of their imagination to beat obedience into you." Her grip tightened on Rift.

Dented his metal around the tips of her finger nails. Then twisted around her fingers as she continued to press.

"Vala—" a distorted voice fizzled as the ink in his eye dried up. One more compression of her hand and the jade sphere cracked, the metal shards fell to the ground.

Vala starred. Unable to look away. Hollowed. Without thought.

The Dragon's Queen tilted her hand to slowly let the sphere fall off her fingers. "I am above beating a misbehaving mutt."

*　　*　　*

DISTANCE BETWEEN ECHOES

A scream tore up a man's throat so violently it crackled and broke into a dry heave. The sizzle of human flesh pressed to white hot iron reverberated down the cement hallways. An image of bubbled flesh folding over metal entered the minds of every cellmate.

The air was hard to swallow. Thick with sulphur and void of heat. Blue lips shook as they fought to swallow each gasp. Inmate throats collapsed then pulsated as they held the air in and struggled to find the strength to exhale.

The cells were bare. Most closed off to the world aside the bars to the hallway. However, one, on the end, had been recently renovated. A hole punched into the side with jagged bars to seal the victim. A crimson sphere hung in the air.

The River's red heat illuminated into Vala's chamber. She lay, sprawled out in its image. Energy sapped from her. She constantly shivered. Like a parasite she leeched off the planet's heat. It was the closest thing she had seen to a sun in weeks. Forced to rely on the River's heat for survival, its warmth gut wrenchingly soothing.

Vala played with her food with nailless fingers. They were swollen and blackened by scabs; dried, flaking white skin wrapped around the fire in her fingertips. The constant exposure left her entire body covered with dry, beet red skin which spotted blood whenever she stretched or moved.

The entire cell draped in a black shadow. It expanded outwards of the cell window like teeth, mimicking rays of light. Vala was unable to make sense of any object in the room. Unable to focus her mind on anything. As if having a word on the edge of her tongue, Vala fought to comprehend her surroundings. The room was lit enough to make sense of its shape and size, but the shadow kept the information away from her mind. Light extended off her skin in waves, seeping into the cement to dissipate centimetres away from her body.

Her only source of entertainment was to touch her food, bleed light into the blackened object to reveal it to be mouldy bread.

Isolation had emptied her mind. With emptiness came the release of weighted responsibility. With no distraction to new friends, growing powers, or the aid of defensive humour, Vala's life had gotten much simpler. Life reduced to one aspect, the endeavour of her daily torture.

Part of it familiar. Parts of it a strange deja vu. Parts of it leaked into the void of her mind and flooded it for brief moments of thought. Reflections of a stupid little girl, doing stupid big life altering decisions. Choices that sank relationships, broke down the image her peers had of her and permanently scarred her body, both internally and externally. Layers of self doubt fueling motivations bled from false reflections.

Lying mirrors portraying imaginary weight manifested from misguided thought. A loneliness within confused by the spotlight she received from her classmates. Centre of attention, but centre to nobody's world.

A busy father, a distracted mother, objective pressure from boys and, worse yet, two-faced friends; all brought a soul crushing conclusion that something was wrong with her.

A quick fix birthed from the inability to consider outside stimulants would dictate the next few months. Her solstice would be collapsing legs, a stuttering heart, strained lungs, and a shrouded mind. A trip to the hospital would enlighten parents to their daughter's situation. One would ignore it, and one would close in on herself.

Days. Alone. Weeks. In tears. Struggling to rebuild who she was without losing everything she was meant to be. Thoughts would drift to razor blades and high places. Warm, crimson baths and plunging off tall buildings would fill daydreams.

Dreams would bring smiles, then reality would bring crushing defeat as balled hands would dig into eyes. Red faced screams would fill the hospital hallways, and the embarrassment from the attention it all drew would only dig her further into herself. To toss her further down the hole.

One day, footsteps would come. At first her mind would be drifted to a daydream. Her teeth gritted from the thought of peaceful oblivion. But then around the corner would come a hum and a smile. A moment of wide eyes as they took in the horror they landed on, but soon they would swell up and be warm.

As an angel would sit down next to Vala with textbooks in hand. Chelsea would be funny. She would be thoughtful. She would be supportive. But above all of that, she would be the first friend Vala had ever truly had. The person to reach down and pull Vala kicking and screaming out of that hole. To save Vala from herself. To put purpose into her life, even if at its most basic stage was only to keep on living.

After all, she was a high school student. There needn't be anything complicated about her life outside the need to experience it. To hold onto it. To love it. To—

Footsteps came. These were heavy. They scraped the ground as they went. They were cold. Their echo traced the pleas of the tortured men that filled the atmosphere with their hollers.

Returned to the present, Vala grabbed her bread, and rolled over to place her back to the cell entrance. With the insight of a child, she relied on out of sight, out of mind. As the steps continued, she played with her food.

It was useless to pray for the steps to be meant for someone else. Vala was well aware that this place was as far from God as the cosmos allowed. Each time she expected to be brought to the edge of hell, she was dragged even further.

The steps stopped. Part of her wondered who they had been for. What was in store for that person? Yet, she also didn't care. It was comforting to pull herself away from her peers. Not knowing their names or their faces helped in dehumanizing them. Helped her cope with their sobs and screams in the night. But she did know their voices...

The sound of rusted iron grinded along the cement floor. Vala cringed. Pulled her legs up as she balled a hand into her chest. As the door to her cell opened, her mind shot to her daily routine. The cloth around her face pushed back her nose, forced her lips still, and caused white flares of light from the pressure against her eyes. The freezing water would have sent shivers down her entire body if she had the luxury to worry about the temperature. Instead, the back of her nose burned as water flooded her throat and filled her lungs.

With a gasp and wide eyes, Vala was thrown back into the present. The steps shuffled along the cell. For the first time she realized that the man walking must have a limp. First a step then a drag. Then a step and then a drag. But with something between both...

"Hello, Vala."

As if fire had been pressed to her spine, Vala shot up and away from the voice. As she did, she kicked a dish of water. Her foot ignited light into the dented saucer. It spun and spilled its contents along the floor. Water droplets sprayed through the air, catching the crimson reflection of the River, then slowly losing energy to become part of the shadow.

Vala scurried to the far reaches of the warmth, but when her four legged dash came to the edge of the River's light, she stopped.

She stared at her shaking hand as it reached out and danced between the light and the dark. She wanted to be as far from the voice as she could, but a part of her couldn't bring herself to do so.

The voice pulled her back into the light. As he spoke, Vala sat up, pulled her limbs inward, and very slowly looked over her shoulder to the man. "We need to have a conversation about your accommodations," David smiled.

Vala glared back at him, her eyes widened a brief moment on his cane. She recognized it as the strange sound between his foot step and drag. It took her great effort to raise an eyebrow. "Who are you—" her voice was hoarse. It fell into itself and she had to repeat herself so it was recognizable. "Who are you, Willy Wonka?"

"That's a bit rude," David leaned against the wall. Frowned when he realized how dirty it was. He straightened back up to brush the soot off his suit. "You know, I expected you to be happy to see me."

"Yeah?" Vala dragged her hand up her face and through her hair. "For the golden ticket you gave me?"

"No. For saving your life." David glared.

"My life—" With fire in her lungs Vala fell forward onto all fours. The effort to shout exhausted her. Her lungs strained to fill themselves, leaving her voice a pathetic plea, "What the fuck are you talking about?"

"The hotel—"

The world pulled in on itself as Vala kicked back onto her bottom and across the room. She didn't stop moving until her back met the cold wall. Her mind left the room and focused in on a twisted face and distorted voice. Looked past it to the woman it had been, to Maggie's beautiful face. A face full of life that had—Vala cringed. She refused to remember the face. Threw her hands out into the air, trying to literally push the image from her mind.

A pit in her stomach that hollowed her very core out as guilt rushed through her person—Vala's mind shot to a blurry memory of a man carrying her over his shoulder. She remembered her dead weight. Remembered her face bouncing off his back. Remembered the dazed strain to look upwards towards a girl on her knees.

Rivers of tears rolled down pale cheeks. Blonde hair tossed forward. Limbs curled overtop a lifeless body. Crimson pooled around shaking, bent legs. Chelsea shivered overtop her mother's body as she screamed until her lungs were empty. How she didn't wait for them to fill before her gasps for air were pushed out again with such force blood vessels popped in her eyes.

"You were there…" Vala's words so faded that they became transparent. She couldn't hide the fact that she was a scared little girl, trapped in a foreign place, waiting to die. Her heart seized a moment as fear seeped in to replace guilt.

"Yes. I was." David sighed as he made his way closer to Vala. His voice became low as he did his best to crouch down to her eye level. "I didn't save your life, I simply prolonged it. I'm in the business of doing so for humans, and I'm about to do it again, for you."

"You're," Vala gulped, "going to free me?"

"No," David shook his head, accidentally let laughter trail his tone. "That would get us both killed, sorry. This is all about the preservation of the human race, and I don't think you or your breakfast club are going to be able to do that. So I need to live to keep humanity intact. You need to live longer than today.

"Until I have everything in place. I need more time. So, I am going to give you a crash course on how to live through all of this. Best yet? Do that while still maintaining that insatiable sense of humour you have."

David saw the doubt in her eyes. He did his best to offer a smile. "You can trust me, Vala. We're both Human. I can't slay the beast this time, but I can convince it not to kill you."

"What?" Vala fought for sound in her voice. Guilt came crashing back and washed out the fear. Her ability to chain thoughts together were overwhelmed with the images of Maggie. "What do you mean?" Her mind was still a muddled mess. She tried to place herself in the moment with David, but her mind kept trying to drift into the past. To Maggie's beautiful green eyes and red hair. To her smile. To her scent. To her warmth. To her—

"They didn't tell you, did they," David went wide eyed. "You think you killed her, don't you?"

Vala looked up with a low brow and shivering eyes. Her mouth opened, but no words followed. Lungs deflated by what felt like a collapsed rib cage. A heavy pressure all around her body pulled inwards as she tried to sink into herself. To vanish from existence.

"Typical," David smirked. "They treat us mortals like pawns. Doesn't matter which side. We are nothing more than tools to be moved along the chessboard. They made you think you killed a woman to fuel your need to redeem yourself. For their purpose. To be their weapon."

David tightened both his eyes and his words. "You're a God, Vala. A fucking God and they're using you as a vessel to a means."

He gathered himself before he retrieved a silver box from his jacket. He smiled as he placed it on the ground. Vala watched as his fingertips left it, she expected the silver to fade into shadow but it stayed lit.

"You're Human," David didn't snap his fingers, but he may as well have. The tone broke Vala out of her disconnected thought and compacted everything into a singularity that she was able to hone onto. Her mind was brought back to the moment, and to his words. "I don't care what garbage they've been feeding you. The person you think you are. The person who has hopes and dreams. Who fears. Who breathes in air and who prays before she goes to bed that there will be a morning to greet her. That is a Human. You and everything you recognize as you is Human."

"This," David gestured his hand to the River. "This isn't you or me. Humans weren't meant to get in the middle of all of this. They might be feeding you stories about how you are some savior from another lifetime. How the Echo you are connected to is some selfless creature from the beyond, but think for a moment. Two all powerful creatures are warring over a bunch of ants. One of them for the ants? Please."

David tapped the box to draw Vala's attention to it. "We aren't ants. We are fuel, Vala. And just like every war that has ever been waged, this one is about resources. You girls are nothing more than fuel for their tanks. The rest of us? Salt for their meat. Opium for their leisure. Goddamn tea leaves to be spent entertaining guests."

David opened the box. Sparks of green and brown flickered from within. With each lash of light came a scream from a bodiless voice. It had no face, but Vala's mind instantly crafted one for it. She knew this voice. It screamed day in and day out at the edge of the hallway. Only yesterday had its screams vanished from the choir of the other voices.

Vala's eyes widened as the power reached out to her. She didn't fight it as it bled into her blood. Surged with the warmth inside her chest. Fuelled her wounds close. Light flickered behind her eyes. The power felt like her armour had returned to her, yet she still sat in her rags.

David snapped the box shut. It cut off the power. "That should buy you some more time."

David rose between Vala and the River to lay a daunting shadow over her. Vala fought to swallow a breath. As the unspeakable power pulsated through her veins, and slowly died out, she quivered in fear. Though the man in front of her was certainly human, there was a demonic sense to his determination.

*　　*　　*

Each step of lead ended in a series of tremors. Every vibration a reminder that gravity was a moment away from betraying her. Every vibration a surge of pain on top of the endless burning that ran throughout her entire body. Every vibration a missing frame of thought causing a disjointed grasp of self awareness.

It had been weeks since David had brought her the Atom of God. The guards had noticed right away that her wounds had healed. Feared she had transformed when they were not around, so she was given around the clock guards.

With no food or water for a week, Vala shuffled her feet as she was transported from her cell towards the Dragon's Queen throne. Dried blood and layers of dirt clung to every part of her body. Every cut and burn ached but they were nothing compared to the pain of dehydration shooting through her body.

The doors came. Vala wasn't sure how. The hallway had been a long mindless journey of disjointed images. She swore she had noticed the doors at the end but they had suddenly emerged ahead of her.

The world swayed a bit as she shifted her weight to keep balance. Each ankle on fire if favoured too long.

Another disjointed image and she was standing midway into the throne room. Vala blinked rapidly as she attempted to grasp what was going on. She must have taken too long because a guard's elbow came to her spine.

This threw her to the ground on all fours. Vala dry-heaved a scream from the pressure of her own weight. She struggled with the chains as she attempted to get back to her feet, but it was in vain. After several attempts without so much as getting a leg straight, she gave up.

Like a dog, Vala crawled on all fours over to the steps of the throne. When she reached them, it took a moment for her mind to realize what they were. The darkened layer slightly lit up as she touched them.

Vala looked up in a haze when she reached out to the stairs to find the Dragon's Queen standing by the glass. A heavy sigh as she struggled to throw her elbow up and over the step.

She dug her bone into the top of the step as she threw the rest of her body's weight onto it. She cried as she dragged her rib cage, then hip, up and over the step. Sitting on the step, Vala had to catch her breath.

Every breath fed the heat in her throat. It traveled down into her lungs to inflate them with what felt like lava eating away at her core. After several minutes, Vala caught her breath, or as close to it as she thought possible.

The second step was attempted. Then the third after a pit stop. Finally she accomplished the climb. Crawled her way after the fourth step towards the Dragon's Queen.

Put her weight up against the glass. It's chill was soothing to the skin. With a moan she reached up for a bar that was used to hold the window in place. Did her best to pull herself up while pushing with her legs. Vala wasn't sure how long it took her to stand but it was embarrassing.

"H-hey." The side of Vala's face pressed against the cold glass. Her eyes closed from exhaustion to embrace the chill. It bled into her and she imagined it touched her entire body for the brief moment she was relaxed.

"Are you willing to summon your armour, now?" the Dragon's Queen watched the River above.

"Totes." Vala gulped, it felt like swallowing a stone.

The Dragon's Queen smiled as she perked up and turned towards Vala with a state of enthusiasm that she had never shown another person.

"I," Vala drew in her breath very slowly, "would do anything," fell forward, but was caught by the Dragon's Queen.

The embrace was gentle and almost felt genuine—Vala felt sicker from it. So, with all of her quaking limbs, burning joints and straining muscles, Vala looked up to glare into the Dragon's Queen's eyes. "I would do anything... for a Klondike Bar."

"*What?*" the Dragon's Queen did not understand the joke but she did understand that one was being made fun of. With the back of her hand, she slapped the laughter out of Vala.

Vala fell to the ground. Screamed as pain came like a tsunami throughout her person. Out of spite, Vala forced laughter through running tears and failing lungs and loose teeth. Blood fell out of her lips with every escape of air.

The Dragon's Queen grabbed Vala by the throat to raise her off the ground as she decided what threat would be best used on the knight.

"You," Vala managed to smile but kept vibrating as the effort to do so was eating up whatever remained of energy, "have the greenest eyes."

Without a facial or verbal response, the Dragon's Queen got her emotion across to Vala in the most effective manner possible. She dislocated Vala's arm.

Vala's scream cracked and broke apart as she struggled but kept falling to a still as she'd tire herself out. Once a moment of rest came, she had more energy and struggled a bit more as she tried to scream again. Everything a confused mixture of instinct towards the pain and defeating exhaustion.

After a few moments the Dragon's Queen began to pull the arm. Slowly but surely she pulled so Vala felt every millimetre of pain as the Dragon's Queen attempted to tear the arm from Vala's socket.

"*Stop!*" Vala dry heaved the scream as she felt her skin began to split. "Please..."

Gold threads crept out of the nothing. The Dragon's Queen's eyes widened in anticipation as the fabric wrapped around Vala's revolting body. As the strings touched Vala's body they turned into her green and brown armour.

*   *   *

Asa cut through a Draugar. Slicing up the core buried within. Cutting off any possibility of reforming. She then let her blade curl up into an orb in her hand and tossed it towards the final Draugar. The stone was lodged free from the explosion towards Mei Ling. Two quick slashes from Mei Ling's wrist blades.

"We did it." Asa stretched with interlocked fingers to crack them over head.

"Y-yeah." Mei Ling grabbed her arms, a blinding pain surged through them. Her world shook as breath was lost and mind went numb. Everything was slow as gravity dragged her to the ground.

The ice shield fell. Cold water fell on top both Chika and Dawn. Soaking them entirely.

"*The hell!*" Dawn rolled to her side to cough her lungs free of water without realizing her restraints had vanished.

Chika snapped upright with a howler. Panic dulled as a state of disbelief took over her. Slowly, she regained her boundaries. With an exhausted mind, Chika looked herself over, "Why am I wet?" She slowly pulled her wet bangs from her eyes.

"Ask Mei Ling," Dawn pushed herself up to glare at Mei Ling, but instead of seeing the grin from the expected prankster, Dawn instead saw the back of Asa. Bent over something. Dawn felt the world stutter as she realized that *something* was Mei Ling.

"*Dawn!*" Asa shrieked as Mei Ling violently shook. Asa had her hands white knuckled around Mei Ling's biceps in a reactive attempt to still her. "Something's wrong with Mei Ling!"

Running on empty, Dawn slipped in the mud. Chika leapt with little effort.

Asa stepped to the side as Chika knelt over Mei Ling and took everything in. She ran her hand over Mei Ling's chest but couldn't feel a heartbeat. Colour left Chika's face as acid kicked up in the back of her throat. With a stern gulp, she fought the vomit down.

DISTANCE BETWEEN ECHOES

Chika placed the heel of her hand in the centre of Mei Ling's chest, the lower half of the sternum. Placed her second hand over top the first. Interlocked her fingers. Kept her elbows straight while bringing her body weight over her hands to help push down vertically.

Chika pushed down firmly and vertically about four centimetres. Relaxed and changed which arm she used for force, then repeated the compression. Between compressions, Chika relaxed the pressure on Mei Ling's chest without her hands losing contact with the sternum.

"One. Two. Three. Four." Chika counted out loud. Mentally trying to space the compressions at a rate of one-hundred a minute. On the thirtieth, Chika tilted Mei Ling's head back. Lifted her chin to clear the airway. Pinched Mei Ling's nose with two fingers to prevent any air leaking. Chika took a deep breath.

Chika sealed her mouth over Mei Ling's. Breathed slowly into Mei Ling for two seconds to inflate Mei Ling's chest. Chika watched Mei Ling's chest to see if it rose as she breathed.

There was some resistance. Chika held Mei Ling's head further back and tilted her chin again. The chest now rose. With the airway cleared, Chika breathed into Mei Ling two more times.

Chika went back to CPR. Compressing Mei Ling's chest thirty times then breathing into her twice. Repeated.

Unable to take her eyes off of Chika's performance, Asa white knuckled her skirt. Inside her head, Asa prayed to every god she had ever heard of.

Pleas to save her best friend followed by vows to devote her life to good wills: helping the less fortunate, going to church regularly, getting A's in school, and no longer cutting her knuckles against the teeth of preppy girls.

Behind Asa stood Dawn, peering over in a nauseous state. She attempted to look serious and focused, but her stance only managed to be that of quaking thighs. It was all she could do to keep from buckling under her own weight. A huge wave of guilt ran from her head down to her toes as she shivered.

Her mind didn't reach out for God. Dawn was pretty convinced that there wasn't one. But watching Chika at such a young age take over the situation so calmly made Dawn believe in biblical Angels.

Unable to watch for long, Dawn looked over to Ozazi. Tried to plea for help but there was no reflected expression from the Light.

Finally a gasp for air, followed by wide darting eyes. Rampant breath as claws clung to Chika's bicep. Mei Ling frantically accepted she was alive.

"Mei Ling." Chika softly smiled as she pulled Mei Ling towards her. Ran her hand over Mei Ling's back as she attempted to calm her. "You just had a heart attack. I was able to perform CPR and artificial respiration on you. You were gone for a minute, but I brought you back. You're going to be okay." Chika stuck to her training. The script she had been given. Her years of swimming finally paying off.

Chika felt Mei Ling smile against her chest before slipping into unconsciousness. Chika sighed with heavy relief as she held her friend, moving her only slightly to make sure her airway was free.

"Is she—" Asa fell to her knees, then reached out. The suddenly limp body cut through her vows and pleas to damns and regrets.

"She's fine." Chika smiled. "Just tired. We should rest awhile before moving her."

"Oh thank God." Asa fell backwards over her bent knees. Sprawled out her arms and stared up at the sky. "I almost had a heart attack." Asa cringed on her ill timed wording.

A gentle hand found Chika's shoulder. She looked up to see a smiling Dawn who spoke softly, "That was the most amazing thing I have ever seen." Dawn sighed. "Thank you."

Suppressed tears broke out from Chika's eyes as red rushed over her face. She had finally gotten a moment to take it all in. "I want to throw up so badly, but I don't want to get it all over her."

The girls took a moment to share in a laugh. For once in her life Mei Ling took something seriously; only because she was unconscious.

Their victory cut short as they all felt themselves engulfed in a grand shadow. Confusion overtook each girl as they first exchanged looks before looking upwards to see the Dragon's Queen watching them from above.

Her wings were mighty. A hundred foot wing span of a sharp, jagged design. They were featherless and connected with what at a first glance appeared to be torn flesh with thousands of batlike viens. Closer inspection showed the wings were solid rock. The veins, small cracks that further split with each flap. Trails of sand trickled down with each beat of her wings.

The rush of air from each flap reached the girls. Their hair twirled around their gawking faces as each felt their soul be clutched by an invisible hand and strangled by the mere sight of the Dragon's Queen.

"*Move!*" Dawn finally broke the silence. She scooped Mei Ling off the ground and somehow found the strength to leap to the side; fell short and skipped along her bicep a moment before correcting her stance and performing a new leap with perfection.

Asa and Chika were on her heels. All three jumped and just as they fell to the ground, jumped again. The Dragon Queen watched the girls make their way to the mountains. A grin crossed her face as she held up her right hand. An eerie green glow summoned around her fist.

With little effort to actually hit any of the girls, the Dragon's Queen aimed her hand towards the trio. From her hand shot a large blast of plasma.

It expanded on impact sending a rush of energy along the ground. It caught up to the heels of the girls and each of them felt its force lift them off their feet and send them a kilometre as the earth beneath them broke apart from a second, subterranean explosion.

Unable to hold onto Mei Ling, Dawn lost control of her friend. Slammed her shoulder to the ground and spun over and over for what seemed like forever. She managed to use her hand to brace herself and slid along it till she could twist herself to her feet to come to a stop.

Dawn caught Chika in her arms. Reached out for Asa who sped past but their extended fingers didn't quite clasp around each other.

With Asa vanishing into the smoke, Dawn turned back to the explosion. A crater that put anything Dawn had ever accomplished to shame was now where the energy had impacted the ground.

Jesus… we didn't even get hit by it… It took a moment for Dawn to realize the blinding pain running head to heel along the entire back part of her body. Her armour was failing. Dawn felt a strange pull throughout her being, which she recognized as the armour feeding from Dawn's very being to sustain itself.

"Asa! Chika!" Dawn put Chika on her feet. "Hit the sand with everything you've got. We need some cover. *Now!*"

The girls didn't question or argue. Both shot flame and lightning in every direction as quickly as they could.

With a variety of smoke and dust covering the three, Dawn ran past each girl. Tugged on them long enough to get them to rush in the direction she wanted. "Keep shooting!" Dawn ordered as she scooped up Mei Ling and kept running. "We'll make our way to the mountain. Find a cave. We need to hide til we figure out how to recharge."

A snap in the air. Distortion of sound and space as another beam crashed into the ground. The girls were lifted off their feet and sent to the left. The smoke swirled passed them as they rolled along the sand. Dawn managed to keep a hold on Mei Ling this time. The Dragon's Queen had missed.

This time her mind was focused enough. As the ground caved in Dawn felt a rumble through the ground. Twelve times the beam expanded, first on impact and then continued into the bridge itself.

"That's enough." Dawn looked around to confirm there was still enough smoke and sand in the air. She coughed through every word. "She can't see us and we don't need any light giving us away. Follow my voice."

The mountain didn't come quick enough. Dawn was forced to sprint, no more energy to leap. Dawn promised herself if they made it out of this alive, she would never take such a simple action of the armour for granted ever again.

The smoke was too thick, so Dawn found the mountain with her face rather than her eyes. With her nose throbbing she howled to warn the other two. "*Goddammit!*"

Dawn held Mei Ling in one arm while she held the other to the face of the mountain. "Follow me!" She sprinted along it hoping to come across a cave in the foot of the mountain.

A few minutes passed before Asa caught up to Dawn in pace. "Up there!" Asa pointed. Dawn didn't get a chance to reply as Asa scooped both Dawn and Mei Ling up and leapt to the opening just below the height of the cover of smoke. Chika followed.

*　　*　　*

The entire cave rumbled. Each time from a new direction, but no matter where it originated from, the entire mountain ridge vibrated from its intensity.

The rumbles were sequenced in sets of twelve, running a short course of a few seconds. You could quickly bounce a hand off of your knee to the beat. It was low and terrifyingly soothing. A pause came after each set, only to begin again ten seconds later.

The cave went on for awhile but it was yet to be fully

explored. About half way in, Mei Ling bounced her hand along to the eerily soothing rhythm. Her inner musician was on damage control for her psyche.

She wasn't sure how much time had passed while they had sat in the cave, but it felt at least half an hour since she had gained consciousness. Her armour was doing its job to keep her alive but Mei Ling still felt like half the woman she was.

Across with legs drawn up to her chin was Chika. Her face low, arms tightly wrapped around her shaking legs, and her eyes pierced through the dim light towards Mei Ling.

"Sorry." Mei Ling noticed the daggered eyes. A nervous grin and soft eyes steadied her hands.

Chika released a sigh that dwarfed the weight of a dying star. Her tight chest opened up as the burning behind her eyes drifted. She clasped a hand to the base of her neck. That pressure was back. Heavier than ever.

"It's okay, Mei Ling." Chika's eyes were low, mouth hardly oh-ed as she spoke. "How are you feeling?" Face remained drained of colour.

Mei Ling shrugged. A honest gesture as she didn't know if she was exhausted, scared, or nervous; possibly a cocktail of the three.

Chika rolled her neck so her vision tilted out towards the cave's entrance. An eerie green glow vibrated along with the rumbles. Afterwards, the night's soft glow came in ten second bursts. The blue light, though brief, was incredibly captivating.

Between the two girls and the entrance stood Dawn and Asa. The cave's lighting was low, which left them shadowed, masking any details to their form. Chika found it difficult to follow what they were exactly doing, but found a smile to her face at how cool the green glow made the two girls look.

"So Chika," Mei Ling scratched the side of her face. "What kind of music do you listen to, anyways?"

"What?" Chika jerked up, eyes wide and full of surprise. "What kind of question is that?" Her voice high pitched and cracked.

"Well..." Mei Ling closed her eyes. Black and grey threads pulled away to reveal her jeans and bunny hug. "So far I've asked everyone else. Dawn likes country... gross. Asa is into hip hop, which I won't get into. Vala and I like rock, though I feel like she might not really be into music, so she'll listen to just about everything.

"Which is really weird to me." Mei Ling reached out to Chika. The rumbles illuminated her iPod in a soft green glow. "I have like 400 songs. Mostly 80's rock or 70's pop, but as long as you like instruments they'll be something for you here."

"I..." Chika quaked her words as thoughts ran dry. "Don't know what to say."

Chika stood up and took the iPod, slowly put each earbud in. Ran her thumb along the library until she found a family favourite. She filled her ears with "Castle in the Sky".

Immersion brought on by closed eyes allowed escape to seep into Chika's soul.

Down the cave, Asa paced back and forth while Dawn stood still. Asa moved tilted forward and straight armed as she swiftly went the length of the cave, then turned on a heel. Repeated.

Dawn stood closest to the cave entrance. Her eyes watched the little bit of Earth she could see from her position with arms folded, face stern but with vibrations clinging to everything tight. Back in street clothes from her armour finally giving out, her strong exterior was working overtime to hide her soft interior. Slowly, the scared little girl Dawn had spent so many years burying was clawing its way to the surface.

"We are all going to die here." Dawn whispered to herself.

"You say something?" Asa paused on her heel mid rotation. Her eyes lost in the darkness of the back of the cave. She used the rumble's light to slowly run her vision outlining objects in the dark.

Dawn didn't reply right away. Her thoughts were being blocked by absence of will.

Chika walked passed Dawn. Only a quick eye dart to

Dawn before sitting down. Her body was steady but light on her feet. Every action precise and unwasted but Chika's blanked mind was instructing anything but intention. It was busy buried in the past. Present thought had no business at the moment.

Dawn studied Chika with concerned eyes, in an attempt to make sense of the weight on Chika's shoulders.

After what seemed a lifetime, Dawn answered Asa. "I just cleared my throat." Her eyes paused hard during a blink. It took days worth of strength to keep her voice from stuttering. Dawn bit her lip as a release.

"Oh." Asa started her pacing again.

In the back of the cave, Mei Ling sat with her head now tilted upwards, pressed against the damp rock. Eyes closed while the rumble met her spine through the wall and her crossed legs through the floor, almost mimicking a massage chair. Mei Ling smiled in the darkness as her hands danced along her thighs again.

Chika rested her eyes. She doubled the volume of the iPod to drown out the world with the beats of the music. She leaned her chin against her knee cap. Though she couldn't see the faint green light across her body, she felt its heat and rumble. Chika let the heat soothe her body as she let the beat of music sooth her mind, and allow her to drift into herself.

A perverse destiny meant for isolation twisted into a welcoming embrace. Sudden realization that hesitation of an unforeseen future left a pageless past and emptied present. Meaningless was a word distanced to notion as Chika clasped her heart and endured pain as she openly welcomed reality. There would never be balance in this torn heart.

Welcoming smiles attached to family faces, her mind rushed to wrap arms around their bodies. Embrace familiarity of the life that was certain. Safe. A charade of happiness. Past the smiles, just over their shoulders on the horizon, were a set of green powerful eyes and beautiful flowing hair.

An imaginary wind curved the long hairs in rumbled rhythm around pale naked skin. The hairs reached an impossible distance through the crowd of faces. Bodies pushed aside as the blonde warmth embraced Chika. Fair hairs touched caramel skin, to dance along her curves and through swaying fingertips; a strand landed between curled lips.

The blonde pulled Chika through the darkness. Everything spun. Rushed. Twisted. Acid in her stomach. Dried mouth. Hard pressed eyes clung to an undecided between but overworked lungs raced to an anticipating pace.

Dawn jumped to the side of an iced over lake. Red crimson painted on her fists as her Amazon eyes locked on a target who wrapped its mighty hands around Chika. Memory refreshed filters. Chika opened her eyes to the presence of green rumble. Echoes of mother and father gave an imaginary lecture that would never be brought to reality, due to a damning sense of indecision.

The first time Chika had met Dawn had been so awakening. Dawn was fast, powerful, fearless, unstoppable, smart, and most importantly, lying about all the above. Past the military training, through the aged years brought on by weight of responsibility, clouded mind with thick storms of false maturity and if you were willing to push beyond—there was the true Dawn.

Chika saw the girl that Dawn used to be. Nights in tears with screaming teeth dug into bird down. Pushed fists into sides of a pillow. Arched back as strained lungs filled her face with red. Legs stretched and twisted with clawing toenails into a bed spread. Chika saw the girl she used to be.

Chika saw the girl that Dawn was supposed to be. Wearing skirts that drove fear into the hearts of fathers. Tops cut sharper than glares of teenage boys. Vocabulary that had no place coming from a girl who secretly read behind closed doors. A girl finding embraces, dreams, and friends both exciting and dangerous. Chika saw the girl she was supposed to be.

Chika saw the girl Dawn would be. Tall. Strong. Powerful. Destined. Most importantly, alive. Chika saw everything she would never be.

Twelve rumbles came. Chika pushed forward on the

first beat. Straightened legs on the second. Twisted hips on the third. Met stern brown eyes to a wide green set on the fourth. Ball fists on the fifth. Gulped on the sixth. Extended arms on the seventh. Clasped hands on a collar on the eighth. Eyes shut on the ninth. Pulled on the tenth. Pushed on the eleventh.

Had her first kiss on the twelfth.

Soft lips pressed as sloppy technique allowed drool to escape. A spark of electricity ran down Chika's spine as nirvana replaced reality.

Chika pulled away. A strand of spit glistened in the blue light before breaking the parting girls.

Dawn was red faced with darting green eyes, a racing heart, quivering lips, sweat on brow, and a dried voice. "Why did you do that?" Dawn barely spoke.

Without waiting for the rumble to return, Chika followed a clarity that she had never felt before in her entire life. A mixture of self acceptance to her mortal self and the proximity of the River to her Dragonborn soul opened her mind to the possibilities of her true power. She stepped two long strides back as her shoulder blades glowed fire hot.

Fire wings expanded into a hundred foot wing span. Built entirely of fire but still holding physical form, they curved along the edge of the cramped cave. Smoke trailed behind every movement they made.

Wings ignited the entire cave into a furious red heat. Mei Ling startled to her feet. Asa swore in reflex. Dawn hesitated in daze of acceptance of a friend accepting herself for the first time.

Chika pulled her wings back so that they were safely out of the mouth of the cave. Flapped her wings. The force pushed the girls. Both Mei Ling and Asa blocked their eyes with their arms. But Dawn reached out in reaction to the realization of the last moment of her best friend, the tips of her fingers burning from the heat of Chika's wings.

The wings forced Chika off of her feet and out of the cave. They dragged along the walls of the cave causing the mouth to cave in a little.

Through falling rubble, Dawn watched helplessly as Chika sped forward to distant death's certainty.

Asa pulled Dawn away as rock grazed the dazed Angel's face. The stone cut through her flesh sharply just above the eye, but the sting of psychical pain was dwarfed by the crippling internal pain of grasping aimlessly at an unreachable thought of action and left her only with hopelessness.

Chika dove towards the ground. She hit the repeat button on her iPod. The wings dragged Chika across the sky. Each flap brought a white crescent swirl of air. Each sonic boom rocketed her forward. Finger slid across the iPod from six to maxed ten. Brown eyes let tears slip away with every beat of song and every pull of her wings.

CHAPTER SIXTEEN: WAYWARD

Vala's head rattled in place while her numb mind was distant from anything resembling thought. Arms of liquid draped over stone armrests while hands of lead were shackled in place. Hollowed brown eyes stared out the room's large glass window towards Earth, though the fractured mind did not bother recognizing it.

Vala half sat, half laid on a stretched out stone chair made of various carvings of gods and languages she did not recognize. In full armour, she laid virtually lifeless as tubes pumped chemicals to disconnect thoughts from actions.

The room shook with rumbling stone gears embedded into the west and east walls. The entire room was an analog computer created near the beginning of time itself. Brown stone made up most of the room aside from the south and north wall being large glass windows, much like the one found in the Dragon's Queen's throne room. Under the thin layer of stone bricks, both above and below, hundreds of much smaller gears were accompanied by various pumps.

A hatch in the ceiling opened up, from it fell two steel arms attached to rusted braces that strained to hold the arms weight when fully extended. The mechanical arms rested just above Vala.

The arms were a thick tubing made of an ancient metal. They ran along Vala's forearms, flattened around the top of her hand and extended down each finger individually. Within it resided black slimy slugs wedged as compactly as possible.

The presence of Vala sprung life into the hibernating creatures. Slowly they stretched out and attached themselves through openings in the joints and the ends of the arms.

The first layer of slugs bit into Vala's pale skin. Though painful, she wasn't in the state of mind to react to their teeth. As they sucked the energy of the Echo out from Vala, the second layer of slugs came to life and bit into the slug ahead. This leeching chain continued over and over up through the arms, into the machines above, and through a series of pipes.

Hidden behind the walls slept a creature that held no name. It was specifically created by the Dragon for this single task. The beast was a dull red with crusted skin, mimicking an armadillo the way it curled into its shell. Its snout was corkscrewed with jagged teeth escaping at all angles. It held two sets of eyes, one above and one below the snout.

Sensing the surge of energy above, the armadillo spun itself rapidly within its chamber. Its speed picked up until it was generating an intense heat that melted the slugs from above. The energy from Vala seeped through the spinning shell to be absorbed by the pores of the beast.

When enough energy was collected, the beast's twisted black eyes turned a milky white. The side of the chamber was opened by one of the Dragon's Queen's minions who gutted the beast with a double edged serrated blade.

The beast shrieked but its gluttony refused to allow it to slow down. It maintained its momentum as it fed and fed from the energy. The minion continued to gut the beast as Vala's energy kept healing the wound closed.

From the wound fell gold, glowing blood. It fell into a funnel that would seep through a series of pipes into a vat below. The vat was shaped in a circle used as a lens for a large telescope aimed towards the River.

Once filled, the telescope would be activated. The energy of the Atoms of God would be converted into Distance to be sent to the River for the Dragon to weave to his will.

Ahead of Vala, another telescope, the size of a large bus, was being pushed in place. The thin end pointed towards Vala while the large lens pointed towards Earth. Once the telescope was in place, minions retrieved long steel apparatuses. They placed them over top both of Vala's arms and the steel pipes housing the slugs.

The apparatuses looked similar to metal gauntlets with thousands of extended thin metal bars coming off of them. Each bar was the dull end of a needle that the minions slowly pushed into Vala's flesh.

When the final needle was in place, they removed the cap on the telescope lens. Vala was instantly connected at a spiritual level to every human being on planet Earth.

Once the glass of the scope aligned with Earth, everything stepped up in intensity.

The armadillo demon's nostrils flared. It could sense the entire spiritual energy of planet Earth and wanted it all. Every man. Every woman. Every child. Every single Atom of God. Lust for the human soul beyond description.

*　　*　　*

Everything halted on Earth when the telescope aligned. Anything with an Atom of God within its chest felt the alignment instantly.

Infants died. Hundreds of millions of lives lost in a half a second.

There was no time for the confusion of any onlookers. Mothers didn't get to grieve. Nurses didn't gasp in bewilderment. Because the pain.

Every survivor felt the indescribable pain that is having your soul torn from your body. Bit by bit, the world was awakened to the realization that all of their old fables were correct. The soul existed. There was no time for rejoice or praise. Something icy reached into the chest cavities of the people of the world and violently tore the warmth out.

Instantly, many collapsed, while others had heart attacks from the stress or fell into shock—and those were the lucky ones.

It wasn't long before the varied sick and elderly joined those killed from the alignment of the telescope. Within moments, the death toll trumped a billion.

The healthy and young held strong but the number would climb as cars crashed, planes fell, and the desperate ended it themselves; the entire experience was three minutes long, but felt like hours of a hell that would make waterboarding blush.

In three minutes, the planet Earth felt a devastating loss in its population.

*   *   *

Across the cosmos, the Distance stretched to the River. The normally red skies of the River turned a pulsating cyan and navy blue. Every warrior holding sword and shield cheered as they were engulfed in the strange light.

The bellowing howls of the armies awoke the Dragon. His lizard eyes rolled around in his skull to find the sky. Lips curled as his wings stretched so far they collapsed the cave he slumbered in.

Emerging from curbing rock, the largest and most powerful of the Echo race rose to the skies. It was impossible for the Dragon to condense his physical state to anything smaller than that of a skyscraper, but for dramatic flare, he allowed his being to be as large as possible so that his wings could wrap around the widest of cities.

His giant purple eyes aimed upwards to a silver device made up of bent metal making a hollowed sphere. Cyan threads filled the sphere with golden light as the souls of Earth were collected for the Dragon's weaving.

Gigantic wings blacked out the sun as the Dragon rose over his army towards the silver sphere. The beat of the wings caused the warriors below to buckle to one knee. The warriors strained to stand as was custom to show their respects.

Ancient magics kept the sphere aloft near the top of the River's atmosphere. Small specks of gold would appear inside the gigantic orb, each speck a human soul.

Once materialized, a spirit shot around the sphere trying to escape towards the Womb, to reenter the reincarnation cycle, but the magic held them. During the bouncing, the spirit would be beaten from its condensed form, unraveling into string rather than a solid ball of energy.

With a massive claw, the Dragon grabbed the collective orb of Distance. With little effort, he began to funnel the Distance into a bridge. With his laughter came ignition of his breath. Intense white flames raised the temperature of the River by several degrees.

A supernatural darkness replaced the sky as the cyan bridge eclipsed the planet. From the Dragon wove a shadow that seeped into the entire planet. He bent the rules of reality to his will as he joined his planet to the physical manifestation of the Bridge.

*   *   *

Chika slammed a fist into the base of the Dragon's Queen's skull. Pushed her hands together to follow up with a stream of flame that crossed several lengths of a football field. Somewhere between Chika's palms and the tip of the flame screamed the Dragon's Queen.

DISTANCE BETWEEN ECHOES

The Dragon's Queen dove out of the way of the flame, spiraled into a nosedive as her stone wings dissolved into a sand storm. The thick squall of dust extinguished the flames almost instantly. The Dragon's Queen regathered the storm into a set of wings and veered towards Chika without missing a beat of the heart.

Green light shot upwards to Chika. The beam expanded every few metres into a dozen flat discs that stretched outwards. Chika flapped her wings to soar backwards, pulled up her chin as her entire body was engulfed by the eerie glow of the attack. The heat pressed against Chika but due to her natural immunity to the intense temperature, she was left with only the sensation of coming out of a sauna.

Before she could turn her attention downwards to the Dragon's Queen, the Dragon's Queen delivered a sucker punch to Chika's gut. The young knight curled over the warrior's arm. Before Chika could take in the hissing of the Dragon's Queen's cursing, she was already being taken by the ankle and hurled to the ground below.

Thought came back just as quickly as her lungs struggled to fill themselves with air. A second before becoming one with the ground below, Chika pulled out of her dive. Too frightened to look behind, Chika pushed herself forward as fast as she could, by fueling her wings into a blaze to push herself much like a jet.

Several beams were sent downwards to Chika. She pulled to her side and flapped to dodge one then twirled under another and arced upwards and back just skimming her wing span across an expanding disc.

Chika hurled two white hot fireballs. The Dragon's Queen batted the flames away with one of her wings. The quick action had consequence, as it blocked vision of Chika's follow up.

With the Dragon's Queen exposure came Chika's stretched hands. Taking a page out of Asa's dictionary, Chika gouged the Dragon's Queen while wrapping her wings around her to engulf the two in an intense fire.

The heat didn't affect Chika but the howling from the Dragon's Queen indicated to Chika that they were being as effective as intended.

However, to Chika's quick dismay, the screaming broke into laughter, followed quickly by a strong grip to her throat and a piercing nail into her neck. With angelic transformation protecting her from most of the pain, Chika held her grip and attempted to pour more energy into the flames.

A quick jerk to the Dragon's Queen's wrist whiplashed Chika. Watching her victim caught in a moment of agonizing pain, the Dragon's Queen released Chika. Before Chika could pull her wings back to escape into flight, a green glow consumed her vision.

On reflex alone, Chika pulled in her wings to take the brunt of the attack. Her magic fought against the energy as most of it was thrown aside, but enough shot past the safety of flames and into her chest.

Chika spiraled out of control.

Before Chika could pull herself upwards to follow up with her fist into the Dragon's Queen's jaw, she fell into focus of the telescope.

Something cold reached its jagged claws deep into Chika's chest as it tore her soul out so violently that blood trailed from her spiralling body. Like a rag doll, her body smashed into the rock below, cutting flesh, crushing bone, and dislocating limbs.

Luckily for Chika, she was already dead a metre off the ground.

*   *   *

On the third minute, Chika's violently torn soul made its way through the glass of the lens, mechanical gears, through the needles, up Vala's arms and before the slugs could suck it dry from existence, it collided violently with the slumbering Echo deep within Vala.

The mind was no longer numb. Every voice of every soul rushed through Vala's mind. They were so clear, she swore millions of cries were coming directly next her ears.

Vala screamed into awareness. She thrashed herself free. Her flesh tore as her muscles forced her arms off the chair. Blood trailed her descent as she threw herself off of the chair and onto the tile floor.

Gauntlets fell, and Vala kicked them away. Pushed herself so her back was to the chair. Pain being no concern as Vala's hands cupped around her ears. She tried to block out the voices but they were coming from every direction and all at once. Worse yet, they were coming within. Vala's eyes shot as wide as they could go as she began to dry heave.

The realization of being the cause of over a billion deaths tore away at every strand of humanity that Vala had. In a single second she connected to every soul and witnessed any moment that each spirit had ever had the pleasure of witnessing themselves.

At first she was screaming and clawing her fingers into her ears as she shook her face violently to try to push the deafening voices out of her head. Second, came tears as she lost who she was to her own self pity and despair. Third, the naked touch of Chika's soul rushing to the front of the screaming voices flowed through every vein in Vala's body so violently you could see them quaking from the outside.

Vala vanished.

Replaced by her original self.

Golden light exploded out from Vala. Every minion, slug, and beast in the castle reduced to a fine dust, followed shortly by the iron, rock, and the rest of the structure.

The only remaining parts were a conscious decision to keep the floor of the room that Vala stood in above the mountains. Only the odd jagged beam remained of the castle below the analog room.

The Echo rose before returning Vala's mind back to the vessel that was Vala's body. Her armour turned brown. The sleeves expanded to encase her hands in gloves. Her skirt tightened around her body to expand into shorts. Her heels expanded into thick three lace boots that ran up to her kneecaps.

The connection to her former self infused Vala with power she had never before imagined possible. The universe shook with her might. She felt her being reach into the everything to find the nothing. Through it, she found the Womb and dug deep to drag out the warmth of the Echo into reality.

A jacket formed over top her upper half. Its material three times thicker than the rest of her armour. Pink fabric that split just above her navel and extended out to the sides then backwards to form a half button up coat.

Vala's mind settled in her newly imbued body as the acceptance of all the past deaths became buried by the Echo's will. The screams were no longer gasps and hollers for serenity. Instead, they hissed and bubbled behind her ears with a thick presence of fuel being stored.

The inside of the coat burned a bright gold before dulling into normal fabric. Brown belts escaped just above her buttocks and looped over her shoulders to be clipped at the end with gold just below her breast.

The fuel bore its warmth through every centimetre of Vala's body. It ran down her limbs and up to her eyes. Dug deep behind them until the universe was rewritten. Lost its soft and hard edges. Left only by an endless sea of blended threads. Vala's brown, bloodshot eyes were replaced with a golden glow.

Her hair retracted upwards into a fold to shorten the length to just above her shoulders. A gold pin held it in place as pink fabric extended from the base of her neck, came up the back of her skull, and fell just above her eye lids to create a hood.

Every breath pushed her warmth out into the universe. Infected reality with her touch. Bled mental connection into her surroundings. With every pull of air came a blinding pink light to her breath that turned golden when she exhaled.

The pattern of a freshly sprouting branch stretched out from the lower right of the coat up and around her back to show just a tip of the branch folding in around her left bicep.

The armour finished its evolution. Vala continued her ascension.

The coat's shoulder blades parted as mighty wings erupted from Vala. The wings were derived of Vala's natural element, Tree. They were an entanglement of thousands of intertwined branches. Green leaves littered the back side of the wings in a downward position to mimic feathers of a bird. With each flap, several leaves would fall turning orange or red before curling into a brown just as they touched the ground; they were always replaced just as quickly as they had fallen.

With the last ounce of the Echo's conscience driving Vala, she reached outwards and focused on the elements of the universe. A golden staff of pure energy ran the length of Vala's body.

Earth. A pink flicker came at the base of the staff to have a spike of rock.

Fire. A single strand of fire spiraled from base to tip. It rotated clockwise, passing freely past Vala's wrist.

Water. A stream of flowing water twisted like a river around the shaft.

Metal. The golden staff hardened into a white metal.

Tree. From the tip of the staff spouted an unearthly barren tree that contorted itself in a maze of branches.

Distance. Cyan and navy leaves sprouted along half of the branches.

Void. Transparent leaves sprouted along the rest of the branches, each acting as a lens and inverting any colour seen through it.

With her mortal mind back in control, Vala focused. A pressure at her frontal lobe as she strained to maintain her new power. Buried deep within herself was a warmth hidden amongst the burning energy of the Echo. A warmth that was slowly depleting into a cold nothing. Deep within Vala stormed a chaos that was the power of a god; somewhere in that squall was Chika.

*　　　*　　　*

There was nothingness all around Chika. She floated in such blackness that she herself was part of the darkness. A nothingness soaring through a field of nothingness connected to a sea of nothingness in a world of nothingness engulfed in a universe of nothing—light.

Her eyes blinked wildly as colour returned to her body and ahead of her, the golden and pink light ignited into a person. "Vala?"

Chika's eyes darted all around Vala. From her armour, to her hair, to the strange perfection in her skin. "You look gorgeous."

Vala smiled. "You look beautiful." Her voice shook the entire universe. The vibration ran through Chika's very core causing her to shiver under her friend's sheer might.

"That doesn't sound like something Vala would say." Chika accented her folded arms with a set of twisted lips. "Who are you, and what have you done with Vala?"

"Dude," Vala waved her hands skyward. "I'm trying to be all mystical and shit. Don't take this from me."

"Where are we?" Chika ran her hands along her biceps to try to heat herself up. She wasn't sure why she was so cold; she didn't notice it was because the warmth of her soul was missing.

"You're inside of me, Chika." Vala laughed to herself at how funny that sounded as the power died down and she returned to her normal self. Armour removed as street clothes, imperfections in her skin, dyed hair, and contacts returned.

Vala swung her arms and legs to create momentum to float over to Chika. The two caught each other and began to slowly spin clockwise through the nothingness.

"I don't understand," Chika freed a hand to rub her eye with her palm. "I don't remember anything. I can't even remember my friends or family. What is happening to me?"

"I ripped your soul out of your body," Vala bent her shoulders and cocked half a grin. "You can't remember anything because you're detached from your mind. You're only remembering what I need you to remember of yourself to have this conversation. I'm remembering for you."

"I don't," Chika fidgeted as she fought to pull a single thought from the back of her mind. "Am I dead?"

"We don't truly die," Vala jabbed Chika in the chest. "But you already knew that, didn't you?"

"Yeah," Chika rubbed her wound more instinctively than out of necessity, as she didn't feel any pain in this place. Slowly after Vala spoke, Chika's religious beliefs came rushing back. "I did."

"I need you for something very important," Vala took in a deep breath. "I need your power. We need to finish this, to protect everyone."

"You sound weird," Chika pulled back, but Vala didn't let her finish the action.

"Can you help me?" Vala's smile twitched as she fought back tears.

"Yea—" Chika gulped. "Yeah, of course."

*   *   *

Vala returned to the ruined castle with her eyes blinding gold and her armour in place, because she had never truly left. Now that her mind was focused on the outside world, Vala turned to face the Dragon's Queen.

Only a second had passed since the explosion of golden light to the formation of Vala's armour and Chika's conversation to this moment. The Dragon's Queen watched in disbelief as Vala's mighty wings pushed off the ground.

Vala slowly spun around to face the Dragon's Queen. As she did, she let a tiny golden orb escape towards the collective on the River.

The Dragon's Queen fired her green beam of energy. Vala tightened her eyes as she didn't miss a beat. With one motion, Vala sped towards the Dragon's Queen, caught the beam only a centimetre out of the Dragon's Queen's fingers.

Vala didn't break eye contact with the Dragon's Queen as the attack was reduced to nothing more than a light show escaping twelve times through a clenched fist.

"What..." the Dragon's Queen tried to break away. "What are you!?"

"This is for Rift," Vala extended her arm to focus her mind to feel every cell within the Dragon's Queen. She used her connection to the elements of the universe to create a miniature black hole in the core of the Dragon's Queens chest cavity.

Though it was but a second to the outside world, from the Dragon's Queen's perspective her body took a hundred years to finish collapsing in on itself into nothingness. Vala's magic manipulated space and time to create the most hellish torture any living creature had or ever would go through; a permanent stamp of cruelty on the universe that would never be overthrown.

Paying the black hole no mind, Vala moved her attention down below to three sets of wide eyes. Behind her, the miniature black hole collapsed out of existence just as quickly as it had appeared.

Threads of golden light rushed over the three knights. A familiar warmth that matched that of the soul rushed over the girls as they were engulfed by the light. Vala mentally wove the three orbs upwards to her.

"I need your Lights." Vala smiled as she had come down to meet the orbs halfway. "You won't be getting them back."

Before anyone could reply, a cyan portal emerged as Ozazi rolled out. He shared an exchange with Dawn, a simple nod that said more than any words could.

Mei Ling pulled Flea out of her bunny hug. "Get'em, buddy."

"It has been a pleasure." Flea floated towards Vala.

"Hey," Mei Ling ran her hand down her neck. "I never did get your name."

"Didn't you?" Flea turned around for one last glance. "My name is Flea."

Mei Ling smiled. "Damn right it is."

"What's the gameplan?" Asa was the only one still in armour. She focused thought to dematerialize her armour. She gave Nither one last pat on the head before pushing him to Vala.

"We're going to take a less than direct approach on this one." From Vala's finger tips expanded golden threads which wove into Dawn's face to instantly heal it.

Dawn gently touched her face. Her nose was normal. Her eye no longer sat off centred. The scars sunk into themselves to flatten into the rest of her skin. Her face was back to normal. It felt perfect and whole, but none of that mattered to her. With no regard to what the rest of the world thought of her anymore, Dawn let her voice whimper the only thing her mind was capable of focusing on, "Chika..."

Vala smiled. "Let's end this."

The girls exchanged looks while Vala turned to face the River. Their orbs merged into a single one just behind Vala. Threads of grey and black from Mei Ling, white and silver from Dawn, and yellow and orange from Asa, bled through the orb and into Vala.

Vala wove gold threads into each Light before sending them down the Bridge. They expanded to make a large diamond as their energies fused to create beams of golden light leading to each other.

A blinding golden light came from the tip of Vala's staff. She swung it, sending a beam of pink light from its tip.

The pink light was slow at first as it crept along the universe. It stretched out like a root expanding to find water. As the root divided to become new roots, its speed picked up. Over and over it multiplied, until there were hundreds of millions of roots speeding down the bridge towards the River.

Vala raised a free hand, weaving cyan threads, to summon wormholes in front of each root. Each one took a sharp incline before diving forward to dig deep into the wormholes.

The Dragon gripped the orb of Distance between his four claws, his entire body curled over its energy. The metal sphere had expanded as the device was preparing the Atoms for conversion into Distance.

His eyes filled with anticipation as he was eager to finally take his place as the rightful ruler of the universe.

Millions of cyan threads knotted as wormholes appeared from all directions. The Dragon jerked his head to look around as his orb was bombarded with millions of roots. They penetrated the metal sphere's magic, each grabbing a single Atom of God before retracting just as quickly as they had appeared.

The Dragon cried out with flames of pure white. He slashed at the roots when his flames did nothing, catching only a few thousand.

With no regard to the structure of the Bridge, his plans or his own safety, the Dragon sped down the Bridge as quickly as he could. Flames trailed out of his open jaw as his tight eyes focused on the golden light of Vala's staff.

As the Dragon sped down the bridge towards Vala, his mighty energy collided with the sands and mountains. Earthquakes ran through the entire structure. Cracks and explosions soared across the bridge.

Unamused by the Dragon, Vala sent more roots. Focused her thoughts to push the beams at a much faster pace at, around, and past the Dragon. The roots found their souls and quickly retracted towards her.

One of the roots let go of an orb about halfway down the bridge. The blinding golden light contorted as a violent force from inside fought against the abyss to exist. In an explosion of pink threads, Chika became whole.

She ducked just as a mighty wind from the beat of the Dragon's wings came over head. The air pressure tossed her hair back and almost tore her perfectly fitted farm animal pyjamas.

Before Chika could take in the sight of the gigantic beast barrelling through the bridge towards her friends, a cyan portal appeared. Esh tumbled out as the knot faded.

"Hey, little guy," Chika caught Esh.

*   *   *

Vala rested her eyes as she focused on the souls within; like a god, she judged each and every one of them. Pushed the rapists, pedophiles, murderers, and those that hid behind the safety of laws to benefit from the above; into her staff. Race, age, or reasons for committing any of these acts were put aside as her inner rage dictated the worth of over a billion lives.

She began to convert the energy into an unnamed element as she tightened her eyes to meet the glare of the Dragon, who barrelled towards her at speeds that were well past possibility.

Vala swung her staff. From it, billions of streams of Earth, Fire, Metal, Tree and Water expanded into a spiralling lance. Each element extended several kilometres before spiralling downwards in millions of thin strips back to her hand.

The elemental lance caught the Dragon in the side, hurling him into the golden diamond of Lights. The beams of gold expanded towards Esh in order to complete the prison.

*   *   *

"This is going to be our last conversation," Esh lowered his metal shards to show his sadness. "Chat, hearing, conference, yak, gab, talk, moment, word, exchange,"

"How about," Chika smiled as she ran her hand along her friend, "parley."

"I'll miss you," Esh pulled himself out of Chika's grip to aim himself towards the prison.

"Yeah," Chika closed her eyes, as she failed the good fight. Her entire body shook as her voice cracked and tears slide down her cheeks. "I'll miss you too, buddy."

"Pal."

"Partner."

"Amigo."

"Hey," Chika used the back of her forearm to dry her face. "Using different languages is cheating."

"My apologies," Esh eyed up the beam heading towards them. "How about, 'friend'?"

"Yeah," Chika snorted as she cupped both hands around Esh. "Friend sums it up just fine."

The energy connected to Esh and through him to Chika. The two merged spiritually while retaining their physical forms as Chika became the brace to dam the energy at this end of the prison, while Esh became a scope to aim the energy back up the beam to complete the prison.

The backlash of energy wrapped around Chika's body. The warmth inside of her chest reached out to the golden light. Instinctively instructed the energy into threads and then into armour.

*   *   *

The golden beams entrapped the Dragon. His roar shook reality itself as he fought in vain with both claw and flames to break the prison.

With no sign of regret, Vala converted the souls buried within the staff's core into raw energy. Mei Ling watched wide eyed as the staff raised and platinum energy tore through the fabric of space and time. An ungodly shriek of high pitched pleas for the right to exist trailed the energy.

Faces of the damned tore through the flat edging of the beam. They fought to hold themselves together as their arms were pulled and torn apart while they reached out to grab onto the nothingness around them. Hands tore through the clasped jaws of the faces as one soul after the other fought for freedom of the conversion. As one pulled the jaws back of another to drag itself into sight, another soul had already began to force its jaws open. Repeating the process endlessly as the beam freely passed into the prison then collided into the snout of the Dragon.

His skull was forced upwards as the heat of the energy tore down his neck and into his chest. His impossibly resilient scales kept the energy from tearing through him. Instead the beam splashed around him becoming many smaller beams.

Vala tightened her eyes and ground her teeth as she fought to contain the entanglement of souls. Now using both hands on the staff to steady the beam, it was all she could do is keep the souls in a state of energy.

Mei Ling was the first to swallow the horrific sight ahead of her as she placed her hand on Vala's back. She didn't need to be asked and she didn't need to be instructed; something inside of her told how to help.

Every ounce of magic that ever belonged to Mei Ling was fused with the Echo inside of Vala. The two became connected at a spiritual level as both minds worked together to steady the mighty power of the Echo; to focus the endless chaos of pleading spirits.

As Mei Ling's focus poured into Vala's mind, black and grey threads unraveled from Vala's coat. They engulfed Mei Ling's arm. The thick entanglement expanded outwards to rebuild her armour.

With a nod, then a shifting of weight, and finally a hand to Vala's back, Asa lent her power as well. She closed her eyes as tight as humanly possible as she tried to block out everything that was going on.

Dawn followed suit. Her eyes were tight and teeth gritted.

Both girls were entangled by thread. Pulled forward and given their armour back.

With the three backing her, Vala was able to finish the conversion of souls into raw energy. The splash increased around the chest of the Dragon and bounced within the prison held together by straining Lights.

"Oh boy..." Chika was wide eyed as she witnessed the beams ricocheting off the Dragon then curving around him and heading down her thin beam of light. The energy grouped itself into a blob of plasma that barrelled towards her.

Chika held Esh in both hands as she bent her knees and locked her elbows to prepare for the condensed ball of energy. It pushed her, but Chika dug her feet into the nothingness around her, somehow finding a foothold.

Using sheer will alone, Chika kept the energy at bay. The pressure shook her forearms so violently the vibration coursed through her entire being, rattling bone so hard she felt it tearing into her every muscle.

Chika tightened her eyes as she took a moment to run a hand from her forehead, to her stomach, to her right chest, and finally her left. She cried out as she attempted to hold the plasma.

The bleed-over of energy that she couldn't contain found itself to her. Burrowed deep into every pore of her body, filling her with the screaming voices of the damned. Wide eyes quaked in horror as every hope and dream fizzled out for her to witness the extinguish of thousands of souls.

But the strength this gave her was necessary. With her new power, Chika shoved her shoulder into the giant ball that now dwarfed her into a mere speck.

Chika dragged her teeth over themselves as she crushed her eyes and grunted to gain ground as her feet slipped over each other. She took one final stomp before screaming every ounce of energy of her being into Esh and through him into the balled energy.

The condensed ball was shattered into thousands of beams of light that were redirected back towards the prison.

Each Light received its own quantity of the beams. Each redirected them along the bars of the bridge to cement them into a permanent state of reality.

With the prison now complete, it was safe for Vala to release the remaining souls in her body back into the womb. Returning them to their former lives was an impossibility but Vala was able to keep the innocent within the reincarnation cycle of humanity.

The Echo's job was complete. Vala exhaled golden light as she collapsed forward. As she fell, the threads of her friend's armour followed suit.

Mei Ling reached out and grabbed Vala by hooking an arm under her armpit. The weight pulled Mei Ling down, but Asa was quick to grab Vala by the arm and aid Mei Ling into pulling the tired Echo into the safety of their bubble.

Green eyes shook seas worth of water as a hoarse voice screamed to decibels never before witnessed in human speech. "*Chika!*" Dawn reached out as far as her arm could extend, but the bubble only allowed her to get as far as her shoulder out of its safety.

The broken time and space between the two halves of the bridge were collapsing onto itself. An unnatural blackness slowly engulfed the space outwards going in. It wouldn't be more than a minute before Chika was nothing but a waving hand through the nothingness.

"I'm coming back!" Dawn slammed a fist against the bubble. "Chika, I swear to God!"

Threads of red and purple pulled back over Chika's shoulders. She stood in the nothing in only her favourite animal pyjamas. Isolated from her power, she never felt more at peace. A warmth from within pulsated up her being and behind her eyes. They began to burn and quake. She swallowed the memory of their kiss. A content smile accompanied satisfied eyes, "I know."

Chika reached forward to press extended fingertips to an invisible wall.

Dawn's fist shook. Fell apart into tight digits that dragged down the wall of the bubble until they dulled.

Bubbles retreated the girls to where their ends of the bridge lead. Chika alone towards the River, while the others aimed towards Earth. They all watched each other as long as they could before the final speck of nothingness took over and they no longer could see beyond their half of the bridge, leaving the Dragon some place between the two dimensions in a sort of nothing for all of time.

Mei Ling sat down cross legged as she held Vala's head in her lap. Brushed the sweat soaked bangs of hair off her face. Vala looked so at peace, Mei Ling couldn't help but smile; even though the back of her throat ached, quaked, and fought to swallow emotion between breaths.

An emptiness was inside each of the girls as they fought to accept the reality that Chika was never coming back. Their chest cavities felt icy, completely drained of magic. Their bodies desperately reached outward with thought to find a way to fill the void.

Dawn broke into a dry heave as she tightened everything in her body to resist a breakdown. Fire clawed at the back of her eyes as she buried her tears.

"Whoa," Asa looked over to Mei Ling and Vala for support. Seeing Dawn show any sign of weakness was the last thing to overload the weight on Asa's shoulders. She fell to her knees, curled over them, and bent her neck inwards while using her arms to support her weight.

Dawn backpedaled. From her perspective, the entire universe was shaking uncontrollably. The imaginary tremors caused her legs to buckle and she fell backwards, catching her shoulder blades on the back of the bubble, she slowly slid down into a sitting position. With heart on fire, she made no effort to pull her limbs inwards as she stared into the nothingness ahead.

EPILOGUE

14:34 26th of June, 2003

Vala opened her eyes to a strange white ceiling. The fluorescent bulbs pushed themselves deep into the back of her mind. She cringed, and when she did she rotated her body. Her stomach felt rotten inside and out. Pain shot up and she wanted to vomit. Nausea ran rampant but she was too weak to even gag.

A sharp pain flared over Vala's right eye. She could measure her pulse by the heartbeats in her temples. The migraine was unbearable. Sounds of the room felt like they shook her entire body. Quakes ricocheted through her boney structure.

The sound of alien beeps and a strange exhale of air came from her right. Brown eyes rolled around her skull towards the sounds. The medical equipment seemed to tower over her from her hospital bed. Vala recognized the machines from a year ago, it was as if they had never been moved and she had never left their shadow.

She noticed a warm pressure on the side of her leg. The angle Vala was at cut off sight to whatever was next to her. Despite her wishes to stay laying down forever, until the end of time and beyond that, Vala fought to sit up by digging her elbows into the bed.

The mattress felt like needles to her skin. Dragging her elbows along it to hoist herself upwards felt like she was grinding bone into dust. She bit down on her teeth as she teared through closed eyes.

Her joints ached. Her muscles felt tight. She swore she could feel her bones shift. The room kept in a spin. Her vision darkened as she rose. It took light a moment to penetrate the head rush.

Once up, she fought to catch her breath. The air was fire. It scorched down her throat and ravaged her lungs. She couldn't find the oxygen in it. Vala panicked. Over worked her lungs to scourer for the oxygen. Her expanded lungs cut against the knives of her rib cage.

She fell forward from the pain. "Shit," she choked on the word. Mostly pushed out air in a fit of pain rather drawing any inward.

It took a moment for her mind to steady itself. Vala fought to figure out why she was where she was. Was she not just fighting for all of humanity? Didn't she possess amazing powers? Was it all a fantasy?

As she fought to understand, her body slowly fought itself down into a restful state. Everything ached and felt heavy against her brittle body, but Vala managed to ground her mind in the moment.

Next to her leg was a long haired woman. Though Vala couldn't see her face due to folded arms being used as a pillow, she knew it was her mother. Vala felt the back of her throat burn up as she fought to swallow emotion.

Weeks in isolated captivity had convinced Vala that she would never see her mother again. With shaking, blue finger tipped hands, Vala reached outwards to her sleeping mother; and brushed her hair slowly. It was tangled and knotted as if she hadn't showered in a few days. The pull of the hairs didn't seem to bother Emily in the least. A strange huff of air followed by a smile from her, Vala assumed she must be dreaming about something nice.

Vala rubbed the kink out of her neck. It felt like she hadn't moved in days. Not wanting to disturb her mother's sleep or have the painful task of having her various needles removed from her body, Vala leaned back on her bed.

As her hand clasped the back of her neck. Her fingers danced along exaggerated boney bumps of her spine. She could trace out her bones as if they were exposed to the world. She pictured skinless bone bleeding into the back of her bed. From open eyes that dare not blink, water swelled and fell.

With a gasp she let her hand fall to her collar bone. The skin around it sank in. It was dry, felt like leather along her fingers. The bones were just as exposed. With a whimper Vala investigated what she already knew to be true. She ran her hand down herself to her shoulder. It shot out jagged like a spike. Vala couldn't find an ounce of fat on her. She remembered all of this.

Remembered how heavy the outside world felt. How hollow her chest cavity felt. How cold she was. The wide eyed looks she got, followed by the cringe. The bombardment of self accusation. The constant feeling of being put under a microscope. Being picked apart to figure out what was wrong with her. But that was all self induced.

Vala also remembered how no one else seemed to care how she got here. Only that it was her fault. That she had to get out. Why couldn't she get out? Why couldn't she eat? Why couldn't she be normal? Why was it taking so long?

Reality spun out of control as Vala's lungs overworked themselves. Fought the flames of air to find any soothing oxygen to ease the mind. The room twisted and her concept of time stuttered. Vala felt her mind fade. Pull back on itself. The light expanded outwards from the bulbs of the room and into the corner of her eyes. With the light dragged a darkness that began in the centre of her vision and bled outwards.

When Vala opened her eyes again, she was alone in the room. Her torment began once more, but she fought to bear it. Fought to accept what she had done to herself. Fought the second damning of her choices.

After several minutes of mentally cutting herself, Vala let her vision fall to the side of her pillow. She was determined to stare out the hospital door forever and ever until all existence was not.

But something caught her eye. On top of the night stand was her cellphone. Vala twisted her face as she almost didn't recognize the symbols on the outer display. The device was old, a model she had traded in months ago. Vala flipped her phone open to see 37 missed calls, 189 text messages and the date: a lapse in time just shy of a year.

Some messages were saved, locked so they couldn't be deleted. A few from friends and other numbers in her phone that she recognized spread throughout the last couple of days. But most of the phone held texts from the last hour. Numbers Vala had never seen before.

Her mother had kept the phone on for everyone to reach out to her. Vala remembered the act. It was something she had used to motivate Vala. But these recent messages were new. A part of no memory.

Vala opened a few of the unknown.

I'll fucking kill you!

You took my baby from me!

I will find you and end you!

Get the hell off our planet!!

I hope they arrest you!

You deserve to die!

Vala stopped reading the texts. Her heart raced so hard in her chest that she swore her ribs were cracking. In a panic, she looked around for someone to ask for help and, in doing so, noticed the door to the room was ajar.

The shoulders and elbows of two police officers standing on either side of the door from the hallway were in view. Vala felt her world spin so hard she had to bring up her hand to steady her mind.

Catching herself in her own hands, Vala dug her palms into her eyes as hard as she could. Lights lit up her vision through closed eyelids as she attempted to tear her own face muscles in a fit of frustration.

Pressure burrowed deep into her mind through ringing ears. The build-up pushed and twisted her mind as the world began to spiral out of control. Vala's stomach folded in on itself as her lungs collapsed.

Hands clasped a beating chest. She grasped for air. The air was dry and felt like sandpaper all the way down into her burning lungs. Vala dug her hands deep into the folds of the blanket as she arched over and fought to find herself.

Helplessness was thrown aside by teenage angst. A flurry of emotion rushed from the emptiness inside; as air filled her body, so did rage. As the control over her breathing took hold, she lost the reins to everything else.

Swiftly she dug her thumbs into her phone as she violently assaulted the device with every strike to delete every message she saw. Even those she recognized, all of it a muddled mess of reality that she was not willing to be a part of.

Until she reached the first saved message. The one that must have inspired her mother to keep the other messages and fight to delete the assault of bad ones.

You can call me, okay?

Vala's entire body quaked as reality was pulled back, only leaving herself and the text message; more specifically, the name of its sender.

"Chelsea."

ABOUT THE AUTHOR

Brayden Bechtold is a new adult author of urban fantasy / science fiction. He focuses in realistic dialogue, dynamic fight scenes and anime inspired themes. In his spare time he enjoys playing board games or video games with his best friend — his wife Laura — and their sons.

BRAYDEN BECHTOLD